A Christmas Party

A SEASONAL MURDER MYSTERY

GEORGETTE HEYER

sourcebooks
landmark

Published by Sourcebooks Landmark, an imprint of Sourcebooks, Inc.
P.O. Box 4410, Naperville, Illinois 60567-4410
(630) 961-3900
Fax: (630) 961-2168
www.sourcebooks.com

Originally published as *Envious Casca* in 1941 in Great Britain by Hodder &
Stoughton, London. This edition issued based on the paperback edition pub-
lished in 2010 in the United States by Sourcebooks Landmark, an imprint of
Sourcebooks, Inc.

Library of Congress Cataloging-in-Publication data is on file with the publisher.

Printed and bound in the United States of America.
VP 10 9 8 7 6 5 4 3 2 1

One

~~~~~~~~~~~~~~~~~

It was a source of great satisfaction to Joseph Herriard that the holly trees were in full berry. He seemed to find in this circumstance an assurance that the projected reunion of the family would be a success. For days past he had been bringing prickly sprigs into the house, his rosy countenance beaming with pleasure, and his white locks (worn rather long, and grandly waving) ruffled by the December winds. 'Just look at the berries!' he would say, thrusting his sprigs under Nathaniel's nose, laying them on Maud's card-table.

'Very pretty, dear,' Maud said, her flattened voice divesting her words of even the smallest vestige of enthusiasm.

'Take the damned thing away!' growled Nathaniel. 'I hate holly!'

But neither the apathy of his wife nor the disapproval of his elder brother could damp Joseph's childlike enjoyment of the Festive Season. When a leaden sky heralded the advent of snow, he began to talk about old-fashioned Christmases, and to liken Lexham Manor to Dingley Dell.

In point of fact, there was no more resemblance between the two houses than between Mr Wardle and Nathaniel Herriard.

Lexham was a Tudor manor house, considerably enlarged, but retaining enough of its original character to make it one of the show-places of the neighbourhood. It was not a family seat of long standing, Nathaniel, who was a wealthy man (he had been an importer from the East Indies), having purchased it a few years before his retirement from an active share in his flourishing business. His niece, Paula Herriard, who did not like the Manor, could not imagine what should have induced an old bachelor to saddle himself with such a place, unless – hopefully – he meant to leave it to Stephen, her brother. In which case, she added, it was a pity that Stephen, who did like the place, should take so few pains to be decent to the old man.

It was generally supposed, in spite of Stephen's habit of annoying his uncle, that he would be Nathaniel's heir. He was his only nephew, so unless Nathaniel meant to leave his fortune to his only surviving brother, Joseph, which even Joseph admitted to be unlikely, the bulk of the estate looked like coming into Stephen's graceless hands.

In support of this theory, it could perhaps have been said that Nathaniel seemed to like Stephen rather more than he liked any other member of his family. But few people liked Stephen very much. The only person who stoutly maintained belief in the sterling qualities to be detected beneath his unprepossessing exterior was Joseph, whose overflowing kindness of heart led him always to believe the best of everyone.

'There's a lot of good in Stephen. You mark my words, the dear old bear will surprise us all one of these days!' Joseph said staunchly, when Stephen had been at his most impossible.

Stephen was not in the least grateful for this unsolic-
ited championship. His dark, rather saturnine face took on
such an expression of sardonic scorn that poor Joseph was
momentarily abashed, and stood looking at him with an
absurdly crestfallen air.

'Surprising weak intellects isn't a pastime of mine,'
said Stephen, not even troubling to remove his pipe from
between his teeth.

Joseph smiled with a bravery which prompted Paula to
take up the cudgels in his defence. But Stephen only gave a
short bark of laughter, and buried himself in his book, and by
the time Paula had told him, with modern frankness, what she
thought of his manners, Joseph, whose invincible cheerfulness no brutality could long impair, had recovered from his
hurt and archly ascribed Stephen's snap to a touch of liver.

Maud, who was laying out a complicated Double Patience,
her plump countenance betraying nothing but a mild interest
in the disposition of aces and kings, said in her toneless voice
that salts before breakfast were good for sluggish livers.

'Oh, my God!' said Stephen, dragging his lanky limbs out of
the deep chair. 'To think that this house was once tolerable!'

There was no mistaking the implication of this savage
remark, but as soon as Stephen had left the room, Joseph
assured Paula that she need not worry on his account, since
he knew Stephen too well to be hurt by the things he said.
'I don't suppose poor old Stephen really grudges us Nat's
hospitality,' he said, with one of his whimsical smiles.

Joseph and Maud had not always been inmates of Lexham
Manor. Joseph had been, in fact, until a couple of years

previously, a rolling stone. In reviewing his past, he often referred to square pegs and wanderlust; and, that nothing should be wanting to exasperate Stephen, would recall past triumphs behind the footlights with a sigh, a smile, and a gently-spoken: '*Eheu fugaces!*'

For Joseph had been on the stage. Articled in youth to a solicitor, he had soon abandoned this occupation (the square peg) for the brighter prospects of coffee-growing (wanderlust) in East Africa. Since those early days he had flitted through every imaginable profession, from freelance prospecting for gold to acting. No one knew why he had left the stage – for since he had belonged to colonial and South American travelling companies it could scarcely be ascribed to the wanderlust that was responsible for his throwing up so many other jobs, for he seemed designed by nature to grace the boards. 'The ideal Polonius!' Mathilda Clare once called him.

It was during this phase of his career that he had met and married Maud. Incomprehensible though it might appear to the young Herriards, knowing Maud only in her fifties, she had once held an honourable place in the second row of the chorus. She had grown plump with the years, and it was difficult to trace in her fat little face, with its tiny mouth embedded between deep creases of pink cheek, and its pale blue, slightly starting eyes, the signs of the pretty girl she must once have been. She rarely spoke of her youth, such remarks as she from time to time let fall being inconsequent, and holding little clue to what Paula chose to think the mystery of her past.

The young Herriards, and Mathilda Clare, a distant cousin, knew Joseph and Maud only as legendary figures until the sea washed them up on the shores of England two years previously – at Liverpool. They had come from South America, solvent, but without prospects. They had gravitated to Lexham Manor, and there they had remained, not too proud, said Joseph, to be Nathaniel's pensioners.

Nathaniel extended his hospitality to his brother and his sister-in-law with surprising readiness. Perhaps, hazarded Paula, he felt that Lexham needed a mistress. If so, he was disappointed, for Maud showed no inclination to take the reins of household government into her small hands. Maud's idea of human bliss seemed to consist of eating, sleeping, playing interminable games of Patience, and reading, in a desultory fashion, chatty biographies of royal personages or other celebrities.

But if Maud was static, Joseph was full of energy. It was nearly all benevolent, but, unfortunately for Nathaniel, who was not gregarious, he delighted in gathering large parties together, and liked nothing so much as filling the house with young people, and joining in their amusements.

It was Joseph who had been inspired to organise the house-party that was looming over Nathaniel's unwilling head this chill December. Joseph, having lived for so many years abroad, hankered wistfully after a real English Christmas. Nathaniel, regarding him with a contemptuous eye, said that a real English Christmas meant, in his experience, a series of quarrels between inimical persons bound to one another only by the accident of relationship, and thrown together by a worn-out convention which decreed that at Christmas families should forgather.

But this acrid pronouncement only made Joseph laugh, clap Nathaniel on the back, and accuse him affectionately of growing into a regular curmudgeon.

It said much for Joseph's powers of persuasion that Nathaniel did, in the end, invite 'the young people' to spend Christmas at the Manor. As he had quarrelled with his nephew Stephen only a month previously, and had been resolutely refusing, for rather longer, to give financial backing to a play which his niece Paula wished to appear in, it took some time to talk him into letting bygones be bygones.

'You know, Nat,' Joseph said, rather ruefully, 'old fogies like you and me can't afford to quarrel with the younger generation. Why, where should we be without them, with all their faults, bless their hearts!'

'I can afford to quarrel with anyone I like,' replied Nathaniel, with perfect truth. 'I don't say that Stephen and Paula can't come to stay if they want to, but I'm not going to have that young woman of Stephen's poisoning the air with her filthy scent; and I won't be badgered by Paula to back a play by a fellow I've never heard of, and don't want to hear of. All your precious young people are out for is money, and well I know it! When I think of the amount I've squandered on them, one way and another—'

'Well, and why shouldn't you?' said Joseph cheerfully. 'Oh, you can't deceive me! You like to make out that you're a skinflint; but I know the joy of giving, and nothing will make me believe you don't know it too!'

'Sometimes, Joe,' said Nathaniel, 'you make me feel sick!'

Nevertheless, he consented, after a good deal of persuasion, to invite Stephen's 'young woman' to Lexham. In the end, quite a number of persons forgathered at the Manor for Christmas, since Paula brought with her the unknown dramatist to whom Nathaniel had taken such violent exception; Mathilda Clare invited herself; and Joseph decided, at the last moment, that it would be unkind to break the custom of years by excluding Nathaniel's business-partner, Edgar Mottisfont, from the party.

Joseph spent the days immediately preceding Christmas in decorating the house. He bought paper-chains, and festooned them across the ceilings; he pricked himself grievously in countless attempts to fix sprigs of holly over all the pictures; and he hung up bunches of mistletoe at all strategic points. He was engaged on this work when Mathilda Clare arrived. As she entered the house, he was erecting an infirm step-ladder in the middle of the hall, preparatory to securing a bunch of mistletoe to the chandelier.

'Tilda, my dear!' he exclaimed, letting the step-ladder fall with a crash, and hurrying to meet this first arrival. 'Well, well, well, well!'

'Hallo, Joe!' returned Miss Clare. 'Yule-tide-and-all-that?'

Joseph beamed, and said: 'Ah, I catch you at a disadvantage! See!' He held up the mistletoe over her head, and embraced her.

'Cave-man,' said Mathilda, submitting.

Joseph laughed delightedly, and, slipping a hand in her arm, led her into the library, where Nathaniel was reading the paper. 'Look what the fairies have brought us, Nat!' he said.

Nathaniel looked up over his spectacles, and said in somewhat discouraging accents: 'Oh, it's you, is it? How are you? Glad to see you.'

'Well, that's something, anyway,' said Mathilda, shaking hands with him. 'Thanks for letting me come, by the way.'

'I suppose you want something,' said Nathaniel, but with a twinkle.

'Not a thing,' replied Mathilda, lighting a cigarette. 'Only Sarah's sister has broken her leg, and Mrs Jones can't oblige.'

As Sarah was the devoted retainer who constituted Miss Clare's domestic staff, the reason for her visit to the Manor was felt to have been satisfactorily explained. Nathaniel grunted, and said that he might have known it. Joseph squeezed Mathilda's arm, and told her not to pay any attention to Nat. 'We're going to have a real Christmas jollification!' he said.

'The deuce we are!' said Mathilda. 'All right, Joe: I'll co-operate. The perfect guest: that's me. Where's Cousin Maud?'

Maud was discovered presently in the morning-room. She seemed vaguely glad to see Mathilda, and gave her a cheek to kiss, remarking somewhat disconcertingly: 'Poor Joseph is so set on an old-fashioned Christmas!'

'All right, I've no objection to helping him,' said Mathilda. 'Shall I make paper-chains, or something? Who's coming?'

'Stephen and Paula, and Stephen's fiancée, and of course Mr Mottisfont.'

'It sounds like a riot of fun. Stephen would make any party go with a swing.'

'Nathaniel does not care for Stephen's fiancée,' Maud stated.

'You don't say!' remarked Miss Clare vulgarly.

'She is very pretty,' said Maud.

Mathilda grinned. 'So she is,' she admitted.

Mathilda was not pretty. She had good eyes, and beautiful hair, but not even in her dewy youth had she been able to deceive herself into thinking that she was good-looking. She had sensibly accepted her plainness, and had, she said, put all her money on style. She was much nearer thirty than twenty; she enjoyed private means; lived in a cottage not uncomfortably far from London; and eked out her income by occasional journalism, and the breeding of bull-terriers. Valerie Dean, who was Stephen's fiancée, vaguely resented her, because she dressed so well, and made her plainness so arresting that she attracted a good deal of attention at parties at which Valerie had confidently expected to draw all eyes upon herself.

'Of course, darling, it isn't that I don't like your cousin,' Valerie told Stephen, 'but it's so silly to call her striking. Because she's practically hideous, isn't she, Stephen?'

'Sure,' said Stephen.

'Do you think she's so frightfully clever, Stephen? I mean, *do* you?'

'Never thought about it. She's a damned good sort.'

'Oh, darling, that sounds absolutely foul!' said Valerie, pleased. 'Don't you wish she weren't going to be at Lexham?'

'No.'

'Oh, Stephen, you are a swine! Why don't you?'

'I like her. I wish you'd shut your pretty little trap. I hate being yapped at when I'm driving.'

'You are a low hound, Stephen. Do you love me?'

'Yes, damn you!'

'Well, it doesn't sound as though you did. I'm pretty, aren't I?'

'Yes, my little bonehead, you're lovely – Aphrodite and Helen rolled into one. Stop drivelling!'

'Oh, I can't think why I ever fell for you, darling. I think you're foul!' said Miss Dean cooingly.

He vouchsafed no answer to this remark, and his betrothed, apparently realising that his mood was not propitious, sank her chin into the collar of her fur coat, and relapsed into quiescent silence.

Their arrival at Lexham Manor coincided with that of Edgar Mottisfont, and all three were welcomed into the house by Joseph, who came trotting out into the porch, beaming with pleasure, and claiming the privilege of an old stager to embrace Valerie.

His rapt appreciation of the truly lovely picture she presented made Stephen look more than ordinarily sardonic, but was well received by his target. Miss Dean, who was indeed lovely, liked to hear her charms enthusiastically praised, and was not above responding to the arch sallies of old gentlemen. She lifted her large blue eyes to Joseph's face, and told him that she knew he was dreadfully wicked, a pronouncement which delighted Joseph, and made Stephen say ill-naturedly: 'A case of *si vieillesse pouvait*!'

'Well, Stephen!' said Edgar Mottisfont, descending from the car which had been sent to fetch him from the station.

'Hallo!' said Stephen indifferently.

'This is an unexpected pleasure,' said Mottisfont, looking at him with disfavour.

'Why?' asked Stephen.

'Now, now, now!' chided Joseph, overhearing this interchange, and bustling forward. 'My dear Edgar! Come in, come in! You must be frozen, all of you! Look at the sky! We're going to have a white Christmas. I shouldn't be surprised if we found ourselves tobogganing in a day or two.'

'I should,' said Stephen, following the others into the house. 'Hallo, Mathilda!'

'I thought I heard your mellow accents,' said Mathilda. 'Spreading goodwill, my sweet?'

Stephen allowed his bitter mouth to relax into a smile at this greeting, but as Nathaniel came into the hall at that moment, and favoured him with nothing more than a nod, and a curt 'Glad to see you, Stephen,' the disagreeable expression returned to his face, and he immediately laid himself out to be objectionable to everyone within range.

Nathaniel, having shaken hands in a perfunctory fashion with Miss Dean, and said 'Oh!' dampingly to her announcement that she simply loved coming to spend Christmas in his perfectly fascinating house, lost no time in whisking himself and Edgar Mottisfont into his study.

'Remind me some time to give you some hints and tips on how to put yourself over with your Uncle Nat,' Mathilda said kindly to Miss Dean.

'Blast you, shut up!' snapped Stephen. 'God, I wonder why I came?'

'Probably because you couldn't think of anywhere else to go,' said Mathilda. Catching sight of Joseph's absurdly dismayed countenance, she added: 'Anyway, now you are here, behave yourself! Would you like to go up to your room now, Valerie, or have tea first?'

Miss Dean, whose major preoccupation in life was the possibility of her hair becoming disarranged, or her complexion impaired, chose to go to her room. This put Joseph in mind of his wife, but by the time he had run her to earth in the drawing-room, Mathilda had escorted Valerie upstairs.

Maud, gently chided by Joseph for not having come out to welcome the visitors, said that she had not heard their arrival. 'I have a very interesting book here,' she said. 'I got it out of the library today. It is the one you or Nat had out a little while ago, and which you thought I should not care for, about the poor Empress of Austria. Fancy, Joseph! She actually rode in a circus!'

Joseph, who possibly had a very fair idea of what the company would have to suffer from his wife's perusal of this, or any other, book, suggested tactfully that it should be put away until after Christmas, and reminded her that she was Valerie's hostess, and should have showed her the way to her room.

'No, dear,' replied Maud. 'I'm sure I had nothing to do with inviting Valerie here. Nor do I see why I shouldn't read my book at Christmas as well as at any other time. She could sit on her hair. Fancy!'

There did not seem to be much hope of dragging Maud's attention away from the Empress's peculiarities, so, with a fond pat on her shoulder, Joseph bustled away again, to irritate the servants by begging them to put tea forward, and to trot upstairs to tap on Valerie's door, and ask if she had everything she wanted.

Tea was served in the drawing-room. Maud laid aside the *Life of the Empress Elizabeth of Austria*, and poured out. She sat on the sofa, a dump of a woman behind a staggering array of embossed silver, and when each of the visitors came into the room, she extended her small plump hand with the same mechanical smile, and the same colourless phrase of welcome.

Mathilda sat beside her, and laughed when she saw the title of the book Maud had been reading. 'Last time I was here it was the *Memoirs of a Lady-in-Waiting*,' she said, teasing Maud.

Mockery slid off the armour of Maud's self-sufficiency. 'I like that kind of book,' she replied simply.

When Nathaniel came in with Edgar Mottisfont, Stephen dragged himself out of a deep armchair, saying ungraciously: 'Got your chair, uncle.'

Nathaniel accepted this overture in the spirit in which it was presumably meant. 'Don't disturb yourself, my boy. How have you been keeping?'

'All right,' Stephen said. He added, with a further effort towards civility: 'You look very fit.'

'Except for this wretched lumbago of mine,' Nathaniel said, not quite pleased that Stephen should have forgotten his lumbago. 'I had a touch of sciatica yesterday, too.'

'Bad luck,' said Stephen.

'The ills the flesh is heir to!' said Mottisfont, shaking his head. 'Anno domini, Nat, anno domini!'

'Nonsense!' said Joseph. 'Look at me! If you two old fogies would take my tip, and do your daily dozen every morning before breakfast, you'd feel twenty years younger! Knees bend – touch your toes – deep breathing before the open window!'

'Don't be a fool, Joe!' growled Nathaniel. 'Touch my toes indeed! Why, there are some mornings when I should be set fast if I stooped an inch!'

Miss Dean offered her contribution to the discussion. 'I do think exercises are the most ghastly bore, don't you?'

'Shouldn't be at your age,' said Nathaniel.

'A dose of salts every morning would do most people a great deal of good,' said Maud, handing a cup-and-saucer to Stephen.

Nathaniel, after casting a malevolent look at his sister-in-law, at once began to talk to Mottisfont. Mathilda gave a gurgle of laughter, and said: 'Well, that's settled that topic, at any rate!'

Maud's pale eyes met hers, uncomprehending, devoid of any hint of humour. 'I find salts very beneficial,' she said.

Valerie Dean, who was looking entrancingly pretty in a jersey-suit which exactly matched the blue of her eyes, had been taking stock of Mathilda's tweed coat and skirt, and had reached the conclusion that it did not become her. This made her feel friendly towards Mathilda, and she moved her chair nearer to the sofa, and began to talk to her. Stephen, who seemed to be making a real effort to behave nicely, joined in his uncle's conversation with Mottisfont, and Joseph, radiant now that his party looked like being a success after all, beamed on everyone impartially. So patent was his satisfaction that Mathilda's eyes began to twinkle again, and she offered, after tea, to help him to hang up his paper-chains.

'I'm glad you've come, Tilda,' Joseph told her, as she gingerly mounted the rickety steps. 'I do so want this party to go well.'

'You're the World's Uncle, Joe,' said Mathilda. 'For God's sake, hang on to these steps! They feel most unsafe to me. Why did you want this family reunion?'

'Ah, you'll laugh at me if I tell you!' he said, shaking his head. 'I think, if you hang your end just above that picture it would just reach to the chandelier. Then we could have another chain over to that corner.'

'Just as you say, Santa Claus. But why the reunion?'

'Well, my dear, isn't it the season of goodwill, and isn't it all working out just as one hoped it would?'

'Depends what you hoped,' said Mathilda, pressing a drawing-pin into the wall. 'If you ask me, there'll be murder done before we're through. Nat's patience will never stand much of little Val.'

'Bosh, Tilda!' said Joseph roundly. 'Bosh and nonsense! There's no harm in the child, and I'm sure she's pretty enough to eat!'

Mathilda descended the steps. 'I don't think that Nat prefers blondes,' she said.

'Never mind! It doesn't matter what he thinks of poor

little Val, after all. The main thing is that he shouldn't carry on a silly quarrel with old Stephen.'

'If I'm to fix this end to the chandelier, move the steps over, Joe. Why shouldn't he quarrel with Stephen, if he wants to?'

'Because he's really very fond of him, because quarrelling in families is always a pity. Besides—' Joseph stopped, and began to move the steps.

'Besides what?'

'Well, Tilda, Stephen can't afford to quarrel with Nat, the silly fellow!'

'You should worry!' said Mathilda. 'You aren't going to tell me that Nat has at last brought himself to make a will? Is Stephen the heir?'

'You want to know too much,' said Joseph, giving her a playful smack.

'Sure I do! You're very mysterious, aren't you?'

'No, no, upon my word I'm not! I only feel it would be very foolish of Stephen to go on being on bad terms with Nat. Shall we hang this big paper-bell under the chandelier, or do you think a bunch of mistletoe would be better?'

'If you really want my opinion, Joe, I think they look equally lousy.'

'Naughty girl! Such language!' Joseph said. 'You young people don't appreciate Christmas as my generation did. Doesn't it mean *anything* to you?'

'It will, by the time we're through,' replied Mathilda, once more ascending the steps.

TWO

PAULA HERRIARD DID NOT ARRIVE AT THE MANOR UNTIL after seven, when everyone else was changing for dinner. Her appearance on the scene was advertised, even to those in remote bedrooms, by the unusual amount of commotion heard downstairs. Paula's entrances always commanded attention. It was not that she deliberately staged them: merely, her personality was rather overpowering, her movements as impetuous as her vivid little face. In fact, Mathilda said with gentle malice, she seemed to have been born with the hall-marks of a great emotional actress.

She was several years younger than her brother Stephen, and resembled him scarcely at all. She was pretty, in the style made popular by Burne-Jones, with thick, springy hair, a short, full upper lip, and dark eyes set widely under discontented brows. There was an air of urgency about her; you could see it in her restless movements, in the sudden glow in her changeable eyes, and in the hungry line of her mouth. She had a beautiful voice, like a stringed instrument. It was mellow, and flexible, which made her the ideal choice for a Shakespearean rôle. It cast into shocking relief the light,

metallic tones of her contemporaries, with their clipped vow-
els, and the oddly common inflexions they so carefully cul-
tivated. She knew how to throw it, too: no doubt about that,
thought Mathilda, hearing it float upstairs from the hall.

She heard her own name. 'In the Blue Room? Oh! I'll
go up!'

Mathilda sat back on her dressing-stool to await Paula's
entrance. In a minute or two there was a perfunctory knock
on the door, and before she could call Come in! Paula had
entered, bringing with her that uncomfortable feeling of
impatience, of scarcely curbed energy.

'Mathilda! Darling!'

''Ware my make-up!' Mathilda exclaimed, dodging the
embrace.

Paula chuckled, deep in her throat. 'Idiot! I'm so glad to see
you! Who's here? Stephen? Valerie? Oh, that girl! My dear,
if you *knew* the feeling I have here about her!' She struck her
chest as she spoke; her eyes quite blazed for a moment, but
then she blinked her thick lashes, and laughed, and said: 'Oh,
never mind that! Brothers – ! I've brought Willoughby.'

'Who is Willoughby?' demanded Mathilda.

There was again that disconcerting flash. 'One day no one
will ask that question!'

'Pending that day,' said Mathilda, intent on her own eyebrows, 'who is Willoughby?'

'Willoughby Roydon. He has written a play…'

It was strange how much that throbbing voice and
those fluttering hands could express. Mathilda said: 'Oh?
Unknown, dramatist?'

'So far! But *this* play – ! Producers are such fools! We must have backing. Is Uncle Nat in a good mood? Has Stephen upset him? Tell me everything, Mathilda, quick!'

Mathilda laid down the eyebrow-pencil. 'You haven't brought your playwright here in the hope of winning Nat's heart, Paula? My poor girl!'

'He must do it for me!' Paula said, impatiently pushing back the hair from her brow. 'It's art, Mathilda! Oh! When you have read it – !'

'Art plus a part for Paula?' murmured Mathilda.

The shaft glanced off Paula's armour. 'Yes. A part. Such a part! It was written for me. He says I inspired it.'

'Sunday performance, and an audience composed of intellectuals. *I* know!'

'Uncle has got to listen to me! I must play it. I must, Mathilda, do you hear me?'

'Yes, my sweet, you must play it. Meanwhile, dinner will be ready in twenty minutes' time.'

'Oh, it doesn't take me ten minutes to change!' Paula said impatiently.

Mathilda reflected that this was true. Paula never bothered about her clothes. She was neither dowdy nor smart; she flung raiment on, and somehow one never knew what she was wearing: it didn't count, it was nothing but a covering for Paula's thin body: you were aware only of Paula herself. 'I hate you, Paula; my God, how I hate you!' Mathilda said, knowing that people remembered her by the exquisite creations she wore. 'Go away! I'm less fortunate.'

Paula's gaze focused upon her. 'Darling, your clothes are perfect.'

'I know they are. What have you done with your playwright?'

'I don't know. Such an absurd fuss! As though the house weren't big enough – ! Sturry said he'd see to it.'

'Well, as long as your playwright doesn't wear soft shirts and a plume of hair – !'

'What do these things *matter*?'

'They'll matter fast enough to your Uncle Nat,' prophesied Mathilda.

They did. Nathaniel, introduced without warning to Willoughby Roydon, glared at him, and at Paula, and could not even bring himself to utter conventional words of welcome. It was left to Joseph to fill the breach, and he did so, aware of Nat's fury, and covering it up with his own overflowing goodwill.

The situation was saved by Sturry, announcing dinner. They went into the dining-room. Willoughby Roydon sat between Mathilda and Maud. He despised Maud, but Mathilda he liked. He talked to her about the tendency of modern drama, and she bore it very meekly, realising that it was her duty to draw his fire.

He was a sallow young man, with rather indeterminate features, and an over-emphatic manner. Listening, a little inattentively, to his conversation, Mathilda pictured him against a middle-class background of indifference. She felt sure that his parents were worthy people, perhaps afraid of their clever son, perhaps scornful of a talent they could not understand. He was unsure of himself, aggressive from very lack of poise. Mathilda felt sorry for him, and schooled her features to an expression of interest in what he was saying.

Paula, seated beside Nathaniel, was talking to him about Roydon's play, forgetting to eat her dinner in her earnestness, annoying him by gesticulating with her thin, nervous hands, insisting on his attending to her, even though he didn't want to, wasn't interested. Valerie, on his right, was bored, and taking no pains to hide it. She had pretended at first to be deeply interested, saying: 'My dear, how marvellous! Do tell me about your part! I shall adore coming to see you in it!' But Paula didn't want to capture Valerie's interest; she brushed her aside with that careless contempt which made her look suddenly like Stephen. So Valerie sighed, patted her sleek curls into position, and despised Paula for wearing a dress which didn't suit her, and for combing her hair so casually off her face.

It was being a bad evening for Valerie. She had wanted to come to Lexham (in fact, she had insisted on Stephen's bringing her) because she knew that Nathaniel did not like her. She hadn't doubted her ability to captivate him, but even the Chanel model she was wearing had failed to bring that admiring look into his eyes which she was accustomed to see in men's eyes. Joseph had twinkled appreciation, but that was no use (though pleasant) because Joseph had no money to leave.

The arrival of an unexpected male guest had been exciting, but he seemed to be absorbed in conversation with Mathilda. Valerie wondered what men saw in Mathilda, and glanced resentfully across at her. It happened that Roydon looked up at that moment, and their eyes met. He seemed to see her for the first time, and to be shaken. He stopped in the middle of what he was saying, flushed, and picked up the thread again in a hurry, Valerie began to feel more cheerful. Playwrights! One never knew about them; they became famous overnight, and made pots and pots of money, and were seen about everywhere with the best people.

Joseph, whom Nathaniel suspected of having connived from the start at Willoughby's arrival, said that he could smell the sawdust again, a figure of speech which apparently left Roydon with the impression that he had been a circus-artist. Joseph speedily disillusioned him. 'I remember once in Durban, when I was playing Hamlet...' said Joseph.

'Go on, Joe! You never played Hamlet in your life!' interrupted Mathilda. 'Your outline's all wrong.'

'Ah, the days when I was young!' Joseph said.

But Roydon wasn't interested in Joseph's Hamlet. He shrugged Shakespeare aside. He said that he himself owed a debt to Strindberg. As for Pinero's comedies, which Joseph had played in, he dismissed them with the crushing label: 'That old stuff!'

Joseph felt depressed. He had a charming little anecdote to tell, about the time he had played Benedick, in Sydney, but it didn't seem as though Roydon would appreciate it. A conceited young man, thought Joseph, dispiritedly eating his savoury.

When Maud rose from the table, Paula was obliged to stop telling Nathaniel about Roydon's play. She glowered at being interrupted, but went out with the other women.

Maud led the way to the drawing-room. It was a big room, and it felt chilly. Only two standard-lamps, placed near the fireplace, lit it, and the far corners of the room lay in shadow. Paula gave a shiver, and switched on the ceiling-lights. 'I hate this house!' she said. 'It hates us, too. You can almost feel it.'

'Whatever do you mean?' asked Valerie, looking round half-fearfully, half-sceptically.

'I don't know. I think something happened here, perhaps. Can't you feel how sinister it is? No, I suppose you can't.'

'You don't mean that it's haunted, do you?' Valerie asked, her voice rising slightly. 'Because nothing would induce me to spend a night here, if it is!'

'No, I don't mean that,' Paula answered. 'But there's something about it – I'm always conscious of it. Cigarette, Mathilda?'

Mathilda took one. 'Thank you, my love. Shall we gather round the fire, chicks, and tell ghost stories?'

'Oh, don't!' shuddered Valerie.

'Don't let Paula impress you!' Mathilda advised her. 'She is just being fey. There's nothing wrong with this house.'

'It is a pity that there are no radiators in this room,' said Maud, ensconcing herself by the fire.

'It isn't that,' said Paula curtly.

'I expect that's what gives Nat lumbago,' said Maud. 'Draughts –'

Valerie began to powder her nose before the mirror over the fireplace. Paula, who seemed to be restless, drifted about the room, smoking a cigarette, and nicking the ash on to the carpet.

Mathilda, taking a chair opposite to Maud, said: 'I wish

you wouldn't prowl, Paula. And if you could refrain from badgering Nat about your young friend's play I feel that this party might go with more of a swing.'

'I don't care about that. It's vital to me to get Willoughby's play put on!'

'Love's young dream?' Mathilda cocked a quizzical eyebrow.

'Mathilda! Can't you understand that love doesn't come into it? It's art!'

'Sorry!' Mathilda apologised.

Maud, who had opened her book again, said: 'Fancy! The Empress was only sixteen when Franz Josef fell in love with her! It was quite a romance.'

'What Empress?' demanded Paula, halting in the middle of the room, and staring at her.

'The Empress of Austria, dear. Somehow one can't imagine Franz Josef as a young man, can one? But it says here that he was very good-looking, and she fell in love with him at first sight. Of course, he ought to have married the elder sister, but he saw Elizabeth first, with her hair down her back, and that decided him.'

'What on earth has that got to do with Willoughby's play?' asked Paula, in a stupefied voice.

'Nothing, my dear; but I am reading a very interesting book about her.'

'Well, it doesn't interest me,' said Paula, resuming her pacing of the room.

'Never mind, Maud!' said Mathilda. 'Paula has a one-track mind, and no manners. Tell me more about your Empress!'

24

'Poor thing!' said Maud. 'It was that mother-in-law, you know. She seems to have been a very unpleasant woman. The Archduchess, they called her, though I can't quite make out why she was only an Archduchess when her son was an Emperor. She wanted him to marry Hélène.'

'A little more, and I shall feel compelled to read this entrancing work,' said Mathilda. 'Who was Hélène?'

Maud was still explaining Hélène to Mathilda when the men came into the drawing-room.

It was plain that Nathaniel had not found the male company congenial. He had apparently been buttonholed by Roydon, for he cast several affronted glances at the playwright, and removed himself as far from his vicinity as he could. Mottisfont sat down beside Maud; and Stephen, who appeared to sympathise with his uncle, surprised everyone by engaging him in perfectly amiable conversation.

'Stephen being the little gentleman quite takes my breath away,' murmured Mathilda.

Joseph, standing near enough to overhear this remark, laid a conspiratorial finger across his lips. He saw that Nathaniel had observed this gesture, and made haste to say, in bracing accents: 'Now, who says Rummy?'

No one said Rummy; several persons, notably Nathaniel, looked revolted; and after a pause, Joseph, a little crestfallen, said: 'Well, well, what shall it be?'

'Mathilda,' said Nathaniel, fixing her with a compelling eye, 'we want you to make up a fourth at Bridge.'

'All right,' said Mathilda. 'Who's playing?'

'Stephen and Mottisfont. We'll have a table put up in the

library, and the rest of you can play any silly – can do any-thing you like.'

Joseph, whose optimism nothing could damp, said: 'Just the thing! No one will disturb you earnest people, and we frivolous ones can be as foolish as we like!'

'It's no good expecting me to play!' announced Roydon. 'I don't know one card from another.'

'Oh, you'll soon pick it up!' said Joseph. 'Maud, my dear, I suppose we can't lure you into a round game?'

'No, Joseph, I will do a Patience quietly by myself, if someone will be kind enough to draw that table forward,' replied Maud.

Valerie, who had not been at all pleased to hear that her betrothed proposed to spend the evening playing Bridge, bestowed a dazzling smile upon Roydon, and said: 'I'm sim-ply dying to ask you about this play of yours. I'm utterly thrilled about it! Do come and tell me all about it!'

Since Willoughby, sore from the lack of appreciation shown by Nathaniel, at once moved across to Miss Dean's side, only Paula was left to make up Joseph's round game. He seemed to feel the impossibility of organising anything very successful under such conditions, and with only a faint, quickly suppressed sigh, abandoned the project, and sat down to watch his wife playing Patience.

After continuing to walk about the room for some time, occasionally joining in Roydon's conversation with Valerie, Paula cast herself upon a sofa, and began to flick over the pages of an illustrated paper. Joseph soon moved over to join her, saying in a confidential tone: 'Tell your old uncle all about it, my dear! What sort of play is it? Comedy? Tragedy?'

'You can't label it like that,' Paula answered. 'It's a most subtle character-study. There isn't another part in the world I want to play more. It's written for me! It *is* me!'

'I know exactly how you feel,' nodded Joseph, laying a hand over hers, and pressing it sympathetically. 'Ah, how often one has been through that experience! I daresay it seems funny to you to think of your old uncle on the boards, but when I was a young man I shocked all my relations by actually running away from a respectable job in a solicitor's office to join a travelling company!' He laughed richly at the memory. 'I was a romantic lad! I expect a lot of people called me an improvident young fool, but I've never regretted it, never!'

'I wish you'd make Uncle Nat listen to reason,' said Paula discontentedly.

'I'll try, my dear, but you know what Nat is! Dear old crosspatch! He's the best of good fellows, but he has his prejudices.'

'Two thousand pounds wouldn't make any difference to him. I can't see why I shouldn't have it now, when I need it, instead of having to wait till he dies.'

'You bad girl! Counting your chickens before they are hatched!'

'I'm not. He told me he'd leave me some money. Besides, he's bound to: I'm his only niece.'

It was plain that Joseph could not quite approve of this cool way of putting the matter. He said tut-tut, and squeezed Paula's hand again.

Maud, who had brought the Diplomat to a triumphant conclusion, was inspired to suggest suddenly that Paula should recite something. 'I am very fond of a good recitation,' she said. 'I remember that I used to know a very touching poem about a man who died of thirst on the Llano Estacado. I forget why, but I think he was riding to some place or other. I know it was extremely dramatic, but it is many years since I last did it, and I have forgotten it.'

Everyone breathed again. Paula said that she didn't go in for recitations, but that if Uncle Nat had not elected to play Bridge, she would have asked Willoughby to read his play to them.

'That would have been very enjoyable, I expect,' said Maud placidly.

It was not Nathaniel's custom to keep late hours, nor was he the kind of host who altered his habits to suit the convenience of his guests. At eleven o'clock, the Bridge-players came back into the drawing-room, where a tray of drinks was awaiting them, and Nathaniel said that for his part he was going to bed.

Edgar Mottisfont ventured to say: 'I had hoped to have a chat with you, Nat.'

Nathaniel darted a look at him from under his bushy brows. 'Can't talk business at this hour of night,' he said.

'Well, I want a word with you, too,' said Paula.

'You won't get it,' Nathaniel replied, with a short laugh.

Maud was gathering up her cards. 'Dear me, eleven already? I think I shall go up too.'

Valerie looked rather appalled at this prospect of having to retire at such an unaccustomed hour, but was relieved to hear

Joseph say cheerfully: 'Well, I hope no one else means to run off yet! The night's young, eh, Valerie? What do you say to going into the billiard-room, and turning on the wireless?'

'You'd be a great deal better in bed,' said Nathaniel, on whom Joseph's high spirits seemed to exercise a baleful influence.

'Not I!' Joseph declared. 'I'll tell you what, Nat: you'd be much better enjoying yourself with us!'

His evil genius prompted him to clap his brother on the back as he said this. It was plain to everyone that the playful blow fell between Nat's shoulders, but Nathaniel, who hated to be touched, at once groaned, and ejaculated: 'My lumbago!'

He left the room with the gait of a cripple, holding his hand to the small of his back, in a gesture which his relatives knew well, but which made Valerie open her lovely eyes very wide, and say: 'I'd no idea lumbago was as bad as that!'

'It isn't. That's just my dear Uncle Nat playing up,' said Stephen, handing a whisky-and-soda to Mathilda.

'No, no, that isn't quite fair!' protested Joseph. 'Why, I've known poor old Nat to be set fast with it! I'm a stupid fellow: I daresay I did jar him. I wonder if I had better go after him?'

'No, Joe,' said Mathilda kindly. 'You mean well, but you'll only annoy him. Why is our little Paula looking like the Tragic Muse?'

'This awful house!' ejaculated Paula. 'How any of you can spend an hour in it and not *feel* the atmosphere – !'

'Pray silence for Mrs Siddons!' said Stephen, regarding her with a sardonic eye.

'Oh, you can scoff!' she flung at him. 'But even you must feel the tension!'

'Well, do you know, it's an awfully funny thing, because I'm not a bit psychic, or anything like that, but I do see what Paula means,' said Valerie. 'It's a kind of an atmosphere.' She turned to Roydon. 'You could write a marvellous play about it, couldn't you?'

'I don't know that it would be quite in my line,' he replied.

'Oh, I have an absolute conviction that you're the sort of person who could write a marvellous play about simply anything!' said Valerie, raising admiring eyes to his face.

'Even guinea-pigs?' asked Stephen, introducing a discordant note.

The playwright flushed. 'Very funny!'

Mathilda perceived that Mr Roydon was unused to being laughed at. 'Let me advise you to pay little if any heed to my cousin Stephen!' she said.

Stephen never minded what Mathilda said to him; he only grinned; but Joseph, at no time remarkable for tact, brought the saturnine look back to his face by saying: 'Oh, we all know what an old bear Stephen likes to pretend to be!'

'God!' said Stephen, very distinctly.

Paula sprang up, thrusting the hair back from her brow with one of her hasty gestures. 'That's what I mean! You're all of you behaving like this because the house has got you! It's the tension: something stretching and stretching until it snaps! Stephen's always worse when he's here; I'm on edge; Valerie flirts with Willoughby to make Stephen jealous; Uncle Joe's nervous, saying the wrong thing: not wanting to, but impelled to!'

'Well, really!' exclaimed Valerie. 'I *must* say!'

'Let no one think I'm not enjoying myself!' begged Mathilda. 'Yule-tide, children, and all that! These old-fashioned Christmases!'

Roydon said thoughtfully: 'I know what you mean, of course. Personally, I believe profoundly in the influence of environment.'

'"After which short speech,"' quoted Stephen, '"they all cheered."'

Joseph clapped his hands. 'Now, now, now, that's quite enough! Who says radio?'

'Yes, let's!' begged Valerie. 'The dance music will be on. Mr Roydon, I just know you're a dancer!'

Willoughby disclaimed, but was borne off, not entirely unwillingly. He was a little dazzled by Valerie's beauty, and although a sane voice within him told him that her flattery was inane, he did not find it unpleasant. Paula was a more stimulating companion, but although she admired him, and had an intelligent appreciation of his work, she was apt to be exhausting, and (he sometimes thought) distinctly over-critical. So he went off with Valerie and Joseph, reflecting that even geniuses must have their moments of relaxation.

'I must say, I don't blame Uncle Nat for barring your intended, Stephen,' said Paula fairly.

Stephen did not seem to mind this candid opinion of his taste. He strolled over to the fire, and lowered his long limbs into an armchair. 'The perfect anodyne,' he said. 'By the way, I don't think your latest pick-up so bloody hot.'

'Willoughby? Oh, I know, but he's got genius! I don't

care about anything else. Besides, I'm not in love with him. But what you can see in that brainless doll beats me!'

'My good girl, what I see in her must be abundantly plain to everyone,' said Stephen. 'This playwriting wen of yours sees it too, not to mention Joe, whose tongue is fairly hanging out.'

'Close-up of the Herriards,' said Mathilda, lying back in her chair, and lazily regarding brother and sister. 'Cads, both. Carry on: don't mind me.'

'Well, I believe in being honest,' said Paula. 'You are a fool, Stephen! She wouldn't have got engaged to you if she hadn't thought you'd come in for all Uncle Nat's money.'

'I know,' said Stephen blandly.

'And if you ask me she came down here with you on purpose to mash Uncle Nat.'

'I know,' said Stephen again.

Their eyes met; Stephen's lips twitched suddenly, and, while Mathilda lay and watched them, he and Paula went off into fits of helpless laughter.

'You and your Willoughby, and me and my Val!' gasped Stephen. 'Oh, lord!'

Paula dried her eyes, instantly sobered by the mention of her playwright. 'Yes, I know it's funny, but I'm serious about that, because he really has written a great play, and I'm going to act the lead in it, if it's the last thing I do. I shall get him to read it aloud to you all tomorrow –'

'What? Oh, God, be good to me! Not to Uncle as well? Don't, Paula, it hurts!'

'When you've quite finished,' said Mathilda, 'will you

explain the exact nature of this treat you have in store for us, Paula? Are you going to read your own part, or is it to be a one-man show?'

'I shall let Willoughby read nearly all himself. He does it very well. I might do my big scene, perhaps.'

'And you actually think, my poor, besotted wench, that this intellectual feast is going to soften your Uncle Nat's heart? Now it's my turn to enjoy a laugh!'

'He's got to back it!' Paula said fiercely. 'It's the only thing I've ever wanted, and it would be too wickedly cruel not to do it for me!'

'I will lay you odds you're in for a disappointment, ducky. I don't wish to throw a damper on your girlish enthusiasm, but the moment doesn't seem to me propitious.'

'It's all Stephen's fault for bringing that sickening blonde here!' Paula said. 'Anyway, I've got Uncle Joe to put in a word for me.'

'That'll help a lot,' mocked Stephen. 'Just fancy!'

'Lay off Joe!' commanded Mathilda. 'He may be God's own ass, but he's the only decent member of your family I've ever been privileged to meet. Besides, he likes you.'

'Well, I don't like being liked,' said Stephen.

Three

There was a light covering of snow on the ground on Christmas Eve. Mathilda, sipping her early tea, reflected with a wry smile that Joseph would talk of a white Christmas all day, perhaps hunt for a pair of skates. He was a tiresome old man, she thought, but disarmingly pathetic. No one was trying to make his party a success, least of all Nathaniel. Yet how could he have expected such an ill-assorted gathering of people to mix well? Pondering this, she was forced to admit that such imperceptive optimism was part and parcel of his guileless nature. She suspected that he saw himself as the beloved uncle, everybody's confidant.

She began slowly to eat one of the thin slices of bread-and-butter which had been brought up with the tea. What on earth had made Stephen come to Lexham? Generally he came when he wanted something: money, of course, which Nathaniel nearly always gave him. This time it was Paula who wanted money, not, apparently, Stephen. From what she had heard, Stephen had had rather a serious quarrel with Nathaniel not so many weeks since. It hadn't been their first quarrel, of course: they were always quarrelling; but the cause of it – Valerie – still existed. Extraordinary that Joseph should have prevailed upon Nat to receive Valerie! Or did Nathaniel believe that Stephen's infatuation would burn itself out? Recalling his behaviour on the previous evening, she had to admit that this seemed very likely to happen, if it had not already happened.

Valerie, of course, saw herself as the mistress of Lexham: a horrible prospect! And, thought Mathilda, that was odd too, when you came to think of it. Odd that Stephen should have risked bringing his Valerie into close contact with Nathaniel. Enough to ruin all his chances of inheriting Nathaniel's fortune, you would suppose. Stephen looked upon himself as Nathaniel's heir; sometimes Mathilda wondered whether Nat had made his will after all, overcoming that unreasoning dislike he had of naming his successor. Like Queen Elizabeth. Strange, in a man usually so hard-headed! But they were strange, these Herriards: one never got to the bottom of them.

Paula: now, what had she meant by all that nonsense about the evil influence of the house? Did she really mean it, or was she trying to instil a distaste for the place in Valerie's feather-brain. She would be quite capable of that, Mathilda thought. If there were something wrong, it wasn't the house, but the people in it. There was an uneasiness, but what on earth possessed Paula to try to make it worse? Queer, flame-like creature! She lived at such high pressure, wanted things so desperately, gave such rein to her uncurbed emotions that you could never be sure when you were seeing the real Paula, and when the unconscious actress.

The playwright: Mathilda, no sentimentalist, felt sorry for him. Probably he'd never been given a fair chance; never would be given one. Quite likely his play would be found to be a clever piece of work, possibly morbid, almost certainly lacking in box-office appeal. He was obviously hard-up: his dinner-jacket was badly cut, and had worn very shiny, poor kid! There was a frightened look behind the belligerence in his eyes, as though he saw some bleak future lying before him. He had tried to interest Nathaniel, falling between his dread of seeming obsequious and his desperate need of enlisting support. He wouldn't get a penny out of Nathaniel, of course. What a cruel little fool Paula was, to have bolstered him up with false hopes!

Stephen: Mathilda stirred restlessly as her thoughts drifted towards Stephen. Cross-grained, like his Uncle Nathaniel. Yes, but he was no fool, and yet had got himself engaged to a pretty nit-wit. You couldn't ascribe all Stephen's vagaries to his boyhood's sick disillusionment. Or could you? Mathilda put down her empty teacup. She supposed adolescent boys were kittle-cattle: people said they were. Stephen had adored another feather-brain, his mother, unlike Paula, who had never cherished illusions about Kitten.

Kitten! Even her children had called her that. What a name for a mother! thought Mathilda. Poor little Kitten, in the widow's weeds which had suited her so well! Lovely little Kitten, who had to be protected from the buffets of this cruel world! Clever little Kitten, who had married, not once, but three times, and who was now Mrs Cyrus P. Thanet, indulging her nerves and her extravagant tastes in Chicago! Yes, perhaps Stephen, who had seen through her so reluctantly, and had taken it so hard, had been soured by his discovery. But what the devil possessed him, then, to get engaged to Valerie, surely a second Kitten? He was regretting it, too, if his indecent laughter last night were anything to go by.

Valerie herself? Resolutely stifling an impulse to write her off as a gold-digger, Mathilda supposed she might have been attracted by those very peculiarities in Stephen which would most quickly disgust her: his careless rudeness, his roughness, the indifferent, sardonic gleam in his deep-set grey eyes.

Mathilda found herself wondering what Maud thought about it all, if she thought anything: a question as yet undecided. Maud, with her eternal games of Patience, the chatty biographies of royal personages which she wallowed in! Mathilda felt that there must be more to Maud than Maud chose to reveal. No mind could be quite so static, surely! She herself had sometimes suspected that Maud's placidity masked a good deal of intelligence; but when, idly curious, she had probed Maud to discover it, she had been foiled by the armour of futility in which Maud so securely encased herself. No one, Mathilda was ready to swear, knew what Maud really thought about her preposterous husband, about her brusque brother-in-law, about the quarrels that flared up between Herriard and Herriard. She did not seem to resent, or even to notice, Nathaniel's contempt of Joseph; apparently she had acquiesced in the arrangement which made her a guest on sufferance in her brother-in-law's house.

That Joseph found nothing to irk him in his position as hanger-on could not surprise anyone who knew him. Joseph, thought Mathilda, had a genius for twisting unpalatable truth to pleasing fiction. Just as Joseph saw Stephen as a shy young man with a heart of gold, so he would, without much difficulty, see Nathaniel as a fond brother, devoted (in spite of every evidence to the contrary) to himself. From the day of his first foisting himself and his wife on Nathaniel's generosity, he had begun to build up a comforting fantasy about himself and Nat. Nat, he said, was a lonely man, age-ing fast; Nat did not like to admit it, but in reality he leaned much on his younger brother; Nat would, in fact, be lost without Joe.

And if Joe could see Nat in such false colours, in what roseate mist did he clothe his own, faintly ridiculous person? Mathilda thought that she could read Joe clearly enough. A failure in life, it was necessary to his self-esteem that he should see himself as a success at least in his crowning part of Peacemaker, Beloved Uncle. Yes, that would explain Joe's insistence on this dreadful family gathering.

A laugh shook Mathilda as she flung back the bedclothes, and prepared to get up. Poor old Joe, trotting from member to member of this house-party, and pouring out quarts of what he fondly believed to be balm! If he did not drive Nat at least to distraction, it would be a miracle. He was like a clumsy, well-meaning St Bernard puppy, dropped amongst a set of people who were not fond of dogs.

When she walked into the dining-room presently, Mathilda found that her first waking fears were already being fulfilled. 'Good morning, Tilda! A white Christmas, after all!' Joseph said.

Nathaniel had breakfasted early, and had gone away. Mathilda sat down beside Edgar Mottisfont, and hoped that he would not think it necessary to entertain her with conversation.

He did not. Apart from some desultory comments on the weather, he said nothing. It occurred to her that he was a little ill-at-ease. She wondered why, remembered that he had wanted a private interview with Nathaniel on the previous evening, and hoped, with a sinking heart, that more trouble was not brewing.

Valerie, breakfasting on half a grape-fruit and some dry toast, and explaining why she did so, wanted to know what they were all going to do. Only Joseph seemed to welcome this desire to map out the day's amusements. Stephen said that he was going to walk; Paula declared that she never made plans; Roydon said nothing at all; and Mathilda only groaned.

'I believe there are some very pretty walks in the neighbourhood,' offered Maud.

'A good tramp in the snow! Almost you tempt me, Stephen!' Joseph said, rubbing his hands together. 'What does Val say, I wonder? Shall we all brave the elements, and blow the cobwebs away?'

'On second thoughts,' said Stephen, 'I shall stay indoors.' Joseph bore up under the offensiveness of this remark, merely wagging his head, and saying with a laugh: 'Someone got out of bed on the wrong side this morning!'

'Aren't you going to read your play to us, Willoughby?' asked Valerie, turning her large blue eyes in his direction.

It never took Valerie more than a day to arrive at Christian names, but Roydon felt flattered, rather excited, at hearing his on her lips. He said, stammering a little, that he would like to read his play to her.

Paula at once threw a damper on to this scheme. 'It's no use reading it just to Valerie,' she said. 'You're going to read it to everybody.'

'Not to me,' said Stephen.

Roydon bristled, and began to say something rather involved about having no desire to bore anyone with his play.

'I hate being read to,' explained Stephen casually. 'Now, now!' gently scolded Joseph. 'We are all longing to hear the play, I'm sure. You mustn't pay any attention to old Stephen. What do you say to giving us a reading after tea? We'll gather round the fire, and enjoy a real treat.'

'Yes, if Willoughby starts to read it directly after tea, Uncle Nat won't have time to get away,' said Paula, brightening.

'Nor anyone else,' interpolated her brother.

This remark not unnaturally involved Roydon in a declaration of his unwillingness to inflict the literary flowers of his brain upon an unsympathetic audience. Stephen merely said Good! but everyone else plunged into conciliatory speeches. Finally, it was agreed that Roydon should read his play after tea. Anyone, said Paula, casting a dagger-glance at her brother, incapable of appreciating Art might absent himself with her goodwill.

It next transpired that Joseph had instructed the head-gardener to uproot a young fir tree, and to bring it up to the house for decoration. He called for volunteers in this festive work, but Paula evidently considered a Christmas tree frivolous, Stephen was apparently nauseated by the very mention of such a thing, Edgar Mottisfont thought it work for the younger members of the party, and Maud, plainly, had no intention of exerting herself in any way, at all.

Maud had been reading more of the *Life of the Empress of Austria*, and created a diversion by informing the company that the Hungarians had all worshipped Elizabeth. She feared, however, that her mind had not been stable, and suggested to Roydon that she would provide an excellent subject for a play.

Roydon appeared bewildered. He said that costume pieces (with awful scorn) were hardly in his line.

'She seems to have had a very dramatic life,' persisted Maud. 'It wouldn't be sword-and-cloak, you know.'

Joseph intervened hastily, saying that he thought it would hardly be suitable, and could he not persuade Maud to lay aside the book and help him with the tree?

He could not. In the end, only Mathilda responded to his appeal for assistance. She asserted her undying love for tinsel decorations, and professed her eagerness to hang innumerable coloured balls and icicles on to the tree. 'Though I think, Joe,' she said, when the company had dispersed, 'that no one else feels any sympathy with your desire for a Merry Christmas.'

'They will, my dear; they will, when it comes to the point,' said Joseph, incurably optimistic. 'I have got a collection of little presents to hang on the tree. And crackers, of course!'

'Does it strike you that Edgar Mottisfont has got something on his mind?' asked Mathilda.

'Yes,' Joseph replied. 'I fancy there is some little matter connected with the business which has gone wrong. You know what a stick-in-the-mud Nat is! But it will blow over: you'll see!'

Judging from Mottisfont's crushed demeanour at luncheon, his interview with his sleeping partner had not been in keeping with the Christmas spirit. He looked dejected, while Nathaniel sat in disapproving gloom, repulsing all attempts to draw him into conversation.

Valerie, who seemed during the course of the morning to have made great headway with the dramatist, was unaffected by her host's blighting conduct, but everyone else seemed to feel it. Stephen was frankly morose, his sister restless, Mathilda silent, the dramatist nervous, and Joseph impelled by innate tactlessness to rally the rest of the guests on their lack of spirits.

The gloom induced by himself had the beneficent effect of raising Nathaniel's spirits at least. To find that his own ill-humour had quenched the gaiety of his guests appeared to afford him considerable gratification. Almost he rubbed his hands together with glee; and by the time the company rose from the table, he was so far restored to equanimity as to enquire what his guests proposed to do to amuse themselves during the afternoon.

Maud broke her long, ruminative silence by announcing that she would have her rest as usual, and very likely take her book up with her. Still cherishing the fancy that the life of the Empress would make a good play, she said that of course it would be rather difficult to stage that erratic lady's travels. 'But I daresay you could get over that,' she told Roydon kindly.

'Willoughby doesn't write that sort of play,' said Paula.

'Well, dear, I just thought it might be interesting,' Maud replied. 'Such a romantic life!'

Nathaniel, perceiving from the expressions of weary boredom on the faces of his guests, that the *Life of the Empress Elizabeth* was not a popular subject, at once, and with ill-disguised malignity, affected a keen interest in it. So everyone, except Stephen, who lounged out of the room, had to hear again about the length of the Empress's hair, the circus-horses, and the jealousy of the Archduchess.

'Who would have thought,' murmured Mathilda in Mottisfont's ear, 'that we undistinguished commoners should be haunted by an Empress?'

He gave her a quick, perfunctory smile, but said nothing.

'Who cares about Elizabeth of Austria, anyway?' asked Paula impatiently.

'It's history, dear,' explained Maud.

'Well, I hate history. I live in the present.'

'Talking of the present,' struck in Joseph, 'who is going to help Tilda and me to finish the tree?'

He directed an appealing look at his niece as he spoke. 'Oh, all right!' Paula said ungraciously. 'I suppose I shall have to. Though I think it's nonsense myself.'

Since it had begun to snow again, and no other entertainment offered, Valerie and Roydon also joined the tree-decorating party. They came into the billiard-room with the intention of turning on the radio, but they were quite unable to resist the lure of glittering tinsel, packets of artificial frost, and coloured candles. Roydon was at first inclined to lecture the company on the childishness of keeping up old customs, and Teutonic ones at that, but when he saw Mathilda clipping candlesticks on to the branches, he forgot that it was all very much beneath him, and said: 'Here, you'd better let me do that! If you put it there, it'll set light to the whole thing.'

Valerie, finding several boxes of twisted wire icicles, began to attach them to the tree, saying at intervals: 'Oh, look! it really is rather sweet, isn't it? Oh, I say, here's a place with absolutely nothing on it!'

Joseph, it was plain to see, was in the seventh heaven of delight. He beamed triumphantly at Mathilda, rubbed his hands together, and trotted round and round the tree, extravagantly admiring everybody's handiwork, and picking up the rickety steps whenever they fell over, which they frequently did. Towards teatime, Maud came in, and said that it looked quite a picture, and she had never realised that the Empress was a cousin of Ludwig of Bavaria, the mad one who had Wagner to stay, and behaved in such a peculiar, though rather touching, way.

Paula, who, after an abortive attempt to discuss with Mathilda the probable duration of Nathaniel's life, had bearded her uncle in his study, interrupting him in the middle of a business talk with Mottisfont, joined the Christmas-tree party midway through the afternoon in a mood of glowering bad temper. Apart from making a number of destructive criticisms, she offered no help with the decorations, but walked about the room, smoking, and arguing that, since

Nathaniel meant to leave her money in his will, she might just as well have it before he was dead. No one paid much attention to this, except Mathilda, who advised her not to count her chickens before they were hatched.

'Well, they are hatched!' said Paula crossly. 'Uncle told me he was leaving me quite a lot of money, ages ago. It isn't as though I wanted it all now: I don't. A couple of thousand would be ample, and after all, what are a couple of thousand pounds to Uncle Nat?'

Roydon, who presumably found this open discussion embarrassing, turned a dull red, and pretended to be busy fitting candles into their holders.

But nothing could stop Paula. She went on striding about the room, and maintaining a singularly boring monologue, which only Joseph listened to. He, trying to pour oil on troubled waters, said that he knew just how she felt, and well recalled his own sensations on a somewhat similar occasion, when he was billed to appear as Macbeth, in Melbourne.

'Go on, Joe! You never played Macbeth!' said Mathilda.

Joseph took this in very good part, but insisted that he had played all the great tragic rôles. It was a pity that he had not observed his wife's entry into the room before he made this boast, because Mathilda at once called upon her to deny so palpable a lie.

'I don't remember his ever appearing as Macbeth,' said Maud, in her placid way. 'But he was very good in character-parts, very good indeed.'

Everyone immediately saw Joseph as the First Gravedigger, and even Paula's lips quivered. Maud, quite unconscious of the impression she was making, began to recall the various minor rôles in which Joseph had appeared to advantage, and threw out a vague promise of looking out a book of press-cuttings, which she had put away somewhere.

'That'll be another book to be filched from her, and disposed of,' remarked Stephen in Mathilda's ear, rather too audibly.

She started, for she had not heard him come into the room. He was standing just behind her, with his hands in his pockets, and his pipe between his teeth. He looked sardonically pleased; life had quickened in his eyes; and there was a suspicion of a smile playing about his mouth. Knowing him, Mathilda guessed that he had been enjoying a quarrel, probably with his uncle. 'You're a fool,' she said abruptly.

He looked down at her, eyebrows a trifle raised. 'Why?'

'You've been quarrelling with your uncle.'

'Oh, that! I usually do.'

'You're almost certainly his heir.'

'So I understand.'

'Did Nat actually tell you so?' she asked, surprised.

'No. Improving homily from dear Uncle Joe.'

'When?'

'Last night, after you'd gone to bed.'

'Stephen, did Joe say that? That Nat had made you his heir?'

He shrugged. 'Not as tersely as that. Arch hints, winks, and nudges.'

'I expect he knows. You'd better watch your step. I wouldn't put it beyond Nat to change his mind.'

'I daresay you're right,' he said indifferently.

She felt a sudden stab of exasperation. 'Then why annoy him?'

His pipe had gone out, and he began to relight it. Over the bowl his eyes glinted at her. 'Bless your heart, I don't annoy him! He doesn't like my intended.'

'Do you?' she demanded, before she could stop herself.

He looked at her, evidently enjoying her unaccustomed discomfiture. 'Obviously.'

'Sorry!' she said briefly, and turned away.

She began, somewhat viciously, to straighten the little candles on the tree. As well as one knew Stephen one still could not get to the bottom of him. He might be in love with Valerie; he might have grown out of love with her; he might even be merely obstinate. But fool enough to whistle a fortune down the wind from mulishness? No man would be fool enough for that, thought Mathilda cynically. She glanced sideways at him, and thought, *Yes, you would; you'd be fool enough for anything in this mood. Like my bull-terriers: bristling, snarling, looking for trouble, always convinced you've got to fight, even when the other dog wants to be friendly. Oh, Stephen, why will you be such an ass?*

She looked at him again, not covertly this time, since his attention was not on her, and saw that he was watching Valerie, whom Joseph had drawn into one of the window-embrasures. He was not quite smiling, but he seemed to Mathilda to be enjoying some hidden jest. She thought, *Yes, but you're not an ass; I'm not at all sure that you're not rather devilish, in fact. You're cold-blooded, and you have a twisted sense of humour, and I wish I knew what you were thinking.* Then another thought flashed across her mind, startling her: *I wish I hadn't come here!*

As though in answer, Paula said suddenly: 'O God, how I hate this house!'

Stephen yawned. It was Roydon who asked: 'Why?'

She detached the stub of her cigarette from its long holder, and threw it into the fire. 'I can't put it into words. If I said it was evil, you'd laugh.'

'No, I shouldn't,' he said earnestly. 'I believe profoundly in the influence of human passions on their surroundings. You're tremendously psychic: I've always felt that about you.'

'Oh, Willoughby, don't!' implored Valerie, instantly distracted from her *tête-à-tête* with Joseph. 'You make me feel absolutely ghastly! I keep thinking there's something just behind me all the time.'

'Nonsense, young people, nonsense!' said Joseph robustly. 'No ghosts at Lexham Manor, I assure you!'

'Oh – ghosts!' said Paula, with a disdainful shrug.

'I often think,' offered Maud, 'that when one gets fanciful it's because one's liver is out of order.'

Paula looked so revolted by this excellent suggestion that Mathilda, to avert an explosion, said hastily that it must be time for tea. Joseph at once backed her up, and began to shoo everyone out of the room, adjuring them to go and 'wash and brush up.' He himself, he said, had one or two finishing touches to make to the decorations, and he would ask Valerie if she would just hold a few oddments for him.

The oddments consisted of two streamers, a large paper bell, a sprig of mistletoe, a hammer, and a tin of drawing-pins. Valerie was by this time bored with Christmas decorations, and she received the oddments rather sulkily, saying: 'Haven't we hung up enough things, don't you think?'

'It's just the staircase,' Joseph explained. 'It looks very bare. I meant to do it before lunch, but Fate intervened.'

'It's a pity Fate didn't make a better job of it,' said Stephen, preparing to follow Mathilda out of the room.

Joseph shook a playful fist at him, and once more picked up the step-ladder. 'Stephen thinks me a dreadful old vandal,' he told Valerie. 'I'm afraid period-stuff makes very little appeal to me. You'll say I'm a simple-minded old fellow, I expect, but I'm not a bit ashamed of it, not a bit! I like things to be cheerful and comfortable, and it doesn't matter a bit to me whether a staircase was built in Cromwell's time or Victoria's.'

'I suppose the whole house is pretty old, isn't it?' said Valerie, looking with faint interest at the staircase.

'Yes, quite a show-piece in its way,' replied Joseph, mounting the four shallow stairs which led to the first half-landing, and trying to erect the steps on it. 'Now, this is going to be tricky. I thought if I could reach that chandelier we could hang the bell from it.'

'Mr Herriard must be awfully rich, I should think,' said Valerie, pursuing her own train of thought.

'Awfully!' said Joseph, twinkling down at her.

'I wonder –' She broke off, colouring a little.

Joseph was silent for a moment; then he said: 'Well, my dear, perhaps I know what you wonder; and though one doesn't like to talk of such things, I have been meaning all day to have a little chat with you.'

She turned enquiring eyes upon him. 'Oh, do! I mean, you can say absolutely anything to me: I shall quite understand.'

He came down the stairs again, abandoning the steps, and took her arm. 'Well, I expect you've guessed that I have a very soft corner for old Stephen.'

'I know, and I think it's marvellous of you!' said Valerie.

As Stephen's treatment of his uncle was cavalier to the point of brutality, this remark was less fatuous than it sounded.

'Ah, I understand Stephen!' Joseph said, changing under her eyes from the skittish uncle into a worldly-wise observer of life. 'To know all is to forgive all.'

'I always think that's frightfully true,' said Valerie, adding after a moment's reflection: 'But has Stephen – I mean, is there anything – ?'

'No, no!' Joseph replied rather hastily. 'But life hasn't been easy for him, poor old chap! Well! life hasn't been easy for me either, and perhaps that helps me to understand him.'

He smiled in a whimsical way, but as Valerie was not at all interested in the difficulties of his life, she did not realise that he had stopped being wordly-wise, and was now a Gallant and Pathetic figure. She said vaguely: 'Oh yes, I suppose so!'

Joseph was finding her a little difficult. A less self-centred young woman would have responded to this gambit, he felt, and would have asked him sympathetic questions. With a sigh, he accepted her disinterest, and said, resuming his rôle of kindly uncle: 'But that's quite enough about me! My life

51

is nearing its close, after all. But Stephen has his all before him. Ah, when I look back to what I was at Stephen's age, I can see so many points of similarity between us! I was ever a rebel, too. I expect you find that hard to believe of such a respectable old fogy, eh?'

'Oh no!' said Valerie.

'*Eheu fugaces!*' sighed Joseph. 'When I look back, do you know, I can't find it in me to regret those carefree years?'

'Oh?' said Valerie.

'No,' said Joseph, damped. 'But why should I bore a pretty young thing like you with tales of my misspent youth? It was about Stephen I wanted to speak to you.'

'He's been utterly foul all day,' responded his betrothed with great frankness. 'It makes it absolutely lousy for me, too, only he's so damned selfish I don't suppose he even thinks of that. As a matter of fact, I've got a complete hate against him at the moment.'

'But you love him!' said Joseph, taken aback.

'Yes; but you know what I mean.'

'Perhaps I do,' said Joseph, with a wise nod. 'And I'm relying on you to bring your influence to bear on the dear old fellow.'

'What?' asked Valerie, turning her large eyes upon him in astonishment.

He pressed her arm slightly. 'Ah, you're not going to tell me that you haven't got any! No, no, that won't do!'

'But what on earth do you expect me to do?' she demanded.

'Don't let him annoy his uncle,' he said. 'Try to get him to behave sensibly! After all, though I suppose I'm the last person to preach wisdom, as this world knows it (for I'm afraid I've never had a scrap of it my whole life long!), it would be silly, wouldn't it, to throw away all this just out of perversity?'

A wave of his hand indicated their surroundings. Valerie's eyes brightened. 'Oh, Mr Herriard, is he really going to leave everything to Stephen?'

'You mustn't ask me that, my dear,' Joseph replied. 'I've done my best, that's all I can say, and now it depends on Stephen, and on you, too.'

'Yes, but I don't believe Mr Herriard likes me much,' objected Valerie. 'It's funny, because generally I go over big with old men. I don't know why, I'm sure.'

'Look in your mirror!' responded Joseph gallantly. 'I'm afraid poor Nat is a bit of a misogynist. You mustn't mind that. Just keep that young man of yours in order, that's all I ask.'

'Well, I'll try,' said Valerie. 'Not that he's likely to pay any attention to me, because he never does.'

'Now you're talking nonsense!' Joseph rallied her playfully.

'Well, all I can say is that it seems to me he pays a darned sight more attention to Mathilda Clare than he does to me,' said Valerie. 'In fact, I wonder you don't set her on to him!'

'Tilda?' exclaimed Joseph. 'No, no, my dear, you're quite wrong there! Good gracious me, as though Stephen would ever look twice at Tilda!'

'Oh, do you honestly think so?' she said hopefully. 'Of course, she isn't in the least pretty. I mean, I like her awfully, and all that sort of thing, but I shouldn't call her attractive, would you?'

'Not a bit!' said Joseph. 'Tilda's just a good sort. And now we must go and wash our hands, or we shall both be late for tea, and I shall be making Stephen jealous! I'll just lean the steps up against the wall, and finish the decorations after tea. There! I don't think they'll be in anyone's way, do you?'

Since the half-landing was a broad one, the steps were not, strictly speaking, in anyone's way, but Nathaniel, when he came out of the library, a few minutes later, took instant exception to them, and said that he wished to God Joe would come to the end of all this tomfoolery. Stephen, descending the stairs, identified himself with this wish in no uncertain tones.

'Now then, you two wet-blankets!' said Joseph. 'Tea! Ah, there you are, Maud, my dear! We wait for you to lead the way. Come along, Nat, old man! Come along, Stephen!'

'Makes you feel quite at home, doesn't he?' Stephen said, grinning at Nathaniel.

Joseph's heartiness so nauseated Nathaniel that this malicious remark made him feel quite friendly towards his nephew. He gave a snort of laughter, and followed Maud into the drawing-room.

Four

J OSEPH MANAGED TO TELL MATHILDA DURING THE COURSE
of tea that he had (as he expressed it) tipped the wink to
Valerie. She thought his impulse kind but misguided, but
he triumphantly called her attention to the better relationship already existing between Stephen and Nathaniel.
Whether this arose from the exertion of Valerie's influence,
or whether, faced by the prospect of having a play read
aloud to them by its author, they had been drawn momentarily together by a bond of mutual misfortune, was a point
Mathilda felt to be as yet undecided, but it was evident that
Stephen was making an effort to please his uncle.

The thought of the approaching reading lay heavy on
Mathilda's brain. At no time fond of being read to, she thought
the present hour and milieu so ill-chosen that nothing short
of a miracle could save this party from disruption. Glancing at
Roydon, who was nervously crumbling a cake, she felt a stir of
pity for him. He was so much in earnest, torn between his belief
in himself and his natural dread of reading his play to what
he could not but recognise as an unsympathetic audience. She
moved across the room to a chair beside him, and said, under

cover of an interchange of noisy badinage between Valerie and Joseph: 'I wish you'd tell me something about your play.'

'I don't suppose you'll any of you like it,' he said, with a sulkiness born of his nervousness.

'Some of us may not,' she replied coolly. 'Have you had anything put on yet?'

'No. At least, I had a Sunday-night show once. Not this play. Linda Bury was interested in it, but it didn't come to anything. Of course, it was very immature in parts. I see that now. The trouble is that I haven't any backing.' He pushed an unruly lock of hair off his brow, and added defiantly: 'I work in a bank!'

'Not a bad way of marking time,' she said, refusing to see in this belligerent confession anything either extraordinary or pathetic.

'If I could only get a start, I'd – I'd never set foot inside the place again!'

'You probably wouldn't have to. Has your play got popular appeal?'

'It's a serious play. I don't care about popular appeal, as you call it. I – I *know* I've got it in me to write plays – good plays! – but I'd sooner stick to banking all my life than – than –'

'Prostitute your art,' supplied Mathilda, unable to curb an irrepressible tongue.

He flushed, but said: 'Yes, that's what I do mean, though I've no doubt you're laughing at me. Do you think – do you suppose there's the least hope of Mr Herriard's being interested?'

She did not, but although she was in general an honest woman, she could not bring herself to say so. He was looking at her with such a dreadfully anxious expression on his thin face that she began, almost insensibly, to turn over vague plans in her mind for cajoling Nathaniel.

'It wouldn't cost much,' he said wistfully. 'Even if he doesn't care about art, he might like to give Paula a chance. She's quite marvellous in the part, you know. He'll see that. She's going to do the big scene, just to show him.'

'What is her part?' Mathilda enquired, feeling herself incapable of explaining that Nathaniel profoundly disliked his niece's association with the stage.

'She's a prostitute,' said the author simply.

Mathilda spilt her tea. Wild ideas of imploring Roydon not to be fool enough to read his play gave way, as she dried the skirt of her frock, to a fatalistic feeling that nothing she could say would be likely to prevent this young man from rushing on to his doom.

Stephen, who had strolled across the room to the cake-stand, saw her spill her tea, and tossed her his handkerchief. 'Clumsy wench! Here, have this!'

'Tea stains things absolutely fatally,' said Valerie.

'Not if you rub hard enough,' returned Mathilda, using Stephen's handkerchief vigorously.

'I was thinking of Stephen's hanky.'

'I wasn't. Thanks, Stephen. Do you want it back?'

'Not particularly. Come over to the fire, and steam off!'

She obeyed, rejecting various pieces of helpful advice proffered by Maud and Paula. Stephen held out a plate of small cakes. 'Take one. Always fortify yourself against coming ordeals.'

She looked round, satisfying herself that Roydon, at the other end of the long room, was out of earshot, and said in an anguished undertone: 'Stephen, it's about a prostitute!'

'What is?' he asked, interested. 'Not this misbegotten play?'

She nodded, shaken with inward laughter. Stephen looked pleased for the first time that day. 'You don't mean it! Won't Uncle enjoy himself! I meant to go away, to write mythical letters. I shan't now. I wouldn't miss this for a fortune.'

'For God's sake, behave decently!' she begged. 'It's going to be ghastly!'

'Nonsense, my girl! A good time is going to be had by all.'

'Stephen, if you're unpleasant to the poor silly young ass, I shall have a shot at murdering you!'

He opened his eyes at her. 'Sits the wind in that quarter? I wouldn't have thought it of you.'

'No, you fool. But he's too vulnerable. It would be cruelty to children. Besides, he's in deadly earnest.'

'Over-engined for his beam,' said Stephen. 'I might get a rise.'

'More than you'd bargained for, I daresay. I always play safe with that unbalanced, neurotic type.'

'I never play safe with anyone.'

'Don't talk to me in that showing-off way!' said Mathilda tartly. 'It doesn't impress me!'

He laughed, and left her side, returning to his seat beside Nathaniel on the sofa. Paula was already talking about Roydon's play, her stormy eyes daring anyone to leave the room. Nathaniel was bored, and said: 'If we've got to hear it, we've got to. Don't talk so much! I can judge your play without your assistance. Seen more good, bad, and indifferent plays in my time than you've ever dreamt of.' He rounded suddenly on Roydon. 'What category does yours come into?'

The only weapon to use against these Herriards, Mathilda knew, was a directness as brutal as their own. If Roydon were to reply boldly, *Good!* Nathaniel would be pleased. But Roydon was out of his depth, had been out of it from the moment Nathaniel's butler had first run disparaging eyes over him. He was wavering between the hostility born of an over-sensitive inferiority-complex and nourished by his host's rudeness, and a desire, which had its root only in his urgent need, to please. He said, stammering and flushing: 'Well, really, that's hardly for me to say!'

'Ought to know whether you've done good work or bad,' said Nathaniel, turning away.

'I'm quite sure we're all going to enjoy ourselves hugely,' interposed Joseph, with his sunniest smile.

'So am I,' drawled Stephen. 'I've just told Mathilda I wouldn't miss it for worlds.'

'You talk as though Willoughby were going to read you a lively farce!' Paula said. 'This is a page out of life!'

'A problem-play, is it?' said Mottisfont, with his meaningless little laugh. 'There used to be a great vogue for them at one time. *You'll* remember, Nat!'

This was said in propitiating accents, but Nathaniel, who seemed still to be cherishing rancorous thoughts about his business-partner, pretended not to hear.

'I don't write problems,' said Roydon, in rather too high a voice. 'And enjoyment is the last thing I expect anyone to feel! If I've succeeded in making you think, I shall be satisfied.'

'A noble ideal,' commented Stephen. 'But you shouldn't say it as though you thought it unattainable. Not polite.'

This sally not unnaturally covered Roydon with confusion. He flushed deeply, and floundered in a morass of disclaimers and explanations. Stephen lay back, and watched his struggles with the interest of a naturalist.

The entrance of Sturry, followed by a footman, to bear away the tea-things saved Roydon, but it was evident that Stephen's remark had shaken his already tottering balance. Paula rent Stephen verbally for several blistering minutes, and Valerie, feeling herself ignored, said that she couldn't see what there was to make such a fuss about. Joseph, divining by what Mathilda could only suppose to be a sixth sense that the play was in questionable taste, said that he was sure they were all broad-minded enough not to mind.

Nathaniel at once asserted that he was not at all broad-minded, if, by that elastic term, Joseph meant that he was prepared to stomach a lot of prurient nonsense, which was all any modern play seemed to consist of. For a minute or two, Mathilda indulged the hope that Roydon would feel himself sufficiently insulted to refuse to read the play at all; but although he did indeed show signs of rising anger, he allowed himself to be won over by Paula and Valerie, who both assured him, inaccurately, that everyone was longing to hear his masterpiece.

By this time, the butler and the footman had withdrawn, and the stage was clear. Joseph began to bustle about, trying to rearrange the chairs and sofas; and Paula, who had been hugging the typescript under one arm, gave it to Roydon, saying that he would find her word-perfect when he wanted her.

A chair and a table were placed suitably for the author, and he seated himself, rather white about the gills, but with a belligerent jut to his chin. He cleared his throat, and Nathaniel broke the expectant silence by asking Stephen for a match.

Stephen produced a box from his pocket, and handed it to his uncle, who began to light his pipe, saying between puffs: 'Go on, go on! What are you waiting for?'

'*Wormwood*,' said Roydon throatily. 'A play in three acts.'

'Very powerful title,' nodded Mottisfont knowledgeably.

Roydon threw him a grateful look, and continued: 'Act I. *The scene is a back-bedroom in a third-rate lodging-house. The bedstead is of brass, with sagging springs, and two of the knobs missing from the foot-rail. The carpet is threadbare, and the wall-paper, which is flowered in a design of roses in trellis-work tied up with blue ribbons, is stained in several places.*'

'Stained with what?' asked Stephen.

Roydon, who had never considered this point, glared at him, and said: 'Does it matter?'

'Not to me, but if it's blood you ought to say so, and then my betrothed can make an excuse to go away. She's squeamish.'

'Well, it isn't! I don't write that kind of play. The wall-paper is just stained.'

'I expect it was from damp,' suggested Maud. 'It sounds as though it would be a damp sort of a place.'

Stephen turned his mocking gaze upon her, and said: 'You shouldn't say that, Aunt. After all, we haven't heard enough to judge yet.'

'Shut up!' said Paula fiercely. 'Don't pay any attention to Stephen, Willoughby! Just go on reading. Now, all of you! You must make your minds receptive, and absorb the atmosphere of the scene: it's tremendously significant. Go on, Willoughby!'

Roydon cleared his throat again. '*Nottingham lace curtains shroud the windows, through which there can be obtained a vista of slate-roofs and chimney-stacks. A tawdry doll leans drunkenly on the dressing-table; and a pair of soiled pink corsets are flung across the only armchair.*' He looked round in a challenging kind of way as he enunciated this, and appeared to wait for comment.

'Ah yes, I see!' said Joseph, with a deprecating glance at the assembled company. 'You wish to convey an atmosphere of sordidness.'

'Quite, quite!' said Mottisfont, coughing.

'And let us admit freely that you have succeeded,' said Stephen cordially.

'I always think there's something frightfully sordid about corsets, don't you?' said Valerie. 'Those satin ones, I mean, with millions of bones and laces and things. Of course, nowadays one simply wears an elastic belt, if one wears anything at all, which generally one doesn't.'

'You'll come to it, my girl,' prophesied Mathilda.

'When *I* was young,' remarked Maud, 'no one thought of not wearing corsets. It would have been quite unheard-of.'

'You corseted your minds as well as your bodies,' interpolated Paula scornfully. 'Thank God I live in an untrammelled age!'

'When I was young,' exploded Nathaniel, 'no decent woman would have mentioned such things in public!'

'How quaint!' said Valerie. 'Stephen, darling, give me a cigarette!'

He threw his case over to her. Roydon asked, trying to control his voice, whether anyone wished him to continue or not.

'Yes, yes, for heaven's sake get on!' snapped Nathaniel testily. 'If there's any more about underwear, you can leave it out!'

'You'll have to, anyway,' added Stephen.

Roydon ignored this, and read aloud in an angry voice; '*Lucetta May is discovered, seated before her dressing-table. She is wearing a shoddy pink négligée, which imperfectly conceals –*'

'Careful!' Stephen warned him.

'*It is grimy round the edge, and the lace is torn!*' said Roydon defiantly.

'I think that's a marvellous touch!' said Valerie.

'It's surprising what a lot of dirt you can pick up from carpets, even where there's a vacuum-cleaner, which I don't suppose there would be in a place like that,' said Maud. 'I know those cheap theatrical lodging-houses, none better!'

'It is not a theatrical lodging-house!' said Roydon, goaded to madness. 'It is, as you will shortly perceive, a *bawdy* lodging-house!'

Maud's placid voice broke the stunned silence. 'I expect they're just as dirty,' she said.

'Look here!' began Nathaniel thunderously.

Joseph intervened in a hurry. 'Too many interruptions! We shall be putting Roydon off if we go on like this! I'm sure we're none of us so old-fashioned that we mind a little outspokenness!'

'Speak for yourself!' said Nathaniel.

'He is speaking for himself,' said Stephen. 'To do him justice, he is also speaking for most of the assembled company.'

'Perhaps you would rather I didn't read you any more?' suggested Roydon stiffly. 'I warn you, it is not meat for weak stomachs!'

'Oh, you must go on!' Valerie exclaimed. 'I know I'm going to adore it. Do, everybody, stop interrupting!'

'*She sits motionless, staring at her reflection in the mirror*,' suddenly declaimed Paula, in thrilling accents. '*Then she picks up a lipstick, and begins wearily to rub it on her mouth. A knock falls on the door. With a movement of instinctive coquetry, she pats her curls into position, straightens her tired body, and calls, "Come in!"*'

The spectacle of Paula enacting these movements in the improbable setting of a respectable drawing-room proved to be too much for Mathilda. She explained between chokes that she was very sorry, but that recitations always had this deplorable effect on her.

'What you can possibly find to laugh at I fail to see!' said Paula, a dangerous light in her eyes. 'Laughter was *not* the reaction I expected!'

'It wasn't your fault,' Mathilda assured her penitently. 'In fact, the more tragic recitations are the more I feel impelled to laugh.'

'I know so well what you mean!' said Joseph. 'Ah, Paula, my dear, Tilda is paying you a greater tribute than you know! You conveyed such a feeling of tension in those few gestures that our Tilda's nerves frayed under it. I remember once, when I was playing in Montreal, to a packed house, working up to a moment of unbearable tension. I felt my audience with me, hanging, as it were, on my lips. I paused for my climax; I knew myself to be holding the house in the hollow of my hand. Suddenly a man broke into laughter! Disconcerting? Yes, but I knew *why* he laughed, why he could not help laughing!'

'I wouldn't mind hazarding a guess myself,' agreed Stephen.

This pleased Nathaniel so much that he changed his mind about banning the reading of *Wormwood*, and bade Roydon, for the third time, to get on with it.

Roydon said: '*Enter Mrs Perkins, the landlady,*' and doggedly read a paragraph describing this character in terms revolting enough to have arrested the attention of his hearers had not this been diverted by Maud, who was moving stealthily about the room in search of something.

'The suspense is killing me!' Stephen announced at last. 'What are you looking for, Aunt?'

'It's all right, my dear: I'm not going to disturb anyone,' replied Maud untruthfully. 'I just wondered where I had laid my knitting down. Please go on reading, Mr Roydon! So interesting! It quite takes one back.'

Stephen, who had joined Mathilda in the search for the knitting, remarked, *sotto voce*, that he had always wondered where Joe had picked Maud up, and now he knew. Mathilda, unearthing an embryo sock on four steel needles from behind a cushion, told him he was a cad.

'Thank you, my dear,' said Maud, settling herself by the fire again. 'Now I can be getting on with it while I listen.'

The rest of Roydon's play was read to the accompaniment of the measured click of Maud's needles. It was by no means a bad play; sometimes, Mathilda thought, it hovered on the edge of brilliance; but it was no play to read to a drawing-room audience. As she had expected, it was often violent, always morbid; and it contained much that could with advantage have been omitted. Paula enjoyed herself immensely in the big scene; and neither she nor Roydon seemed capable of realising that the spectacle of his niece impersonating a fallen woman under tragic circumstances was unlikely to afford Nathaniel the least gratification. Indeed, it was only by a tremendous effort of will-power that Nathaniel was able to control himself; and while Paula's deep voice vibrated through the room, he grew more and more fidgety, and muttered under his breath in a way that boded ill for both dramatist and actress.

It was past seven o'clock before the play ended, and during the last act Nathaniel three times consulted his watch.

Once, Stephen said something in his ear which made him smile grimly, but when Roydon at last laid down his typescript there was no trace of a smile on his face. He said in awful tones: 'Very edifying!'

Paula, carried away by her own performance, was deaf to the note of anger in his voice. Her dark eyes glowed; there was a lovely colour in her cheeks; and her thin, expressive hands were restless, as always when she was excited. She started towards Nathaniel, holding out those hands. 'Isn't it a wonderful play? Isn't it?'

Mathilda, Joseph, Valerie, and even Mottisfont, whom *Wormwood* had profoundly shocked, hurried into speech, drowning whatever blistering things Nathaniel meant to say. Stephen lounged at his ease, and watched them derisively. Dread of what Nathaniel might yet say to Roydon made them praise the play in exaggerated terms. Roydon was pleased, and triumphant, but his eyes kept travelling to his host's face with an expression on them of so much anxiety that everyone felt sorry for him, and repeated that the play was arresting, original, and quite made one think.

Paula, with an obtuseness which made Mathilda want to shake her, brushed aside the compliments she was receiving on her acting, and again attacked her uncle. 'Now that you've heard it, Uncle Nat, you will help Willoughby, won't you?'

'If by that you mean will I give you the money to squander on a piece of what I can only call salacious balderdash, no, I won't!' he responded, not, however, in a loud enough voice to be overheard by the author.

Paula stared at him, as though she scarcely grasped his meaning. 'Can't you see – can't you *see* that the part is made for me?' she asked, with a little gasp.

'Upon my soul!' exploded Nathaniel. 'I should like to know what the world is coming to when a girl of your breeding can stand there and tell me the part of a harlot is made for her!'

'That out-of-date rubbish!' Paula said contemptuously. 'We are talking of Art!'

'Oh, we are, are we?' said Nathaniel, in a grim voice. 'And I suppose that is your idea of Art, is it, young woman? Well, all I have to say is that it isn't mine!'

It turned out, unfortunately for everybody else, that this was an understatement. Nathaniel had a good deal more to say, on subjects which ranged from the decadence of modern drama and the puppyishness of modem dramatists to the folly of all women in general and of his niece in particular. He added a rider to the effect that Paula's mother would have done better to have stayed at home to look after her daughter than to spend her time gadding about marrying every Tom, Dick, and Harry she met.

It was now felt by all who were privileged to hear these remarks that it would be advisable to get Roydon out of the way until Nathaniel's wrath had had time to cool. Mathilda very nobly put herself forward, and told Roydon that she had been immensely interested in *Wormwood*, and would like to have a talk with him about it. Roydon, who, besides being rather impressed by Mathilda, was naturally eager to talk about his play, allowed himself to be manoeuvred out of the room just as Joseph joined the stricken group about his brother, and, with ill-timed jocosity, smote him lightly on the back, saying: 'Well, well, Nat, we're a couple of old-stagers, eh? A crude, sometimes a violent piece of work. Yet not without merit, I think. What do you say?'

Nathaniel at once became a cripple. He said: 'My lumbago! Damn you, don't *do* that!' and tottered to a chair, one hand to the small of his back and his manly form bent with suffering.

'Why, I thought it was all right again!' said Valerie innocently.

Nathaniel, who had closed his eyes, opened them to cast a baleful glance in her direction, and replied in the voice of one whose days were attended by anguish bravely borne: 'The least touch brings it on!'

'Rubbish!' said Paula, with quite unnecessary emphasis. 'You weren't even thinking about your lumbago a minute ago! You're a miserable humbug, Uncle Nat!'

Nathaniel rather liked being abused, but he resented having his lumbago belittled, and said that the day might come when Paula would be sorry she had said that.

Maud, who was rolling up her knitting-wool, said in her sensible way that he had better have some antiphlogistin, if it was really bad.

'Of course it's bad!' snapped Nathaniel. 'And don't think I'm going to have any of that muck on me, because I'm not! If anyone had the least consideration – But I suppose that's too much to expect! As though it isn't enough to have the house filled with a set of rackety people, I'm forced to sit and listen to a play I should have thought any decent woman would have blushed to sit through!'

'When you talk about decent women you make me sick!' flashed Paula. 'If you can't appreciate a work of genius, so much the worse for you! You don't want to put your hand in your pocket: that's why you're making all this fuss! You're mean, and hypocritical, and I despise you from the bottom of my soul!'

'Yes, you'd be very glad to see me laid underground! I know that!' said Nathaniel, hugely enjoying this refreshing interlude. 'Don't think I don't see through you! All the same, you women: money's all you're out for! Well, you won't get any of mine to waste on that young puppy, and that's flat!'

'All right!' said Paula, in the accents of a tragedienne. 'Keep your money! But when you're dead I shall spend every penny you leave me on *really* immoral plays, and I shall hope that you'll know it, and hate it, and be sorry you were such a beast to me when you were alive!'

Nathaniel was so pleased by this vigorous response to his taunt that he forgot to be a cripple, and sat up quite straight in his chair, and said that she had better not count her chickens before they were hatched, since after this he would be damned if he didn't Make a Few Changes.

'Do as you please!' Paula said disdainfully. 'I don't want your money.'

'Oho, now you sing a different tune!' Nathaniel said, his eyes glinting with triumph. 'I thought that that was just what you did want – two thousand pounds of my money, and ready to murder me to get it!'

'What are two thousand pounds to you?' demanded Paula, with poor logic, but fine dramatic delivery. 'You'd never miss it, but just because you have a bourgeois taste in art you deny me the one thing I want! More than that! You are denying me my chance in life!'

'I don't care for that line,' said Stephen critically.

'You shut up!' said Paula, rounding on him. 'You've done all you can to crab Willoughby's play! I suppose your tender regard for me makes you shudder at the thought of my appearing in the rôle of a prostitute!'

'Bless your heart, I don't care what sort of a rôle you appear in!' replied Stephen. 'All I beg is that you won't stand there ranting like Lady Macbeth. Too much drama in the home turns my stomach, I find.'

'If you had a shred of decency, you'd be on my side!'

'In that case, I haven't a shred of decency. I don't like the play, I don't like the dramatist, and I object to being read to.'

'Children, children!' said Joseph. 'Come now, this won't do, you know! On Christmas Eve, too!'

'Now I *am* going to be sick,' said Stephen, dragging himself up, and lounging over to the door. 'Let me know the outcome of this Homeric battle, won't you? I'm betting six to four on Uncle Nat myself.'

'Well, really, Stephen!' exclaimed Valerie, with a giggle. 'I do think you're the limit!'

This infelicitous intervention seemed to remind Nathaniel of her existence. He glared at her, loathing her empty prettiness, her crimson fingernails, her irritating laugh; and gave vent to his feelings by barking at Stephen. 'You're as bad as your sister! There isn't a penny to choose between you! You've got *bad taste*, do you hear me? This is the last time either of you will come to Lexham! Put that in your pipe, and smoke it!'

'Tut-tut!' said Stephen, and walked out of the room, greatly disconcerting Sturry, who was standing outside with a tray of cocktails, listening with deep appreciation to the quarrel raging within.

'I beg your pardon, sir; I was about to enter,' said Sturry, fixing Stephen with a quelling eye.

'What a lot you'll have to regale them with in the servants' hall, won't you?' said Stephen amiably.

'I was never one to gossip, sir, such being beneath me,' replied Sturry, in a very grand and despising way.

He stalked into the room, bearing his burden. Paula, who was addressing an impassioned monologue to her elder uncle, broke off short, and rushed out; Joseph urged Valerie, and Maud, and Mottisfont to go up and change for dinner; and Nathaniel told Sturry to bring him a glass of the pale sherry.

While this family strife had been in full swing, Mathilda, in the library, had been explaining to Willoughby, as tactfully as she could, that Nathaniel was not at all likely to finance his play. He was strung up after his reading, and at first he seemed hardly to understand her. Plainly, Paula had led him to suppose that her uncle's help was a foregone conclusion. He went perfectly white when the sense of what Mathilda was saying penetrated his brain, and said in a trembling voice: 'Then it's all no use!'

'I'm afraid it's no use as far as Nat is concerned,' Mathilda said. 'It isn't his kind of play. But he isn't the only potential backer in the world, you know.'

He shook his head. 'I don't know any rich people. Why won't he back it? Why shouldn't p-people like me be g-given a chance? It isn't fair! People with money – people who don't care for anything but –'

'I think you'd be far better advised to send your play to some producer in the usual way,' said Mathilda, in a bracing voice calculated to check hysteria.

'They're all afraid of it!' he said. 'They say it hasn't got box-office appeal. But I know – I *know* it's a good play! I've – I've sweated blood over it! I can't give it up like this! It means so much to me! You don't know what it means to me, Miss Clare!'

She began gently to suggest that he had it in him to write other plays, plays with the desired box-office appeal, but he interrupted her, saying violently that he would rather starve than write the sort of play she meant. Mathilda began to feel a little impatient, and was quite glad to see Paula stride into the room.

'Paula!' said Roydon despairingly, 'is it true, what Miss Clare says? Is he going to refuse to put up the money?'

Paula was flushed and bright-eyed, stimulated by her quarrel with Nathaniel. She said: 'I've just told him what I think of him! I told him –'

'Well, we don't want you to tell us,' said Mathilda, losing patience. 'You ought to have known that there wasn't a hope!'

Paula's gaze flickered to her face. 'I shall get the money. I always get what I want, always! And I want this more than I've ever wanted anything in my life!'

'Judging by those of Nat's remarks which I was privileged to hear –'

'Oh, that's nothing!' Paula said, tossing back her hair. 'He doesn't mind having rows. We none of us do. We like rows! I shall talk to him again soon. You'll see!'

'I hope to God I shan't!' said Mathilda.

'Ah, you're so un-understanding!' Paula said. 'I know him much better than you do. Of course I shall get the money! I know I shall!'

'Don't buoy yourself up with false hopes: you won't!' said Mathilda.

'I've got to get it!' Paula said, looking rapt, and tense. 'I've *got* to!'

Roydon glanced uncertainly from her glowing face to Mathilda's discouraging one. He said in a dejected voice: 'I suppose I'd better go and change. It doesn't seem much use –'

Paula said: 'I'm coming too. It is of use, Willoughby! I always get my own way! *Really!*'

A merry Christmas! Mathilda thought, watching them go. She took a cigarette from the box on the table, and lit it, and sat down by the fire, feeling quite limp. *All this emotional strain!* she thought, with a wry smile. It was not her affair, of course, but the threadbare playwright, tiresome though he was, had roused her pity, and Paula had a disastrous way of dragging even mere onlookers into her quarrels. Besides, one couldn't sit back and watch this ill-starred party going to perdition. One had at least to try to save it from utter ruin.

She was forced to admit that she could not immediately perceive any way of saving it from ruin. If Paula's folly did not precipitate a crisis, Joseph's balm-spreading would. There could be no stopping either of them. Paula cared only for what concerned herself; Joseph could never be convinced that his oil was not oil but vitriol. He saw himself as a peacemaker; he was probably peacemaking now, Mathilda reflected: infuriating Nat with platitudes, making bad worse, all with the best intentions.

A door opened across the wide hall; Nathaniel's voice came to Mathilda's ears. 'Damn you, stop pawing me about! For two pins, I'd turn the whole lot of them out of doors, bag and baggage!'

Mathilda smiled to herself. *Joseph at it again!*

'Now, Nat, old fellow, you know you don't mean that! Let's talk the whole thing over quietly together!'

'I don't want to talk it over!' shouted Nathaniel. 'And don't call me old fellow! You've done enough, inviting all these people to my house, and turning it into a damned bazaar! Paper-streamers! Mistletoe! I won't have it! Next you'll want to dress up as Santa Claus! I hate Christmas, do you hear me? Loathe it! abominate it!'

'Not you, Nat!' Joseph said. 'You're just an old curmudgeon, and you're upset because you didn't like young Roydon's play. Well, I didn't care for it either, if you want to know, but, my dear old chap, youth must be served!'

'Not in my house!' snarled Nathaniel. 'Don't come upstairs with me! I don't want you!'

Mathilda heard him stump up the four stairs which led to the first half-landing. A crash which she had no difficulty in recognising followed. Nathaniel, she deduced, had knocked over the steps.

She strolled to the door. The steps lay on the ground, and Joseph was tenderly assisting his brother to rise from his knees.

'My dear Nat, I'm so sorry! I'm afraid it was my fault,' he said remorsefully. 'I'm a careless fellow! I had meant to have finished my poor little decorations before this!'

'Take them down!' ordered Nathaniel in a strangled voice. 'All of them! This instant! Clumsy jackass! My *lumbago*!'

These dread words struck Joseph to silence. Nathaniel went upstairs, clinging to the handrail, once more a helpless cripple.

'Oh dear!' said Joseph ridiculously. 'I never thought they would be in anyone's way, Nat!'

Nathaniel returned no answer, but dragged his painful way upstairs to his bedroom. Mathilda heard a door slam, and laughed.

Joseph looked round quickly. 'Tilda! I thought you'd gone up! Oh dear, dear, did you see what happened? Most unfortunate!'

'I did. I knew those steps of yours would be the death of someone.'

Joseph picked them up. 'Well, my dear, I don't want to tell tales out of school, but Nat's a naughty old man. He deliberately knocked them over! All that fuss!'

'I could wish that you hadn't left them there,' Mathilda said. 'Lumbago, I feel, will be our only topic of conversation this evening.'

He smiled, but shook his head. 'No, no, that isn't quite fair! He has got lumbago, you know, and it *is* very painful. We must put our heads together, you and I, Tilda.'

'Not me,' said Mathilda vulgarly.

'My dear, I'm relying on you. Nat likes you, and we *must* smooth him down! Now, I'll just put these steps out of harm's way, and then we'll think what can be done.'

'I,' said Mathilda firmly, 'am going upstairs to change.'

Five

~~~~~~~~~~~

WHILE JOSEPH BORE THE STEP-LADDER AWAY TO SAFETY in the billiard-room, Mathilda went back into the library to pick up her handbag. She had reached the top of the stairs before he overtook her, but he did overtake her, and, tucking a hand in her arm, said that he did not know what they would any of them do without her.

'No soft soap, thanks, Joe,' replied Mathilda. 'I'm not going to be the sacrifice.'

'Sacrifice indeed! What an idea!' He lowered his voice, for they had reached the door of Nathaniel's room. 'My dear, help me to save my poor party!'

'No one can save your party. You might do a bit towards it by removing all paper festoons and mistletoe from his outraged sight.'

'Sh!' Joseph said, with an absurdly nervous glance towards Nathaniel's shut door. 'You know Nat! That was only just his way. He doesn't really mind my decorations. I'm afraid the trouble is more difficult to deal with than that. To tell you the truth, Tilda, I wish Paula hadn't brought that young man here.'

'We all wish that,' said Mathilda, coming to a halt outside her own bedroom. 'But don't you worry, Joe! He may have added to Nat's annoyance, but he isn't the cause of it.'

He sighed. 'I did so hope that Nat would have taken to Valerie!'

'You're an incurable optimist.'

'I know, I know, but one had to try to ease things for poor old Stephen! I must confess I am a little bit disappointed in Valerie. I've tried to make her realise just how things are, but – well, she doesn't co-operate, does she?'

'That, Joe, is meiosis,' said Mathilda dryly.

'And now there's this bother with Mottisfont,' he went on, a worried frown creasing his brow.

'What's he been up to?'

'Oh, my dear, don't ask me! You know what an impractical old fool I am about business! He seems to have done something that Nat very much disapproves of, but I don't know all the ins and outs of it. I only know what Mottisfont told me, which was really nothing but hints, and very mysterious. But there! Nat's bark is always worse than his bite, and I daresay it will all blow over. What we've got to do is to think of some way of keeping Nat in a good humour. I don't think this is quite the moment for me to approach him about Mottisfont's affairs.'

'Joe,' said Mathilda earnestly, 'you can count me out in your benevolent schemes, but I'll give you a piece of advice! Don't approach Nat about anyone's affairs!'

'They all look to me, you see,' he said, with one of his whimsical smiles.

She supposed that he really did see himself as a general mediator, but she was feeling tired, and this resumption of his peacemaking rôle exasperated her. 'I haven't noticed it!' she said.

He looked hurt, but nothing could seriously impair his vision of himself. A couple of minutes later, Mathilda, turning on the taps in the bathroom they both shared, could hear him humming to himself in his dressing-room. He hummed the first few phrases of an old ballad inaccurately and incessantly, and Mathilda, who had an ear for music, thumped on the door leading from the bathroom to his dressing-room, and begged him either to learn the ditty or to gag himself. Then she was sorry, because, finding that by raising his voice a trifle he could easily converse with her, he became very chatty, and favoured her with some sentimental reminiscences of his careless youth. Occasionally he would interrupt himself to ask her if she was listening, but he did not seem to need the stimulus of intelligent comment, and, indeed, went on talking happily for quite some time after she had left the bathroom. However, he was not at all offended by the discovery that for quite ten minutes his conversation had reached her only as an indistinguishable burble of sound, but laughed good-humouredly, and said, Alas, he found himself living very much in the past nowadays, and feared he must be turning into a dreadful old bore. After that he returned to his Victorian ballad, alternately humming and singing it until Mathilda began to nourish thoughts of homicide.

She called out to him: 'Are you sure you never appeared in Grand Opera, Joe? What a Siegfried you'd have made! Figure and all!'

'Naughty, naughty!' he replied, with an archness which made her understand Stephen's brutality to him. 'Tilda dear, are you dressed yet?'

'Nearly. Why?'

'Don't go down without me! I've got an idea!'

'You're not laying your head together with mine, Joe: don't think it!'

He only laughed at this, but he must have kept an ear cocked, for when she opened her door a few minutes later, he instantly emerged from his room, rubbing his hands together, and saying gleefully: 'Ah, you can't fox your old uncle, you bad girl!'

'Let me point out to you, Joe, that you're not my uncle, and that even my best friends don't call me a girl.'

He linked arms with her. 'Wasn't it the Immortal Bard who wrote, *To me, dear friend, you never can be old*?'

Mathilda closed her eyes for an anguished moment. 'If we are going to quote at one another, I warn you, you'll come off the worst!' she said. 'I know a song which runs, *Your parents missed a golden opportunity: They should of course have drowned you in a bucket as a child.*'

He squeezed her arm, chuckling. 'Oh, that tongue of yours, Tilda! Never mind! I don't care a bit! not a little bit! Now, just you listen to the plan I've made! You're going to play Piquet with Nat after dinner.'

'Not on your life.'

'Yes, yes, you are! I had thought of Bridge again, but that would mean Mottisfont, and he doesn't seem to be a very strong player, and you know how seriously Nat takes his game! And then I suddenly remembered those grand battles you and he had the last time you stayed here, and how much he enjoyed them. I suggest that after dinner you should challenge Nat to a rubber, while I keep the others amused in the billiard-room. Charades or Clumps, or one of those other good, old-fashioned round games.'

'If the choice lies between Piquet and a good, old-fashioned round game, you've sold your idea, Joe. I'll co-operate.'

He beamed with gratitude, and might, she felt, have patted her on the back had they not by this time reached the drawing-room.

Neither Stephen nor Mottisfont had as yet come downstairs, but the other three guests had assembled, and were standing about, drinking cocktails, while Maud, who said that she never touched spirits, was hunting ineffectively for the *Life of the Empress*, which she remembered having laid down somewhere, though she wasn't sure where. She rather unwisely asked Paula if she had seen it, and Paula, who was wrapped in gloomy reflection, came to earth with a start, and a gesture of insupportable irritation.

'I?' she said. 'What, in God's name, should I want with your book?'

'I only wondered, dear,' said Maud mildly. 'I remember having it here after lunch. Or did I take it up with me when I went for my rest?'

Paula threw her an exasperated glance, and began to pace about the room, once more wrapped in her dark thoughts.

Valerie, after making several vain attempts to flirt with Roydon, who seemed as dejected as Paula, flounced over to the fire, looking sulky. Here Joseph joined her, paying her a few fulsome compliments, and really doing his best, Mathilda thought, to entertain her.

But Valerie did not want to flirt with Joseph; Valerie was finding the party very dull, and since she did not belong to a generation trained to be polite to its elders she snubbed Joseph, and told Maud that she hadn't seen her book and wouldn't know it from another if she did see it.

Roydon brought a cocktail to Mathilda, and lingered undecidedly beside her. After a few desultory remarks, he suddenly said in a burst of confidence: 'I've been thinking over what you've said, and I've come to the conclusion you're right. I shall try it out again. After all, I haven't tried Henry Stafford. He might like it. He put on *Fevered Night*, you know, and it only ran for a week. I shan't bother about backers any more. You're quite right: the play is strong enough to stand on its own legs.'

Mathilda could not recall having made such a statement, but she was glad that Roydon, who, so short a time since, had been in despair over Nathaniel's refusal to back his play, had recovered his optimism, and she cordially applauded his decision. Edgar Mottisfont then came in, saying that he hoped he hadn't been keeping everyone waiting, and was chatty, in a determined way, until Joseph asked him if he had seen Nat or Stephen. This seemed to bring the memory of his interview with Nathaniel unpleasantly to mind, and he said No, he hadn't seen either of them, and relapsed into a depressed silence.

Stephen lounged in a few minutes later, similarly

taciturn, and everybody glanced at the clock, and wished that Nathaniel would hurry up.

At half-past eight, Sturry appeared to announce dinner, saw that his master was not present, and went away again, looking affronted. Joseph said hopefully that he was sure Nat would be down in a minute, but when ten minutes had elapsed, he said that Nat must have forgotten the time, and suggested to Stephen that he should go upstairs to fetch his uncle down.

Stephen was pouring himself out another glass of sherry, and replied with his customary brusqueness that if Joe was so anxious for Nat's presence he had better go and fetch him for himself.

'Come, come, Stephen!' said Mottisfont. 'Not very civil of you, eh, my boy?'

'Oh, I don't pay any heed to that old bear of a nephew of mine!' Joseph said sunnily. 'Stephen and I understand one another. Paula dear, suppose you were just to run up, and tap on your uncle's door?'

'No, thank you!' Paula said, with an angry little laugh. 'I've already tried that, because I wanted to speak to him, but he wouldn't even answer.'

Stephen grinned. 'No flies on Uncle Nat. Let's go in to dinner.'

Valerie looked as though Nathaniel's absence from his board would be a relief to her, but said: 'Oh, but we can't, without Mr Herriard, can we?'

'What a nice sense of convention you have, my pretty!' said Stephen.

'You're a set of lazybones!' Joseph told them. 'I see I shall have to trot up myself.'

'I didn't phrase it quite like that, but you've interpreted my meaning correctly,' said Stephen.

Paula gave an unwilling laugh, but said, as Joseph left the room: 'You're in a sweet mood, brother!'

'Matching yours, sister,' he replied, smiling at her with an amiability belied by his shut teeth.

'I think I'm suffering from an overdose of Herriard,' said Mathilda.

Maud, who had abandoned the search for her book, and was seated in her usual place beside the fire, looked up fleetingly from Stephen and his sister to Mathilda. Her face was expressionless, but she moved her plump little hands, clasping them in her lap rather tightly.

'I wonder how you stand it, Maud,' Mathilda said.

'I'm used to it, dear,' Maud replied.

Joseph's voice was heard calling to Stephen from the head of the stairs. 'Stephen, old chap, just come here a minute, will you?'

Edgar Mottisfont said: 'Oh dear! I hope nothing's wrong!'

'What should be wrong?' said Stephen, strolling to the door. 'What do you want, Joe?'

'Come up, my boy, will you?'

He shrugged, and went out.

'What *can* be the matter?' wondered Valerie. 'Do you suppose Mr Herriard's ill, or something?'

'Ill? Why should he be? He was perfectly well when I saw him last,' said Mottisfont.

'My lumbago,' murmured Mathilda.

Stephen, leisurely mounting the stairs, found Joseph, and Nathaniel's valet, Ford, standing outside Nathaniel's door. They both looked worried. Stephen said, 'Well, what's wrong?'

'Stephen, my boy, I don't quite like it,' Joseph replied. 'Nat doesn't answer my knock and Ford tells me he didn't answer his, half an hour ago.'

'So what?' retorted Stephen. 'Perhaps he's fed up with the human race, and who shall blame him?'

'Don't joke, old chap! I'm afraid something must be wrong. I think we ought to break down the door.'

'There isn't a sound to be heard, sir,' Ford said, his ear to the crack. 'I've called repeatedly, Mr Stephen.'

Stephen raised his brows. 'Oh? Uncle Nat! Uncle Nat, are you all right?'

There was no answer. Frowning, Stephen set his shoulder to the door. Under the combined efforts of himself and Ford, the lock burst at last, and both men were precipitated into the room.

It was a large, wainscoted apartment, with a four-poster bed, and heavy black oak furniture. The curtains had been drawn across the windows, and the lights were turned on. A red fire glowed in the hearth, and not far from it, beside a ladder-back chair, Nathaniel Herriard lay on the floor, with his head on his arm, as though asleep.

'Good God, he must have fainted!' Stephen exclaimed, striding forward, and dropping to his knees beside Nathaniel. 'Get some brandy, Ford! Don't stand there staring!'

Joseph came bustling up in a twitter of concern. 'Oh dear, how can this have happened? Nat, old man, Nat!'

'It's no use yapping at him,' Stephen said, looking rather white. 'He's dead.'

'Stephen!' gasped Joseph. '*Dead?* Nonsense! He can't be! He's fainted, that's all!'

Stephen rose from his knees. 'Feel him,' he said crudely.

'No, no, no, I won't believe it!' Joseph stammered, in his turn kneeling beside Nathaniel's body, and picking up one of his life-less hands. 'Fetch a mirror! If we hold it in front of his lips –'

'You fool, can't you see he's dead?' Stephen snapped.

Joseph gave a moan, and began distractedly to chafe the hand he held. 'But how could he be? He wasn't ill, Stephen! Nat, my dear Nat!'

'I don't know. Stroke, I suppose. What do we do now?'

'A doctor, quickly! No, no, he can't be dead!'

'Yes, I suppose we ought to send for a doctor,' Stephen said, his voice jumpy under its studied nonchalance. 'Ford had better ring up. Cheerful Christmas party, yours, Joe.'

'Don't!' Joseph begged, in broken tones.

The valet came hurrying back into the room with the brandy decanter, and a glass, but was checked on the thresh-old by Stephen, who said: 'That won't be wanted. He's dead. Go and ring up his doctor, will you?'

'Dead, sir?' said Ford, turning a sickly colour. 'Not the *master*, Mr Stephen?'

'Who else, fool? On second thoughts, you can give me that brandy. Go and get hold of a doctor, and be quick about it, see?'

'Ford!' Joseph said, in a strangled voice. 'Say nothing of this to anyone!'

'Why not?' demanded Stephen. 'They've got to know. Not proposing to carry on with your blasted festivities, are you?'

'Stephen, Stephen, you are in the presence of death!'

'That's what I told you,' Stephen replied hardly, pouring himself out some brandy. 'Unnerving, isn't it?'

'Go, Ford!' Joseph said. 'Just tell Dr Stoke that Mr Herriard has met with an accident, and beg him to come at once!'

'Why the euphemism?' enquired Stephen, as the stricken valet withdrew.

Joseph said, hushed: 'Come here a moment, my boy. It wasn't a stroke. Oh, my God, Stephen, Nat has been murdered!'

'Have you gone mad?' Stephen demanded, the brandy half-way to his lips.

'Look!' said Joseph, holding up his hand.

The palm of it was stained with blood. Stephen set down his glass with a jarring sound on the mantelpiece, and came back to Nathaniel's body. 'How – ? Where – ? What the devil are you driving at?'

Joseph dragged his handkerchief from his pocket, and passed it over his face. 'I was trying to straighten him,' he said unsteadily. 'I felt something sticky on his back. He's been stabbed, Stephen! My brother Nat!'

'Damn it, he was in here with the door locked!' Stephen said. 'He can't have been stabbed!'

'Look!' Joseph said, averting his face. 'You must forgive me, but I can't. Stupid of me, but I can't. Not again!'

'The brandy's on the table,' Stephen said, turning Nathaniel's body on to its face. 'My God, you're right!'

Joseph rose from his knees, tottered to the table, and sank into a chair by it, dropping his head in his hands, and groaning. Nathaniel's coat, over the lower lumbar region, was sticky with congealing blood. There was a slit in the material, clotted round the edges with blood. Stephen said curtly: 'He must have bled internally. Hardly any outside. Now we are in a mess!'

'It doesn't seem possible! I can't believe it! Nat, of all people!'

'Here, have some brandy!' Stephen said, fetching his glass from the mantelpiece.

Joseph gulped down the neat spirit, and achieved a wan smile. 'Yes, yes, we must be calm! We must try to think. This is a terrible business, Stephen. One's brain seems to be numb. Those young people downstairs, making merry in their innocence, while here, in this room, you and I confront –'

'Can it!' said Stephen brutally. 'Merriment is not the predominant note of this sanguinary party, and you know it! And as for innocence – I wonder who the devil did this?'

This reflection seemed to pull Joseph together. He sat up, and gave a gasp. 'One had not thought of that! I suppose the shock of it – Stephen, this is appalling! Who *could* have done so terrible a thing?'

Stephen walked over to the windows, and twitched the curtains apart. After a brief inspection, he turned, and said: 'Do you realise that the door was locked, and every window shut?'

Joseph, who was wandering about the room in a distracted way, blinked at him. 'The bathroom! That's how the murderer must have got in!'

Stephen's eyes went swiftly to the door leading into the bathroom. It stood ajar, and a light showed beyond it. He walked into the room. A bath had been prepared for Nathaniel; his towels were laid over the hot rail; the bathmat had been spread on the floor. The door was locked, and only the ventilator above the casement window was open.

'That door's locked too,' Stephen said, returning to the bedroom. 'Work that out, if you can!'

'The door locked?' Joseph said blankly. 'Are you *sure*, Stephen?'

'Of course I'm sure!'

Ford came back into the room. 'The doctor will be round immediately, sir. And Miss Paula's coming up, sir. I couldn't stop her. Well, I didn't rightly know what to say, Mr Joseph.'

'Stephen, this is no sight for a woman!' Joseph exclaimed. 'She mustn't come in!'

Stephen threw him a contemptuous glance, and made no movement to intercept his sister's entrance.

Paula came in in her usual tempestuous way, saying: 'What is it? Why don't you come down? What is all the mystery?'

'That will be a puzzle for the police,' replied Stephen.

She saw Nathaniel's body, and her eyes narrowed. She stood staring down at it for a moment, growing a little pale, and then asked in a tight voice: 'Is he dead?'

'Oh yes!' Stephen answered.

'What killed him?'

'You have the wrong word. Not what: who.'

She looked at him, something hard and anxious in her eyes. 'Was he murdered, then?'

'Stabbed in the back.'

She shuddered. 'How horrible! How horrible!'

There was a silence. Joseph broke it. 'You oughtn't to be here, Paula,' he said feebly.

'Why not?'

'Dewy girlhood,' Stephen explained.

'Oh!' She hunched a scornful shoulder. 'What are we to do?'

'I suppose we ought to notify the police. In fact, I may as well do so at once,' Stephen said, moving to the door.

'On Christmas Eve!' Joseph groaned, as though he found this an added torture. 'Oh, Paula, Paula!'

She flashed round upon him. 'Why do you say that? Do you suppose I had anything to do with this?'

'Oh, my dear, no!' he said, shocked. 'Of course you didn't!'

'Who did? Have you any idea?'

'I can't think, my dear. It's too hideous! I try to realise it, to pull myself together –'

'This house! This wicked, horrible house!' She burst out, looking wildly round. 'You laughed at me when I told you it was evil!'

'My dear, you're overwrought!' he said, looking somewhat taken aback. 'The house can't have killed poor Nat!'

'Its influence! Acting on us all, impelling *one* of us –'

'Hush, Paula, hush!' he said. 'That's nonsense! There, my poor child, there! Come away! It isn't fit for you to be here.' He put his arm round her, and felt how tense she was, yet trembling a little.

'It wasn't one of us,' she said, speaking with difficulty. 'It couldn't have been. Someone through the window – robbery, perhaps. The door was locked!'

'Paula dear, did Ford tell you that?'

'I knew it! I tried to get in, before I went downstairs! He wouldn't answer when I knocked.'

'Oh, Paula, why didn't you tell us?' he exclaimed.

'I didn't think anything of it. Only that he was sulking. We'd had a row. *You* know what he was! Besides, I did tell you, when you asked me to go up and call him.'

'Too late!' he said tragically.

'It must always have been. I suppose he was dead when I knocked on the door.'

He winced. 'Paula dear, not that *hard* voice!'

There was a look of Stephen in her face as she answered: 'It's no use expecting me to sentimentalise. I'm honest, anyway. I didn't like him. I don't even care that he's dead. He was mean and tyrannical.'

This was very shocking to Joseph. He looked really pained, and rather anxious too, and said: 'We mustn't let ourselves become hysterical, Paula. You don't mean that. No, no, your old uncle knows you better than that!'

She shrugged. 'I hate being idealised.'

He took one of her thin hands, and fondled it. 'Gently, my dear, gently! We must keep our heads, you know.'

She understood this to mean that she must keep hers, and said: 'You mean that the police will think I did this, because of my quarrel with him? All right! Let them!'

'No, my dear, they could never suspect a girl of your age, I feel sure. But don't talk unkindly of poor Nat! And, Paula! try to make Stephen guard his tongue too! *We* know how little that manner of his means, but others don't, and some of the things he says – only for effect, the silly fellow! but I dread his doing it before the police! Oh dear, I never thought when I planned this party that it would end like this. I meant it all to be so jolly and happy!'

'We'd better go downstairs,' she said abruptly.

He heaved a sigh. 'I suppose it's foolish of me, but I don't like to leave him here alone.'

It was plain from her expression that she thought this very foolish, so after looking down at Nathaniel's body for a moment he accompanied her out of the room, saying in a melancholy tone: 'My last leave-taking! Perhaps it will not be for so long, after all.'

Ford was standing at the head of the stairs, conversing in whispers with one of the housemaids. The girl, after the manner of her kind, was torn between excitement and a conventional impulse to burst into tears. She scuttled away when she saw Joseph. Paula flushed, and said through her teeth: 'Gossip already! That's what we shall have to face!'

Joseph pressed her arm admonishingly, told the valet to mount guard over Nathaniel's bedroom, and escorted his niece downstairs. 'Stephen will have broken the terrible news to them by now,' he said.

Stephen had indeed performed this office. Having notified the local police-station, five miles distant, he had walked into the drawing-room, where the rest of the party was still assembled, in varying degrees of impatience and uneasiness, and had said at his most sardonic: 'No use waiting for Uncle Nat. As you've no doubt guessed, he's dead.'

'Dead?' Mathilda exclaimed, after a moment's stupefied silence. 'Are you joking?'

'I am not. To put it plainly, someone stuck a knife in his back.'

Valerie gave a scream, and clutched at the nearest support, which happened to be Roydon's arm. He paid no heed to her, but stood staring at Stephen, with his jaw dropping.

Mottisfont said in an angry, querulous tone: 'I don't believe it! This is one of your mistaken ideas of humour, Stephen, and I don't like it!'

Maud's hands were still clasped in her lap. She sat still, a plump, upright little figure, with a rigid back. Her pale eyes studied Stephen, travelled on to Mottisfont, to Roydon, to Valerie, and sank again.

'It's true?' Mathilda said stupidly.

'Unfortunately for us, quite true.'

'You mean he's been murdered,' said Roydon, as though the words stuck in his throat.

'Oh no! I can't bear it!' Valerie whimpered. 'It's too ghastly!'

Mottisfont passed a hand across his mouth. He asked in a voice which he tried hard to keep level: 'Who did it?'

'I've no idea,' Stephen replied. He took a cigarette from

the box on the table, and lit it. 'Interesting problem, isn't it?' he drawled.

Six

HIS WORDS WERE FOLLOWED BY A RATHER STUNNED silence. He smoked for a moment, looking round in malicious amusement at the various countenances turned towards him. It was impossible to read the thoughts behind them; they looked shut-in, suddenly guarded, even a little furtive. He said cordially: 'Really, no one would know which was the actor amongst us! we're damned good, all of us.'

Maud looked at him, expressionless, but said nothing. Edgar Mottisfont said angrily: 'A remark – a remark in the worst of bad taste!'

'Herriard,' Mathilda said succinctly.

Joseph came in with Paula. She looked pale, exchanged a glance with her brother, and asked him curtly for a cigarette. He put his hand in his pocket, withdrew it again, and nodded to the box on the table. Joseph had gone over to his wife, and had taken her hand in both of his. 'My dear, we are bereaved indeed,' he said, with a solemn depth of tone which made Mathilda feel an insane desire to giggle.

'Stephen says that Nathaniel has been murdered,' Maud said calmly. 'It seems very strange.'

The inadequacy of this comment, although typical of Maud, momentarily robbed Joseph of the power to display deeper emotions. He looked disconcerted, and said that he could see that the shock had numbed her. The rest of the company perceived that whatever feelings of grief or of horror might inhabit Joseph's inmost soul he would not for long be able to resist the opportunity thus afforded him to seize the centre of a tragic stage. Already he was seeing himself, Mathilda thought, as the chief mourner, the brave mainstay of a stricken household.

Attention swerved away from him to Valerie. Fright had enlarged the pupils of her lovely eyes; her mouth drooped; she said in a soft wail: 'I wish I hadn't come! I want to go home!'

'But you can't go home,' Stephen replied. 'You'll be wanted by the police, like the rest of us.'

Tears spangled her lashes. 'Oh, Stephen, don't let them! I don't know anything! I can't be of any use, and I know Mummy would not like me to be here!'

'Nobody could possibly suspect you!' Roydon said, looking noble, and glaring at Stephen.

'My poor child!' Joseph said, creditably, everyone felt, in face of so much folly. 'You must be brave, my dear, and calm. We must all be brave. Nat would have wished it.'

A certain pensiveness descended upon the company, as each member of it pondered this pronouncement. Mathilda felt that Joseph would soon succeed in making them forget the real Nathaniel, and accept instead the figment of his rose-coloured imagination. She said: 'What do we do now?'

'We have already sent for the doctor,' Joseph said, with a glance of fellowship thrown in his nephew's direction. 'There is nothing that we can do.'

'We can have dinner,' said Paula, brusquely putting into words the unworthy thought in more than one mind.

There was an outcry. Valerie said that it made her sick to think of eating; Mottisfont remarked that it was hardly the time to think of dinner.

'How much longer do you want to wait?' asked Stephen. 'It's already past nine.'

Mottisfont found Stephen so annoying that he could hardly keep his animosity out of his voice. Stephen made him feel a fool, and some evil genius always prompted him to follow up one ineptitude with another. He now said: 'Surely none of us means to have dinner tonight!'

'Why not tonight, if we mean to eat tomorrow?' Stephen enquired. 'When will it be decent for us to eat again?'

'You make a mock of everything!'

Joseph stepped forward, laying one hand on Stephen's shoulder, the other on Mottisfont's. 'Oh, my dear people, hush!' he said gently. 'Don't let us forget – don't let us allow our nerves to get the better of us!'

'I will ring the bell,' said Maud, doing so.

'Have you sent for the police?' Paula asked her brother.

'We won't talk of that, dear child,' said Joseph, with misplaced optimism.

Paula's words appeared to let loose pent-up excitement. Even Mathilda heard herself saying: 'But who could it have possibly been?' In the middle of this valueless babel, Sturry came in, his countenance schooled to an expression of rigid gloom. He stood by the door, a mute at the funeral.

'Ah, here is our good Sturry!' said Joseph, drawing him into the family circle by this affectionate address.

Sturry would not be so drawn. He stood immovable, despising people who did not know their places. 'You rang, sir?' he asked frigidly.

'Yes, yes!' Joseph said. 'You have heard the terrible news? I need not ask you!'

'No, sir. The news was conveyed to the Hall by Ford. I am extremely sorry to hear of the occurrence, sir.'

'Ah, Sturry, you must feel it too! What a tragedy! What a terrible shock!'

'Indeed yes, sir,' Sturry replied, conveying by these simple words some impression of the affront he had suffered. No one could feel that he would have engaged himself to wait on Nathaniel if he could have foreseen these vulgar events. It seemed reasonable to suppose that he would hand in his notice at the first opportunity.

A little damped, Joseph said: 'You had better serve dinner. The master would not have wanted his guests to make any difference, would he?'

'Very good, sir,' said Sturry, declining to give an opinion on this moot point.

He withdrew, but the shreds of his disapproval remained behind. Remembering the overwrought questions and exclamations which his entrance had interrupted, Nathaniel's guests felt uneasily that they had lapsed into bad form. Mottisfont cleared his throat, and remarked that one hardly knew what to do.

'I *know*!' Valerie said. 'I mean, I've simply never dreamed of such a thing happening to me! Oh, Stephen, Mummy will be utterly furious! I do think I ought to go home!'

'The trains are very infrequent over Christmas,' stated Maud. 'And, of course, when there is snow they get held up.'

'Oh, I couldn't go by train!' Valerie said. 'Stephen brought me in his car.'

'Sorry,' said Stephen. 'I can't leave.'

'But, Stephen, you could come back, couldn't you? I don't want to be a nuisance, or anything, but actually my nerves aren't awfully strong, and the least little thing like this upsets me for weeks! Literally!'

He returned no answer. His look of derision had given place to one of strain; even her absurdity failed to conjure up his familiar mocking devil. It was left for Roydon to respond to her. 'I wish I could take you home,' he said. 'I can see you're one of those tremendously highly-strung people whose awareness is almost hyper-acute.'

'Actually, Mummy says I simply live on my nerves,' Valerie confided.

'You haven't a nerve in your whole insensate body!' said Paula, with shattering effect.

Valerie had never sustained such an insult in her life. She flushed poppy-red; her eyes flashed becomingly, and it seemed as though the tension was to be relieved by a very satisfying exchange of personalities between the two ladies.

Sturry came back into the room to announce dinner. The quarrel petered out; and Nathaniel's guests filed out of the room in depressed silence.

Sturry had swept away the knives and forks from Nathaniel's place at the head of the table. This vacancy struck everyone immediately, and brought his death suddenly and foolishly nearer. Joseph was inspired to exclaim: 'It will seem strange to me, and melancholy, to see another in Nat's place. It must come: I know it, and I shall accept it bravely, but I can't help feeling glad that for just this one evening I see only Nat's empty chair.'

No comment seemed to be required; indeed, it would have been impossible for anyone except Stephen, Mathilda reflected, to have made any. Half expecting him to utter some blistering remark, she glanced across the table towards him. A wryness about his mouth informed her that the tactlessness of the reminder had not gone unobserved, but he gave no other sign of having heard Joseph.

Joseph whispered: 'Help me, Tilda! We must be natural! We must try not to let this horror get on top of us!'

What he hoped she might be able to do she had no idea. An attempt to inaugurate a conversation upon any other subject than Nathaniel's death would be regarded as callous, and must fail. She began to drink her soup, ignoring Joseph.

Valerie, growing momently more temperamental, refused soup, saying that it seemed awful to be sitting at dinner with Mr Herriard dead upstairs.

'You don't drink soup because you think it's bad for your figure. You told us so,' said Paula.

'Some people think a great deal of the Hay Diet,' suddenly remarked Maud. 'I daresay it is very good, though I myself have never had any trouble with my digestion.

But Joseph has to be more careful. Rich food never agrees with him.'

Sturry, who had been conferring with the footman in the doorway, approached Joseph's chair, and bent over it, murmuring bodingly: 'Dr Stoke, sir.'

Joseph leaned forward. 'Stephen, my boy! The doctor!'

'You'd better take him up,' said Stephen.

'You don't wish to be present? You have a right to be there.'

'Thanks, not in the middle of dinner.'

Joseph put back his chair, and rose, with what was felt to be a gallant attempt at a smile. 'It shall be as you like, old fellow. I understand.'

'I imagine you might.'

'Hush! No bitter words tonight!' Joseph said, as he left the room.

He found the doctor in the hall, handing his coat and hat to the footman. 'Stoke!' he said. 'You know why you have been sent for? I needn't tell you.'

'Herriard's man told me that there had been an accident to his master,' the doctor replied. He looked narrowly at Joseph, and said in a sharper voice: 'Nothing serious, I trust?'

Joseph made a hopeless gesture. 'Dead!' he said.

'Dead!' The doctor was plainly startled. 'Good God, what has happened?'

'A terrible thing, Stoke,' Joseph said, shuddering. 'I will take you to him.'

'Is he in his own room?' Stoke asked, picking up his bag.

He was a spare, active man, and he ran up the broad stairs ahead of Joseph. Ford was sitting on a chair outside Nathaniel's door; the doctor glanced frowningly at him, and passed into the room. When he saw the position of Nathaniel's body, he went quickly up to it, and dropped on to his knees. The briefest of inspections convinced him that his patient was indeed dead; he looked up, as Joseph came into the room, and asked curtly: 'The valet spoke of an accident. How did this happen?'

Joseph averted his eyes from Nathaniel's body, saying in a low tone: 'Look at his back, Stoke!'

The doctor looked quickly down. Stephen had left Nathaniel lying much as he had found him, on his left side, exposing the little bloodstained rent in his coat.

There was a short silence; Joseph turned his back upon the doctor's activities, and gazed down into the dying embers in the grate.

The doctor rose from his knees. 'I suppose you realise that this is a case of murder?' he said.

Joseph bowed his head.

'The police must be notified at once.'

'It has already been done. They should be here any minute now.'

'I will wait for them.'

'It has been such a ghastly shock!' Joseph said, after an uncomfortable pause.

The doctor assented. He looked as though he too had suffered a shock.

'I suppose you don't know who – ?' he asked, leaving the sentence unfinished.

Joseph shook his head. 'I almost feel I'd rather not know. If one could be sure he didn't suffer!'

'Oh, probably hardly at all!' Stoke said reassuringly.

'Thank you. It's a relief to know that. I suppose he must have died immediately.'

'Well, within a very short time, anyway,' conceded Stoke.

Joseph sighed, and relapsed into silence. This lasted until the arrival of a police inspector, with various satellites. Stephen brought them upstairs, and Joseph roused himself from his abstraction, greeting the Inspector, whom he knew, with a forced smile, and saying: 'You know Dr Stoke, don't you?'

The room seemed suddenly to be overfull of people. Joseph confided to Stephen that it seemed a desecration. The police-surgeon and Dr Stoke conferred together over Nathaniel's body, and the Inspector, who looked as though he did not like being brought to a murder-case on Christmas Eve, began to ask questions.

'I can't tell you anything,' Stephen said. 'The last time I saw him alive was downstairs in the drawing-room, at about seven-thirty.'

'I understand it was you who broke into the room, sir, and discovered the body?'

'His valet and I. Our finger-prints will be found all over the place.'

'Mine too,' Joseph said unhappily. 'One doesn't think, when a thing like this happens.'

The Inspector's eyes dwelled on the brandy decanter, and the glass beside it. Stephen said: 'No. False scent. The brandy was brought to revive my uncle before we realised he was dead. I drank it.'

'Very understandable, sir, I'm sure. When you came in, was the deceased lying as at present?'

'Not quite,' Stephen said, after a moment's reflection. 'He was rather more on his face, I think.'

'I wonder if you would be so good, sir, as to replace the body as you found it?'

Stephen hesitated, distaste in his face. Joseph said pleadingly: 'Inspector, this is terribly painful for my nephew! Surely –'

'Shut up!' Stephen said roughly, and went to Nathaniel's body, and arranged it. 'More or less like that.'

'Do you agree with that, sir?' the Inspector asked Joseph.

'Yes, yes!' Joseph said. 'His head was on his arm. We never dreamed – we thought he had fainted!'

The Inspector nodded, and asked who slept in the next bedroom, which lay beyond Nathaniel's bathroom. He was told that it was a single spare-room which Roydon had been put into, and took a note of this. Having scrutinised the windows, both in the bedroom and in the bathroom, and looked meditatively at the half-open ventilator, he ascertained that these had not been tampered with since the finding of Nathaniel's body, and at last suggested that further questions might best be answered in some other room.

Both Joseph and Stephen were glad to get away from the scene of the crime, and they led the Inspector downstairs to the morning-room, leaving the photographer, the finger-print experts, and the ambulance-men in possession.

The morning-room fire had been allowed to go out, and the room felt chilly. The Inspector said that it was of no consequence, and he would be obliged to question everyone in the house. Joseph gave a groan, and ejaculated: 'Those poor young people! If they could have been spared this horror!'

The Inspector did not waste his breath answering this; he knew his duty, and he had no time to spare for irrelevancies. He should have been filling his children's stockings by right, not taking depositions at Lexham Manor. It wasn't as though the case was likely to do him much good, he reflected. He wasn't the Detective-Inspector, but merely deputising for that gentleman, who was in bed with influenza. The Chief Constable, a nervous man, would be bound to call in Scotland Yard, he thought, and some smart London man would get all the credit for the case. He waited for Joseph to lower the hand with which he had covered his eyes before saying: 'Now, sir, if you please! I understand you have a number of guests staying in the house? If I might have their names?'

'Our Christmas party!' Joseph said tragically.

'We shall at least be spared your rollicking festivities,' Stephen said.

The Inspector glanced at him rather narrowly. That was a queer way to speak of his uncle's murder, he thought. It didn't do to set too much store by what people said in moments of shock, but if he were asked he would be bound to admit that he hadn't taken a fancy to young Herriard, not by a long chalk.

Joseph caught his glance, and rushed to Stephen's support. 'My nephew's very much upset,' he said. 'It's been a dreadful blow – and I'm afraid the modern youth makes a point of hiding its feelings under a mask of flippancy.'

Stephen grimaced, but allowed this explanation to pass without comment. He dived a hand into his pocket for his pipe and his tobacco-pouch, and began to fill the pipe, while Joseph told the Inspector about the other guests.

Joseph had a kind word for everybody. Roydon was a most promising playwright, a great friend of his niece. The niece? Ah yes! this young man's sister: an actress, and quite her poor dead uncle's favourite. Then there was Miss Dean – a smile towards Stephen – his nephew's fiancée. He might say that this party had really been arranged on her account. She had never stayed with them before, and they had so much wanted to get to know her. Miss Clare, too! a cousin, quite a *persona grata* in the house. Remained only Edgar Mottisfont, Nathaniel's partner, and close friend for many years. There were, of course, the servants, but he was quite sure none of them could have had anything to do with the murder.

This was unpromising stuff, but the Inspector did not allow himself to be unduly cast-down. He wanted to know whether there had been any quarrel between the deceased and any of his guests.

'Oh no, no! Not what I should call a quarrel!' Joseph said quickly. 'I'm afraid all we Herriards are inclined to be testy, but there has been nothing of a serious nature. Nothing – *nothing* to warrant this dreadful thing!'

'But there has been quarrelling, sir?'

'Just a few family tiffs! What I call the give and take of family life. My brother was a sufferer from lumbago, and you know what that does to a man's temper, Inspector. There may have been a little crossness here and there, but we knew that Uncle Nat's bark was worse than his bite, didn't we, Stephen?'

Not even his own predicament, which he must have known to be dangerous, could induce Stephen to join forces with Joseph. He said 'Did we?' in a non-committal tone which did much to destroy the good impression Joseph was making.

The Inspector turned towards him. 'Would you say that there had been a quarrel, sir?'

'No, I wouldn't. I'd say my uncle had quarrelled with every one of us, with the exception of Miss Clare.'

'Did you have words with him, sir?'

'Many,' said Stephen coolly.

'Stephen, don't be silly, old man!' Joseph interposed. 'Whatever may have passed between you and Nat earlier in the day, I for one can bear witness to the fact that you and he were on the friendliest terms by teatime! Inspector, this stupid fellow loves to make himself out to be a regular old bear, but I saw him with my own eyes link arms with my brother as they came in to tea, and no one could have been nicer to him thereafter than he was! Indeed, I noticed it particularly, and was so happy to see it!'

The Inspector's appraising gaze travelled from his face to Stephen's. 'But there had been a quarrel between you and the deceased today, sir?'

Stephen shrugged. 'Well, I hadn't been thrown out of the house.'

'I should like a plain answer, if you please, sir.'

'Yes, then,' Stephen said.

'But, Stephen, you're giving a false impression!' Joseph said. 'We all know you and Nat rubbed one another up the wrong way, but he was very fond of you, and you of him!'

'You'd better examine my uncle,' Stephen told the Inspector roughly. 'He apparently knows all the answers.'

'Was your quarrel of a serious nature, sir?'

'I've already told you that I wasn't thrown out of the house.'

'Am I to take it that at the time the deceased was last seen alive you were on friendly terms with him?'

'Temporary truce,' said Stephen.

'When did you last set eyes on the deceased, sir?'

Stephen took a moment to think this over. 'Not sure of the time. I left the drawing-room when Roydon had finished reading his play. Probably about half-past seven.'

'When you state that you left the drawing-room, am I to understand that you left the deceased there?'

'Everyone was there.'

'And between that time, and the time when you discovered his body, you did not see him?'

'No.'

'What were you doing during that period?'

'Changing, in my room.'

'Thank you, sir,' said the Inspector, making a note.

'Done with me?' Stephen asked. 'Dinner – probably spoilt by now, of course – is still before me, I would respectfully point out to you.'

Cold-blooded devil! thought the Inspector. He said: 'That will be all for the present.'

Stephen walked out of the room. Joseph, who had been watching him with a good deal of anxiety, smiled at the Inspector, and said: 'He doesn't mean the things he says, you know. The fact of the matter is he's very like my poor brother. Both of them hasty-tempered, and bitter-tongued. A quick flare-up, and all over. Nothing sulky!'

The Inspector received this information politely if not very enthusiastically. He asked Joseph when he had last seen Nathaniel.

'Miss Clare and I must have been the last people to have seen him alive,' Joseph answered. 'Everyone else had gone upstairs. I was going up with him. I wanted to have a talk with him. Alas, that I did not!'

'How was that, sir?'

Joseph looked momentarily disconcerted, but apparently decided that since his tongue had betrayed him he must make the best of it. 'To tell you the truth, Inspector, my brother was in a very bad temper, and I wanted to smooth him down! But he said he didn't want to talk. Well, I mustn't conceal anything, must I? I had stupidly left a step-ladder on the stairs, and my brother knocked it over, and – yes, he was very cross with me indeed! So I thought it wisest to let him cool off. Miss Clare and I went upstairs together a few minutes later.'

'What had put Mr Herriard in a bad temper, sir?'

'Oh, a mere nothing! Mr Roydon had been reading his play to us, and my brother didn't like it.'

'That doesn't seem to be much of a reason, sir.'

Joseph gave an unhappy laugh. 'I'm afraid it was quite

enough reason for him, Inspector. That's just the sort of thing that did upset him.'

The Inspector pondered this, and at length produced: 'If he didn't like to have it read to him, sir, why was it read?'

Complications were clearly arising. Joseph said: 'Mr Roydon is a guest in the house. It would have been very difficult to have forbidden him to read his play, wouldn't it?'

'Seems queer-like to me, sir,' was all the Inspector vouchsafed. 'I'd like to see this Mr Roydon, please.'

'Certainly, but I'm sure he knows nothing about the crime. I mean, it would be too preposterous! My brother had never laid eyes on him before he came down here yesterday. Shall I send him in to you?'

'Yes, please,' said the Inspector.

He was clearly an unresponsive man. His stolid manner and frozen stare quite put poor Joseph out. He went away, looking unhappy, to find Roydon.

The house-party was in the dining-room, where Stephen, unmoved by the late gruesome events, was eating his interrupted dinner. Everyone else had reached the coffee stage, and, with the exception of Maud, was plying him with eager questions. They all turned, as Joseph came in, and Paula asked if the police had finished.

'Alas, my poor child, I'm afraid it will be a long time before they do that!' said Joseph, with a heavy sigh. 'They have only just begun. Willoughby, the Inspector wants to see you. He is in the morning-room.'

Roydon at once flushed, and his voice jumped up an

octave. 'What on earth does he want to see me about? I can't tell him anything!'

'No, that's what I assured him. I am afraid he is a stupid sort of a man. It came out that you had been reading your play to us – dear me, it seems already as though that was in another life!'

'Did you tell him so?' said Stephen, looking up under his brows.

Joseph's absurdly cherubic countenance set into worried lines. 'Well, yes, but I never dreamed he'd take me up as he did!'

Paula's eyes stabbed him. 'Did you tell him that Willoughby wanted Uncle Nat's backing?'

'Of course I didn't! I didn't say a word about that. It's quite irrelevant, and I don't think there's the least need to mention it.'

Roydon stubbed out his cigarette, and got up. 'I suppose I'd better go along and see the man,' he said. 'Not that I can throw the least light on the affair, but that's by the way!'

He went out, and Stephen, watching him critically, said to his sister: 'Are you vitally concerned in your boy-friend's fate? With any luck, I should say he'll incriminate himself good and proper.'

'He had nothing to do with it!' Paula said.

'How do you know?' jeered Stephen.

She stared at him. 'Well, I don't know,' she said slowly. 'I don't know who did it.'

'I should like to think that someone quite unconnected with any of us was the guilty man,' said Joseph. 'May we not assume that, children, and try not to say bitter, hurtful things to one another?'

The only person to respond to this appeal was Mathilda, who said handsomely that he at least could not be accused of this vice. He threw her a grateful smile, but shook his head, saying that he was afraid he was a very imperfect mortal.

'As though I hadn't had enough to put me off my food already!' growled Stephen.

Valerie, who had been fidgeting with her coffee-spoon, let it fall into the saucer, and exclaimed: 'I wonder it doesn't make you sick to think of eating anything! I think you're the most callous person I've ever met in all my life!'

'I shouldn't be surprised,' agreed Stephen.

'And if the police want to question me, it's no earthly use, because I don't know a thing about it, and my nerves just won't stand it! I feel as though I'm going mad!'

'Oh, do shut up!' said Paula.

'I won't shut up! I didn't come here to be insulted, and I don't see why I should be expected to put up with it!'

'Leave her alone, Paula,' ordered Stephen, getting up, and walking over to the sideboard, where some chocolate mousse had been left for him.

'I'm not doing anything to her. If she doesn't like my behaviour she can leave the room, can't she?' said Paula, becoming belligerent.

'I wish I could leave the house!' cried Valerie.

'I believe it is still snowing,' remarked Maud, as unperturbed by this bickering as by all the other events of the day.

'I don't care! I'd rather walk all the way to London than stay here now!'

'It's an engaging thought,' said Stephen. 'Orphan of the Storm.'

'Oh, you can laugh at me! but if you think I could possibly sleep a wink here you're mistaken! I simply shan't dare to close my eyes all night. I shall be *petrified*!'

'Well, really, I don't think that's very sensible,' objected Mathilda. 'What do you suppose is going to happen to you?'

'You wouldn't understand,' said Valerie, adding in a lofty tone: 'I expect you're one of those lucky people who just haven't got any nerves, and don't feel a thing. But the thought of Mr Herriard, lying there in that room – Oh, I simply can't bear it!'

'You won't have to,' said Stephen. 'The body will be removed to the police-mortuary. Probably has been by this time.'

This brutal truth made Joseph wince. He said: 'Stephen, Stephen!' in an imploring voice.

'I think,' said Maud, getting up, 'that I shall go and sit in the drawing-room with my book.'

Joseph glanced at her with humorous affection. 'Yes, my dear, do that!' he said. 'Try to put it all out of your mind! How I wish that I could do the same! But I am afraid the Inspector will want to see you.'

'Oh yes!' she said, uninterested.

'There is nothing to be afraid of, you know. He is quite human.'

'I am not afraid, thank you, Joseph,' she replied placidly.

Paula barely waited until she had left the room before

ejaculating: 'If I've got to listen to extracts from that ghastly book on top of everything else, I think *my* nerve will crack!'

'Keep calm, sister: Aunt has lost the book.'

'Stephen!' exclaimed Joseph. 'No, that's too bad of you! If you've hidden it, you must give it back to her at once.'

'I haven't touched it,' said Stephen curtly.

Neither Mathilda nor Paula believed this, but as Joseph showed signs of pressing the point, they intervened to prevent an explosion. Mathilda said that no doubt it would turn up; and Paula wondered how Roydon was getting on with the Inspector.

He was not, as a matter of fact, getting on very well. Policemen represented to him, quite irrationally, his personal enemies. He did not like them; they made him nervous, in much the same way that butlers did, so that he felt that his clothes were shabby and his hands too large. To conceal this discomfort, he assumed a grand manner, and was inclined to overact his unconcern. He said: 'Ah, Inspector, you want a word with me, don't you? I'm quite ready to tell you anything I know, of course, but I'm afraid that won't be much. I'm only down for the week-end, as I daresay you've heard. In fact, I hardly knew Mr Herriard.'

He ended on his nervous laugh. He hadn't meant to say all that; he knew it must have sounded artificial, but somehow he was unable to stop himself. To occupy his hands, he lit a cigarette, and began to smoke it, rather too fast. He wished the Inspector would stop staring at him so unblinkingly. As though he were a wild beast in a show! he thought resentfully.

The Inspector asked him for his name and address, and

slowly wrote these down in his notebook. 'Were you acquainted with the deceased previous to your arrival here?' he asked.

'No. Well, naturally I knew *of* him, but I hadn't actually met him. I came down with Miss Herriard. She invited me.'

'I understand you are occupying the bedroom next to the deceased's?'

'Oh well, yes, in a way I suppose I am!' conceded Roydon. 'Only there's a bathroom in between, so naturally I didn't hear anything, if that's what you mean.'

'When you left the drawing-room after tea, did you go straight upstairs to your room?'

'Yes. At least, no! Now I come to think of it, Miss Clare and I went into the library. As far as I remember, Miss Herriard joined us there. It was after that that I went up to change. I've no idea where Mr Herriard was by that time. I never saw him again after I left the drawing-room.'

The Inspector thanked him, and requested him to ask Miss Herriard to come to him.

Paula was not afraid of policemen. She answered the Inspector's questions impatiently; and when he asked her if she had had any quarrel with Nathaniel, said that no one could possibly live for half a day with Nathaniel without quarrelling with him. But when the Inspector wanted to know why she had quarrelled with her uncle, she replied haughtily that it was none of his business.

This did nothing to prejudice him in her favour, and since under his remorseless probing she very soon lost her temper it was not long before he had learnt that she had wanted

Nathaniel to give her money for some undivulged purpose, and that he had refused.

'But if you think that that's got anything to do with the murder you're a fool!' Paula said. 'I shouldn't have told you, only that the whole house knows it, so that you were bound to find it out sooner or later. Do you want to know anything else?'

'Yes, miss, I want to know what you did when you left the drawing-room after tea.'

'Oh, I don't know!' she said. 'Do you think I keep a record of my movements?'

'Did you go straight upstairs?'

She condescended to give the matter a little thought. 'No; I went into the library. I went upstairs later, with Mr Roydon.'

'Did you go to your own room?'

'Of course! Where else should I go?'

'And you did not come out of it again until you joined the rest of the party downstairs?'

'No,' she replied briefly.

He let her go, and sent for Edgar Mottisfont. If she had been belligerent, and Roydon patronising, Mottisfont provided a contrast to them both by using an ingratiating manner. That he was nervous was plain to be seen, but they were all nervous, the Inspector thought, and no wonder. Mottisfont seemed more shocked than any of them, reiterating his horror, and his incomprehension. He had been intimately acquainted with Nathaniel for close on thirty years; for many years he had spent Christmas with Nathaniel. Nothing like this, he said, unconscious of absurdity, had ever happened before.

'I understand there had been some unpleasantness,' the Inspector said.

'He was a hard man. Out of touch with the younger generation, you know. It was Miss Herriard's fault for bringing Roydon here. She should have known better! However, that's not my affair. I've never pretended to understand that couple. Seemed to take a delight in annoying their uncle! I don't know why Herriard put up with them, but there's no doubt he was fond of them, in his way.'

'May I ask, sir, if Miss Herriard had any particular reason for bringing Mr Roydon here?'

Mottisfont seemed to feel that he had said too much. He replied evasively: 'You'd better ask her. It had nothing to do with me.'

'There was no quarrel between yourself and Mr Herriard?'

As he put the question, the Inspector knew that there had been a quarrel. It was as though a curtain was drawn swiftly over Mottisfont's face, shutting him in. He had been a little off his guard, talking querulously about the young Herriards, but now he was wary again, trying to make up his mind, the Inspector guessed, what he should say. Probably he didn't know who might have overheard his quarrel; didn't dare lie; didn't want to tell the truth. All the same, these nervous witnesses! The Inspector waited, keeping his gaze steady on Mottisfont's face.

The weak grey eyes behind Mottisfont's spectacles shifted. 'Not a quarrel. Oh, dear me, no! Nothing of that sort! Why, we've been in partnership for twenty-five years! What an idea! We merely disagreed about a matter purely concerned with the business. Herriard was more or less of a sleeping-partner, you know, but very fond of interfering with the actual running of the business, if you gave him the chance. A little old-fashioned: didn't move with the times. Many's the battle-royal we've waged! But I think I may claim to have been able to handle him!'

Considering him: weak eyes, harassed brow, peevish mouth; and remembering Nathaniel's dominant personality, the Inspector disbelieved him, but he did not press the matter. He thought the whole pack of them were lying, one way or another, some to shield others, some from fear. No sense in getting oneself bogged in a swamp of misstatements until he'd heard what the experts, busy in Nathaniel's room upstairs, had gleaned. He seemed, therefore, to accept Mottisfont's statements, and asked the inevitable question: 'When you left the drawing-room, where did you go?'

He'd known what the answer would be, of course. Mottisfont had gone up to his room, to change for dinner, and had not come out of it again until he had joined the rest of the party in the drawing-room.

The Inspector dismissed him, suppressing a sigh. Alibis were the bane of a detective's life, but he felt he would have welcomed one now. Gave one something to catch hold of, in a manner of speaking. You might have a chance of disproving an alibi: more of a chance, at any rate, than of disproving that these people had all been in their own rooms when Nathaniel was killed.

Consulting his notebook, the Inspector sent for Miss Dean. As soon as Valerie came into the room, he saw that she was badly frightened. He did not think, critically surveying her, that she would be capable of stabbing anyone, but he thought she could be scared into talking, and felt more hopeful.

Her first words were an agitated disclaimer of any knowledge at all of the crime, and a demand to be allowed to go home at once. He told her that she had nothing to be afraid of, if she was quite frank with him.

She said: 'But I don't know anything! I went straight up to my room to change. *I* never had any quarrel with Mr Herriard! I can't think why you should want to question me. I should have thought Miss Herriard was the person who could tell you most. It was all her fault!'

'What makes you say that, miss?'

'Because it was! Of course, they'll all be furious with me for saying so, but I don't see why I should sacrifice myself to protect them! She wanted Mr Herriard to let her have two thousand pounds to finance Mr Roydon's play – though I'm absolutely certain he had nothing to do with it, because he's not that kind of person at all. But Paula was furious because Mr Herriard didn't like Willoughby's play, silly old fool, and she had a simply frantic row with him, and absolutely slammed out of the room. Actually, it's a marvellous play, but Mr Herriard was definitely moth-eaten, and he rather loathed it. Besides which he was in a stinking temper already, because I rather think he'd been having a row with Mr Mottisfont.'

'What about?' asked the Inspector quickly.

'Oh, I don't know, only Mr Mottisfont was utterly sunk

in gloom – of course, he's wet all round the edges too – and everything was ghastly, one way and another.'

'In what way, miss?'

'Oh, on account of Stephen's being in one of his foul moods, and Paula doing nothing but stride about the place in a temper, and Mathilda Clare thinking herself very clever, and completely monopolising Stephen, just as though *she* were the only person who counted! And she isn't even moderately good-looking. In fact, she's haggish.'

There did not seem to be very much to be made of this, although the disclosure that Paula wanted money for Roydon's play would bear looking into, the Inspector thought.

'The only person who's been in the least decent,' pursued Valerie, now fairly launched on a flood of grievances, 'is Uncle Joseph. I wish I'd never come, and I know my mother will be utterly livid when she hears what's happened! It isn't as if it was even any use my coming, because I never had a chance to get to know Mr Herriard, which was the whole idea. I think he was a woman-hater.'

'Indeed, miss? Didn't you and him get on together?'

'Well, we never had a chance, what with one thing and another. I must say, I thought he was frightfully rude, but Stephen was just about as tactless as he could be, goodness knows why! and Paula would keep on about Willoughby's play, when anyone could see it was only making Mr Herriard worse.'

She continued in this strain for several minutes, leaving the Inspector with the impression that the household contained few, if any, persons who would have been unwilling to have murdered Nathaniel.

This somewhat irresponsible testimony was contradicted by Maud, who when summoned to the morning-room came in with the deliberate tread of all stout persons, and betrayed neither alarm nor any particular interest.

Maud baffled the Inspector. She answered readily any questions put to her, but her face told him nothing, and she seemed either to be very stupid or very much too clever. She said that she had been in her bedroom from the time she had left the drawing-room until she had returned to it, just before dinner. The Inspector had expected that: it would be quite a shock, he reflected bitterly, if any of these people said anything else. Maud said that no doubt her husband could corroborate her statement, since he had been in his dressing-room, next door. The Inspector nodded, and asked her if there had been much unpleasantness in the house.

Maud's pale eyes stared at him. 'I didn't notice anything,' she said.

In face of what he had heard from the other witnesses, this startled the Inspector. He looked suspiciously at Maud, and said: 'Come, come, Mrs Herriard! Isn't it a fact that there had been a good deal of quarrelling going on between the deceased and certain members of the house-party?'

'I daresay,' said Maud indifferently. 'I didn't pay any attention. My brother-in-law was a very quarrelsome man.'

'Oh!' said the Inspector. 'Then you wouldn't say that there had been anything out of the ordinary in the way of unpleasantness?'

'No,' she said. 'There is always unpleasantness in this house. Mr Herriard was very disagreeable.'

The Inspector coughed. 'You've lived here for some time, haven't you, madam?'

'Two years,' she said, without a change in her expression.

'Then I may take it that you know most of the ins and outs of the place, as one might say?'

'I never interfered,' said Maud.

'No, madam, I'm sure…Would you say that there had been any serious trouble between the deceased and any of his guests?'

'No. There is usually trouble when my husband's nephew and niece visit Lexham. They do not try to please their uncle. The Herriards are like that.'

'Quarrelsome, do you mean?'

'Yes. Mr Herriard liked it.'

'He liked having his relations quarrel with him?' asked the Inspector incredulously.

'I don't think he minded. He never seemed to like people who were civil to him. He was very rude himself, very. He didn't mean anything by it.'

'Would you say that there had been serious trouble over this play which Miss Herriard wanted her uncle to spend money on?'

'Oh no!' Maud said calmly. 'He didn't care about the play, that's all. I didn't either.'

'Did he refuse to put up any money?'

'I expect so. I daresay he would have in the end, however. He was very fond of Paula. It was a stupid moment for her to have chosen, that's all.'

'Why was it a stupid moment, madam?'

Her eyes slowly turned towards him again. 'Mr Herriard was annoyed about the party.'

'In what way?'

'He didn't want a party.'

'But if he didn't want it, why did he have it?'

'It was my husband's doing. He is not at all like his brother. He thought it would be a good thing. But Mr Herriard very much disliked Miss Dean, and that upset him.'

The Inspector pricked up his ears. 'He disliked Miss Dean? He didn't want his nephew to marry her?'

'No. But I don't suppose he will. I always thought he had made a mistake. I expect he stuck to it to annoy his uncle.'

This seemed fantastic to the Inspector. 'Stuck to it to annoy his uncle?'

'He likes annoying people,' said Maud.

This matter-of-fact opinion, stated with a simplicity that could not but carry weight, confused the Inspector's mind. He began to perceive that he had to deal with extraordinary people, and it was with misgiving that he presently confronted Mathilda Clare.

His first thought was that she was no beauty, his second that she had very shrewd eyes. Her indefinable air of expensive *chic* slightly alarmed him, but he found her perfectly easy to get on with, if not very helpful.

She corroborated Maud's testimony. She had never yet, she told him, stayed at Lexham Manor without finding herself pitchforked into the middle of a family quarrel. 'Though I'm bound to say,' she admitted, 'that things weren't usually as sultry as they have been this Christmas. That was Joseph

Herriard's fault. He meant it all for the best, but he's one of those tactless creatures who spend their whole lives putting their feet into it. This time he's surpassed himself, for not content with getting Miss Dean into the home he allowed Miss Herriard to bring Mr Roydon here.'

'I understand that Mr Roydon came to get Mr Herriard to finance a play of his?'

'That was the general idea,' admitted Mathilda. 'But Mr Herriard thought not.'

'Very upsetting for Mr Roydon,' said the Inspector invitingly.

'Not at all. He is now determined to let the play stand on its merits.'

'Oh! And Miss Herriard?'

'Miss Herriard,' responded Mathilda coolly, 'treated the assembled company to a dramatic scene – she's an actress, good in emotional rôles. I wasn't present, but I'm told that she and Mr Herriard had a really splendid quarrel, and enjoyed themselves hugely.'

'Seems a funny way to enjoy yourself, miss.'

'It would seem funny to you or to me, Inspector, but not, believe me, to a Herriard.'

He shook his head dubiously, and asked, without much hope, where she had been between seven-thirty and dinner-time.

'Changing in my room,' she replied. 'Joseph Herriard will bear me out. His dressing-room communicates with my bathroom, and we not only went upstairs together, but he chat – talked to me all the time I was changing.

What's more, we came downstairs together. That's my alibi, Inspector.'

He thanked her gravely, refusing to be drawn, and said that he would like to interview the servants.

'Just ring the bell,' said Mathilda, rising, and walking to the door. 'You will then be able to start on the butler.'

She rejoined her fellow-guests in the drawing-room. 'Well?' said Stephen.

'I did what I could for you,' she replied. 'He's now about to pump Sturry.'

'That ought to finish us,' he said grimly. 'Sturry was listening outside the door when the storm broke.'

Seven

T HE INSPECTOR, WHO HAD BEEN CONFRONTED WITH condescension in Roydon, hostility in Paula, now encountered, as Sturry majestically advanced into the morning-room, a lofty disdain which would have caused a more sensitive soul to shrink.

'You rang, Inspector?' said Sturry, conveying a suggestion of astonishment.

The Inspector felt in a vague way that he had committed a solecism, but he was strong in the consciousness of his duty, and he replied firmly: 'Yes, I rang. I want to ask you a few questions. Is your name Albert Sturry?'

'My name, Inspector, is Albert Reginald Sturry.'

The Inspector repressed an impulse to beg his pardon, and wrote the name in his notebook. 'You are employed here as butler?'

'I have served Mr Herriard in that capacity for four years and seven months,' replied Sturry. 'Previous to that, I was with the late Sir Barnabas Lancing, of Lancing Towers, and Upper Eaton Place.'

The Inspector made a note of this, but wisely thrust Sir Barnabas into the background. He said: 'Now, what do you know about this business?'

The arctic light in Sturry's eye plainly informed him that if he imagined he could address a respectable butler in this fashion he would find himself much mistaken. 'I regret that I am unable to assist you,' said Sturry. 'It being no part of my duties to pry into the affairs of my employers.'

The Inspector perceived that he had taken a false step. He said: 'Naturally not, but a man in your position is bound to know the ins and outs of a house.'

Sturry acknowledged this tribute by a slight bow, and waited.

'By all accounts the deceased was a difficult man to get on with, eh?'

'I experienced no difficulty, Inspector. Mr Herriard had his idiosyncrasies, no doubt. Latterly his temper became impaired by rheumatic complaints, as was understandable.'

'Made him quarrelsome?'

'I would not go so far as to ascribe the distressing quarrels which have taken place under this roof wholly to Mr Herriard's lumbago,' said Sturry.

It became clear to the Inspector that the butler was big with news. It was equally clear that while he had a human desire to impart his news, he was mindful of what was due to his dignity, and must be handled with tact and respect. 'Ah!' the Inspector said, nodding. 'And I daresay you knew him as well as anyone. Stands to reason, being in your position, and with him over four years.'

'I believe Mr Herriard had no reason to be dissatisfied with me,' conceded Sturry, unbending a little. 'It has been my endeavour to fulfil my functions to the best of my ability, whatever the behaviour of certain of Mr Herriard's guests.'

'Must have been difficult for you, I daresay.'

'Not so much difficult as distasteful,' said Sturry, putting him in his place again. 'Accustomed as I have been for thirty-five years to serving in the best families – for I commenced as under-footman to the late Earl of Belford, when I was hardly more than a Lad – there have been Incidents at Lexham Manor which I could only deplore.'

The Inspector made a tut-tutting noise, and tried to look sympathetic.

'I need scarcely say,' added Sturry, 'that I shall be giving notice at the earliest opportunity.'

'You know your own business best, but the house is likely to be kept on, isn't it? There's bound to be an heir.'

'I should not care,' said Sturry, with a quiver of disgust, 'to demean myself by remaining in any house where a murder had been committed. It is not what I am accustomed to. It is impossible to imagine such an occurrence taking place under the late Earl's roof, or, indeed (though the baronetcy was of quite recent creation) under the roof of the late Sir Barnabas.' He drew in his breath through his teeth. 'Nor, I may add, would it suit me to take a post either in Mr Joseph Herriard's household, or in Mr Stephen Herriard's.'

'Oh?' said the Inspector, deeply interested, and trying not to show it. 'Not your money, eh?'

This vulgarity brought a look of pain to Sturry's countenance, but being by this time launched on the cumulative tide of his disclosures, he decided to overlook it. 'Mr Joseph Herriard is a very well-meaning gentleman,' he said, 'but the Peculiar Circumstances of his life have made him, I regret to say, forgetful of his dignity. He is Familiar with the Staff.'

The Inspector nodded feelingly. 'I know what you mean. What about the young one? Cross-grained-looking chap, I thought.'

'Mr Stephen Herriard,' said Sturry, 'is not a gentleman with whom I could ever contemplate taking service. Mr Stephen's temper is quite as violent as his late uncle's, and although I would not wish to imply that he is not Quite the Gentleman, he is careless of appearances to a degree which I could not bring myself to overlook. He has, moreover, become engaged to a young lady who will not, in my opinion, Do for Lexham Manor.' He paused, fixing the Inspector with a basilisk eye. 'I could not, in any case, reconcile it with my conscience to serve any gentleman who had been on such inimical terms with the late Mr Herriard,' he said.

Here it comes at last! thought the Inspector. 'I'd heard that they quarrelled a good bit,' he said. 'Bad, was it?'

Sturry closed his eyes for an expressive moment. 'At times, Inspector, it has been what I should call Shocking, both Mr Stephen and Mr Herriard raising their voices in a manner very unbecoming to their stations, and not caring who might be within hearing. Indeed, upon one occasion Mr Stephen had Words with his uncle in front of the Tweeny.'

The enormity of this did not, perhaps, impress the Inspector as forcibly as it was meant to, but he looked shocked, and said he wondered why Stephen came to Lexham so often.

'If you were to ask me, Inspector,' said Sturry, 'I should say that both Mr Stephen and Miss Paula came for what they could get out of the late Mr Herriard.'

'Is Stephen Herriard the heir?'

'That, Inspector, I could not take it upon myself to say, not being in the late Mr Herriard's confidence. It is generally believed in the Hall that he is, Mr Herriard having had an unaccountable fondness for him. But there has been a good deal of unpleasantness lately over Mr Stephen's Unfortunate Entanglement, Mr Herriard having taken exception to Miss Dean in a way one cannot wonder at. There was Quite a Scene between them after lunch.'

'About Miss Dean?'

'I could not say, I am sure,' said Sturry primly. 'But when I was about to enter the drawing-room this evening with the cocktail-tray, I heard Mr Herriard shout at Mr Stephen that he was quite as bad as his sister, and that it was the last time either of them should come to Lexham.'

'Is that so?' said the Inspector, very much on the alert. 'He was quarrelling with Miss Herriard too, was he?'

'Mr Herriard was in general very indulgent with Miss Paula,' said Sturry. 'Though I have reason to believe that he looked with disfavour upon her connection with the stage.

But Miss Paula most regrettably brought down with her to spend Christmas a Person of the name of Roydon.'

The Inspector knew what this method of referring to Roydon implied, and was inclined to sympathise with Sturry. 'He didn't like Roydon?'

'I gathered, Inspector,' said Sturry grandly, 'that he considered Miss Paula's friendship with the young man Unsuitable.'

'I could see he wasn't out of the top-drawer.'

'Mr Roydon,' said Sturry, with impressive reserve, 'is a very estimable young man, I am sure, but he is Out of Place in an establishment where eight indoor servants are employed.'

The Inspector's sympathy veered momentarily towards Roydon. 'I understand he wanted the deceased to put up some money for a play, or something?'

'That, Inspector, was Miss Paula's object in bringing him to Lexham. Two thousand pounds was the figure I heard her name to Mr Herriard.'

'That's a lot of money,' said the Inspector.

'It would seem so to some, no doubt,' said Sturry, in an odiously patronising way. 'Miss Paula referred to it as Paltry.'

'I take it that Mr Herriard refused to let her have it?'

'Mr Herriard, Inspector, said that Miss Paula should have none of his money to waste on Mr Roydon. To which Miss Paula replied that when he was dead she would spend every penny he left her on Immoral Plays.'

The Inspector was shocked. 'That's a nice way to talk!' he exclaimed.

'Miss Paula,' said Sturry forbearingly, 'is not one to Mince Matters.'

'What did Mr Herriard have to say to that?'

'Mr Herriard said that she had better not count her chickens before they were hatched, since he would possibly be Making a Few Changes.'

'Oh, he spoke of changing his will, did he? How did the young lady take that?'

'Being, as one might say, in a Passion, Miss Paula said that she did not care, and did not want Mr Herriard's money. Mr Herriard then said that he thought that that was just what she did want, two thousand pounds of it.' He paused for his final effect. '"And ready to murder me to get it!" Mr Herriard said.'

'He actually used those words?' demanded the Inspector.

'Those were his very words,' replied Sturry solemnly, 'I heard him with my own ears, being, as I have informed you, Upon the Point of bringing in the cocktails.'

He fixed the Inspector with a glassy stare as he spoke. The Inspector, reading the message thus haughtily conveyed to him, quite understood that the butler had stood with his ear to the door during this painful altercation, and had no intention of admitting it. He nodded his comprehension, and asked: 'Was it then that Mr Herriard said that Mr Stephen was as bad as his sister?'

'Immediately consequent upon Mr Stephen's refusing to support his sister,' said Sturry.

'Oh, he didn't support her?' said the Inspector, like a terrier with its nose to a rat-hole.

'Somewhat to my surprise, Inspector, no,' Sturry replied. 'Mr Herriard, who was by that time in Quite a Taking, then turned on Mr Stephen, if I may be permitted to use the expression.'

'What happened next?'

'I could not say,' answered Sturry, with a return to his cold reserve. 'Following my entrance into the drawing-room, Mr Stephen left it.'

'And Mr Herriard had told him that he wouldn't have him here any more?'

'That was what Mr Herriard said.'

'Had he said that before at any time?'

'Never, Inspector, to *my* knowledge. Quite remarkable it was, the way he put up with Mr Stephen. It has been, I may say, a Wonder to us in the Hall.'

The Inspector looked at him for a reflective moment. 'Where were you between the time the deceased went upstairs and the time he was discovered dead in his room?'

'I was occupied about my Duties,' replied Sturry, 'between the dining-room and My Pantry.'

'Did you see any of the guests during that period?'

'No, Inspector, but I have reason to believe that Mr Herriard's valet and the second-housemaid can give you some information on this point.'

'Well, you can send them in,' said the Inspector. 'I'll see the valet first. Has he been here long?'

'Only a matter of a few months,' Sturry replied. 'It was not customary for the late Mr Herriard's personal servants to remain long in his employment.'

'Difficult master?'

'Mr Herriard was very particular, and not, I regret to say, above throwing his shoes, or, upon occasion, even weightier articles at his valet, when his rheumatic complaints troubled him. Modern servants, as no doubt you are aware, do not Hold with that sort of thing.'

'Doesn't seem to have bothered you,' remarked the Inspector humorously.

'I need hardly say,' said Sturry coldly, 'that the late Mr Herriard never so demeaned himself with Me.'

He then withdrew in a very stately manner, softly closing the door behind him.

Ford, who, in a few minutes, presented himself, was looking a little scared. He would not admit that he had found Nathaniel a hard master; he seemed, instead, anxious to assure the Inspector that he had got on well with him, and had liked the place. Swallowing, he said, as though he had keyed himself up to it, that he had been upstairs between seven-thirty and eight-thirty, and had tried to enter his master's room. He thought that that would have been at ten to eight, or perhaps a little later. He had previously run a bath for Mr Herriard, as was his custom, and had laid out his evening clothes.

'Why did you go back?' asked the Inspector.

'Mr Herriard used very often to like me to help him to dress after his bath,' explained Ford.

'Did you find the door locked?'

'Yes, Inspector.'

'Did you knock?'

'Only the once,' faltered the valet.

'Was there any answer?'

'No. But I didn't make anything of that, thinking Mr Herriard might still be in his bath.'

'Was it usual for Mr Herriard to lock his door?'

'Not to say usual, Inspector, nor yet unusual. I have known him do it, if he was put out, or didn't wish to be disturbed.'

'Well, what did you do?'

'I went away again.'

'Where to?'

'Just along the upper hall to the sewing-room, meaning to wait a little while. Maggie – that's the second-housemaid – was in there, pressing a skirt, which Miss Paula had asked her to see to. And on my happening to pass the remark that the master had locked his door, she said she had seen Miss Paula only a minute or two before coming away from the door in her dressing-gown.'

'She did, did she? Did you see anyone on the upper hall?'

'Not to say see them, Inspector, but when I came up the backstairs I heard a footstep in the hall, and as I came through the archway that leads to the back-landing I saw Mr Roydon's door shut.'

'Do you mean Mr Roydon had just come upstairs to change?'

'Oh no, Inspector! Mr Roydon had been in his room some little time, Maggie having seen him come up with Miss Paula, and the pair of them standing talking together just inside Miss Paula's room.'

'I'll see this Maggie presently. How long did you stay in the sewing-room?'

'Well, I couldn't exactly say, Inspector, but I daresay it would have been twenty minutes or so.'

'And during that time you didn't see anyone in the upper hall?'

'Well, I wasn't looking. I heard everyone go down – that is, naturally I didn't count them, not knowing it might be important; but I remember hearing Mrs Joseph Herriard come out of her room, and Miss Paula, because Miss Paula called to Mr Roydon, and they went down together. Then I heard Miss Clare and Mr Joseph joking together, a few minutes later. Now I come to think of it, I don't remember hearing Mr Mottisfont go down, nor Miss Dean; but I did hear Mr Stephen, for he let his door bang. It was shortly after this that I began to think it was funny Mr Herriard hadn't come out of his room.'

'Oh, you knew he hadn't?'

'Well, I wouldn't say that exactly, but I'd had an ear cocked, as you might say, in case his bell should ring, which I could have heard in the sewing-room, the door being open, and the room just at the top of the backstairs. So I went along to try the door, and when I found it was still locked I took the liberty of calling to Mr Herriard. Then, of course, he didn't answer, nor I couldn't hear a sound inside the room, and I began to get a bit scared. Several times I called, and never any answer. And then Mr Joseph came up, and he called to Mr Stephen, and Mr Stephen and I, we broke the lock open, and found Mr Herriard lying there.' He ended with a shudder, and pressed his handkerchief to his lips. 'Horrible, it was! I hope I may never have to see such a sight again!'

'The chances are you won't,' the Inspector said unemotionally. 'What did Mr Joseph and Mr Stephen do?'

'They thought at first he'd fainted, like I did myself. Mr Stephen sent me off to fetch some brandy. By the time I'd come back, they'd discovered Mr Herriard was dead. "That won't be wanted," Mr Stephen said, meaning the brandy. "He's dead." I give you my word I nearly dropped the tray, it was such a shock to me!'

'Must have been a shock for Mr Stephen and Mr Joseph too,' said the Inspector.

'Oh yes, it must indeed! Mr Joseph was quite distracted, rubbing poor Mr Herriard's hands, and seeming as though he couldn't believe he was dead. Very devoted to Mr Herriard, he was.'

'Was Mr Stephen much upset?'

'Well, Inspector, Mr Stephen's not one to wear his heart on his sleeve, as the saying is, but it stands to reason it must have upset him, particularly when he hadn't been on good terms with Mr Herriard, by all accounts. He looked very white, and spoke to me very curt. He told me he could do with the brandy himself, and he took the tray out of my hands, and told me to go and ring up the doctor. Mr Joseph was nearly crying, and he said not to speak of Mr Herriard's death to anyone else. He was a bit upset by Mr Stephen's manner, Mr Stephen having a rough tongue, as anyone will tell you. But there's many as will cover up what they feel by a rough manner, and I didn't set any store by anything Mr Stephen said, for I saw his hand shaking, and I could see he'd had a jolt. What's more, Mr Stephen doesn't get on with Mr Joseph, being crossgrained, and never having liked Mr Joseph's coming to live at Lexham, by all accounts. Mr Joseph sort of brings out the worst in him, if you take my meaning.'

'Jealous of him, was he?'

'I wouldn't like to say that, Inspector, though I have heard it said that Mr Stephen was afraid Mr Joseph would put his nose out of joint. But I never believed that, because Mr Stephen's no fool, and anyone could see Mr Joseph's as innocent as a newborn babe, with no more notion of that kind of thing than nothing at all. In my opinion, it was just Mr Joseph's *way* that got Mr Stephen's goat.'

'H'm!' said the Inspector. 'You like Mr Stephen, don't you?'

'I've never had any cause to dislike him. He's always been pleasant enough to me, whenever I've waited on him, which I often have.'

'Got a temper, by what I hear.'

'Yes, like Mr Herriard he is, in some ways, except that he's not one to tell the world what he's thinking, by any means. You knew where you were with Mr Herriard, but Mr Stephen's no talker, and you wouldn't get to the bottom of him in a hurry. And I don't think the worse of him for that.'

'No reason why you should,' said the Inspector, closing the interview.

Maggie, when summoned to the morning-room, twisted her apron between her fingers, and said in a frightened gasp that she didn't wish to get anyone into trouble. When her alarms had been allayed, and she had been permitted to unburden herself of a highly coloured account of her own reactions to the crime, which included such interesting details as Coming Over Ever So Queer, and suffering equally from palpitations and a total inability to believe that anyone could have murdered the master, she admitted that she had seen Miss Paula and Mr Roydon go into Miss Paula's room, and had heard the murmur of their voices, the door having been left ajar. Later, when she had come up the backstairs with Miss Paula's dress, which she had gone downstairs to fetch, having had it in the kitchen to dry, because of the stain on it which Miss Paula had asked her to wash out, she had caught a glimpse of Miss Paula outside the master's door, just coming away, as though she had been in to speak to him.

There was nothing more to be got out of her, nor did an interrogation of the rest of the staff produce any other information than that Mrs Fratton, the cook-housekeeper, had no expectation of ever recovering from the shock; that the kitchen-maid had been having strong hysterics all the evening, her being a seven-months child, and delicate from birth; and that Preston, the head-housemaid, had seen Disaster in her teacup only the day before, and had told the rest of the staff to Mark her Words, there was Trouble coming for Someone.

By the time the Inspector, confronted by a gustily sobbing kitchen-maid, had somewhat hastily informed Mrs Fratton, who supported and encouraged this damsel by adjurations to give over, and stop acting so silly because the policeman wasn't going to eat her, that he had no more questions to ask, the experts upstairs had finished their various tasks, and Nathaniel's body had been conveyed to the waiting ambulance.

Several finger-prints had been discovered upon the panels and handle of Nathaniel's door, and upon various articles of furniture in the room. Some of these were Nathaniel's own prints, as might have been expected; and although the others would have to be identified there did not seem to be much hope that this line of investigation would prove to be very helpful. The expert was engaged, Sergeant Capel told the Inspector, in taking the finger-prints of all the inmates of the house, a task calling for a great deal of tact and patience, since Valerie Dean was tearfully sure that her mother would object, and the female half of the domestic staff apparently considered the operation to be the first step to the gallows.

Both doctors were agreed that the blow had been dealt with a thin knife, and that death had followed within a few minutes, but no trace of the weapon had so far been found. A careful inspection of the windows had not revealed any sign of the fastenings having been tampered with, and although finger-prints were clearly visible upon the glass it was expected that these would prove to be the valet's, since he freely admitted that he had shut the windows some time before Nathaniel had come upstairs. The door-keys belonging both to the bedroom and the bathroom would be subjected to a more minute inspection, and the ventilator above the bathroom window had already been exhaustively studied, without, however, yielding any clue. The only article of interest which had been discovered in Nathaniel's room was a flat gold cigarette-case, which had been found on the floor, lying half under the armchair beside the fire, out of sight of a cursory survey of the room.

The Inspector looked narrowly at this. It bore a monogram composed of the letters S and H. 'Any finger-prints?' he asked.

'No, sir.'

'What, none?'

'No, sir. I reckon they got rubbed off.'

'I suppose they must have. All right, I'll take charge of it.'

'Yes, sir,' said the young detective.

'And I'll see Miss Paula Herriard again. Send her in!'

This second summons to the morning-room apparently discomposed Paula, for she came in presently with a heightened colour, and more than her usual impetuosity. Without giving the Inspector time to speak, she demanded angrily what more he could possibly want with her. 'I call it utter incompetence!' she said, scorn vibrating in her voice.

The Inspector was unmoved by this stricture. Plenty of people, he reflected, when they were frightened tried to conceal it under a blustering manner. He thought, watching her restless hands and over-brilliant eyes, that Paula was decidedly frightened. 'I should like to go over your evidence again, miss,' he said, turning back the pages of his notebook.

'Bright!' she commented, with a sharp, unmirthful laugh.

He paid no heed; she didn't even annoy him; in fact, the more she lost her temper the better pleased he would be. 'You stated, miss, that when you went up to your room to change for dinner, you didn't come out of it again until you joined the rest of the party in the drawing-room.'

Her eyes were fixed on him, never wavered from his face, but he thought she breathed more rapidly. 'Well?'

'Do you wish to add anything to that?' asked the Inspector, giving her back look for look.

He had rattled her, just as he'd known he would. He could see the flicker of doubt in her eyes, the half-concealed alarm. He could have sworn she'd play for time, and she did, saying defensively: 'Why should I?'

'My information is that you were seen coming away from the deceased's bedroom in your dressing-gown,' he answered, at his most stolid.

He was startled by the sudden leap of flame into her eyes, the rush of colour to her cheeks. She was a dangerous piece of goods, and no mistake! he thought.

'My God, what does this house *do* to people? Who's been spying on me? Did I have a bloodstained dagger in my hand?'

He was shocked by her brutality, but although he was not an imaginative man, he thought he could readily picture her as a villainess in the kind of good old-fashioned melodrama you never seemed to see nowadays. He replied dampingly: 'No, miss.'

'You astonish me! Now tell me this: Was I seen coming out of my uncle's room? Was I?'

'Never mind asking me questions, miss, if you please! Did you go to your uncle's room after you had gone upstairs to change for dinner?'

'No, I didn't. I went to the door of his room, and no further.'

'How was that, miss?'

She jerked up one shoulder. 'He wouldn't let me in. I suppose he was dead.'

'When you say he wouldn't let you in, what do you mean?'

'Oh my God, must you have every I dotted, and every

T crossed? The door was locked; he didn't answer when I knocked.'

'Did you speak to him?'

'I don't know. Yes, I think so. I said, "It's I, Paula," or something of that sort. What does it *matter*?'

He ignored this. 'And he didn't answer?'

'I've already said so.'

'Didn't that strike you as a bit queer?'

'No.'

'When you knocked on his door, and called to him, and he didn't answer, you didn't think it in any way queer?' he persisted.

'No, I tell you!' She saw that he was incredulous, and added in a goaded voice: 'I knew he didn't want to see me.'

'Why not?'

'That's got nothing to do with you!'

'Oh yes, it has, miss! The fact is that you were wanting money from your uncle, which he wouldn't give you, and you'd quarrelled with him on account of it. Isn't that so?'

'You know it all, don't you?' she sneered.

'I advise you to consider your position,' he said.

'There's nothing to consider! You can't prove I ever went into my uncle's room! All you can prove is that we quarrelled, and if you take the trouble to enquire a little farther into our affairs, you'll find that we've quarrelled hundreds of times before!'

'Let me remind you, miss, that when I first asked you what you did when you got upstairs this evening, you never said a word about going to your uncle's room.'

'No! Because I could see from the look of you what sort of a fool you'd make of yourself if I told you that!'

She had succeeded at last in nettling him. He told her that she had better be careful what she said, but when she ironically thanked him for his warning, and asked if he had anything more to say, prudence made him swallow his irritation, and reply in an even tone that she might go.

The young detective, who had been a silent spectator of this scene, remarked that she was a hard-boiled dame. The Inspector grunted, refusing to commit himself.

'I thought you'd have pushed her a bit more, sir,' ventured the detective.

'I daresay you did. The difference between us is that I wasn't born yesterday,' replied the Inspector. 'There's no knowing with her sort. Send Roydon in to me!'

Willoughby strolled in presently, with the butt of a cigar between his fingers, and addressed the Inspector with a rather overacted air of tolerance. 'Well, Inspector, what is it now?' he said.

Confronted with the valet's evidence, he changed colour, but said with more annoyance than guilt: 'Look here, what are you getting at? If you think I went to Mr Herriard's room, you're damned well wrong!'

'When I put the question to you, sir, you stated that you did not leave your room until you came down to dinner. I have reason to believe that you did.'

'Naturally when you asked me that I thought you meant did I go to Mr Herriard's room!'

'But that wasn't what I asked you sir. Did you or did you not leave your room before you went down to the drawing-room?'

'Oh well, if you insist on such accuracy, yes, I did! Not that it has the least bearing on the case, which is why I didn't mention it.'

'I'll be the judge of that, thank you, sir. Why did you leave your room? Where did you go to?'

'Good God, where do you suppose I went to?' asked Roydon. 'You policemen must be pretty hard-up for clues if you're reduced to suspecting a man just because he is a man and not an angel!'

'Oh!' said the Inspector, rather blankly. 'Seems to me you might have told me that before, sir.'

'I probably should have if I'd remembered it,' said Roydon. 'And if that's all you want to know –'

'A minute ago, sir, you said you would have told me if you'd thought it had any bearing on the case.'

'Well, so I should have, only it hadn't, which is probably why I forgot it,' replied Roydon. 'Is there anything else?'

'That'll be all for the present,' said the Inspector.

Roydon walked out of the room. The young detective remarked that it looked fishy to him. 'Telling lies like that, for no reason!'

'People do,' said the Inspector. 'Afraid of getting mixed up in things. I don't see my way yet, and that's a fact.' His eye alighted on the gold cigarette-case. He picked it up. 'Where's Esher taking the finger-prints?'

'In the library. The old gentleman showed him in there. Miss Dean kicked up a fuss about it. The old man had his work cut out, jollying her along. Esher ought to be about through by this time.'

'We'll go and have a look,' said the Inspector, moving towards the door.

He arrived in the library in time to see Mathilda submitting her well-manicured hand to the expert.

'Of course, I quite see that this will seriously cramp my style if ever I decide to take to a life of crime,' she said.

'If you think that that's why I absolutely loathe the idea of having mine done –' began Valerie hotly, and broke off at sight of the Inspector.

Mathilda glanced over her shoulder. 'Ah, Torquemada in person!'

Joseph went up to the Inspector, saying: 'Come in, Inspector! We're just finishing, as you can see.'

'Very sorry to have to ask you to submit to this, sir, but –'

'Nonsense! Of course we understand that it must be!'

'Well, I think it's absolutely degrading!' interrupted Valerie. 'As though one was a common criminal, or something! I never thought I should be so insulted!'

Even Joseph's patience showed signs of cracking. He said with a touch of asperity: 'My dear child, don't be a silly little goose! Do you want any of us, Inspector? Can you tell me anything, or mustn't I ask?'

'Nothing to tell you so far, sir. I would like to know which of you gentlemen owns this, if you please.'

They all looked at the cigarette-case. The monogram

was plainly to be read. The Inspector's gaze was fixed on Stephen. Stephen was looking at the case; his harsh face gave nothing away. Joseph, after one glance, cast a swift, startled look at Mathilda, half-questioning, half-appalled.

'Well, it's not mine!' said Roydon.

'It's mine,' said Stephen coolly, raising his eyes to the Inspector's. 'Where did you find it?'

'Had you mislaid it, sir?'

Stephen did not answer for a moment. Joseph said with uneasy jocularity: 'I don't suppose he knows whether he had or not! I'm afraid my nephew's always leaving things about, aren't you, Stephen? Where did you pick it up, Inspector? We don't want any mysteries, if you don't mind!'

'It was discovered, sir, in the late Mr Herriard's bedroom,' replied the Inspector.

Joseph's airy manner momentarily deserted him. He gave a gasp, and said in a hurry: 'Oh, there might be dozens of explanations to account for that! Why – why, my nephew probably put it down there when we were in the room together, or very likely – or at least quite possibly my brother found it lying somewhere, and took it up, meaning to give it back to him. Oh, I can think of any number of explanations!'

'Well, don't!' said Stephen ungratefully. 'Mind telling me precisely where this was found, Inspector?'

'It was lying on the floor, half under the chair by the fire.'

'Oh, then the thing's perfectly plain!' said Joseph, still labouring in Stephen's defence. 'I expect it slipped out of your pocket, old man, and in the agitation of the moment you didn't notice it. When you were bending over poor Nat. That would be it!'

'The case was not found anywhere near the body of the deceased, sir,' interpolated the Inspector.

'Oh! Well, I daresay it got kicked across the room,' said Joseph, in a despairing way. 'I'm sure we were all so much upset that anything could have happened! Stephen, why don't you say something? There's nothing in this! We all know that! There's no need to be silly about it! All the Inspector wants to know is –'

'So far, I've had damned little chance of saying anything,' said Stephen. 'If you've quite finished handing out a line of talk which wouldn't convince a half-wit, I will state two facts. I don't know how my case got into my uncle's room. It did not fall out of my pocket, possibly because my agitation didn't lead me to stand on my head, but more certainly because I hadn't it on me when I entered the room.'

The Inspector took no trouble to conceal his scepticism. Joseph plunged again into deep waters. 'Depend upon it, my brother took it upstairs with him! Really, there's no need –'

'And dropped it on the floor, sir?'

'Pushed it under the chair, apparently,' said Stephen. 'Or is that what I'm supposed to have done, Inspector?'

'I wouldn't say that,' answered the Inspector. 'It might have fallen off the chair – if someone sitting there thought he'd put it in his pocket, but happened to drop it into the chair instead, and then got up. Someone a bit careless, maybe.'

'I object to that!' Joseph interrupted. 'That's deliberately twisting a perfectly innocent remark of mine to mean something I never intended, and which is absurd – quite absurd!'

'Shut up!' said Stephen. 'I admit it's my case; I accept your statement that it was found in my uncle's room. So what, Inspector?'

'You'd better consider your position, sir.'

Mathilda, who had preserved a somewhat ominous silence throughout this interchange, moved forward. 'Quite finished?' she enquired. 'Because if so I'll speak my little piece. I saw Mr Stephen Herriard give his cigarette-case to Miss Dean before ever he left the drawing-room after tea.'

Stephen laughed. Valerie said furiously: 'You shan't put it on to me! I never had his beastly case! I left it on the table! I don't know what became of it! He probably picked it up before he went out of the room. You're the filthiest, meanest *beast* I ever met, Mathilda Clare!'

'And you, my little pet,' said Mathilda, with great cordiality, 'are a bitch!'

Eight

THE INSPECTOR LOOKED A GOOD DEAL TAKEN ABACK BY THIS exchange of compliments. It did not fit in with his ideas of how the gentry behaved, and he made no attempt to cope with the situation. Roydon seemed to share his feelings, but Paula, who had stalked into the library at the outset of hostilities, said in approving accents: 'Good for you, Mathilda!'

As usual it was Joseph who had to intervene. He shook his head at Mathilda, although with a sympathetic twinkle in his eye, and suggested to Valerie that she was overwrought.

'She's trying to make you think I murdered Mr Herriard!' said Valerie tearfully.

'My dear child, no one could possibly think anything so absurd!' Joseph assured her. 'Nobody as pretty as you could be suspected of hurting a fly!'

She was a little mollified by this tribute, and when Roydon said emphatically 'Hear, hear!' she threw him a pathetic smile, and said: 'Oh, I don't know about that, but I don't even remember Stephen's giving me his case, and I certainly never took it out of the room. It's much more likely that I simply tossed it back to him.'

'Oh, it is, is it?' said Mathilda. 'Why "tossed"?'

Valerie's face turned crimson. 'I don't know. I –'

'Yes, you do. You know perfectly well that Stephen threw his case over to you. So let's have less of this convenient aphasia!'

Valerie flung round to face Stephen. 'Are you going to stand there allowing that woman to insult me?' she demanded.

'Where on earth did you dig out a line like that?' enquired Paula.

'She's got a lousy taste in literature,' Stephen explained. 'Mathilda, I forbid you to insult my intended.'

'You and who else?' retorted Mathilda crudely.

'Children, children!' implored Joseph.

The Inspector cleared his throat. 'If you please, ladies! Miss Dean, is it a fact that Mr Stephen Herriard gave his cigarette-case to you before he went up to change?'

'I tell you I don't know! I simply don't remember! Anyway, I never took it out of the room!'

Maud, who had come into the library behind Paula, said in her flattened voice: 'You asked him for a cigarette, dear, and he threw his case over to you.'

'You're all against me!' Valerie declared, tears spangling the ends of her lashes.

'No, dear, but it is always better to speak the truth. I have often thought it a pity that girls should smoke so much. It is very bad for the complexion, but I make it a rule never to interfere in what doesn't concern me.'

'Let that be a lesson to you!' Paula said to Valerie, quite in Stephen's manner.

The Inspector, possibly feeling that of all the women present Maud was the most rational, turned to her, and asked: 'Did you see what Miss Dean did with the case, madam?'

'No,' Maud replied. 'I expect something happened to divert my attention. Not that I was watching particularly, because there was no reason why I should.'

'If she had given the case back to Mr Herriard, do you think you would have noticed it?'

'Oh no, I don't suppose I should!'

'She didn't give it back to him,' Mathilda said.

'Well, what did she do with it, miss?'

'I don't know. Like Mrs Herriard, I didn't notice.'

'I simply put it on the table!' Valerie said. 'Willoughby was in the middle of reading his play. I don't know what became of it afterwards.'

'Look here, miss!' said the Inspector patiently. 'We'll get this settled once and for all, if you please! Did Mr Herriard give you his case, or did he not?'

'I don't call it *giving* me his case just because I asked him for a cigarette, and he hadn't the decency to get up and hand me one, but just chucked his case at me! And I don't see why –'

'He *did* throw his case to you?'

'Yes, but –'

'Then don't keep on saying you don't remember!' said the Inspector severely. 'Now then, sir: are you sure you hadn't got the case on you when you left the room?'

'Perfectly.'

'That's true!' Joseph exclaimed. 'Now I come to think of it, *you* asked him for a cigarette, Paula, when we came down from poor Nat's room, and he put his hand in his pocket, as though to pull out his case, and then just nodded to the box –' He stopped short, as the infelicitous nature of his testimony apparently dawned on him. 'Not that that proves anything!' he added, in a hurry.

'No, sir,' agreed the Inspector dryly, and turned from him to Valerie again. 'You say you put the case down on the table, miss –'

'I didn't say I *actually* did! I only said I most *probably* did!' replied Valerie, who seemed to have decided that her only safety lay in prevarication. 'And it's no use badgering me, because –'

'Valerie, my child!' Joseph said, taking one of her hands, and holding it between both of his. 'The Inspector only wants to get at the truth of what happened! You mustn't think that you'll be incriminating anyone just by telling him quite frankly what you did with Stephen's case.'

'I don't care about that,' said Valerie, stating a self-evident fact. 'But I know quite well Mathilda's trying to put it onto me, and it isn't fair!'

'No, no; Tilda never had any such idea, had you, Tilda? She knows you couldn't have done it.'

It now seemed good to Paula to pour oil on sinking flames. 'Indeed!' she ejaculated. 'How, may I ask, does she know that?'

'Good God, Paula, she hasn't got the guts, let alone the ingenuity!' replied Mathilda.

'Mathilda! Paula!' expostulated Joseph despairingly. 'No, really! Really, my dears!'

'Oh yes, I've no doubt you both think I'm a fool!' said Valerie. 'Just because I don't do the things you do! But as a matter of fact I very nearly went to *college*, and I should have, only that it seemed the most frightful waste of time!'

'I think that was very sensible of you,' remarked Maud, without any malice at all. 'I daresay it's all very well for some people, but I never went to college, and look at me!'

Quite a number of those present obeyed this behest, in a fascinated kind of way. The Inspector, feeling that the command of the situation was slipping out of his grasp, cleared his throat, and said loudly: 'No one, least of all the police, wants to put anything on to an innocent person; but I warn you, Miss Dean, you don't do yourself any good by refusing to speak the truth. Did you put Mr Herriard's case down on the table?'

After this question had been relayed in a gentler form by Joseph, and Roydon had made a rather involved speech, the gist of which seemed to be that it was the height of injustice to expect nervous subjects to speak the truth, Valerie was induced to admit that she had put the case down on the table. Nobody remembered having seen it there, but that, as Mathilda delicately suggested, was hardly surprising, since everyone's attention had been fully occupied by Roydon's reading, and the exciting scene that had followed it.

The Inspector then went to look at the table in question, everybody tramping after him, and it was found to be a Chippendale piecrust table, which Sturry preferred to designate as an Incidental Table. It bore a small bowl of flowers, an ashtray, and a silver match-box, and Sturry, questioned, stated that when he had entered the drawing-room before dinner, to make sure that James, the footman, had Set it to Rights, no cigarette-case had been visible. James was equally sure that it had not been on the table when he had emptied the ashtray, so that left everyone, as Mathilda kindly pointed out, exactly where they were before this exhaustive enquiry had been inaugurated.

'No, miss, there I cannot agree with you,' said the Inspector darkly.

'The fact is, anyone could have picked it up without attracting the least attention,' she said.

Edgar Mottisfont took instant exception to this. 'I don't see that at all!' he said. 'Are you suggesting that someone tried to steal Stephen's case? Why should anyone but Stephen have picked it up? We all knew it didn't belong to us!'

Joseph said, as angrily as anyone of his mild temper could: 'Edgar, do think before you speak! What – I ask you – are you trying to insinuate? What reason have you to try to stab Stephen in the back?'

'I wasn't trying to stab him in the back!' retorted Mottisfont. 'All I said was –'

'What you meant us to infer was obvious!' said Joseph. 'I should have thought that after all the years you've known Stephen –'

'I don't say that he stabbed Nat!' said Mottisfont, a spot of colour on his cheekbone. 'It's not my business to find out who did that! I'm only saying that the most likely person to have picked up the case was its owner! Of course, I know very well you Herriards always stick together, but I'm not a

Herriard – I'm just a plain man, and I object to the fantastic idea you're trying to foster, that someone else pocketed a valuable case which didn't belong to them!'

'Edgar, old friend, if anything I've said gave you the impression that I was in league with Stephen against you –'

'Nothing I have said could have given you that impression,' interpolated Stephen.

'Hush, Stephen! – if I've given you that impression, I heartily beg your pardon! I never for one moment meant to insinuate that *you* had touched the case!'

It was generally felt that Joseph had now surpassed himself; but it was plain, from his guileless countenance, that he had no notion of having said anything that might have been more felicitously expressed. Mathilda would have allowed the matter to rest. Stephen, however, said sardonically: 'Why stop there? Whom do you suspect of having taken my case?'

'Stephen! Why will you always take me up wrongly? I don't suspect anyone! Good gracious, how could I possibly –'

'This is the most useless discussion I've ever taken part in!' declared Paula. 'Are we to sit up all night while you and Joe make fools of yourselves? I'm tired to death, and I'm going to bed!'

This last announcement was flung at the Inspector's head. He said nothing to dissuade her. He was feeling tired too; he wanted to consider the case quietly; and he could not think that a prolongation of his investigations into the night-watches would yield any very valuable results. Like many laymen, he had a deep faith in the skill of specialists, and his dependence was now placed on the findings of the police experts. He said formally that he had no further questions to put to anyone.

Valerie at once reiterated her demand to be allowed to go home, and her conviction that she would be unable to sleep a wink if compelled to remain at Lexham. The Inspector, having informed her that her presence was necessary to the conduct of the case, very meanly left her fellow-guests to convince her that a journey to London from Lexham at eleven o'clock on Christmas Eve would be most difficult to accomplish, and rejoined his assistants in the morning-room. Twenty minutes later, the police-cars were heard to start up in the drive, and Valerie, until she discovered that a constable had been left to mount guard over the premises all night, showed signs of recovering her equilibrium.

Maud, whose stagnant calm had been to all outward appearances undisturbed by the shocking events of the day, exasperated everyone by resuming her search for the *Life of the Empress of Austria*; Paula, saying that she must be alone or go mad, swept upstairs to her room; and Stephen gratified Mathilda, but revolted everyone else, by saying that a drink was clearly called for. Even Joseph said that it did not seem to be quite the moment for carousing: an expression which had the effect of driving everyone else instantly over to Stephen's side. Mottisfont said that he thought they had all earned a drink. Upon reflection, he said that that wasn't quite what he had meant, but when Stephen asked him with false amiability what he had really meant, he found himself unable to explain, and foundered in a morass of unfinished sentences.

Sturry, gathering that his superiors were determined to debauch themselves, apologised in a quelling way for having forgotten, under the stress of circumstances, to bring the usual tray into the drawing-room, and went away to rectify his omission.

Valerie, who had been silent for quite ten minutes, suddenly announced her intention of ringing up her mother. No one put forward any objection, though from the look which descended on to Stephen's face it was generally inferred that he was not in favour of the operation.

When Valerie had left the room, Mathilda moved across to Stephen's side, and asked softly: 'Who's the heir?'

He shrugged.

'You?'

'I don't know. Don't think he made a will.'

'Joe's been hinting all day that he did.'

'Oh – Joe!'

'He ought to know, if anyone does.'

'The answer being that no one does. Sorry you've been let in for this.'

'Don't waste any pity on me: I've got an unbreakable alibi,' she replied lightly. 'Far be it from me to cast any aspersions on your word, Stephen, but there is one appeal I should like to address to you in the name of us all.'

He looked at her with a suddenly lowering expression on his brow. 'Well?'

'If you purloined Maud's book, do for God's sake give it back to her!'

He gave a laugh, but it seemed to her that it was perfunctory. 'I haven't got her book.'

'Don't quibble!' said Mathilda severely.

'I'm sick of the damned book!' he snapped. 'I've already told you once that I don't know where it is!'

He got up, as he spoke, and walked away to the other end of the room. She saw that his nerves were on edge, and was sorry that she had teased him. Sturry came in with a tray of drinks, and set it down on a side-table. Maud asked him if he had seen the book she was reading. Sturry said in a very despising way that he had not noticed it, but would make enquiries.

'It is very unfortunate,' stated Maud. 'I wish I could remember where I laid it down. I always read for twenty minutes in bed before I put the light out. It is very calming to the mind. I had just got to the part about Rudolph. The one who committed suicide.'

'What do you find so calming about that?' asked Stephen, over his shoulder.

'It takes one's mind off things,' she answered vaguely.

It said much for Joseph's kindliness, Mathilda thought, that with no more than a sigh, immediately suppressed, he got up from his chair, and offered to help in the search for the book. Mathilda was afraid that he would ask Stephen for it, but although he did glance speculatively at that unresponsive profile he appeared to feel the moment to be unpropitious, and said nothing. It seemed rather unfair that he, upon whom the brunt of the evening's burden had fallen, should be obliged to undertake a singularly futile search single-handed, so Mathilda got up, and offered to assist him. Maud thanked her placidly, and went back to her seat by the fire.

'She might have put it down in the billiard-room,' Mathilda suggested. 'She came in there just before tea, didn't she?'

The billiard-room yielded no clue to the book's whereabouts, but the sight of the Christmas tree, glittering under the lights, brought home to Mathilda and to Joseph the gruesome nature of the events of the day. Joseph swallowed twice, and made a tragic gesture towards the coloured balls and the twinkling tinsel.

'What are you going to do about it?' asked Mathilda. 'It does seem a trifle out of place, doesn't it?'

Joseph blew his nose. 'It must be taken away. Oh, Tilda, is this all my fault? Was I wrong to coax Nat into giving this party? I meant it to be so different!'

'I don't see that you could have known that Nat would be murdered,' she replied.

He shook his head, putting out a hand to finger one of the icicles that depended from a laden branch.

'Joe, did he make a will?'

He raised his eyes. 'Yes. I don't know whether it's still in existence, though. Perhaps it would be better if he'd destroyed it.'

'Why?'

'It was when he had pleurisy, in the spring,' Joseph said. 'I persuaded him to make a will. I thought it right, Tilda! If only one could see into the future!'

'Was it in Stephen's favour?'

He nodded. After a moment, she said: 'Well, Stephen didn't know it, anyway.'

He glanced up quickly, and down again.

'Unless you told him,' she added.

'I? No, I never said so! Not in so many words! But when I saw what sort of a mood he was in, I did rather hint to Valerie that a word from her might be advantageous. She may tell the Inspector so. She's such a thoughtless child! And you know what an impression Stephen must be giving the police by that silly, boorish manner he puts on! Oh, Tilda, I feel worried to death!'

She was silent for a moment. 'Did the police ask you who was the heir?' she said presently.

'Yes, but I think I shelved the question. I gave them the name of Nat's solicitor.'

'Do you suppose that the will is in his charge?'

'I don't know,' he said reluctantly. 'If it isn't, I shall have to say where I think it might be. I mean, I can't do Stephen out of his inheritance, can I? Besides, they'd be bound to find it sooner or later. I don't know what to do for the best.'

Mathilda felt strongly inclined to advise him not to meddle, but she refrained. He said: 'I wish you'd exert your influence, Tilda! Don't let him alienate the police through sheer perversity! He won't listen to me.'

'I expect he knows his own business best,' she said shortly. 'In any event, I have no influence over him.'

'Sometimes I fear that no one has,' said Joseph, with one of his gusty sighs. 'It's as though he was born cussed! Now, what in the world can have possessed him to hide poor Maud's book? That's the sort of silly, schoolboy mischief that puts people against him so!'

Mathilda thought that anyone less schoolboyish or mischievous than Stephen would have been hard to find, but she merely observed that Stephen denied all knowledge of the book's whereabouts.

'Oh well, perhaps I'm wronging him!' said Joseph, visibly brightening. 'Anyway, it doesn't seem to be in this room.'

They returned to the library, their arrival synchronising with that of Valerie, who had apparently derived some benefit from a protracted and expensive telephone-call to her mother. She announced that Mummy was coming down to Lexham on the following day.

'Oh, my God!' said Stephen audibly.

'I'm sure she must want to be with you at such a time,' said Joseph hastily. 'We shall be very glad to have her, shan't we, Maud? One only wishes that her visit were taking place under happier circumstances.'

'Mummy says she's sure it will all be cleared up satisfactorily, and we just mustn't worry!' said Valerie.

This valuable piece of advice plunged everyone into a state of profound gloom. After thinking it over, Mottisfont said that he didn't see how it could be cleared up satisfactorily.

'No,' said Stephen cordially. 'Not when you consider that one of us is an assassin.'

'I find that remark gratuitously offensive!' said Mottisfont.

'Why?' asked Stephen.

'Now, now!' Joseph intervened. 'We mustn't let this thing get on top of our nerves! I myself feel convinced that Nat was murdered by someone from outside.'

'You would,' said Stephen.

'Damn it all, why not?' demanded Mathilda.

He shrugged. 'Windows all latched on the inside.'

'But the ventilator was open!' Joseph reminded him. 'An agile man might have got in that way, I believe. Of course, it wouldn't have been easy, but although you may not believe it I used to be a bit of an athlete in my younger days, and I'm pretty sure I could have done it.'

'You couldn't do it now, Joe,' said Mathilda. 'Too much *enbonpoint*.'

'Ah, you love to make fun of your poor old uncle!' he said, shaking his fist at her. 'Yet when I was a young man I was as slim as Roydon there. I well remember when I was playing Romeo once – But what am I about, telling stories of my youth when our minds are full of graver matters? Maud, my dear, we will have a thorough search for your book tomorrow, I promise. You have had a wearing day: you should be in bed, you know.'

'I daresay I may have left it upstairs,' she said, winding up her knitting-wool. 'I do not want anyone to worry about it. I expect it will turn up.' She rose, said good night in a general way, and departed.

'I shall follow her example,' said Mathilda. 'Are you coming up, Valerie?'

Valerie replied reluctantly that she supposed she would have to, but that the thought of having a policeman in the house was too ghoulish to permit of her closing her eyes all night.

'I shouldn't worry. I believe policemen are a very moral set,' said Mathilda unkindly. 'Lock your door, if you're nervous.'

'I do think you're the limit!' exclaimed Valerie, giggling.

'I don't suppose any of us will sleep much,' remarked Mottisfont, when she had left the room. 'I know I shan't. I feel as though I'd had a knock-out. Nat! It still doesn't seem possible!'

'Personally,' said Roydon, with ill-assumed indifference, 'I feel pretty done-in, and I daresay I shall sleep like a log. After all, it's different for me. I mean, it isn't as though I *knew* Mr Herriard.'

This implication, that he stood aloof from the crime and its consequences, did nothing to advance his popularity with the three other men. Even Joseph shook his head in a fore-boding way; and Mottisfont went so far as to say that they were all in it, one just as much as another.

'I'm afraid I can hardly agree with you!' said Roydon, in a head-voice. 'I don't want to cast any aspersions on anyone, but *I* had no quarrel with Mr Herriard!'

'Just what do you mean by that, young man?' Mottisfont demanded, his eyes snapping behind his spectacles.

Stephen yawned. 'That you and I did. I wonder if I'm as boring as the rest of you? Perhaps I'd better go to bed. What's the name of Uncle Nat's solicitor, Joe?'

'Filey, Blyth, and Blyth,' answered Joseph. 'But John Blyth has always handled poor Nat's affairs.'

'Know his home address?'

'No; but I expect it's in the Telephone Directory, for I'm nearly sure he lives in London. Why? Do you think we ought –'

'I'll ring him up in the morning,' Stephen said, and lounged out.

Mottisfont watched him go, his expression one of open dislike. 'Taking a lot on himself, isn't he?' he said disagreeably.

Joseph, who had looked a little surprised, rallied, and said briskly: 'Nonsense! Stephen knows what a muddle-headed old fellow I am. Quite right of him! Good gracious, Edgar, I hope you aren't trying to make me jealous of my own nephew! That would be rather too much of a good thing!'

'Oh, as long as you don't mind, I suppose it has nothing to do with me!' said Mottisfont.

'Stephen and I understand one another,' said Joseph, becoming the indulgent uncle again. 'Now, I think we had better all go to bed, don't you? We are a little overwrought, and, indeed, how could we fail to be? Perhaps the night will bring counsel.' He went to the door, but looked back as he opened it to say with a wistful smile: 'We feel the blank in our lives already, don't we? Perhaps I more than anyone. To go to bed without that good night to Nat! It will be long before I can accustom myself to it.'

Mottisfont and Roydon both suffered the Englishman's inevitable reaction to such indecent pathos. Mottisfont reddened, and coughed; Roydon stared at his feet, and muttered: 'Quite!' Joseph sighed, and said: 'But I mustn't intrude my private grief upon you. We've all got to keep stiff upper lips, haven't we?'

Neither of his listeners could lower himself sufficiently to respond adequately to this, so Joseph went away with a heavy tread and another sigh.

'Well, considering I never heard Mr Herriard say a decent word to him – !' began Roydon.

Mottisfont resented Joseph's attempt to play upon his emotions quite as profoundly as Roydon, but he had known the Herriards for many years, and he was not going to join a long-haired playwright in running them down. He said repressively: 'The Herriards take a good deal of knowing. They've all got sharp tongues, except Joe, but I've never set any store by that. You can't judge by appearances.'

'It seems to me that they all play into one another's hands!' said Roydon. 'In fact, it wouldn't surprise me to discover that Stephen's filthy rudeness to Joseph Herriard is just so much eyewash! You can't help noticing how they all hang together, once it comes to the pinch!'

Mottisfont had been thinking much the same thing, but he was not going to admit it. He merely said that there was nothing surprising in families hanging together, and made for the door.

Roydon followed him upstairs, remarking in a disgruntled way that it wasn't his idea of a Christmas party.

He was by no means alone in this view of the matter. The Chief Constable, receiving Inspector Colwall's report on the case, said that this was the sort of thing that would happen when Bradford was sick.

'Yes, sir,' agreed Inspector Colwall, swallowing the insult.

'Christmas Eve, too!' said the Chief Constable, in an exasperated tone. 'To my mind, it's a case for Scotland Yard.'

'Perhaps you're right, sir,' responded the Inspector, thinking of the complexities of the case, the lack of evidence, and the difficulties of dealing with the kind of witness he had found at Lexham Manor.

'And that being so,' said the Chief Constable, 'I'll get on to London right away.'

The Inspector was in complete agreement over this. If Scotland Yard was to take over the case, he for one did not want to be told that the scent had been allowed to grow cold, and that the Yard should have been called in days earlier. That was the kind of thing that happened when the local police tried to solve their cases, and failed; and it didn't do a man any good to be made to look like a fool who'd been trying to make things difficult for Scotland Yard.

So the Chief Constable put through a call to London, and was connected in due course with a calm person who said he was Detective-Superintendent Hannasyde. The Chief Constable gave him the particulars of the case, and after asking several questions Superintendent Hannasyde said that he would send a good man down to assist him next morning.

That was polite of the Superintendent, but when his words were repeated to Inspector Colwall, the Inspector only said, Yes, in a dispirited tone. The good man from Scotland Yard would automatically take charge of the case, and very likely tick everyone off into the bargain, he thought, uneasily aware of his own shortcomings as a detective. He went off duty in a frame of mind almost as gloomy as anyone's at Lexham Manor, and very nearly as resentful as that of the good man from Scotland Yard, who, far from feeling any elation at being given a promising case to handle, told his subordinate that it was just his luck to be sent into the wilds of Hampshire on Christmas Day.

Sergeant Ware, an earnest young man, ventured to say that the case sounded as though it might be interesting.

'Interesting!' said Inspector Hemingway. 'It sounds to me like a mess. I don't like the lay-out, I don't like the locality, and if I don't find a whole crowd of suspects, all telling a lot of silly lies for no reason at all, my instinct's wrong, and that's all there is to it.'

'Well, perhaps it is, this time,' suggested Ware.

The Inspector fixed him with a bright and fulminating eye. 'Don't you get insubordinate with me, my lad!' he warned him. 'I'm never wrong.'

The Sergeant grinned. He had worked with Inspector Hemingway many times, and had almost as great a respect for his foibles as for his undoubted ability.

'And don't stand there smirking as though you were off on a Cheap Day Excursion, because if I were to burst a blood-vessel you'd very likely get blamed for it!'

'Why should I, sir?' asked Ware, diverted.

'Because that's the way things turn out in the Force,' said the Inspector darkly.

Nine

THERE WAS NO APPARENT REASON TO SUPPOSE, ON THE following morning, that Inspector Hemingway was regarding the case with a less jaundiced eye. On the journey into Hampshire, he spoke bitterly and at length on the subject of the play which he had been helping to produce in his hometown, and which was to be performed on Boxing Day. He saw no prospect of being present upon this interesting occasion, and the trend of his remarks led Ware to infer that without his masterful hand upon the reins the play had little chance of succeeding, if, indeed, it could be performed at all.

The Drama was one of the Inspector's pet hobby-horses, and the Sergeant sat back in his corner of the railway compartment, and resigned himself to the inevitable. The expression of interest which concealed his almost total inattention did not deceive the Inspector for an instant. 'Yes, I know you aren't listening,' he said. 'If you listened more, you'd be a better detective, besides being a lot more respectful to your superiors. The trouble with you young chaps is that you think you've got nothing to learn.'

The Sergeant had never been disrespectful to his superiors

in all his blameless life, and his painstaking efforts to broaden his knowledge were notorious, but he attempted no protest. Merely he grinned, and said that he had never been much of a one for the theatre.

'You needn't tell me!' said Hemingway disgustedly. 'I'll bet you spend all your off-time at the pictures!'

'Well, I don't, sir. I was brought up very strict. I generally do a bit of carpentering.'

'That's worse,' said Hemingway.

After a discreet pause, the Sergeant ventured to enquire what were his chief's impressions of the case they were bound for.

'It's a great mistake to start off with a lot of preconceived ideas,' replied Hemingway. 'Which is why you'll never see me do such a thing. It'll be time enough for me to go getting impressions when I've had a look at the dramatis personae. Not that I want to look at them, mind you! From what the Superintendent told me, you'd find it hard to pick out a set of people I wouldn't rather not look at.'

'Sounds to me as though it might be an interesting sort of a case,' suggested the Sergeant, in cajoling accents. 'Stands to reason it's going to be a teaser, or the locals wouldn't have called us in.'

'That's where you're very likely wrong,' said the disillusioned Inspector. 'Whenever we get called in to a crime in classy country surroundings, you may bet your life it's because the Chief Constable plays golf with half the suspects, and doesn't want to handle the thing himself.'

Events were to prove him to be to a certain extent justified.

Almost the first thing that the Chief Constable said to him was: 'I'm not going to pretend I'm not glad to hand over this business to you, Inspector. Very awkward case: most astounding! I've known the murdered man for years. Know his brother too. I don't like it.'

'No, sir,' said the Inspector.

'What's more,' said the Chief Constable, 'it's a damned queer business! Can't see myself how the murder can possibly have been committed. Of course, our Detective-Inspector's away, sick. This is Inspector Colwall, who's had charge of the case up till now.'

'Glad to know you,' said Hemingway, mentally writing Colwall down as a painstaking man who had probably missed every vital point in the case.

'Inexplicable!' pronounced Major Bolton, but not, it was gathered, with reference to Hemingway's polite remark. 'You'd better go through it from the start. Take a chair!'

Hemingway obeyed this invitation, nodded to his Sergeant to follow his example, and turned a bright, enquiring eye upon the Major.

'The murdered man,' said Major Bolton, 'was a wealthy bachelor. He bought Lexham Manor some years ago. Sort of show-place: oak panelling, and that kind of thing. Cost a packet: never could make out why he wanted it. Not that sort of man, on the face of it. Made his money in trade. Head of a firm of importers, but been a sleeping-partner for some years now. East Indian stuff: spices, and that kind of thing. Mind you, I'm not saying he was a self-made man! Perfectly respectable family, and all that. Don't know anything about his parents: believe the father was a country solicitor. There were three children: Nathaniel, the murdered man, Matthew, and Joseph. Matthew doesn't come into it. Dead for years. His widow's in America, with her third husband. Never met the lady myself, but I know her children. They're both in it, up to the neck. Couple of years ago, Joseph – bit of a rolling-stone: no harm in him, but a feckless sort of a fellow – came home from wherever he'd been – South America, I believe, but that's nothing: he's been all over the world at one time or another – and took up his residence at Lexham Manor. Never had much use for Nat Herriard myself, but to give him his due, he treated his family well. Better than any of 'em deserved, if you ask me. Not that there's anything against Joseph. What you might call a well-meaning ass. Sort of Peter Pan, if you get my meaning. Got a wife. Gossip says he picked her up out of the chorus. Don't know anything about that. Colourless kind of woman. Pretty once, run to fat now. Never could make anything of her. Either deep as the devil, or a born fool. Know the type?'

The Inspector nodded. 'I do, sir, and what's more I wish I didn't.'

Major Bolton gave a snort of laughter. 'Mind you, I haven't anything on her, and I don't myself see her sticking a knife into her brother-in-law. All the same, no one in these parts could ever understand her consenting to live at Lexham, sponging on Nat. However, she's a placid kind of a woman, and I daresay she'd had enough of roaming about the world with Joseph. Tiresome sort of man, Joseph. No money-sense. No sense at all, if you ask me. Ever see a play called *Dear Brutus*?'

'Barrie,' responded the Inspector. 'If you've a taste for him, it's in his best manner. Myself –'

'Well, Joe's always put me in mind of one of the characters in it,' said the Chief Constable, ruthlessly interrupting what Sergeant Ware knew would have been a pithy lecture on the Drama. 'Silly old footler who danced about in a wood. Know the one I mean?'

'Coade,' said Hemingway.

'Well, I'm a plain man myself,' said the Chief Constable, conveying in these simple words his contempt for all whimsies. 'However, they say it takes all sorts to make a world. Next we come to Stephen and Paula Herriard. They're Nat's nephew and niece, Matthew's children. Always treated Lexham Manor as a second home. I know 'em both, and I don't like either of 'em. Stephen's a rough-tongued young man with no manners, and not enough to do; and Paula – nice-looking girl, if you like that stormy type – is on the stage. Both got small private means: enough to make 'em independent, but not enough to make a splash with. It's always been assumed that Stephen was Nat's heir. Stands to reason he would be. Only a few months ago he got engaged to a girl. Never set eyes on her myself, but Nat couldn't stand her. Said she was a gold-digger. Daresay he was right. You didn't take to her, did you, Colwall?'

'No, sir. Silly little thing, and not, in my opinion, the right sort for a gentleman to marry.'

'Well, she's in it too. I don't mean that she committed

the murder, for from what Colwall tells me it doesn't look as though she's the sort of girl who could do such a thing, but she was one of the people staying in the house at the time. Stephen brought her down, presumably to introduce her to Nat. According to what the servants say, they didn't get on at all. Quite possible that Nat's annoyance over her may have precipitated matters.'

'Precipitated matters?' repeated Hemingway.

'Don't know that it's quite fair to say that,' amended the Major. 'But there seems to have been a row between Nat and Stephen. Of course, if Nat threatened to cut Stephen off with a shilling if he married the girl – well, you never know, do you? I wouldn't put it beyond Stephen to stick a knife into someone. Always seemed to me a callous young devil. Then there's this Roydon-fellow.'

From the Major's expression it could easily be deduced that he disapproved profoundly of Mr Roydon. The reason was at once made apparent. 'He calls himself a playwright, or some such nonsense,' said the Major.

'He does, does he?' said Hemingway. 'Well, that's very interesting, sir. What did you say his name was?'

'Willoughby Roydon. Don't suppose you've heard of him; I know I hadn't. As far as I can make out, he hasn't had anything put on – really put on, I mean.'

The Inspector appeared to appreciate the distinction, nodding, and saying sapiently: 'Sunday evenings, eh? Uplift and Modernism. I know. What's he doing in the case, sir?'

'Friend of Paula Herriard. He's written a play which she

wanted her uncle to back. Don't know what it was about. Daresay it would be all the same to me if I did. I don't go in for that kind of thing. Can't stand highbrows at any price. Point is, Nat didn't like it. This Roydon-fellow seems to have read the thing aloud to him yesterday afternoon, and Nat lost his temper over it, and there was a general sort of a row. Well, I'm a fair-minded man, and, after all, you can't be surprised, can you? I mean, coming down to stay with a man, and then reading stuff aloud to him! Never heard of such a thing!'

'Did Mr Herriard quarrel with Mr Roydon, then?' asked Hemingway.

'That we can't make out, can we, Colwall? Roydon says he didn't.'

'Well, sir, it's a bit more than that,' said Colwall. 'They didn't any of them say as Mr Herriard had actually had words with Mr Roydon. It was Miss Herriard he quarrelled with. According to what the butler told me, Mr Herriard threatened to cut her out of his will, and said he wouldn't have her, nor Mr Stephen either, to stay again. Of course, there's no denying he was a violent-tempered kind of man. No saying whether he meant it or not. If he did, and Mr Stephen knew that he did, it puts an ugly complexion on the matter, that's what I say.'

'Yes, yes!' said the Major, elbowing him out of the discussion. 'All very well, but we mustn't exclude the other possibilities. There's Mottisfont, for instance. I consider he will bear looking into. He's been Nat's partner for a great many years, Inspector, and there's plenty of evidence to show that he's been up to something Nat didn't like. The servants say that he was shut up with Nat yesterday, and that there was a quarrel between them. You didn't feel satisfied about him, did you, Colwall?'

'Not altogether, I didn't, sir. Very nervous gentleman, for a man of his years. He didn't speak the truth to me, or at least not all of it, that I am sure of.'

'They never do,' said Hemingway. 'Are there any more suspects?'

'Properly speaking, there aren't,' said Colwall. 'There's Miss Clare, but she's got an alibi. Besides, there doesn't seem to be any motive. Kind of cousin, she is. Otherwise, there's only the servants. Most of them couldn't have had any reason to murder their master. I don't know that any of them had, except that Mr Herriard was very rough with his valet, by what the butler told me. Threw things at him when he was out of temper. Quite one of the Old School, as you might say.'

Hemingway was unimpressed. 'Nothing to stop him giving notice, if he couldn't stand Mr Herriard,' he said. 'Unless, of course, he'd got a legacy coming to him?'

'That I don't know, not having seen the will, but I should not think he had. He'd only been with Mr Herriard a matter of a few months. Mind you, he never said Mr Herriard was a hard master! It was the butler told me that. Ford spoke very nicely about his master. Spoke up for Mr Stephen, too.'

'What's he like?' demanded Hemingway.

'Wiry little chap, about thirty-five or six, I'd say. Bit scared of me, he was, but he spoke out quite honest and aboveboard, and didn't try to throw suspicion on to anyone – except Mr

Roydon, maybe, though he was only telling me what it was his duty to, after all.'

'What about the butler?'

'I'd say he was all right. Very starchy he is, but not above putting his ear to keyholes. He doesn't like Mr Stephen, but that's nothing. He's been some time with Mr Herriard.'

'Might be coming in for a legacy, of course,' said the Chief Constable. 'He'd hardly commit a murder for it, though. Not a man like Sturry. Besides –' He paused, frowning, and then said, shooting a look at Hemingway from under his brows: 'Not the point. I told you this was the devil of a case, Inspector. The suspects aren't worrying me: it's how the deuce the murder was committed at all.'

'What, you aren't going to tell me this is one of these locked-door cases you read about, sir?' exclaimed Hemingway incredulously.

'It is, just that. Now, you listen to the facts as we know them! Roydon read his play to the rest of the house-party after tea yesterday. It ended in a general row; the party split up, and went off upstairs to change for dinner, leaving Miss Clare in the library, and Joseph Herriard trying to smooth his brother down in the drawing-room. Nat then went up to his room, still furious. Miss Clare, who came out of the library just as he was going upstairs, heard him slam his bedroom door. She and Joseph then went up together. They were the last people except the murderer, of course – to see Nat alive. Some time between then, which must have been between seven-thirty and eight, and when the party gathered in the drawing-room again for cocktails, Nat was stabbed to

GEORGETTE HEYER

death in his bedroom. When he didn't join the party, Joseph went up to tell him they were all waiting for him. He found Ford outside Nat's door, pretty worried at getting no answer to his knocking. The door was locked, and when Ford and Stephen Herriard forced the lock, Nat was lying dead on the floor, with the windows latched securely, both the door into his bedroom and that from his bathroom on to the upper hall locked on the inside, and only the ventilator above the bathroom window open.'

'What kind of a ventilator?' asked Hemingway.

'The ordinary sort, opening outwards, which you often get above a casement-window.'

'Big enough for anyone to get in through it?'

The Chief Constable looked at Inspector Colwall, who said slowly: 'Well, it is, and it isn't, if you take my meaning. A man would have to be pretty small to do it, and, what's more, he'd need to be clever. It isn't as though the room's on the ground-floor, you see. What with having to climb up to it, and then squirm in without making any noise – well, I don't see how it could have been done, I'm bound to confess. Nor I couldn't discover any signs of footprints on the sill, but you can't go by that entirely, for it was snowing hard all yesterday evening, and they might easily have been covered up.'

'Any finger-prints?'

'Only on the insides of the windows, and they were Ford's, just as you'd expect. It was he who shut the windows after tea, and drew the curtains.'

'What about the door-keys?'

'That's just it,' said the Major. 'We've had them carefully examined, and we can't detect any of the scratches you'd expect to find if they'd been turned in the locks from outside.'

'That's queer,' said Hemingway, with the bird-like look in his eye which his Sergeant knew betokened lively interest. 'Sounds like a classy case, after all. Any signs of a struggle in the room, sir?'

'None whatsoever.'

'Looks as though he wasn't expecting trouble from his visitor, then. Those the photographs, sir? Thank you.' He considered them for a moment or two, and remarked: 'Still in his day-clothes.'

'Yes; there were no signs that he'd started to change. Ford had prepared his bath, and laid out his dinner-jacket and things.'

'He didn't have this Ford in to help him dress?'

'Apparently he did sometimes, but not always. He rang if he wanted Ford.'

'Oh! Weapon?'

'The doctors are agreed that the blow was struck with a thin, sharp instrument, probably a knife. You'll see the position of the wound. There was scarcely any external bleeding, but death, I'm informed, must have followed within a very few minutes.'

'I see, sir. Weapon not found?'

'Not so far. But to my mind it hasn't been looked for,' said the Major, casting a severe glance towards Inspector Colwall.

The Inspector reddened. 'It was looked for in the deceased's room, sir, but you know as well as I do that it's a very big house, and what with that, and the number of people all staying there, with their baggage – well, it's a tall order to find the weapon, and I didn't like to turn the place upside-down.'

The Major looked unconvinced, but Hemingway said: 'No, you'd have been at it all night and half today, I daresay.'

'Well, that's where it is,' said Colwall gratefully.

'I don't know that the weapon's going to interest me much,' pursued Hemingway. 'What with all these thrillers that get written nowadays by people who ought to know better than to go putting ideas into criminals' heads, there's no chance of any murderer forgetting to wipe off his finger-prints. Sickening, I call it. Now, how do you figure the murderer got into that room, Inspector?'

Colwall shook his head. 'It's got me beat. If there wasn't any hanky-panky with the key – and that's an expert's job, when you come to think of it – I don't see how anyone could have got in.'

'No; but there's one piece of evidence we mustn't forget,' interposed the Chief Constable. 'Stephen Herriard's cigarette-case was found lying on the floor by the fire, half-hidden by an armchair.'

'That doesn't look so good for Stephen Herriard,' said Hemingway. 'Does he own it?'

'Yes, he owned it, but Miss Clare deposed that he had given it to Miss Dean before he went up to change for dinner.'

'What did she have to say to that?' asked Hemingway, addressing himself to Colwall.

Inspector Colwall sighed. 'She had a lot to say, being one of those who can't give you a plain yes or no. Anyone would have thought she expected to be charged with having committed the murder, simply through admitting she'd had the case! In the end, she did say she'd had it, but she swore she never took it out of the drawing-room. Her theory is that Mr Stephen himself must have picked it up, and I'm bound to say it's likely he did.'

'What did he say?'

'He didn't say much,' answered Colwall reflectively. 'He didn't, so to speak, get much chance, for Miss Clare started in to tell Miss Dean off good and proper, and what with that, and Mr Joseph trying to make me believe the case might have slipped out of Mr Stephen's pocket after the murder had been discovered, when he was bending over the body –'

'Could it?' interrupted Hemingway.

'Not a chance, seeing where it was found. Mr Stephen saw that himself. If he'd been sitting in a chair by the fire, though, and took out his case for a cigarette, and put it back sort of careless, so that it didn't slip into his pocket, but fell into the chair instead, and maybe slid off when he got up – well, that might account for it.'

'Sat down with his uncle for a chat and a quiet smoke, and then murdered him when he wasn't looking?' demanded Hemingway. 'Cold-blooded chap he'd have to be!'

'He is,' said the Major shortly. 'Anyone will tell you that.'

'That's right,' agreed Colwall. 'Cold as a fish, that's what he is. Why, from all I could see, he doesn't even care two pins for that girl of his! Didn't turn a hair when Miss Clare said that she'd had his cigarette-case. You don't catch him trying to shield anyone!'

'Well, that's a comfort, anyway,' said Hemingway. 'If there's one thing that gets my goat more than another, it's coming up against a man with a lot of silly, noble ideas in his head which don't do any good to anyone. Is that all the evidence we've got, Inspector?'

'Not quite, it isn't. One of the housemaids saw Miss Herriard coming away from her uncle's door in her dressing-gown. A bit after, the valet heard a footstep in the front hall, as he was coming up the backstairs. He just saw Mr Roydon's door shut. But Mr Roydon gave a perfectly reasonable explanation for that; and as for Miss Herriard, she made no bones about admitting she'd tried to get into her uncle's room, to have her row out with him. She says she found the door locked, and didn't get any answer to her knock.'

'Didn't that strike her as funny?'

'It didn't strike anyone as funny. They all bear one another out that it was just like Mr Herriard not to answer, if he was in a bad temper.'

'It sounds like a nice family,' remarked Hemingway.

The Inspector permitted himself to smile. 'It is that, and no mistake. You'll see!'

'Seems to me I'd better go up there as soon as I can,' said Hemingway. 'I'd like to have a word with the police-surgeon, if you please, sir.'

'Yes, of course. You'll want to see the finger-prints too, I daresay,' said the Major, passing him on to Inspector Colwall.

'Half that gang up at the Manor,' confided Colwall, as he closed the door of the Chief Constable's room, 'will just about throw fits when they realise you're from Scotland Yard.'

'Excitable people, are they?'

'I believe you! Miss Herriard's a real tragedy-queen, and Miss Dean's the sort who'd go off into hysterics for two pins.'

'That's young Herriard's blonde, isn't it? I've got a fancy to meet her.'

'You won't get anything out of her, not to rely on,' Colwall said, staring.

'Ah, but I've always had a weakness for blondes!' Hemingway said.

Inspector Colwall looked at him suspiciously, but could not bring himself to believe that the good man from Scotland Yard was being flippant. 'Well, you may be right,' he said. 'I wouldn't set any store by what she says myself. But of course I've never gone in for your branch of the service. Never had a fancy for it. I daresay it comes easy to you chaps, but if I had to spend many evenings like I did last night I should go potty. You don't know what you're up against with that crowd, Inspector.'

'That's all right,' said Hemingway cheerfully. 'As long as there's one blonde I've no complaints coming.'

There were, unknown to him, two blondes now awaiting him at Lexham Manor, Mrs Dean having arrived in a hired car at an alarmingly early hour.

None of the inmates of the house had, from their appearances, enjoyed unbroken rest during the night. Valerie, indeed, declared that she had not once closed her eyes; and even Stephen seemed more than usually morose. The party met at the breakfast-table. Joseph, who came in last of all, greeted the company with a tremulous smile, and said: 'Alas, that I can't wish you all a merry Christmas! Yet it seems unfriendly, and sad, doesn't it, to let this day pass without one word to mark its character?'

There was no immediate response to this. Finally, Valerie said: 'It doesn't seem like Christmas, somehow.'

'Personally,' said Roydon, 'I set no store by worn-out customs.'

'If anyone is going to church,' said Maud, apparently deaf to this remark, 'Ledbury is bringing the car round at twenty minutes to eleven.'

'I'm afraid none of us feels quite in the mood for our usual Christmas service,' said Joseph gently. 'But you must go, of course, if you wish to, my dear.'

'I always go to church on Christmas Day,' replied Maud. 'And on Sundays, too.'

'One had not realised that there were still people who did!' said Roydon, with the air of one interested in the habits of aborigines.

This was felt to be an observation in such bad taste that Mathilda at once offered to accompany Maud, and Stephen – although not going to these lengths – ranged himself on Maud's side by telling the dramatist to shut up, and get on with his breakfast.

'Hush, Stephen!' said Joseph, yet with a sympathetic gleam in his eye.

'You shut up too!' said Stephen. 'We've listened to enough nauseating twaddle to last us for a fortnight. In case it inter- ests anyone, Uncle Nat's solicitor is coming down here by the eleven-fifteen from Waterloo. If Ledbury is fetching you from church, Aunt Maud, you'll have to drive on to pick Blyth up at the station afterwards.'

Maud showed herself perfectly ready to fall in with this plan, but Mottisfont, who had been making only the barest pretence of eating, said with a good deal of meaning: 'Very high-handed! Let us hope that someone is not in for a disappointment.'

Stephen showed his admirable teeth in a singularly disagreeable smile. 'Is that meant for me?'

Mottisfont shrugged. 'Oh, if the cap fits – !'

'For heaven's sake, Edgar!' interposed Joseph. 'Surely if anyone has the right to object to Stephen's taking charge of things it is I!'

'Well, if I were you I wouldn't put up with it for a moment.'

Joseph tried to exchange a smile with Stephen. 'Ah, but I'm not a clever business man like you, Edgar! I'm only a muddleheaded old artist – if I may be so bold as to lay claim to that title – and Stephen knows well that I'm grateful to him for all that he's doing.'

Paula, who had been crumbling a roll in glowering abstraction, intercepted the offensive reply which everyone felt to be hovering on Stephen's tongue by saying suddenly: 'How long will it be before we get probate?'

Everyone was rather startled by this, and as no one else seemed inclined to answer her Joseph said: 'My dear, I'm afraid we aren't thinking of such things just yet.'

She cast him one of her scornful, impatient glances. 'Well, I am. If Uncle Nat's left me the money he always said he would I shall put *Wormwood* on.'

Roydon flushed, and muttered something unintelligible. Valerie said that she would make a point of going to see it. She gave it as her opinion that it would be marvellous. Mathilda hoped, privately, that this appreciation would in some measure compensate Roydon for the marked lack of enthusiasm displayed by everyone else. She rose from the table, and went away to smoke a cigarette in the library.

Here she was soon joined, rather to her annoyance, by Mottisfont, who, after remarking aimlessly that one missed one's morning paper, began to wander about the room, fidgeting with blind-cords, matchboxes, cushions, and anything else that came in the way of his unquiet hands.

After a few minutes, Mathilda laid down her book. 'You seem worried, Mr Mottisfont.'

'Well, who wouldn't be?' he demanded, coming to the fire. 'I don't know how you can go on as though nothing had happened! Apart from anything else, Stephen's manner –'

'Oh, Stephen!' she said. 'You ought to know him by now, surely!'

'Ill-mannered cub!' he muttered. 'Taking things into his own hands, without so much as a by-your-leave! I call it thoroughly officious, and why on earth he must needs drag Nat's solicitor down here on Christmas Day, God alone knows! Anxious to get his hands on Nat's will, I suppose. Indecent, I call it!'

'The solicitor ought to come at once,' she replied rather shortly. 'The police are bound to want to go through Nat's papers, for one thing.'

It struck her that he winced slightly at this. He said: 'They aren't likely to find anything.'

'You never know,' Mathilda said.

'Everyone knows that Nat was a hot-tempered old – a hot-tempered man who said a lot of things he didn't mean. Why, I, for instance, have had dozens of quarrels with him! They always blew over. That's what the police don't understand. They'll go picking on things that have no bearing on the murder at all, and try to make out a case from them against some unfortunate person who had nothing to do with it.'

She had a strong suspicion that the unfortunate person he had in mind was himself. 'Oh, I shouldn't think they'd do that!' she said, in a reassuring tone. 'After all, they must have realised by now that Nat quarrelled with everyone.'

'Yes, but –' He stopped, reddening, and took off his glasses, and began to polish them. 'I haven't any opinion of that Inspector we had here last night. Unimaginative fool, I thought. Rather offensive too. What do you think of his locking Nat's study? As though any of us would dream of touching anything in it! Very uncalled-for! Sheer officialdom!'

Mathilda now felt reasonably certain that there was in existence some document which Mottisfont wanted to get his hands on. She returned a noncommittal answer, and was relieved of the necessity of sustaining any more of a difficult dialogue by the entrance of Roydon.

Edgar Mottisfont looked at him in an exasperated kind of way, but Roydon seemed to have come in search of Mathilda, and took no notice of him. 'Oh, there you are, Miss Clare! Are you really going to church?'

'Yes,' said Mathilda firmly.

'Well, could I have a word with you before you go? It isn't important! – at least, it doesn't really *matter* – but I thought I'd like to.'

Mathilda reflected that fright had had an appalling effect upon Mr Roydon's powers of self-expression. 'All right, as long as it hasn't anything to do with the murder,' she said.

'Oh no, nothing to do with that!' he assured her.

'I suppose you want me to go?' said Mottisfont.

Roydon disclaimed, not very convincingly, but Mottisfont said with a short laugh that he knew how to take a hint, and left the room.

'Well?' said Mathilda.

'It's nothing much, but you took such an intelligent interest in my work that I wanted to tell you that I've thought over what you said, and come to the conclusion you were right. Either *Wormwood* is good enough to stand on its own merits, or it had better be chucked into the incinerator. I daresay that you heard Paula say that she would put it on. Well, I shan't let her. The whole idea of getting a backer was wrong.'

'I see,' said Mathilda, more than a hint of dryness in her voice.

'I felt I'd like you to know.'

'Yes, I quite see.'

'Of course, Paula doesn't quite understand. She's so keen to play the part. As a matter of fact, the idea of getting her uncle to back the play was hers, not mine. I don't really think I ought to have let her talk me into it. I never was quite happy about it, and then when you said what you did, I made up my mind that I wouldn't be under an obligation to anyone over it. Paula doesn't see it in that light yet. Of course, it's very generous of her, but –'

'But equally embarrassing,' supplied Mathilda.

'Oh, I don't know about that exactly! Only, I thought that you might be able to make her understand my point of view. I mean, if she says anything to you about it.'

'I should think,' said Mathilda, extracting the butt of her cigarette from its holder, and throwing it into the fire, 'that she would be quite capable of appreciating your point of view without any assistance.'

He looked sharply at her; she met his challenging stare steadily, and after a few moments his eyes shifted from hers, and he said lamely: 'You see, she's tremendously keen on the play. It's rather difficult for me to say anything.'

'Yes, I should think it might be,' she agreed.

He said in an injured tone: 'I thought you would understand the way I feel.'

'I do.'

'Well, then –' he began uncertainly. He did not seem to know how to continue, and started again. 'Besides which, I don't think it's altogether wise of her to talk so openly about what she means to do with her legacy, do you? I mean, it might so easily give people a totally wrong impression.'

'Of her, or of you?'

The colour rushed up into his face; he looked very much discomposed, but after a moment blurted out: 'Of both of us, I suppose.'

'Yes,' said Mathilda. 'I like you so much better when you're honest, Mr Roydon.'

'I wasn't aware that I had ever been anything else,' he said stiffly.

She saw that she had deeply offended him, and was not sorry that Paula should choose that moment to stalk into the room.

'Why,' demanded Paula, in her deep, throbbing voice, 'are the police letting us alone this morning?'

'I can't think. I was merely thankful,' replied Mathilda.

'There's nothing to be thankful for. I believe it means Scotland Yard.'

Roydon gazed at her with something of the expression of a fascinated rabbit. 'Why should it mean that?'

'My dear Willoughby, can't you see how obvious it was from the start that Scotland Yard would be called in? Think! Uncle Nat was murdered in a locked room! Do you imagine that the local police can cope with that? If I weren't so closely connected with the crime, I think I should find it absorbingly interesting,' she added, considering the matter dispassionately.

'Anyone is welcome to my ring-seat,' said Mathilda. 'I do hope you're wrong about Scotland Yard.'

'You know I'm not.'

'Well, if you're not, I do think you ought to be more careful of what you say, Paula!' said Roydon.

Her brilliant gaze drifted to his face. 'Why? In what way?'

'About my play, for instance. I was just saying to Miss Clare, when you came in, that you might easily give people a wrong impression by talking of backing it. Besides, though I'm awfully grateful, I've changed my mind about it. Miss Clare made me see yesterday that it would be a mistake to rely on a backer.'

The expression of contempt which swept over Paula's face made her look suddenly like Stephen. 'You've got cold feet,' she said. 'Whether you like it, or whether you don't, I'm going to put your play on.'

'It's extremely generous of you, but –'

'It's nothing of the kind. I'm not doing it from any personal motive, but because I believe in the play. I don't know how you came to write it, but you did, and that's all that concerns me.'

He did not know how to interpret these remarks, and merely said: 'Yes, but it's sheer folly to tell everyone what you mean to do.'

'You're wrong! Stupidly wrong! Everyone knows that I care desperately about *Wormwood*. I made no secret of it. You heard what I said to Uncle Nat! I should be a fool to change my tune now that Uncle's dead. As big a fool as you, Willoughby!'

'I very much resent that implication!' he said.

'Oh, go to hell!' Paula threw at him, over her shoulder.

He walked out of the room with an air of wounded dignity which gave promise of a day of sulks to come.

'You shouldn't have said that,' Mathilda told Paula. 'People not out of the top-drawer are always inclined to be touchy.'

But Paula had as little consideration for the sensibilities

of others as Stephen, and she said disdainfully: 'He's yellow. Odd, how clever he can be on paper, yet how inept in conversation!'

'He's a little out of his depth. Frightened too. He can't cope.'

'Badly frightened. I ought to have known he'd lose his nerve. I can't bear men who go to pieces in a crisis!' She saw the quick, startled look Mathilda cast at her, and added, with a curl of her lip: 'Don't be afraid! I didn't mean to imply that Willoughby was my accomplice.'

'Well, do, for God's sake, be more careful what you say!' recommended Mathilda crossly.

Paula laughed. 'It's getting you down, Mathilda, isn't it? I knew it would. You're beginning to feel suspicious; you listen – oh, without meaning to! – for the underlying motive beneath everything we say. Do you wonder which of us did it? Find your brain sneaking round to that thought, however much you try not to let it?'

'Yes,' Mathilda admitted.

Paula cast herself on to the sofa, setting her elbows on her knees, and sinking her chin into the cup of her hands. 'I know! Ah, but it *is* interesting, isn't it? Confess!'

'No, it's vile.'

'Oh – vile!' The thin shoulders jerked up in a characteristic shrug. 'If you like! But, psychologically speaking, isn't there a fascination? Watching our behaviour, listening for the scared note – voices lift: have you noticed it? People are such fools, they give things away, lose grip, say too much!'

'The trouble with you, my girl, is that you have a morbid mind,' said Mathilda. 'What's that?'

The sound of chains clanking round car-wheels had provoked this exclamation. Paula got up, and moved to the window. It had stopped snowing some hours earlier, but only a single pair of wheel-tracks disturbed the smooth whiteness of the drive and the deep lawn beyond it. A large limousine had drawn up before the front-door, and as Paula reached the window a figure in a Persian lamb coat and a skittish hat, perched over elaborately curled golden hair, alighted.

'I think,' said Paula, 'I *think* it's Mrs Dean.'

'Good God, already?' exclaimed Mathilda, getting up. 'What's she like?'

'Just what you might have expected. Joe has tripped out to meet her.'

'He would!' said Mathilda.

Not only Joseph had gone out to meet this new guest, but Valerie also. Before Joseph could utter his little speech of welcome, she had cast herself upon her parent's awe-inspiring bosom, crying: 'Oh, Mummy, thank goodness you've come! It's all too frightful for words!'

'My pet, of course Mummy has come!' said Mrs Dean, in accents quite as thrilling as Paula's. 'Mummy had to be with her little girl at such a time.' She extended a tightly gloved hand to Joseph, saying with an arch smile: 'I shan't ask my girlie to introduce you. I know that you are Stephen's Uncle Joe! Val told me about you over the 'phone, and how kind you have been to her. You must let a mother thank you, Mr Herriard!'

Joseph turned quite pink with pleasure and responded gallantly that to be kind to Valerie was a privilege requiring no thanks.

'Ah, I can't have you turning my girlie's head!' said Mrs Dean. 'Such a foolish childie as she is!'

'Oh, Mummy, it's been simply foul!' said Valerie. 'I couldn't sleep a wink all night, and that beastly policeman upset me frightfully!'

'I'm afraid our nerves aren't over-strong,' Mrs Dean confided to Joseph. 'We've always been one of the delicate ones, and quite absurdly sensitive.'

'Ah!' said Joseph. 'May I say that it is all too seldom nowadays that one encounters the bloom of innocence?'

While uttering this speech, he had drawn Mrs Dean into the house, and Mathilda and Paula, who had come out of the library into the hall, were privileged to hear it. They perceived at once that Joseph had met a soul-mate, for Mrs Dean threw him a warm smile, and said: 'I have always tried to keep the bloom on both my girlies. How one hates to see that dewy freshness vanish! You must forgive a mother's foolish heart if I say that I can't help wishing that this hadn't happened!'

'I know, and I understand,' said Joseph earnestly.

'If only my Val had not been in the house!' said Mrs Dean, apparently stating her only objection to the murder.

Joseph saw nothing ludicrous in this remark, but shook his head, and said with a heavy sigh: 'How well I know what you must feel!'

'You have young people of your own, I expect,' said Mrs Dean, throwing open her coat and displaying a formidable bust, covered by a tightly fitting lace blouse and supporting a large paste brooch.

'Alas, no! None of my own! But I count Stephen and Paula as my own. They are very dear to me,' said Joseph, getting well into his stride.

'I knew as soon as I saw you that my little girl had not exaggerated 'Uncle Joe's' kindness,' declared Mrs Dean, laying a hand on his arm, and gently squeezing it. 'You can't deceive me! You are the good fairy in the house!'

'Oh no, no, no!' protested Joseph. 'I'm afraid I'm only a foolishly sentimental old fellow who likes to see people happy around him! Ah, here is Paula! Paula, my dear, come and say how-do-you-do to Mrs Dean!'

'My dear!' ejaculated Mrs Dean, turning on her high heels as Paula advanced, and stretching out her hands. 'So this is Stephen's beloved sister! Let me look at you, childie! Yes, I can see something of Stephen. My poor child, this is a terrible time for you, and with your mother so many, many miles away! I shall claim the right of Stephen's mother-in-law to take his sister under my wing too.'

The thought of Stephen's being taken under Mrs Dean's wing momentarily paralysed Paula. By the time she had recovered her breath sufficiently to repudiate the suggestion that she either missed her mother or wanted a substitute, Joseph had drawn Mathilda forward and was introducing her. He then said that Mrs Dean must be cold from her long drive, and begged her to sit down by the fire while he fetched his wife.

'Now, you mustn't make any difference for me, dear Mr Herriard, for I have come to be a help, and not a hindrance! I don't want to cause anyone the least bit of trouble! I'm sure Mrs Herriard must be far too upset and shocked to be troubled by tiresome visitors. You must just not take a scrap of notice of me.'

'You must have a cup of coffee and a sandwich!' he said. 'Do let me persuade you!'

'Well, if you insist! But this is spoiling me, you know!'

Paula, seeing no other way of escape, said that she would give the necessary order, and vanished, leaving Mathilda to cope with a situation that appalled her. Joseph trotted upstairs in search of Maud, and Mrs Dean disposed herself in a chair by the fire, and began to peel off her gloves.

Mathilda, who had had time to observe the lady, had not missed the calculating light in the prominent blue eyes, and now noticed with malicious amusement the quick, appraising glance Mrs Dean cast about her, at her surroundings.

'Mummy, I simply won't be bullied by that ghastly policeman any more!' said Valerie.

'No one will bully you while Mummy is here to protect you, my pet,' responded her parent. 'But, childie dear, you must run up, and change out of that frock!'

'Oh, hell, Mummy, why?'

'Hush, dear! You know Mummy doesn't like her girlies to use that sort of language! You shouldn't have put on the primrose today: it isn't suitable.'

'I know, but I haven't got anything black, and anyway no one else is bothering.'

'No, dear, Mummy knows you haven't anything black, but you have your navy. Now, don't argue with Mummy, but run off and change!'

Valerie said that it was a foul nuisance, and the navy suit made her look a hag, but Mathilda was interested to see that she did in fact obey Mrs Dean's command. She began to suspect that that lady's smile and sugared sweetness masked a will of iron, and looked at her with misgiving.

Mrs Dean, having smoothed out her gloves, now extricated herself from her fur coat, revealing a figure so tightly corseted about the hips and waist, so enormous above as to appear slightly grotesque. As though to add to the startling effect of this method of dealing with a super-abundance of fat, she wore a closely fitting and extremely short skirt. Above the confines of the hidden satin and whalebone, her bust thrust forward like a platform. A short neck supported a head crowned with an elaborate coiffure of rolled curls. Large pearl studs were screwed into the lobes of her ears; and the hat that perched at a daring angle over one eye was very smart, and far too tiny for a woman of her bulk. She was quite as lavishly made-up as her daughter, but could never, Mathilda decided, have been as pretty as Valerie.

Mrs Dean, having taken covert stock of Mathilda, said: 'Such terrible weather, isn't it? Though I suppose one mustn't complain.'

'No,' agreed Mathilda, offering her a cigarette. 'The weather is about the only seasonable feature confronting us. Will you smoke?'

'I wonder if you will think me very rude if I have one of my own? I always smoke my own brand. One gets into the habit of it, doesn't one?'

'Indeed, yes,' said Mathilda, watching her extract an enamelled case from her handbag, and take from it a fat Egyptian cigarette with a gold tip.

'I expect,' said Mrs Dean, 'you are all quite disorganised, and no wonder! On Christmas Eve, too! Tell me all about it! You know that Val was only able to give me the barest details.'

Luckily for Mathilda, who did not feel equal to obeying this behest, Joseph came down the stairs again just then, saying that Maud was dressing for church, and would be with them in a few minutes. Mathilda said that she too must get ready for church, and made good her escape. As she rounded the bend in the stairs, she heard Mrs Dean say in confiding accents: 'And now, dear Mr Herriard, tell me just what happened!'

Ten

~~~

By the time that Maud, dressed in her outdoor clothes, had come downstairs into the hall, Mrs Dean had drawn from Joseph an account of Nathaniel's murder, and was looking considerably startled. It was plain that she had not, from Valerie's agitated telephone communication, grasped to what an extent Stephen might be implicated in the crime. She heard Joseph out with the proper expression of horror and sympathy on her face, but behind the conventionality of her speech and bearing a very busy brain was working fast.

'I'm prepared to go to the stake on my conviction that Stephen had nothing whatsoever to do with it!' Joseph told her.

'Of course not,' she said mechanically. 'What an idea! Still, it's all very dreadful. Really, I had no suspicion! We must just wait and see, mustn't we?'

At this moment Maud appeared from above, descending the stairs in her unhurried way. No greater contrast to Mrs Dean's somewhat flamboyant smartness could have been found than in Maud's plump, neat figure. She might, in the days of her youth, have adorned the second row of the chorus, but in her sedate middle-age she presented the appearance of a Victorian lady of strict upbringing. There was nothing skittish either in the style or the angle of the high-crowned hat she wore on her head. She carried a Prayer-book in one hand, and an umbrella in the other; and on her feet were a pair of serviceable black walking-shoes, with laces. Mrs Dean, running experienced eyes over her correctly deduced that the frumpish fur coat, which made her look shorter and fatter than ever, was made of rabbit, dyed to resemble musquash.

'Ah!' cried Joseph, jumping up. 'Here is my wife! Maud, this is dear little Valerie's mother!'

Maud tucked her umbrella under one arm, and extended a nerveless hand. 'How-do-you-do?' she said, politely unenthusiastic. 'I am just on my way to church, but Joseph will see to everything.'

Joseph, Mathilda, and Paula had all assumed, on Mrs Dean's arrival, that Maud would abandon her expedition to church, but Maud, although she listened to their representations, had no such intention. To Joseph's plea that she should bear in mind her duties as hostess, she replied that she did not consider herself to be a hostess.

'But, my dear!' expostulated Joseph. 'In your position – you are the only married lady here, besides its being your home –'

'I have never thought of Lexham as home, Joseph,' said Maud matter-of-factly.

Joseph had given it up. Mathilda put the affair on another basis by saying that Maud, as doyenne, could not leave the rest of the party to cope with Mrs Dean. Maud said that she did not know what a doyenne was, but she had always made a point of non-interference at Lexham.

'Darling Maud, this isn't a case of interference! Who's going to look after the woman? Show her to her room, and all that sort of thing?'

'I expect Joseph will manage very well,' said Maud placidly. 'It occurred to me last night that I might have left my book in the morning-room, but when I looked today it wasn't there. So tiresome!'

Mathilda too had given it up, and since, like Maud, she did not consider herself a hostess, she did not volunteer to deputise in the part.

So here was Maud, dressed for church, allowing Mrs Dean to clasp her unresponsive hand, and saying: 'You see, I always go to church on Christmas Day.'

'You mustn't dream of letting me upset any of your plans! That I couldn't bear!' said Mrs Dean.

'Oh no!' replied Maud, taking this for granted.

'I ought to apologise for thrusting myself upon you at such a time,' pursued Mrs Dean. 'But I know that you will understand a mother's feelings, dear Mrs Herriard.'

'I haven't any children,' Maud said. 'I am sure no one minds your being here in the least. It is such a large house: there is always room.'

'Ah!' said Mrs Dean, struggling against the odds. 'The joy of always having a room for a friend! How I envy you, living in such a beautiful place!'

'I believe the house is generally very much admired,' said Maud. 'I do not care for old houses myself.'

There did not seem to be anything to say to this, so Mrs Dean tried a new form of attack. Lowering her voice, she said: 'You must let me tell you how very, very deeply I feel for you in your tragic loss.'

The defences remained intact. 'It has all been very shocking,' said Maud, 'but I never cared for my brother-in-law, so I do not feel much sense of loss.'

Joseph fidgeted uncomfortably, and darted an anguished look of appeal at Mathilda, who had by this time joined Maud. But it was Sturry, entering the hall from the back of the house, who came to the rescue. 'The car, madam, is At the Door,' he announced.

'Oh!' cried Mrs Dean. 'I wonder what has happened to my car? There is just a suitcase in it, and my hat-box, and dressing-case. Could someone bring them in, do you think?'

'The chauffeur, madam,' replied Sturry, contemptuous of overdressed women who expected to see their luggage carried in at the front-door, 'drove round to the Back Entrance. Walter has taken up the luggage to the Blue Room, sir,' he added, addressing this last remark to Joseph.

Sturry's grand manner, followed so hard upon Maud's damping calm, quite cowed Mrs Dean. She said Thank you, in a meek voice.

Sturry then moved with a measured tread to the front door, which he opened for Maud and Mathilda, and Joseph unwisely asked him if he had seen Mr Stephen anywhere.

'Mr Stephen, sir,' said Sturry, in an expressionless voice, 'is Knocking the Balls About in the billiard-room.'

'Oh tut, tut, tut!' said Joseph involuntarily, and with an

apologetic glance towards Mrs Dean. 'These young people are so – so thoughtless! He doesn't mean any harm, you know. He just doesn't always think!'

'Oh, I never mind a little unconventionality!' declared Mrs Dean, with a wide smile. 'I know what an odd, wayward creature Stephen is. Let's go and rout him out, shall we?'

Joseph looked a little dubious, but presumably he thought that Stephen must be accustomed to his future mother-in-law's breezy tactics, for he made no demur, but led the way to the billiard-room.

The Christmas tree, still decked with tinsel, at once caught Mrs Dean's eye, and she exclaimed at it admiringly before sailing forward to greet Stephen. 'My dear boy!' she uttered. 'I came as soon as I could!'

Stephen, who was practising nursery-cannons in his shirt-sleeves, carefully inspected the disposition of the balls before replying. Having assured himself that they were still lying well, he straightened his back, and said: 'So I see. How-do-you-do?'

'Oh, *I* am perfectly well!' she said. 'But you, my poor boy! What you must be going through! Don't think I don't understand!'

'Yes, it has been a greater shock to Stephen than he perhaps realises,' agreed Joseph. 'But billiards on *this* day, old fellow? Do you think you should? It isn't that *I* mind, but you don't want to give people a wrong impression, do you?'

Beyond casting an exasperated glance in Joseph's direction, Stephen took no notice of this. He asked Mrs Dean if she had seen Valerie.

'My poor girlie! Yes, she ran straight into my arms when

I arrived. This has been a dreadful shock to her. You know what a sensitive little puss she is, Stevie! We must do our best to spare her any more unpleasantness.'

'That oughtn't to be difficult,' he replied. 'The police aren't likely to suspect her of having killed my uncle.'

Mrs Dean gave a shudder. 'Don't! The very thought of it – ! I must say, Stephen, that if I had had any idea what was going to happen I should never, never, have allowed her to come here!'

'If,' said Stephen, with an edge to his voice, 'you mean to convey by that air of reproach a suggestion that I ought to have warned you, I must point out to you that my uncle's murder was not one of the planned entertainments for the party!'

'Naughty boy!' Mrs Dean scolded, giving his hand a playful slap. 'If I didn't know that wicked tongue of yours, I should be very cross with you! But I understand. I've always said that you're one of those shy people who hide their real feelings under a sort of bravado. Aren't I right, Mr Herriard?'

'Quite right!' Joseph said, trying to slip a friendly hand in Stephen's arm, and being frustrated. 'Stephen loves to try to shock us all, only his old uncle won't be shocked!'

'Ah, that's the way with so many of the young people today,' said Mrs Dean, shaking her head.

'Let me point out to you that there is no fire in this room, and that you could both discuss me in greater comfort elsewhere!' snapped Stephen.

Mrs Dean's eyes might acquire a steely look, but her smile remained. She said: 'You conceited boy, to think I should waste my time discussing you! I have much more important things to do! Indeed, I must unpack the few bits and pieces I brought with me, and just tidy myself a little after the journey.'

Joseph at once offered to escort her to her room, and led her away before Stephen could say something even more outrageous. In the hall, Valerie, now clad in the navy-blue suit which her mother thought more proper to the occasion than primrose-yellow, was flirting mildly with Roydon. As Roydon's mind was preoccupied with the possible consequences of Nathaniel's murder, the flirtation was a desultory affair, but the sight of her daughter, *tête-à-tête* with a young man whom one glance assured her was ineligible, made Mrs Dean intervene at once. She said that she wanted her girlie to come up and help her to unpack.

'Oh, Mummy, why on earth?' said Valerie petulantly. 'The housemaid will do all that.'

'No, my pet; you know Mummy never likes the servants to meddle with her things,' said Mrs Dean. 'Come along!'

'Oh, all right!' said Valerie sulkily. 'See you later, Willoughby!'

Once in the seclusion of the Blue Room, which was a spacious if somewhat sombre apartment over the library, Mrs Dean wasted no time in beating about the bush, but asked abruptly: 'Who is that young man, Val?'

'Willoughby? He's a playwright. He's written the most marvellous play called *Wormwood*. He read it to us yesterday.'

'I've never heard of him,' said Mrs Dean.

'Well, he hasn't actually had anything put on yet, but

he's frightfully brilliant, and I expect *Wormwood* will run for simply years!'

'I'm sure I hope it may,' responded Mrs Dean. 'But you know you can't afford to waste your time on penniless young writers, my pet, and I didn't quite like to see you being so friendly with him.'

'Oh, Mummy, what absolute rot! As though I couldn't be friends with other men just because I'm engaged!'

'You must let Mother know best, my pet. You don't want to make Stephen jealous, now, do you?'

'I don't care,' said Valerie sullenly. 'Besides, I don't believe he would be. He simply pays no attention to me. The only person he's more or less decent to is that sickening Clare-woman. And she isn't even *moderately* good-looking, Mummy!'

'Is she the one who went off to church with Mrs Herriard? Such manners! I wonder what Mrs Herriard was before she was married? I'm sure my little girl has nothing to fear from anyone as plain as Miss Clare. You mustn't be silly, childie. I can see it's high time Mother came to keep an eye on you. I've no doubt you've been getting on the wrong side of Stephen. He isn't the sort you can play tricks with.'

'Well, if it wasn't for being frightfully rich, I don't think I would marry Stephen,' said Valerie, in a burst of frankness.

'Hush, dear! I suppose there's no doubt that Stephen will inherit all this?'

'Oh, I don't know, except that Uncle Joe practically told me he would! Only I simply couldn't live here all the year round, Mummy: I should go mad!'

'Time enough to think of that later.' Mrs Dean glanced

round the room. 'His uncle must have been worth a fortune. You don't run a place like this on twopence-ha'penny a year. But I don't like the sound of this murder, Val. Of course, we don't *know*, and very likely everything will turn out satisfactorily, but I couldn't let my girlie marry a murderer.'

'I wouldn't be able to, would I?' asked Valerie, opening her lovely eyes very wide.

'Of course not, my pet, but it was the engagement I was thinking of. Only one doesn't wish to do anything in haste. Mother has to think of Mavis too, you know.'

'I don't see what Mavis has got to do with my marrying Stephen.'

'Now, don't be silly, childie!' said Mrs Dean, somewhat tartly. 'Heaven knows it isn't easy to find an eligible husband for one daughter, let alone two! Your meeting Stephen at the Crewes' was a piece of very good luck – not that I would want either of my chicks to marry without love, naturally – and young men who are heirs to fortunes don't crop up every day of the week by any means. We shall just have to wait.'

'I don't believe Stephen ever would have proposed to me if you hadn't sort of made him,' said Valerie discontentedly. 'In fact, in a way I rather wish he hadn't.'

'You know Mother doesn't like her girlies to talk in that vulgar way. And she doesn't like to see that sulky look, either. You must just trust her to do what's best, and be your own bright self, my pet.'

'I don't see how anyone could possibly be bright in this house. It's a ghastly place. Paula says it's evil.'

'Nonsense!' said Mrs Dean. 'Now, run along, and don't let Mother hear any more of that kind of rubbish!'

Valerie departed with something very like a flounce, but reappeared a minute later with whitened cheeks, and quickened breath. 'Mummy!' she gasped. 'The most frightful thing! Someone has arrived! Two of them! I saw them from the top of the stairs!'

'Good gracious, Val, why shouldn't people arrive? Who are they?'

'It's an Inspector from Scotland Yard! I heard him say so to Sturry! Oh, Mummy, can't we go home? Can't you get me out of this?'

'Come inside, and shut the door!' commanded Mrs Dean. 'Now, just you drink this glass of water, and stop being silly! I'm not at all surprised that Scotland Yard has been called in. There's nothing for you to worry about. No one thinks you had anything to do with the murder.'

'Yes, they do, because of that foul cigarette-case!'

'What cigarette-case?'

'Stephen's. He sort of threw it to me in the drawing-room, and later it was found in Mr Herriard's bedroom. But I never put it there!'

'Of course you didn't, and the police will realise that just as Mother does. You must just tell them all you know, and stop worrying. Remember, Mother is here to take care of you!'

'I know I shall die if I have to answer any more questions! That policeman yesterday was utterly brutal, and this one's bound to be worse!' said Valerie fatalistically.

Her bugbear, at this moment, was taking stock of Joseph and of Stephen, both of whom had emerged from the billiard-room to receive him. Joseph had a piece of tinsel in his hand, and explained that he was engaged in dismantling the Christmas tree. 'We have no heart for it now!' he said.

'You ought to send it to your local hospital,' said Hemingway helpfully. 'They'd very likely be glad of it.'

'There!' cried Joseph. 'Why didn't I think of that? It's just what my brother would have wished, too! It shall be done! What say you, Stephen?'

'Do what you like with the damned thing!' said Stephen shortly.

The Inspector looked at him with quick interest. 'Mr Stephen Herriard?' he asked.

Stephen nodded. 'Yes. What do you want to do? Visit the scene of the crime, or interrogate us all again?'

'If it's all the same to you, sir, I'd like to visit the scene of the crime first. Perhaps you'd take me up? I understand it was you who discovered Mr Herriard's body?'

'Go with my uncle,' said Stephen. 'He discovered it too, and can tell you quite as much as I can.'

'Stephen!' begged Joseph.

'Oh, that's all right with me, sir!' said Hemingway cheerfully. 'Very understandable that the gentleman shouldn't wish to go into the room again.'

Joseph sighed. 'Very well, Inspector, I'll take you.'

Joseph followed him to the staircase. He cast a knowledgeable eye over this noble erection, and remarked that he didn't know when he'd seen a finer one.

'No; it is supposed to be a perfect example of the Cromwellian,' said Joseph, with an effort. 'I'm afraid I'm a vandal in these matters. My brother was very proud of the house.'

'Went in for antiques, did he?'

'Yes, it was quite a hobby of his.' Joseph glanced over his shoulder, summoning up a brave smile. 'I used to tease him about it! And now this has happened!'

'I daresay you feel it more than most,' sympathised the Inspector.

'Perhaps I do. One doesn't like to be egotistical, but the younger generation have all their lives before them. I feel very much alone now.'

They had mounted the stairs by now, and while the constable who had been left in charge at the Manor cut the tapes that sealed the door of Nathaniel's room, the Inspector took stock of his surroundings. He wanted to know who occupied the various rooms opening on to the main hall, and he asked to be shown the backstairs and the sewing-room. By the time he had looked at these, the door into Nathaniel's room had been opened, and the constable was waiting for him to enter.

The room had not been touched since the removal of Nathaniel's body, and Joseph winced perceptibly at the sight of his dress-clothes, still laid out upon a chair. He turned away, shading his eyes with his hand, while the Inspector's trained gaze absorbed every detail of the room.

The Inspector had studied the photographs taken of the corpse, but when Joseph seemed to have recovered a little from his emotion, he asked him to describe the position in which he had found his brother. He asked more questions, and Joseph soon warmed to his narrative, and might even, by unkind persons, have been thought to have been enjoying himself considerably. His own and Stephen's shock lost nothing in the telling; he had a good memory, and was able with very little prompting to reconstruct the scene of the crime for Hemingway. He even presented him with two separate theories to account for the position in which Stephen's cigarette-case had been found, which, as Hemingway afterwards remarked to his Sergeant, was excessive.

'Nice old chap,' said the Sergeant.

'He's nice enough, but he'll very likely drive me mad before I'm through with this,' returned Hemingway. 'If I get a line on any of his blessed relatives, he'll lie awake all night, thinking up a set of highly unconvincing reasons to account for their doings. Anything strike you about this case?'

The Sergeant stroked his chin. 'I'd say it was a fair stinker,' he volunteered.

'Stinker!' ejaculated Hemingway. 'It couldn't have happened!'

'But it did happen,' the Sergeant pointed out.

'Yes, that's what makes me wish I'd never joined the Force,' said Hemingway. He walked into the bathroom, and gazed up at the ventilator. 'If that was the only thing open, and they're all agreed it was, it looks as though it has a very important bearing on the case. Hand me that stool, will you?'

The Sergeant brought the cork-topped stool to him, and he climbed onto it, to inspect the ventilator more closely.

'If anyone got in that way, he'd have had to be a small man,' said Ware. 'The young fellow we saw downstairs couldn't have done it.'

'No one could have got in without scratching the paint with his shoes.'

'Rubber soles,' suggested the Sergeant.

'You may be right. Assume someone did get in this way. How?'

'I was thinking he might have climbed up by a ladder. There's bound to be one in the gardener's shed, for pruning the fruit trees.'

'That doesn't interest me. What I want to know is, how did he set about oozing through this highly improbable aperture once he had climbed up the ladder?'

The Sergeant considered the ventilator, and sighed. 'I see what you mean, sir.'

'Well, that's something, anyway. Head first, that's how he must have got in, and nothing to catch hold of inside. The inference is he squirmed in, dropped on to his head on the floor, picked himself up, not a penny the worse for wear, and walked in to murder the old man, who hadn't heard a sound.'

'The door may have been shut. He may have been deaf.'

'He'd need to be stone-deaf. Talk sense!'

'I don't see how anyone got in by that ventilator, sir,' said the Sergeant, after thinking it over. 'Looks as though he must have come in through the door after all.'

Hemingway got down from the stool, and returned to the bedroom. 'Very well. We'll take it that he did. For what it's worth, the body was found lying with its back to the door.'

The Sergeant frowned. 'Well, sir, what *is* it worth?'

'Nothing at all,' replied Hemingway. 'You can say that someone stole into Nathaniel's room without his knowing it, and stabbed him in the back; and you can just as easily say that he was facing the other way when he was stabbed, and staggered round before collapsing. May have been trying to get to that bell by the fireplace. I had a talk with the police-surgeon, and he tells me that a stab to the right of the spine, in the lumbar region, wouldn't kill a man instantaneously. So the position of the body doesn't help us much.'

'Was the door locked before the murder, sir?'

'Nobody knows, seeing that nobody knows when he was murdered. If I was one to let my imagination run away with me, which I'm not, I should say Nathaniel locked the door himself.'

'Why, sir?'

'On the evidence. You should always listen to evidence. Half the time it's a pack of lies, but you never know. In this case, all the witnesses say that Nathaniel was in a rag-ing temper; and Brother Joseph admits that he was trying to smooth the old boy down, and getting ticked off for his pains. Followed him half-way up the stairs, he did. Now, if you were Nathaniel in a temper, being followed about by Joseph, what would you do?'

'I don't rightly know,' said the Sergeant, staring.

'Then all I can say is you've taken more of a fancy to Joseph than I have. If I had a wind-bag like that on my tail,

I'd lock my door, and very likely shove a heavy piece of furniture against it as well.'

The Sergeant smiled, but ventured to say: 'That's guess-work, sir.'

'It is, which is why we won't treat it as more than a possibility,' responded Hemingway, moving over to the door. 'If I'm right, and Nathaniel locked this door himself, we haven't got to consider whether the murderer used a pencil and a bit of string to lock the door behind him, because he couldn't have unlocked it that way. What's more, they did have the sense to examine the door for signs of rubbing.'

'Wouldn't hardly notice on these oak doors, would it?' suggested the Sergeant. 'Not like soft paintwork which the string would cut into.'

'No; but you'd be bound to see some trace under a magnifying-glass. Which would lead one to suppose that the murderer found the door locked, and turned the key from the outside.'

'With an *oustiti*,' nodded the Sergeant. 'That's what I was thinking. Only there aren't any scratches on the key. If it weren't for that, I'd say an *oustiti* must have been used.'

'That, and about half a dozen other reasons,' interrupted his superior scathingly. 'You aren't dealing with a professional burglary, my lad: this is an amateur-job; and whoever heard of an amateur having a tool out of a professional's kit?'

'I thought of that, but I don't know but what he might have come by it,' argued the Sergeant.

'He might, but the odds are he didn't,' retorted

Hemingway. 'Not one layman out of a hundred would know there was a tool for turning keys from the wrong side, let alone the name of it.'

'Most people know there is a tool for doing that,' persisted the Sergeant. 'I don't say they'd know the name, but –'

'No; they'd just walk into the nearest ironmonger's and ask for a pair of forceps shaped a bit like eyebrow-pluckers to open locked doors with, I suppose,' said Hemingway, with awful sarcasm.

The Sergeant reddened, but said: 'Well, that's an idea, anyway. Suppose the key *was* turned with a pair of eyebrow-pluckers?'

'I'm not going to suppose anything of the sort,' replied Hemingway. 'For one thing, they wouldn't be anywhere near strong enough, nor pliable enough; and for another, the grooving on them would be horizontal, instead of vertical, and wouldn't give them any grip on the key. Try again!'

'Well, sir, it's all very well, but if an *oustiti* wasn't used, what was? The murderer got into the room somehow. That we do know. Or if the door wasn't locked before the murder, it was after, and there's no sign the key was turned by the old pencil-and-string trick. It beats me.'

'You're a great help,' said Hemingway. 'Ever asked yourself why the murderer took such precious care to lock the door after him?'

The Sergeant considered this. 'I hadn't thought of that,' he admitted. 'Now you put it to me, sir, it does seem queer. Doesn't seem to be any point to it at all, unless it was just done to bamboozle us.'

'Which it probably was,' said Hemingway. 'And I'm bound to say it's succeeding up to the present.'

'Bit of a risk to take, wasn't it? Fiddling about with a door-lock when anyone might have seen him?'

'Whoever committed this murder took the hell of a lot of risks, if you ask me. If I remember rightly, Miss Herriard was seen outside the door in her dressing-gown.'

'You don't think this was a woman's job, sir, do you?' asked the Sergeant incredulously.

'Might have been. Don't you go getting a lot of silly ideas into your head about women! I've known some who'd have put a cageful of tigers to shame. One thing seems pretty certain: Nathaniel wasn't expecting to be stabbed. There are no signs of any struggle, not even a chair pushed out of place. He was taken unawares, and he didn't suspect the murderer of meaning to injure him.'

'Come to think of it,' objected the Sergeant, 'that doesn't point particularly to Miss Herriard. He wouldn't suspect any of the people in the house, would he?'

'He'd suspect them fast enough if they started tampering with the lock of his door,' said Hemingway. 'No, it looks as though the murderer came in in the natural way, all above-board and open, stabbed the old man, and went out again, locking the door behind him by some means which we haven't yet discovered. And somehow I don't believe it.'

The Sergeant saw the frown on his superior's brow, and asked: 'Why not, sir?'

'I've got a feeling it didn't happen that way. What did the murderer lock the door for at all? It's no use saying, to bamboozle the police, because it isn't good enough. If you find a corpse in a locked room, what's the inference?'

'Suicide,' replied the Sergeant promptly.

'Exactly. And if you want a murder to look like suicide you don't first stab the victim in the back, and next remove the knife. There was no idea of making this look like suicide, so the locked door doesn't add up at all.' He looked carefully at the plate in the jamb, which had been torn away. 'In fact,' he said, 'I'm beginning to wonder whether the door ever was locked.'

The Sergeant weighed this suggestion on its merits. 'Three of them said that it was.'

'Four, counting Miss Herriard,' agreed Hemingway.

'Four's too many to be in a conspiracy,' said the Sergeant positively.

'The valet said that he couldn't get any answer to his knock. I don't recall that he said he had tried the door.'

'You mean,' said the Sergeant slowly, 'that you think maybe he only knocked, and when Stephen Herriard came up it was he who forced the latch, and turned the key quickly afterwards, when no one was looking?'

'I don't think anything of the kind,' said Hemingway. 'I have got an open mind.'

'What did you make of the cigarette-case, sir?'

'It doesn't look too good for Master Stephen, on the face of it.'

'No; but that's complicated too, isn't it, sir? I mean, there seems to be plenty of evidence to show that the last person known to be in possession of the case was Miss Dean.'

'Look here!' said Hemingway. 'I can accept the theory that Stephen walked in here to have a quiet chat with his uncle over a cigarette (though, mark you, on the evidence it doesn't seem likely), but what I can't swallow is the suggestion that Miss Dean did. Get hold of the valet for me, will you?'

Ford, when he presently appeared in the Sergeant's wake, showed a slight reluctance to enter the room, and seemed a little nervous. Detectives from Scotland Yard were outside the range of his experience, and although he could look Inspector Hemingway in the eye, he was unable to keep a tremor out of his voice.

When Hemingway asked him if he had tried to open the door into his master's room, he had to think for a moment before replying that he had just turned the handle.

'What do you mean, "just turned the handle"?' asked Hemingway.

'Sort of gently, Inspector, in case Mr Herriard didn't want to be disturbed. The door wouldn't open.'

'So then what did you do?'

'Nothing. I mean, I just waited by the backstairs, like I told the other Inspector.'

'Oh, you did, did you? Well, it seems a funny thing that a man's valet, expecting to help his master to dress, and getting no answer to his knock on the door, *and* finding the door locked, should walk off without so much as thinking that the business was a bit odd.'

Ford stammered: 'I did think it was unusual. Well, not as much as that, but it hadn't ever happened quite like that before.

But Mr Herriard didn't always have me in to help him to dress. Only when his lumbago was troubling him, so to speak.'

'Which I'm told it was,' said Hemingway swiftly.

Ford swallowed. 'Yes, sir, but –'

'So you might have thought you'd be wanted for a certainty, mightn't you? A man with lumbago, for instance, isn't going to bend down to tie up his shoe-laces.'

'No,' admitted Ford sulkily. 'But it's my belief Mr Herriard put it on.'

'Never had lumbago at all?'

'I wouldn't go as far as to say that. He did have it sometimes pretty bad, but it wasn't always as bad as he liked to make out. If he was put out over anything, he'd carry on as though he was a cripple.'

'Did he have you in to help him to dress yesterday morning?'

'Yes, he did, but –'

'But what?'

'Nothing, sir, only I didn't think he had it badly. It was mostly temper.'

'Bad-tempered man, wasn't he?'

'Well, that's it, Inspector. He was a fair Tartar when anyone had got his dander up. You never knew how to take him,' Ford explained eagerly. 'I know it sounds funny, me not liking to go into his room last night until he rang for me, but I give you my word this is a funny kind of a house, and you had to watch your step with Mr Herriard. If he was in a good mood you could go in and out as anyone would expect to in my position; but if he had one of his black fits on him you couldn't do right, and that's a fact.'

Hemingway said sympathetically: 'I get it. Violent kind of man, was he?'

The valet grinned. 'I believe you!'

The Inspector, who had once read Ford's original testimony, had a disconcertingly good memory, and, having lured the valet into making this admission, pounced on it. 'Oh! Then how is it that you told Inspector Colwall that he wasn't a hard master, but that you got on well with him, and liked the place?'

Ford changed colour, but said staunchly: 'Well, it was true enough. I wouldn't call him hard exactly. He was all right when no one had upset him. I've been here nine months, anyway, and not given in my notice, which is more than any of his other valets did, by all accounts. He liked me, you see. I never had any unpleasantness. Not to say real unpleasantness.'

'He never threw his boots at you, I suppose?'

'I don't mind that,' Ford said. 'I mean, it didn't happen often. Just a bit of temper. I could generally manage him.'

'You could generally manage him, but you were scared to go into his room without his sending for you?'

'Well, he wouldn't have liked that. I didn't set out to get on the wrong side of him, naturally. I knew he was in one of his bad moods. He didn't like Miss Paula bringing Mr Roydon down here.'

'Was that what had put him out?'

'That, and something Mr Mottisfont had done. He was grumbling on about it yesterday morning, while I was helping him to get dressed.'

'Grumbling to you?'

'Well, not so much to me as to himself, if you take my

meaning, sir. It was quite a habit with him to let off steam to me when any of the family had annoyed him.'

'Seems to me all the family had annoyed him this time.'

The valet hesitated. 'Well, of course, Mr Joseph had properly got under his skin, inviting a party down here for Christmas, and he took a regular dislike to Miss Dean, and he was angry with Miss Paula for making a fool of herself over a long-haired playwright – that's the way he put it, you understand – but it would not be fair to say that he was hot-up against Mr Stephen. He used to hit it off very well with him.'

'Are you telling me he hadn't quarrelled with Mr Stephen?'

'No, I'm not. He was the kind who'd quarrel with his own mother. All I say is that he and Mr Stephen understood one another and there wasn't a bit of ill-will between them.'

'Oh!' said Hemingway, eyeing him strangely. 'So you hadn't any reason to suppose that there was any kind of break between them on account of Miss Dean?'

'It would have blown over,' Ford said, giving him back stare for stare.

'All right, that's all,' said Hemingway curtly.

The Sergeant, who had listened silently to the whole of this interchange, said as soon as Ford had withdrawn: 'I thought you were riding him a bit hard, Chief.'

'If it wasn't for the laws of this country I'd have ridden him harder,' responded Hemingway. 'I don't like his story.'

'Seems a funny kind of a house altogether,' pondered the Sergeant. 'It struck me, remembering what he said to Inspector Colwall, that he's about the only person, barring

Mr Joseph Herriard, who's anxious to give Stephen Herriard a good character.'

'Well, I'm glad something strikes you,' said Hemingway testily. 'What's been striking me from the start is that the only finger-prints found on the windows or on the bathroom key are Ford's.'

'It's reasonable, though, that his finger-prints should be found, isn't it, sir?'

'When I come up against a queer case, I don't like reasonable evidence,' said Hemingway.

'If he's only been here a matter of nine months, I don't see what he's got to gain by murdering his master.'

'Who said he had murdered him? He might have had plenty to gain by lending young Stephen a hand,' said Hemingway. 'What I want to know is who inherits the old man's money. Let's go downstairs.'

Joseph met them in the hall, and was able to explain that Nathaniel's solicitor was on the way to Lexham. He said that the study had been locked up by the local police, and Hemingway replied at once that he should not have the room opened until the solicitor was present.

He had not long to wait. At about half-past twelve, the car which had taken Maud and Mathilda to church drew up outside the door, and the two ladies came in, followed by a short, stout man who looked cold, and rather disgruntled. When introduced to Hemingway, he nodded, and said good morning, but his first thought was to get as near to the fire as possible, and to warm his chilled hands.

The noise of his arrival attracted most of the house-party to the hall, so while Mr Blyth thawed before the fire Hemingway had an opportunity to observe Roydon, Paula, Valerie, and Mrs Dean. Neither Stephen nor Edgar Mottisfont emerged from the billiard-room, whence the click of the ivory balls could faintly be heard, and Maud went upstairs to take off her coat and hat.

Joseph gave Blyth a glass of sherry, and fell into low-voiced conversation with him. Paula, suddenly becoming aware of Hemingway's presence, stared at him for a moment, and then strode over to him, saying abruptly: 'Are you the Inspector from Scotland Yard?'

'Yes, miss, I am.'

'I thought so. I'm Paula Herriard. I wish you luck!' she said with a short laugh.

'That's very good of you, miss, I'm sure. I daresay I'll need it,' said Hemingway equably.

'You will! What do you think of us?'

'Well, I haven't had much time to make up my mind.'

'I may as well warn you that you are now speaking to one of the chief suspects.'

'Fancy that!' he said.

'Oh yes!' she said, tapping a cigarette on her thumbnail. 'My uncle accused me of being ready to murder him for two thousand pounds. Haven't you been told that?'

'And were you?' enquired Hemingway, in an interested tone.

'Of course not! Besides, how could I possibly have done it?'

'That's what I was wondering.'

Joseph's attention had by this time been caught by his

niece's unguarded voice, and he came over to her side, look-ing rather anxious, but saying with an assumption of light-ness! 'Now, what nonsense do I hear our naughty Paula talking? You mustn't take this young woman too seriously, Inspector. I'm afraid she's been trying to shock you.'

'That's all right, sir: I'm very broadminded.'

'That's just as well,' said Paula, disengaging herself from the avuncular arm about her waist, and walking away.

'My niece is a good deal upset by this appalling business,' Joseph confided. 'She was very fond of my brother. Now, Inspector, since Mr Blyth is here I'm sure you would like to go through all the papers and things as soon as possible. Mr Blyth is quite ready. You won't mind if my nephew is pres-ent? I think he has a right to be there.'

'No objection at all,' said Hemingway. 'In fact, I'd like him to be present.'

Eleven

Stephen, fetched from the billiard-room, came with an ill-grace, disclaiming the slightest interest in the contents of his uncle's desk. Mottisfont, who had followed him, surprised everyone by declaring that as Nathaniel's partner he considered he had a right to be present. Joseph seemed to feel that this was mere officiousness, and said that he hardly thought Nat's private papers could be of interest to his business partner. However, the Inspector, whose obliging demeanour was making Valerie open her eyes wider and wider, said that he had no objection to Mottisfont's presence either.

'It seems to me that it is my presence which is entirely superfluous,' said Stephen. 'If you expect me to be able to throw any light on obscurities I can tell you now that I shan't be able to.'

'No, no, Stephen; of course you must be present!' Joseph said, taking his arm.

Valerie said, as soon as they were out of earshot: 'Well! I never expected a Scotland Yard person to be so decent!'

'Too decent by half,' said Paula scornfully.

'Yes,' agreed Roydon. 'You want to be very much on your guard with those smooth-spoken chaps. They're simply trying to trap you.'

Mrs Dean laughed in a very robust way, and said that there were no traps for her girlie to fall into, she thanked God. This had the effect of making everyone recall duties that would remove them to widely distant parts of the house, and the party disintegrated.

Meanwhile, Nathaniel's study, which was situated in the west wing, and approached by a wide corridor, had been unlocked, and entered. Stephen switched on the electric stove, and began to fill his pipe. Joseph permitted himself a slight shudder at the sight of Nathaniel's sanctum, and pulled himself together with an obvious effort. He turned to Blyth, and said: 'I think you know why my nephew sent for you. There is one very important matter –'

'I had better tell you at once that no will was ever drawn up by my firm for your brother, Mr Herriard,' interrupted the solicitor.

'So that's that,' said Stephen.

'In the absence of any will –'

'But there is a will!' Joseph said.

Everyone looked at him, Hemingway not less intently than the rest.

'How do you know?' demanded Mottisfont. '*I* only know that Nat had a stupid dislike of making a will!'

'Yes, yes, but he did make one. I helped him to draw it up.' Joseph looked towards the Inspector, adding: 'I ought to mention, perhaps, that when I was a young man my father mapped out a legal career for me. I'm afraid I was always a feckless creature, however, and –'

'You can spare us the story of your life,' said Stephen. 'Most of us know it already. When did you help Uncle Nat to draw up a will?'

'When he had pleurisy so badly in the spring,' replied Joseph. 'It was on his mind, and, indeed, it had for long been on mine. You mustn't think that I coerced him in any way. I only put it to him that the thing ought to be done, and saw to it that it was all legal, as far as my little knowledge went. I quite thought he'd have deposited it with you, Blyth.'

The solicitor shook his head.

'Well, that accounts for his dark threats yesterday,' remarked Stephen.

'What were they, sir?' asked Hemingway.

Stephen's mocking eyes lifted momentarily to his face. 'Something about making changes. I thought it was mere rhetoric.'

'The question is, if Mr Blyth hasn't got the will, where is it?' asked Mottisfont.

Stephen shrugged. 'Probably in the incinerator.'

'No, no; he wouldn't have done that!' Joseph said. 'Don't talk of him in that cruel way, Stephen! You know there was no one, not even me, he cared for as much as he cared for you!'

'Are you trying to say that I had reason to know there was a will in my favour?' demanded Stephen.

'You ought to have guessed as much, I should have thought,' said Mottisfont spitefully. 'Joseph's been hinting at it ever since *I* came down here!'

At this attack, Joseph instantly ranged himself on the side of his nephew. 'I don't wish to speak harshly at such a time, Edgar, but that is a – a monstrous suggestion! Stephen, did I ever, at any time, tell you anything about poor Nat's will?'

'No.'

'Oh, I haven't known your family for all these years without learning that you always stick together!' Mottisfont said. 'All I can say is that I for one got the impression that Stephen was Nat's heir, and I got it from the remarks you let fall, Joe!'

The Inspector, though not unappreciative of this interchange, intervened, saying apologetically: 'I don't want to interfere with you gentlemen, but if there is a will I'd like to see it.'

'There isn't one,' Stephen said shortly.

The Inspector's eyes were on Joseph's troubled face. 'What do you say to that, sir?'

'My brother did make a will,' Joseph answered. 'Perhaps he subsequently destroyed it. I don't know. But there's a safe in this room, and I think it might be there.'

'A safe in this room?' repeated Stephen.

'Yes, it's hidden behind that picture,' replied Joseph. 'I don't suppose you knew about it. Nat only told me when he was ill, and wanted me to get something out of it.'

'Can you open it?'

'Yes, if the combination hasn't been changed.'

Stephen walked over to the picture Joseph had indicated, and took it down, revealing a small wall-safe. After a good deal of fussing and fumbling, Joseph succeeded in opening it. He then invited Blyth to see what it contained, and stood back, looking anxious.

Blyth drew two bundles of documents out of the safe, and brought them to the desk, where he and Hemingway went through them. Stephen stood frowning by the fireplace, while Mottisfont, who seemed to find it difficult to sit still, polished his spectacles.

After a pause, Blyth said in his precise way: 'Most of these papers are share-certificates, and can have no bearing on the case. I find that there is a will.' He added in a disparaging tone: 'It would appear to be in order.'

'For God's sake – !' said Stephen irritably. 'Since there is a will, let's know how we stand! Who's the heir?'

The solicitor looked austerely at him over the top of his pince-nez. 'It is, as you no doubt perceive, a brief document,' he said. 'Had I been consulted – But I was not.'

'I think it's all right,' Joseph said guiltily. 'My brother wouldn't let me send for you, but I think I remembered enough of my early training to draw it up correctly.'

'It will of course have to be proved,' said Blyth in a cold tone. 'Where such a large sum of money is involved, I should naturally have advised the employment of a solicitor. But I am well aware of the late Mr Herriard's peculiarities.'

'Who – is – the – heir?' demanded Stephen.

Blyth looked affronted, and Mottisfont muttered something about observing a little decency. The Inspector, however, supported Stephen, and said that he too would like to know who was the heir.

'There are two bequests,' said Blyth. 'Miss Paula Herriard inherits fifteen thousand pounds; Mr Joseph Herriard, ten thousand pounds. The residue, including the house and estate, is left to Mr Stephen Herriard, unconditionally.'

There was a moment's silence. Stephen jerked his head round to stare at his uncle. 'What in hell's name did you do that for?' he asked angrily.

Even Blyth looked surprised. The Inspector stood watching Stephen with the interest of a connoisseur. Joseph said: 'It was Nat, old man, not I. I only helped him to draw it up.'

'Encouraged him to leave a fortune to me, I suppose!'

The savage, gibing note in Stephen's voice made Mottisfont's jaw drop. The Inspector looked from Stephen's harsh face to Joseph's worried one, and waited.

'Stephen, I can't bear you to speak so bitterly of Nat!' Joseph said. 'You know he thought the world of you! I didn't have to encourage him to make you his heir! He always meant it to be that way. The only thing I did was to persuade him to make a proper will.'

'Well, I call it very decent of you, Joe!' said Mottisfont, unable to contain himself. 'It isn't everyone who'd have behaved as you've done.'

'My dear Edgar, I hope you didn't think I was the Wicked Uncle of the fairy-stories!'

'No; but I should have expected – You were Nat's brother, after all! Ten thousand only! Well, I never would have believed it!'

Joseph gave one of his whimsical smiles. 'I'm afraid it seems a dreadfully large sum to me. I never could cope with money. You can say I am an impractical old fool, if you like, but I should have been very uncomfortable if Nat had left me more.'

This was so unusual a point of view that no one could think of anything to say. After a pause, Blyth cleared his throat, and enquired whether the Inspector wished to go through his late client's papers.

Joseph sighed. 'If you must, I suppose you must,' he said. 'Somehow one hates the thought of poor Nat's papers being tampered with!'

'I can't see the least sense in it,' said Mottisfont. 'They aren't likely to throw any light on the murder.'

'You never know, sir,' said Hemingway, polite but discouraging.

The contents of Nathaniel's desk, however, afforded little of interest. Evidently Nathaniel had been a methodical man who kept his papers neatly docketed, and did not hoard correspondence. A letter from Paula was discovered, bearing a recent date. Paula's wild handwriting covered four pages, but apart from one petulant reference to her uncle's meanness in not instantly agreeing to support Willoughby Roydon's works there was nothing in the letter to indicate that she felt any animosity towards him. None of the other private letters seemed to have any bearing on the case, and after glancing through them the Inspector turned to the business letters, which Blyth was sorting. These too were uninteresting from Hemingway's point of view, but while he was running through them, Blyth, who had been studying some papers which were clipped together, glanced fleetingly towards Mottisfont, and then silently laid the papers before Hemingway.

'Ah!' said Mottisfont, with a slight laugh. 'I fancy I see my own fist! I can guess what that is!'

Hemingway paid no heed to this remark, but picked up the sheaf, and began to read the first letter.

It had apparently been written in reply to a demand for information, and the terms in which it was couched were too guarded to afford the Inspector any very precise idea of the business the firm of Herriard and Mottisfont had been conducting. Attached to it was the rough draft of a further letter from Nathaniel. Such intemperate expressions as *crass folly*, *unjustifiable risks*, and *staggering impudence* abounded, and had called forth a second letter from Mottisfont, in which he suggested rather stiffly that his partner was behind the times, and had, in fact, been out of the business for too long to realise the exigencies of modern times, or the necessity of seizing any opportunity that offered for lucrative trading.

The fourth and last letter in the clip was again a copy, and in Nathaniel's hand. It was quite short. It stated with crushing finality that 'this business' would be brought to an immediate conclusion. Plainly, although Nathaniel might of late years have taken but little share in the working activities of the business which bore his name, his veto was final, admitting of no argument.

The Inspector laid these papers to one side, and would have continued to run through the dwindling pile before him had not Mottisfont said, with another of his mirthless laughs: 'Well, if that's my correspondence with Mr Herriard over the China business, as I can see it is, I've no doubt you must want to know what the devil it's all about, Inspector!'

'Not now!' Joseph said. 'This isn't quite the moment, do you think?'

'Oh, so Nat told you about it, did he?'

'Good heavens, no! Nat knew me too well to do that! I knew you'd had some sort of a disagreement, of course.'

'Well, I've no objection to having the thing out now, or at any other time.'

'If you feel like that, sir, what is it all about?' asked Hemingway.

Mottisfont drew a breath. 'My firm – it's a private company – deals with the East Indies trade.'

'Just what is the composition of the company, sir?'

'Private limited liability. The shares were held by the three of us: Nathaniel Herriard, Stephen Herriard, and myself.'

'In what proportion, sir?'

'Nathaniel Herriard held seventy per cent of the shares, myself twenty, and Stephen Herriard ten. When Nathaniel virtually retired from active partnership, I became managing director.'

'And you, sir?' asked Hemingway, looking at Stephen.

'Nothing to do with it. Shares wished on to me when I was twenty-one.'

'Oh no, the business was just Nathaniel and me!' said Mottisfont. 'Well, he more or less retired some years ago, leaving me to carry on.'

'What does more or less mean, sir?'

'Less,' said Stephen.

Mottisfont pointedly ignored this interruption. 'Well, I don't suppose anyone who knew Nathaniel will deny that he was by nature an autocrat. He never could keep his fingers out of any pie.'

Joseph protested at this. 'Edgar, I must point out to you that this pie was of his own making!'

'Oh, I'm not saying he wasn't a very clever business man in his day! But you know as well as I do that he was getting past it. Couldn't keep up with the times: lost his vision.'

'Any disagreements between you and Mr Herriard on the firm's policy?' asked Hemingway.

'Yes, many. Trade has been very bad during the last few years, particularly bad for our business. The Sino-Japanese war was a crippling blow. Nathaniel had been out of things for too long to be able to cope with the new situation. I always had to fight to get my own way. Dear me, I can recall occasions when he's threatened me with every kind of disaster! But that was just his way. If you let him bluster himself out, in the end he always listened to reason. Those letters you have under your hand refer to a deal I wanted to put through, and which he was frightened of. I could show you dozens of others just like them, if I hadn't destroyed them.'

'What was this deal, sir?'

'Well, unless you're a business man, I don't suppose you'd understand it,' said Mottisfont.

Stephen's bitter mouth curled. 'Nothing very difficult to understand about it,' he said, his voice harsh enough to make Mottisfont start.

'I was not aware that you were in Nathaniel's confidence!' Mottisfont said, his eyes snapping behind their spectacles.

Stephen laughed. Joseph laid a hand on his arm. 'Gently, old man! We don't want to make mischief, do we?'

'Damn you, don't paw me about!' Stephen said, shaking him off. 'I've been quite sufficiently nauseated by Mottisfont's pretty picture of his own totally non-existent influence over Uncle Nat. So you could handle him, could you? You just let him bluster himself out, did you? By God, I won't have the old devil belittled by a damned little worm like you! You went in mortal dread of him, and well you know it!'

'How dare you speak to me like that?' stammered Mottisfont. 'You know nothing about my relationship with Nat! Nothing! Because you knew no better than to quarrel with him, you think no one had more sense! Well, I was dealing with Nat when you were at a kindergarten! Puppy!'

'Edgar! Stephen!' implored Joseph, wringing his hands. 'This isn't worthy of either of you! What must the Inspector think?'

The futility of this agonised enquiry drew a sound like a snarl from Stephen, but only made Hemingway say cheerfully: 'Oh, you don't want to worry about me, sir! Perhaps, since Mr Stephen Herriard seems to know all about it, he'd like to tell me what this new deal was that his uncle didn't hold with?'

'Gun-running,' said Stephen.

Mottisfont grasped the arms of the chair he was sitting in as though he were about to jump up, and then relaxed again. 'It isn't difficult to believe that you'd stab a man in the back!' he said, in a trembling voice.

'I'd already noticed that you found no difficulty in believing it!' retorted Stephen.

'Stephen, Stephen, don't let *your* tongue betray you into saying what you can only regret! That was unpardonable of you, Edgar, unpardonable!' Joseph said.

'Oh yes, what I say is unpardonable, but what your precious nephew says is quite another matter, isn't it?' Mottisfont sneered.

'Edgar, you know what Stephen is just as well as I do! I'm not excusing him. But as for letting him get a rise out of you with his absurd, nonsense about gun-running – ! For shame, Edgar! Of course, no one believes you were mixed up with anything of the sort! Why, it sounds like one of those lurid films which I, alas, am too much of an old stager to enjoy!'

'Only it happens to be true,' said Stephen.

'Really, Stephen! I hope I'm as fond of a joke as anyone, but is this quite the time, my boy?'

The Inspector, who had been watching Mottisfont, said: 'I don't want to interrupt you gentlemen, but perhaps we'd all of us get along better if I made it plain that I'm not at the moment interested in gun-running, which is what I thought this "China business" of yours might be, Mr Mottisfont.'

Stephen found Mottisfont's expression of mingled relief and uncertainty comic, and began to laugh. Joseph flung up a hand. 'Stephen, please! Edgar, is this thing possible?'

'Good heavens, Joseph, there's nothing to be so tragic about!' said Mottisfont. 'A great many people consider that we are making a criminal mistake not to allow the shipment of arms to China!'

'But it's illegal!' said Joseph, quite horrified. 'You mean to say you wanted to engage in an illegal business?'

'Was engaged in it. Is engaged in it,' said Stephen. 'Lucrative pursuit, gun-running.'

'You seem to know a lot about it,' said the Inspector.

'Not me, no. Only what my uncle told me. You have Mr Mottisfont's word for it that I have nothing to do with the management of the firm.'

'Well, it is a lucrative business,' said Mottisfont, with sudden candour. 'Of course, it's frowned on by the authorities, but we needn't go into that now. There are always two ways of looking at a thing, and I'm not at all ashamed of selling arms to China. What's more, Nat would soon have come round to my point of view.'

'Nat,' said Joseph, in a deep voice, 'was the Soul of Honour. He would never have consented.'

The Inspector looked at him. 'You weren't in his confidence, sir?'

'Not about business matters,' confessed Joseph. 'You see, I've never had the least head for that sort of thing. I chose to follow Art, and though I daresay many people would think me a fool, I've never regretted it.'

'And you, sir?' asked Hemingway, addressing Stephen. 'Just what did you know about this?'

'The bare facts. My uncle had discovered the gun-running racket, and he wasn't pleased about it. In fact, he was damned angry.'

'Nathaniel was too good a business man not to have seen reason, in face of the balance-sheets during the past three or four years!' said Mottisfont. 'I don't mind admitting that we hadn't been doing well.'

The Inspector said: 'If it's all the same to you, sir, I'd like to know how things stand. What are your Articles of Association? What happens to Mr Herriard's shares?'

'They were to be offered to the remaining shareholders pro rata,' replied Mottisfont. 'A very ordinary arrangement.'

'That is to say that you would then have a two-thirds interest in the company, and Mr Stephen Herriard one-third?'

'Certainly.'

'What about the valuation?'

Stephen removed his pipe from his mouth. 'On the last three years' trading. Doesn't the plot thicken?'

'I suppose you know what you mean by that! I can only say that I don't!' snapped Mottisfont.

'I just think that things have panned out very luckily for you,' smiled Stephen.

This remark provoked Mottisfont to such an explosion of wrath that not only Joseph, but Blyth too, intervened. While these three voices strove against each other, Stephen stood smoking his pipe, and grinning sardonically, and the Inspector divided his attention between his demeanour and those of Mottisfont's agitated utterances which he was able to hear.

Again and again, and with tears in his voice, Joseph begged Mottisfont not to say what he must later regret; but the only effect this had on Mottisfont was to make him shout that he had had enough of Joseph's meddling ways, and would not be surprised to find that he had been in league with Stephen from the start.

The obvious inference not only shocked Joseph, but gave him an opportunity of showing his audience that he could enact a tragic rôle just as well as the character-parts in which his wife said he was so good. Horror, grief, and righteous indignation all infused his voice as he refuted this accusation; and, as he turned away from Mottisfont, he almost tottered.

The Inspector, though not unappreciative of the spirited scene he was witnessing, thought it time to bring it to a close. He said that he did not think he need trouble the actors any more at present. Stephen at once strolled out of the room; and after delivering himself of a few trembling remarks about the entire Herriard family, Mottisfont also went away. The Inspector looked at Joseph, but Joseph showed no disposition to follow suit. He said, when the door had shut behind Mottisfont: 'Nerves play strange tricks on us poor humans! I think you, Inspector, must have seen too much to attach importance to the foolish things a man will say under nervous stress. This has been a severe shock to my old friend Mottisfont. It has thrown him off his balance. You must believe that!'

'I do,' replied Hemingway.

'I consider there was a good deal of provocation,' said Blyth dryly.

'Yes, yes, I know there was!' Joseph agreed. 'Stephen has a wicked tongue. I'm not excusing him. But I think I may claim to know him better than most people and I can't let this pass without saying that that remark of his was not by any means unprovoked. Mottisfont's attitude to him ever since my poor brother's death has been little short of hostile.'

'Do you know why?' asked Hemingway.

Joseph shook his head. 'There's no reason, except that I'm afraid my nephew doesn't lay himself out to be very agreeable. He wants knowing, if you understand what I mean. I can't deny that he has – well, an unfortunate manner, very often, but it doesn't mean anything. Then, too, I daresay Mottisfont was inclined to be jealous of him, the silly fellow!'

'Would you say that he had an influence over your brother, sir?'

'Well, hardly that, perhaps. But my brother was very fond of him. And Stephen cared a good deal for my brother too, whatever Mottisfont may choose to think. You know how it is, Inspector! My nephew is not the sort of man to show what he feels, and people are inclined to think him callous. Poor Mottisfont was terribly shocked by my brother's death! Of course, Stephen was too, but he won't show it, and that misled Mottisfont into thinking – well, I'm sure I don't know what he thinks, but that unfortunate business of the cigarette-case made him say one or two things that were quite uncalled-for. But I think I put a stop to that. The old uncle has his uses!'

'Mr Mottisfont thought the finding of that case in Mr Herriard's room suspicious?'

'Oh, I don't know that he went as far as that! In any event, I feel sure the cigarette-case means nothing at all. There are probably a dozen explanations to account for its having been found in my brother's room.'

'Mr Herriard,' said Hemingway, 'did you at any time tell your nephew about the will you helped your brother to draw up?'

'No, indeed I didn't!' Joseph said quickly. 'Why, it would have been most improper of me! You mustn't pay any heed to what poor Mottisfont said! That I'd been hinting that Stephen was the heir! Now, I do assure you, Inspector, that I never did anything of the kind. The only person I ever said anything to – and then only in the most general terms – was Miss Dean.'

'What did you say to her, sir?'

'Really, I can't recall my exact words! It was nothing you could possibly construe into – in fact, I told her my lips were sealed. And I shouldn't have said that, only that – oh dear, oh dear, one tries to act for the best, never imagining that the most innocent motives may lead to all sorts of hideous complications! You'll think me a sentimental old fool, I expect, but my one idea was to smooth out a few wrinkles, if I could.'

'Between Mr Stephen and the deceased?'

'Well, yes,' admitted Joseph. 'It's no use trying to conceal from you that my poor brother was in a very bad humour, for I'm sure you've already been told that. His lumbago was troubling him, and there was this business of Mottisfont's, besides the rather unfortunate affair of young Roydon's play. I did my best to pour oil, and I will readily admit that I was on tenterhooks lest Stephen should upset all his chances by – by irritating his uncle. That's why I spoke to Miss Dean.'

'So that unless Miss Dean told him, you don't think he had any knowledge of his uncle's having made this will?'

'Not from me! I don't know what my brother may have told him, but I can assure you I never said anything about it.'

The Inspector's excellent memory again proved disconcerting. 'But when Mr Herriard and his nephew had words after the reading of Mr Roydon's play, didn't Mr Herriard speak of making a few changes?'

'Really, I don't think I heard him! In any case, it was the sort of thing he might say if he was in a temper.'

'But it would imply, wouldn't it, that he had reason to believe that Mr Stephen knew of the provisions of this will?'

'I suppose it would,' agreed Joseph unhappily. 'But you can't mean to suggest that Stephen – Oh no, no! I won't believe such a horrible thing!'

'I'm not suggesting anything, sir; I'm only trying to get at the truth.'

Joseph wrung his hands in one of his agitated gestures. 'Ah, you think me a foolish old fellow, but I can't but see what you suspect! I know that things do look black against my nephew, but I for one am convinced that the murder wasn't committed by anyone under this roof!'

'How's that, sir? What reason have you to think that?' asked the Inspector quickly.

'Sometimes,' answered Joseph, 'intuition proves to be sounder than reason, Inspector!'

'I'll have to take your word for that, sir,' replied the disillusioned Inspector. 'I haven't found it so myself. Of course, that's not to say I won't.'

'Try to keep an open mind!' Joseph begged.

'I'm paid to do that, sir,' said Hemingway, somewhat acidly. 'And now, if you don't mind, I'll finish what I have to do here with Mr Blyth.'

This was too pointed to be ignored. Joseph went away, his seraphic brow creased with worry. Blyth said, with a slight smile: 'He means well, Inspector.'

'Yes, that's a vice that makes more trouble than any other,' said Hemingway. 'If you ask me, there very likely wouldn't have been a murder at all if it hadn't been for him getting ideas about peace and goodwill, and assembling all these highly uncongenial people under the same roof at the same time.'

'I fear you are a cynic, Inspector.'

'You get to be in my profession,' replied Hemingway.

The inspection of the rest of Nathaniel's papers did not take long, nor was anything of further interest discovered amongst them. The solicitor was soon at liberty to join the rest of the house-party in the library; and Hemingway went off in search of his Sergeant.

Ware met him in the hall, and looked a question.

'Nothing much,' Hemingway said. 'Young Stephen's the heir all right. You have any success?'

'Well, I can't say I have,' Ware replied. 'Can't get much out of the servants – much sense, I mean. But one thing struck me as a bit funny. I was having a look round, and went into the billiard-room, and I found an old lady there. Mrs Joseph Herriard, I believe.'

'I don't see anything funny about that.'

'No, sir, but she was fair turning the room upside-down, looking for something. I watched her for quite a minute before she saw me. One end of the room's fitted out like a small lounge, and she was looking under all the cushions, and running her hands down the sides of the chairs, as though she thought something might have slipped down between the upholstery. She gave a bit of a start when she saw me, but of course that's nothing in itself.'

'Hunting for something, was she? Well, that might be interesting.'

'Yes, that's what I thought, but when I asked her if she'd lost something I'm bound to say she didn't seem at all discomposed, as you might say. She said she'd lost her book.'

'Well, I daresay she had, but I'd like to meet her,' said Hemingway.

'She's still there, sir.'

When Joseph had begun to dismantle the Christmas tree, he had had a small wooden tub brought into the billiard-room. It was half-full of tinsel decorations and crackers, and when the Sergeant showed Hemingway into the room, Maud was engaged in turning these over in her search for the *Life of the Empress of Austria*. She acknowledged the Inspector's arrival with a nod and a small smile. She seemed to think that the Sergeant had fetched him to assist her, for she thanked him for coming, and said that it was extraordinary how things could get mislaid.

'A book, is it, madam?' asked Hemingway.

'Yes, and it is a library book, so it must be found,' said Maud. 'Of course, I expect it will turn up, because things very often do, and in the most unexpected places.'

'Such as in a tub full of Christmas decorations?' suggested Hemingway, with a quizzical look.

'You never know,' said Maud vaguely. 'I once mislaid a shoehorn for three days, and it was eventually found in a coal-scuttle, though how it came there I never could discover. I daresay you will be searching the house yourself, and if you should happen to come upon my book I should be very grateful if you would tell me. It is called the *Life of the Empress Elizabeth of Austria*. A most interesting character: really, I had no idea! It is most annoying that I should have lost it, because I hadn't finished it. She must have been very lovely, but I can't help feeling sorry for her husband. He seems to have been a handsome man when he was young, but of course he grew those whiskers in later life. And then so fat! Not that I think that excused her altogether. No, the book isn't here. So tiresome!'

She smiled, and nodded again, and went out of the room, returning, however, in a few moments to tell the Inspector not to make a special point of looking for the book, as she knew he had other things to think about.

The astonished Sergeant exchanged a glance with his superior, but Hemingway assured Maud that he would keep his eyes open.

'Well!' ejaculated the Sergeant, when Maud had gone away again. 'What do you make of that?'

'I'd say she *was* looking for her book.'

The Sergeant was disappointed. 'It struck me she might be looking for the weapon that killed the old man. Seemed fishy to me.'

'She wouldn't have had to look far,' said the Inspector. 'Not if it's in this room. What's wrong with *your* eyesight, my lad?'

The Sergeant blinked, and gazed about him. Hemingway pointed a finger at the wall above the fireplace. Flanking the head of an antlered deer were two old flint-lock pistols, a pair of knives in ornate sheaths, and various other weapons, ranging from a Zulu knobkerrie to a seventeenth-century halberd.

'Just about as much gumption as the locals, that's what you've got!' said Hemingway scornfully. 'Get up on a chair, and take a look at those two daggers! And don't go fingering them!'

Swallowing this insult, the Sergeant pulled a chair forward, and said that it was funny how you could miss a thing that was right under your nose.

'I don't know what you mean by "you"!' retorted Hemingway. 'I know what I'd mean by it, but that's different. And funny isn't the word I'd use, either. Any dust on those daggers?'

The Sergeant, standing on the chair, reached up, leaning a hand against the wall to steady himself. 'No. At least, yes: on the undersides,' he said, peering at them.

'Both free from dust on the outside?'

'Pretty well. So's this pike-affair. Careful servants in this house. I expect they do 'em with one of those feather dusters on the end of a long stick.'

'Never mind what they do them with! Hand those daggers down to me!'

The Sergeant obeyed, using his handkerchief. Hemingway took them, and closely scrutinised them. It was plain that the sheaths at least had not been taken down recently, since dust clung to the undersides, and a few wispy cobwebs on the wall were revealed by their removal. Indeed, the Sergeant, descending from his perch, and studying the knives, gave it as his opinion that neither had been handled.

'Take another look,' advised Hemingway. 'Notice anything about the hilts?'

The Sergeant glanced quickly at him, and then once more bent over the weapons. As Hemingway held them up the dust on them was clearly visible. Each sheath, where it had lain against the wall, was thinly coated with dust, and so was one hilt. The other hilt had no speck of dust on it, on either side.

The Sergeant drew in his breath. 'My lord, Chief, you're quick!' he said respectfully.

'You can put this one back,' said Hemingway, unmoved by the compliment, and handing him the knife with the dusty hilt. 'It hasn't been touched. But this little fellow has been drawn out of its sheath very recently, or I'm a Dutchman!' He held it up to the light, closely inspecting the hilt for finger-prints. No smudge on its polished surface was visible to the naked eye, and he added disgustedly: 'What's more, when the experts get on to it, they'll find that it's been carefully wiped. However, we won't take any chances. Lend me that handkerchief of yours, will you?'

The Sergeant gave it to him. Carefully grasping the base of the hilt between his finger and thumb through the folds of the linen, Hemingway drew the knife from the sheath. It slid easily, a thin blade which revealed a slight stain close to the hilt. The Sergeant pointed a finger at this, and Hemingway nodded. 'Overlooked that, didn't he? Well, I fancy we have here the weapon that killed Nathaniel Herriard.' Perceiving a look of elation on his subordinate's face, he added damp-ingly: 'Not that it's likely to help us, but it's nice to know.'

'I don't see why it shouldn't help us,' objected Ware. 'It proves the murder was an inside job, anyway.'

'Well, if that's your idea of help, it isn't mine,' said Hemingway. 'Of course it was an inside job! And a nice, high-class bit of work too! There won't be any finger-prints on this. You have to hand it to our unknown friend. Thinks of everything. He chooses a weapon which nine people out of ten would stare at every day of their lives without attaching any importance to. He chooses a time when the house is full of visitors who all have their reasons for wanting old Herriard out of the way; and seizes the moment when everyone's dress-ing for dinner to stab his host, and restore the knife at his leisure. It's an education to have to do with this bird.'

The Sergeant gazed meditatively up at the wall over the fireplace. 'Yes, and what's more, he might have taken the knife at any time,' he said. 'There's no sign he took the sheath as well.'

'There's every sign he didn't.'

'That's what I mean. I daresay no one would have noticed if that knife had been taken out of the sheath quite a while before the murder was committed. It isn't even as if it was on a line with your eyes: you have to look up to catch sight of it.'

'What's more important,' said Hemingway, 'is that it could have been put back at any time. After everyone had gone to bed, as like as not. So now perhaps you begin to see that the chances are that this nasty-looking dagger is going to rank as a matter of purely academic interest.'

Twelve

T HE INSPECTOR HAD BARELY PACKED THE KNIFE AND ITS sheath away into a case when Sturry entered the room, and stood upon the threshold with an expression of lofty resignation on his face. Hemingway, no respecter of persons, said: 'Well, what do you want?'

Sturry gave him a quelling look, and replied with meticulous politeness: 'Mr Joseph, Inspector, desired me to enquire whether you, and the Other Policeman, will be requiring luncheon. If this should be the case, a Cold Collation will be served in the morning-room.'

'No, thanks,' said Hemingway, who had no opinion of cold collations at midwinter.

Sturry bowed slightly. His arctic gaze took in the position of the chair which the Sergeant had used to enable him to reach the knives on the wall, and travelled upwards. He acknowledged the disappearance of one of the pair of knives by a pronounced elevation of the eyebrows, and moved forward to restore the chair to its place against the wall. He then plumped up a couple of cushions, looked with contempt at the partially dismantled Christmas tree, and at last withdrew.

GEORGETTE HEYER

The Sergeant, who had been watching him with considerable disfavour, said: 'I don't like that chap.'

'That's only inferiority complex,' said Hemingway. 'You didn't like being called the Other Policeman.'

'Snooping round,' said the Sergeant darkly. 'He saw the knife had gone all right. He'll spread that bit of news round the house.'

'Then we may get some interesting reactions,' responded Hemingway. 'Come on! We'll take the knife back to headquarters, and get a bit of dinner at the same time. I want to think.'

He was unusually silent during the hot and substantial meal provided by the cook at the Blue Dog inn; and the Sergeant, respecting his preoccupation, made no attempt to converse with him. Only when the cheese was set before them did he venture to say: 'I've been thinking about that weapon.'

'I haven't,' said Hemingway. 'I've been thinking about that locked door.'

'I don't seem to get any ideas about that,' confessed the Sergeant. 'The more I think about it the more senseless it seems.'

'There must have been a reason for it,' said Hemingway. 'A pretty strong one, too. Whoever murdered Nathaniel Herriard, and locked the door behind him, was taking the hell of a chance of being caught in the act. He didn't do it for fun.'

'No,' agreed the Sergeant, thinking it over. 'It looks as though you're right there. But what reason could he possibly have had?'

Hemingway did not answer. After a few moments, the Sergeant said slowly: 'Supposing the murdered man didn't lock the door himself, in the first place? We've no proof that he did, after all. I was just wondering… If the murderer walked into the room, and locked the door behind him –'

'Old Herriard would have kicked up a rumpus.'

'Not if it had been his nephew he wouldn't. He might have thought Stephen wanted to have a straight talk with him, without the valet's coming in to interrupt them.'

'Well?' said Hemingway, showing a faint interest.

'Well, Stephen, or someone else, killed him. You remember the valet telling us that he came along, and tried the door, and found it locked? Suppose the murderer was still in the room then?'

'All right, I'm supposing it. So what?'

The Sergeant caressed his chin. 'I haven't worked it all out, but it does strike me that he may have thought he'd got to leave that door locked when he left the room.'

'Why?'

'Might be the time element, mightn't it? He may have thought that if anyone was to come along and try the door a minute or two later, and find it unlocked, he'd be whittling down the time of the murder a bit dangerously. I don't say I quite see –'

'No, nor anyone else,' interrupted Hemingway.

'There might have been a reason,' persisted the Sergeant doggedly.

'There might have been half a dozen reasons, but what you seem to forget is that it isn't all that easy to turn keys from the wrong side of the door. If the door was locked from the outside, the man who did it must have provided himself with a tool for the purpose. He couldn't have done it extempore, so to speak.'

'He could, by slipping a pencil through the handle of the key, with a bit of string attached.'

'He could, but we haven't any evidence to show that he did. In fact, we've plenty of evidence to show that he didn't.'

'Were there any finger-prints on the key?' asked the Sergeant.

'Old Herriard's, and the valet's, considerably blurred. Just what you'd expect.'

The Sergeant sighed. 'Nothing seems to lead anywhere, does it, sir? I'm blessed if I know how to catch hold of this case.'

'We'll go back to the station,' decided Hemingway. 'I'm going to have another look at that key.'

The key, however, revealed no new clue. It was a large key, and it had been lately smeared with vaseline. 'Which makes it still more unlikely that it could have been turned from outside,' said Hemingway. 'To start with, I doubt if any *oustiti* would have gripped such a greasy surface; and to go on with, we'd be bound to see the imprint of the grooving on the grease. It's disheartening, that's what it is.' He scrutinised the handle through a magnifying glass, and shook his head. 'Nothing doing. I'd say it hasn't been tampered with in any way.'

'Which means,' said the Sergeant weightily, 'that whoever locked that door did it from the inside.'

'And then dematerialised himself like the spooks you read about. Talk sense!'

'What was to stop him hiding in the room until the body had been found, and then slipping out unnoticed, sir?'

'Nothing at all. In fact, you might have got something there, except for one circumstance. All the members of the household were accounted for at the time of the discovery. Think again!'

'I can't,' said the Sergeant frankly. 'Seems as though we've got to come back to the ventilator.'

'The more I think of it, the more that ventilator looks to me like a snare and a delusion,' said Hemingway. 'It's a good seven foot above the floor, to start with, and too small to allow an average-sized man to squeeze through it, to go on with.'

'The valet,' said the Sergeant.

'Yes, I've thought of him, but I still don't see it. Even supposing he could have got through, how did he reach the floor?'

'Supposing he didn't come in that way, but was there all the time, and escaped through the ventilator?'

'Worse!' said Hemingway emphatically. 'Did he go head first down a ladder?'

'Not the way I see it,' said the Sergeant, ignoring this sarcasm. 'I've got an idea he and young Herriard were in this together. It seems to me that if he'd had a chair to stand on he might, if he was clever, have got out through the ventilator. Once his shoulders were through, he could have wormed himself round, and maybe got hold of a drain-pipe, or a bit of that wistaria over the window, to give himself a purchase while he got a leg out. Once he'd got one foot on the ladder he'd be all right.'

'Seems to me he'd have to be a ruddy contortionist,' said the Inspector. 'And what about the chair under the ventilator?'

'He could have moved that back when the door was forced open. Who'd have noticed? The old fellow would have been taken up with his brother's body, and if Stephen was in it he doesn't count.'

'I can't see what you want with young Stephen in this Arabian Nights story of yours. Why don't you let the valet have the whole stage?' demanded the sceptical Inspector.

'Because if Stephen wasn't in it, there wasn't a motive,' replied the Sergeant. 'My idea is that Stephen bribed the valet to help him. I don't say the valet did the killing: that's going too far.'

'Well, I'm glad to know you draw the line somewhere,' said Hemingway. 'And don't you run away with the notion that I'm not pleased with this theory of yours! I've always told you that you haven't got enough imagination, so it's very gratifying to me to see you taking my words to heart, which is a thing I never thought you did. And if it weren't for all the circumstances you've overlooked, it would be a good theory.'

The Sergeant said in a resigned voice: 'I know there are some loose ends, but –'

'Who set the ladder up to be handy?'

'Either of them.'

'When?'

'Any time,' said the Sergeant, adding after a moment's reflection: 'No, perhaps not any time. As soon as it was dark.'

'Have you ever tried to set a ladder up against a particular window in the dark?'

'No, sir, I haven't; but if there was a light in that particular window I'd back myself to do it,' retorted the Sergeant.

'You win,' said Hemingway handsomely. 'I'll give you the ladder. And if you can tell me how Ford managed to be in his master's room and flirting with one of the housemaids at one and the same time, I'll go straight off and arrest him.'

'The way I see it, the murder had been committed by the time he came up the backstairs, and went into the sewing-room.'

'It may have been, but not by him. He was in the servants' hall.'

'That's what he said.'

'Exactly. And if he was as smart as you seem to think, he wouldn't have said that if he couldn't have proved it. You can check up on it: in fact, you must; but if you don't find that he's borne out by the other servants I'll be surprised.'

'Well, I can't get it out of my head that he's the one person who could have gone in and out of the deceased's room as he pleased, and, what's more, have left his finger-prints about without occasioning any suspicion. I suppose no one could have monkeyed about with the bedroom windows?'

Hemingway shook his head. 'You can't slip a knife-blade in between that kind of casement-window and its frame, if that's what you're thinking of.' He frowned suddenly. 'I wonder, though?... My lad, we'll go back to the house! Then you can nose round for a handy garden-ladder, while I have a heart-to-heart with old Joseph Herriard.'

Unaware of the ordeal before him, Joseph had been trying, throughout luncheon, to second Mrs Dean's attempts to introduce what she called a normal note into the party's conversation. Having announced brightly that they must try not to be morbid, Mrs Dean had favoured the company with some anecdotes of a winter spent in the south of France; but as these seemed to lack any other point than the introduction of the names of the well-born people she had met in Nice, no discussion was engendered, and the subject petered out. Maud contributed her mite by recalling that the Archduchess Sophia removed the Empress's children from her care, and shut them up in a wing of the palace. Stephen was heard to groan, and although Mrs Dean, with what Mathilda could not but consider very good manners, showed herself willing to search her memory for further details of the Empress's ill-starred career, Joseph evidently felt that no one else would have the patience to endure more Imperial reminiscences, and hastily changed the subject.

But neither his nor Mrs Dean's efforts could avail to keep the talk away from Nathaniel's murder. It loomed too large in everyone's minds; and although Stephen was taciturn, and Maud detached, it was not long before it had become the sole topic of any sustained conversation. Even Joseph succumbed, and said, for perhaps the sixth time, that he felt sure someone from outside had committed the murder. This led to a discussion on the possible ways by which anyone could have gained access to Nathaniel's bedroom, and Valerie propounded the suggestion that there must be a secret passage behind the oak-panelling. This idea, thrown out on the spur of the moment, took such instant possession of her mind that she reiterated her dread of spending another night under this ill-omened roof; and it might even have induced her to consent to share her mother's bedroom, had she not reflected in time that she would not, in this event, be allowed to smoke in bed, or to read into the small hours.

'My little girl mustn't let her nerves run away with her,' said Mrs Dean bracingly. 'Who could possibly want to murder *you*, my pet?'

A glance at Stephen's face might have provided her with a possible answer, but happily she did not look in his direction.

Paula, somewhat unexpectedly, said: 'I wonder if there is a way into Uncle's room which we don't know about? Is there, Joe?'

'My dear, don't ask me!' said Joseph, laughing at her. 'You know your old uncle has no taste for antiques! For all I know, the house may be riddled with secret passages, and priest-holes, and hidden doors! Or isn't it the right period for those delightfully romantic things? Stephen, you're a bit of an archaeologist! – set your sister's mind at rest!'

Stephen cast him a smouldering look. 'I've no idea,' he said shortly.

'Oh yes, you love to hide your light under a bushel!' Joseph chaffed him. 'Trying to make us believe you're an ignoramus! But he's no such thing, Mrs Dean, I assure you! In fact – but don't say I told you so! – he's a very clever fellow!'

This piece of facetiousness made Stephen scowl more threateningly than ever, and inspired Mottisfont to say in a meaning tone: 'I'm sure if there is a secret way into Nat's room, Stephen would know of it.'

'I don't know of it,' Stephen replied.

Joseph's arch smile vanished. 'What do you mean by that, Edgar?'

Mottisfont raised his brows. 'Merely that it's common knowledge that Stephen shared Nat's love for the house. I naturally thought he must know its secrets, if there are any. You're very touchy, Joe!'

'I don't care for that kind of edged remark,' Joseph said. 'I know this is a period of great strain, Edgar, but we all feel it, some of us perhaps more than you. The least we can do is to refrain from saying malicious things about each other!'

'I wish you'd rid your mind of the belief that I need your support!' said Stephen.

Mrs Dean, realising that a woman's soothing influence was called for, raised a finger, and said: 'Now, Stevie! I shall have to say what I used to say to my girlies, when they were children: birds in their little nests agree!'

'Actually, I believe they don't,' remarked Roydon.

If anything had been needed to set the seal to Mrs Dean's disapproval of an impecunious playwright, this would have been enough. Perceiving a faintly purple tinge in her cheeks, Mr Blyth looked at his watch, and said with rare prudence that he must not miss his train.

This had the effect of breaking up the luncheon-party. Joseph bustled off to see whether the car had been brought round to the door; Mrs Dean said that what the young people wanted was a brisk walk to blow away the cobwebs, adding that Valerie must get Stephen to show her round the estate. Valerie, however, protested that it was a foul day, and filthily cold, and that she thought walking in the snow a lousy form of amusement anyway; and by the time her mother had taken her to task over her choice of adjectives, Stephen had vanished, and Paula had marched Roydon off to discuss the forthcoming production of *Wormwood*.

Mrs Dean had contemplated an afternoon spent *tête-à-tête* with Maud, who, though obviously stupid, must, she thought, be able to enlighten her on various aspects of the Herriard inheritance; but this plan was frustrated at the outset by Maud herself. She said that she expected Mrs Dean would like to lie down after her tiring morning.

'Oh dear me, no!' declared Mrs Dean, with her wide smile. 'I always say that nothing ever tires me!'

'You are very fortunate,' said Maud, gathering up her knitting and a magazine. 'I can never do without my afternoon rest.'

So that was that. Maud went away, and Mrs Dean was left to the company of Edgar Mottisfont.

Mathilda, meanwhile, had joined Stephen in the billiard-room, and was playing a hundred up with him, in a not very serious fashion. As she chalked the tip of her cue, she said: 'Far be it from me to interfere with your simple pleasures, Stephen, but I wish you'd let up on Joe. He means so well, you know.'

'You damn him in four words. Go in off the red.'

'Leave me to play my own game in my own way,' said Mathilda severely, but following out his instruction. 'I find Joe rather pathetic.'

'Broken-down actor. I don't.'

'Thanks, we can all see that. I wish I knew why he is so fond of you.'

'I can honestly say that I have never, at any time, given him cause to be. If you hit the white fairly fine, and with plenty of running side –'

'Be quiet! Why do you dislike him so much?'

'Damned old hypocrite!' said Stephen savagely. 'You haven't had to watch him oiling up to Uncle Nat for two years.'

'If he'd done you out of your inheritance you might have grounds for your dislike,' she pointed out.

'Blast him! I wish he had!'

She could not help laughing. 'Yes, I can understand that, but really it's very unworthy of you, Stephen! I admit that his manner is against him, and that his habit of calling you an old bear gives you some excuse for feeling homicidal, but to give him his due he's treated you remarkably white. I imagine Nat would never have drawn up that will without his persuasion.'

Stephen slammed the red ball into one of the bottom pockets, and straightened his back. 'Being, as he would tell you, cross-grained, so much altruism nauseates me!'

She retrieved the red ball from the pocket, and spotted it for him. 'That's unreasonable. If he were entirely hypocritical, he'd have tried to induce Nat to leave all his money to him.'

He hunched one impatient shoulder. 'The fellow's always acting. I can't stand him.'

'Well, he can't help that: it's second nature. He sees himself in so many rôles. Did you hear him sustaining a spirited dialogue with your prospective mother-in-law?'

'Did I not!' he said, grinning. 'Did *you* hear him relying on my good nature to keep him out of the workhouse?'

'No, I missed that. Are he and Maud going to remain on at Lexham?'

'Not if I know it!'

'I have an idea Maud doesn't want to,' she remarked. 'What do you make of her, Stephen?'

'You can't make anything of a vacuum. Yes, what is it?'

This last sentence was addressed to Sturry, who had entered the room, and was waiting by the door, with a look of patient resignation on his face.

'I beg your pardon, sir, but I thought you would wish to be informed that the Inspector from Scotland Yard is here again.'

'Does he want me?'

'As to that, sir, I could not take it upon myself to say.'

'Well, all right! you can go,' Stephen said irritably.

Sturry bowed. 'Very good, sir. And perhaps I should mention that I have reason to believe that the Inspector Abstracted one of the foreign daggers from this room, and took it away with him before lunch.'

Having delivered himself of this piece of news, he waited to see what the effect of it would be. On the whole, it was disappointing, for although Stephen glanced quickly up at the wall above the fireplace, he made no remark. Mathilda too said nothing, but she did give a faint shudder. Sturry was obliged to be satisfied with this. He withdrew to his own domain, there to regale the more favoured amongst his colleagues with a highly coloured and wholly fictitious account of Mr Stephen's reactions to his disclosure.

For a minute or two after he had left the room, neither Stephen nor Mathilda spoke. Stephen seemed to be intent only on the game. He finished his break, rather sooner than Mathilda had expected, for he was a good player, leaving her an easy shot.

'Curious that it should be so beastly to know the actual weapon,' she said lightly. 'I suppose we ought to have suspected those daggers.'

He made no reply. She saw that the lowering look had descended on his brow again, and found herself once more wishing that she could fathom the workings of his queer, secluded mind. She said abruptly: 'Who picked up your cigarette-case?'

'I've no idea.'

'I know Valerie had it, but no one could suspect her of having gone into Nat's room, much less of having stabbed him. And the more I think of it the more incredible it seems that anyone else should have taken the thing upstairs.'

'Uncle Nat himself,' he suggested.

'I don't believe it. Why should he?'

'To give it back to me, presumably.'

'He wasn't in that kind of a mood when I last saw him,' Mathilda replied. 'Besides, if Valerie really left it on the table by her chair, it would have been perfectly safe there. I'll tell you what, Stephen: there's some mystery attached to that case, and for the life of me I can't solve it.'

He seemed disinclined to discuss the matter, merely giving a kind of grunt, and turning away to mark up her score on the board. A horrid little doubt seized her: what did she know of him, after all? It might be proved that he was in financial difficulties; he might have taken Nat's threats seriously; he might cherish large desires, which he kept hidden in his own guarded heart, and which only a fortune could put within his reach. There was a streak of cruelty in him, of hard ruthlessness, which was betrayed in his treatment of Joseph, and of Valerie. He didn't care how much he hurt people: he had suffered hurt himself, and that was reason enough for his unkindness to others.

Then her mind veered sharply to the consideration of his sister, and she began to feel that she was living in a world of nightmare. Would Paula be capable of stabbing to death an old man who loved her, merely for the sake of a part in an unknown dramatist's play? She didn't know. She had no clue to Paula either; she only knew her as an urgent, unbalanced young woman, always obsessed by the idea of the moment.

Yes, but although Paula had been seen at Nat's door, how had she contrived to get into a locked room, or, more difficult still, to lock it behind her? Mathilda had no knowledge of the means by which doors could be locked and unlocked from the wrong side, but she knew that there were such means. Yet it seemed unlikely that Paula could have employed any of them, for how could she have acquired the necessary tools?

This led to the question, were they in it together, this odd, frustrated brother and sister? It was too diabolical: Mathilda shied away from the thought, miscued, and straightened herself, saying with a breathless laugh: 'Oh, damn! You'll run out now!'

'I wonder what that Scotland Yard man's up to?' Stephen said restlessly.

'Trying to trace the person who handled that dagger,' she suggested.

'He won't do that.'

The confidence in his tone startled her. She looked at him almost fearfully. 'How do you know?'

He bent over the table for his shot. 'Bound to have wiped the finger-prints off it,' he replied. 'Any fool would know enough to do that.'

'I suppose so,' she agreed. 'Whoever did it was pretty ingenious. How could anyone have got into the room? And how was the door locked afterwards?'

'Hell, how should I know?'

'How should any of us know?' she asked. 'This isn't a house full of crooks! We're all ordinary people!'

'Even though one of us is an assassin,' interjected Stephen.

'True; but although I'm not personally acquainted with any assassins –'

'You are personally acquainted with one assassin, my girl.' He saw how quickly her eyes leaped to his, and added, with one of his mocking smiles: 'Since someone in this house is one.'

'Of course,' she said. 'It's rather hard to realise that. I was going to say that I've always imagined that a murderer could be quite an ordinary person. Not like a confirmed thief, I mean. Which of us, for instance, would know how to open a locked door? Of course, I suppose one of the servants might be a crook, but I don't quite see why any of them should have wanted to murder Nat. They none of them gain anything by his death.'

'True,' said Stephen uncommunicatively.

'Could there be anything in that idea of Valerie's? Is there a sliding panel, or anything of that kind?'

'I've never heard of it.'

She sighed: 'No; it does seem rather fantastic. But someone got into that room somehow, and if it wasn't through the door or the window, how was it?'

'Go and present Valerie's idea to the Inspector. It ought to go with a swing, I should think.'

There was a satirical note in his voice, but the Inspector, recalling the oak wainscoting at the Manor, had already thought of this solution, and was occupied at that very moment in sounding the panels in Nathaniel's room. Since two of the walls were outside ones, and one separated the room merely from the bathroom, only that abutting on to the upper hall called for investigation. The closest scrutiny and the most careful tapping revealed nothing; nor was there any moulding to hide a convenient spring to release a sliding panel. The Inspector was forced to abandon this line of investigation, and to turn his attention to the windows.

These were casement, with leaded panes. They fitted closely into their frames, which were also of lead, the windows overlapping the frames sufficiently to make it impossible for the fastenings to be moved by a knife inserted from outside. They were at no great distance from the ground, and the Inspector judged that a gardener's ladder would be amply tall enough to reach them. They were built out into a square bay, with a window-seat running beneath them, the whole being hidden at night by long curtains, drawn right across the bay. The Inspector went thoughtfully downstairs in search of Joseph.

The footman volunteered to find him, and ushered Hemingway into the morning-room. Here Joseph soon joined him, an expression of anxiety on his rubicund countenance.

'Sorry to disturb you again, sir, but I'd like a little talk with you, if you don't mind,' said Hemingway.

'Of course! Can you tell me anything yet, Inspector? This suspense is dreadful! I expect you're inured to this sort of thing, but to me the thought that my brother's murderer may be in the house even now is horrible! Haven't you discovered *anything*?'

'Yes, I've discovered the weapon that killed your brother,' replied Hemingway.

Joseph grasped a chairback. 'Where? Please don't keep anything from me!'

'Over the fireplace in the billiard-room,' said Hemingway.

Joseph blinked at him. 'Over – ?'

'One of a pair of knives stuck up beside a stag's head.'

'Oh! Yes, yes, I know! Then you didn't discover it in anyone's possession!'

'No; I'm sorry to say that I didn't,' said Hemingway.

'*Sorry?* Oh! Yes, I expect you must be. Of course! Only one can't help shrinking from the thought that this ghastly thing might be brought home to someone one knows – one of one's guests, perhaps!'

'That's all very well, sir, but you want to know who killed your brother, don't you?' said Hemingway reasonably.

Joseph threw him a wan smile. 'Alas, it isn't as simple as that, Inspector! Part of me yearns to bring my brother's murderer to justice; but the other part – the incurably sentimental, foolish part! – dreads the inevitable discovery! You assure me that the murder was committed by someone staying in the house. Consider what frightful possibilities this must imply! The servants? I cannot think it. My nephew? my niece? The very thought revolts one! A lifelong friend, then? An innocent child, hardly out of the schoolroom? Or an unfortunate young playwright, struggling gallantly to fulfil his destiny? How can I want any of these to be found guilty of murder? Ah, you think me a muddleheaded old fool! I pray for your sake you may never go through the mental torment I writhe under now!'

The Inspector fully appreciated the fine delivery of these lines, but he was shrewd enough to realise that with the slightest encouragement Joseph would turn a police investigation into a drama centred about his own ebullient personality, and he took a firm line at once, saying prosaically: 'Well, that's very kind of you, sir, I'm sure. But it's no use us arguing about who did it, or who you don't think could have done it. All I want you to do, if you'll be so good, is to cast your mind back to what happened when you and your nephew entered Mr Herriard's room after the murder had been committed.'

Joseph shuddered, and covered his eyes with his hand. 'No, no, I cannot!'

'Well, you can have a try, can't you, sir?' said Hemingway, as one humouring a child. 'After all, it only happened yesterday.'

Joseph let his hand fall. 'Only – yesterday! Is it possible? Yet it seems as though a lifetime had passed between then and now!'

'You can take it from me that it hasn't,' said Hemingway, somewhat tartly. 'Now, when you went upstairs to call your brother down to dinner, you found his valet outside the room, didn't you?'

'Yes. It was he who gave me the first premonition that something was wrong. He told me that he could get no answer to his knocking, that the door was locked. I remember that so distinctly – so appallingly distinctly!'

'And what did you do then?'

Joseph sat down on a chair, and rested one elbow on the table. 'What did I do? I tried the door, I called to my brother. There was no answer. I was alarmed. Oh, I had no suspicion of the dreadful truth! I thought he had been taken ill, fainted, perhaps. I called to Stephen.'

'Why did you want him particularly, sir?'

Joseph made one of his little vague gestures. 'I don't know. Instinctively one wishes for support. I knew too that my strength would not avail to break down the door. He and Ford burst open the lock, and I saw my poor brother, lying on the floor, as though asleep.'

'What happened next, sir?'

'How can I tell you?' Joseph demanded. 'One's heart stood still! The world span round. I suppose one knew then, intuitively, that the worst had happened. Yet one clutched at a frail thread of hope!'

'And what about Mr Stephen, sir? Did he clutch at it too?' asked Hemingway, unimpressed.

'I think he must have. I recall that he sent Ford at once for some brandy. But an instant later he had realised the awful truth. As I dropped to my knees beside my brother's body, he said: "He's dead."'

'It didn't take him long to discover that, did it?'

'I think his instinct must have told him. I could not at first believe it! I told Stephen to fetch a mirror. I *would* not believe it. But Stephen was right. Only he thought that Nat had had a stroke. He said so at once, and for a few moments I was mercifully permitted to think so too.'

'And then?'

'Let me think!' Joseph begged, pressing his fingers to his temples. 'It was all a nightmare. It seemed – it still seems – unreal, fantastic! Ford came back with the brandy. Stephen took it from him, sent him away to ring up the doctor.'

'Oh!' said Hemingway. 'So Ford was hardly in the room at all, what with one thing and another?'

'No. There was nothing he could do. While he was still in the room I had made my ghastly discovery. I was glad to hear Stephen telling him to leave us. At that moment I could not bear that a stranger should be present.'

'What discovery was this, sir?'

'I found that there was blood upon my hand!' said Joseph, in shuddering accents. 'Blood from my brother's coat, where I had touched it! Then, and then only, I saw the little rent, and knew that Nat had been done to death!'

The Inspector, quite carried away by all this, murmured, 'Foully done to death,' before he could stop himself, and then had to cough, to smother his own words. Fortunately, Joseph did not seem to have heard him. Lost in admiration of his own performance, thought Hemingway, wondering how a man who was undoubtedly unnerved could yet dramatise his emotions with such morbid relish.

'Very upsetting for you, sir,' he said. 'I'm sure I don't want to make you dwell on it more than I need, but I do want to know what happened when Ford had gone off to ring up the doctor. When Inspector Colwall came here he found the doors locked, and all the windows shut.'

'Yes, that's what makes it so inexplicable!' said Joseph.

'Did you yourself see that the windows were shut, sir?'

'No, but my nephew did. I was too overcome! It had not even occurred to me that we ought to look at the windows. But my nephew was a tower of strength! He thought of everything, just as one had always felt sure he would, in an emergency!'

'He looked at the windows, did he, sir?'

'Yes, I'm sure he did. I seem to remember that he walked over to them, putting back the curtains. Ah yes! and he asked me if I realised that the doors were both locked, and all the windows shut!'

'You didn't look at the windows yourself, sir?'

'No, why should I? It was enough that one of us had seen that they were shut. I didn't care: I think I was half-stunned!'

'Then I take it that it wasn't you who ascertained that the bathroom door also was locked?'

'Stephen saw to everything,' Joseph said. 'I don't know where I should have been without him!'

The Inspector, who was fast coming to the conclusion that no one at the Manor, including himself, would be in the present predicament but for the activities of Mr Stephen Herriard, agreed heartily, and said that he would not trouble Joseph any further. Then he went off to find Ford.

Ford, twice questioned by the police already, was nervous, and inclined to be sullen, but when he was asked if he had tried the bathroom door in his efforts to get into his master's room on the previous evening, he replied readily that he had, and that it had been locked. Paula, interrupted in the middle of a discussion with Roydon on the advisability of rewriting a part of the second act of *Wormwood*, said impatiently that of course she had not tried the bathroom door, and turned her shoulder to the Inspector. He withdrew, and was fortunate enough to encounter Valerie, crossing the hall towards the staircase. She gave a start on seeing him, and eyed him with mingled trepidation and suspicion.

'You're just the person I was waiting to see, miss,' said Hemingway pleasantly.

'It's no use: I don't know anything about it!' Valerie assured him.

'No, I don't suppose you do,' he replied, surprising her exactly as he had meant to. 'It isn't likely a young lady like you would be mixed up in a murder.'

She gave an audible sigh of relief, but still watched him suspiciously. Correctly divining that she would not object to familiarity, if it were judiciously mixed with flattery, he said: 'If you don't mind my saying so, miss, it's a bit of a surprise to me to find anyone like you here.'

She responded instinctively. 'I don't know what you mean! Do you think I'm so extraordinary?'

'Well, it isn't every day of the week that I meet a beautiful young lady, all in the way of business,' said the Inspector unblushingly.

She giggled. 'Good gracious, I didn't know that policemen paid one compliments!'

'They don't often get the chance,' answered Hemingway. 'You're engaged to be married to Mr Stephen Herriard, aren't you, miss?'

This brought a cloud to her brow. 'Yes, in a way I suppose I am,' she admitted.

'You don't sound very sure about it!' he said, cocking an intelligent eyebrow.

'Oh, I don't know! Only I never thought a thing like this would happen. It sort of changes everything. Besides, I utterly loathe this house, and Stephen adores it.'

'Ah, he's got a taste for antiques, I daresay!' said Hemingway, very much on the alert.

'Well, I think it's all completely deathly, and I simply won't be buried alive here.'

'I wouldn't take on about that, if I were you, miss. I expect Mr Stephen will be only too glad to live wherever you want.'

She opened her eyes at him. 'Stephen? Oh gosh, no! He's the most foully obstinate person I've ever met! You simply can't move him once he's made up his mind.'

'I can see you've been having a pretty uncomfortable time,' said Hemingway sympathetically.

Valerie, already smarting from the sense of her own wrongs, and further aggrieved by her parent's attitude of bracing common sense, was only too glad to have found someone to whom she could unburden herself. She drew nearer to the Inspector, saying: 'Well, I have. I mean, I'm one of those frightfully highly-strung people. I just can't help it!'

The Inspector now had a certain cue, and responded instantly to it. 'I could see at a glance that you were a mass of nerves,' he said brazenly.

'That's just it!' said Valerie, immensely gratified. 'Only none of these people realise it, or care a damn about anyone but themselves. Except Uncle Joe: he's nice; and I rather like Willoughby Roydon too. But the rest have been simply foul to me.'

'Jealous, I wouldn't wonder,' nodded Hemingway.

She laughed, and patted her curls. 'Well, I can't imagine why they should be! Besides, Stephen's as bad as the others. Worse if anything!'

'Perhaps he's jealous too, in a different way. I know I would be.'

'Oh, Stephen's not in the least like that!' she said, brushing the suggestion aside. 'He doesn't care what I do. No, honestly doesn't! In fact, he doesn't behave as though he cared for me a bit, in spite of having brought me down here to get to know his uncle. Of course, I oughtn't to be saying this to you,' she added, with a belated recollection of their respective positions.

'You don't want to worry about what you say to me,' said the Inspector. 'I daresay it's a relief to be able to get it off your chest. I can see you've been through a lot.'

'I must say, I think you're frightfully decent!' she said. 'It's been sheer *hell* ever since Mr Herriard was killed; and that other Inspector was too brutal for words! – I mean, absolute Third Degree! All about Stephen's filthy cigarette-case!'

'I'm surprised at Inspector Colwall!' said Hemingway truthfully. 'What did you happen to do with the case, if you don't mind my asking?'

'I didn't do anything with it. I mean, I simply took a cig-arette out of it, and put the case down on the table in the drawing-room, and never thought of it again until all this loathsome fuss started. Only Mathilda Clare – who's quite the ugliest woman I've ever laid eyes on – practically accused me of having had the case all the time. Of course, she was simply out to protect Stephen, Willoughby says. Because Mr Mottisfont said, who was likely to pick up the case except Stephen himself? which is perfectly true, of course. And if you ask me, Mathilda Clare deliberately tried to throw the blame on to me because she knew Mr Herriard didn't like me!'

'Now that's a thing I can't believe!' said the Inspector gallantly.

'No; but he didn't, all the same. In fact, that's why I came here. It was my mother's idea, actually, that I should have a chance to get to know Mr Herriard. Personally I think he was a woman-hater.'

'If he didn't like you, he must have been. Didn't he want his nephew to marry you?'

'Well, no, as a matter of fact he didn't. Only I feel sure I could have got round him, if only Stephen hadn't made everything worse by annoying him over something or other.

Of course, that's just *like* Stephen! He would! I did try to make him be sensible, because Uncle Joe dropped a word in my ear, but it was no use.'

'What sort of a word?' asked Hemingway.

'Oh, about Mr Herriard's will! He didn't actually say everything was left to Stephen, but I sort of gathered it.'

'I see. Did you tell Mr Stephen?'

'Yes; but he only laughed, and said he didn't care.'

'He seems to be a difficult kind of young man to have to do with,' said Hemingway.

She sighed. 'Yes, and I don't really – Oh well! Only I wish I'd never come here!'

'I'm sure I don't blame you,' said Hemingway, wondering how to get rid of her, now that he had extracted the information he wanted.

This problem was solved for him by Mathilda, who came into the hall at that moment from the passage leading to the billiard-room. Valerie flushed guiltily, and ran upstairs. Mathilda's cool, shrewd gaze followed her, and returned, enquiringly, to the Inspector's face. 'I seem to have scared Miss Dean,' she remarked, strolling across the hall towards him. 'Was she being indiscreet?'

He was slightly taken aback, but hid it creditably. 'Not at all. We've just been having a pleasant little chat,' he replied.

'I can readily imagine it,' Mathilda said.

Thirteen

WHILE THESE VARIOUS ENCOUNTERS HAD BEEN TAKING place, Mrs Dean had been usefully employing her time in conversation with Edgar Mottisfont. Like Valerie, he too was suffering from a sense of wrong, and it did not take Mrs Dean long to induce him to confide in her. The picture he painted of Stephen's character was not flattering, nor did his account of the circumstances leading up to the murder lead her to look hopefully upon the outcome of the police investigation. Really, the case seemed to be much blacker against Stephen than Joseph's story had led her to suppose. She began to look rather thoughtful, and when Mottisfont told her bluntly that if he were Valerie's father he would not let her marry such a fellow, she said vaguely that nothing had been settled, and Valerie was full young to be thinking of marriage.

It was really a very awkward situation for a conscientious parent to find herself in. No one had informed her of the actual size of Nathaniel Herriard's fortune, but she assumed it to be considerable, and it was a well-known fact that rich young men were not easily encountered in these hard times. But if Stephen should be convicted of having murdered his uncle, as seemed to be all too probable, the money would never come to him, and Valerie would reap nothing but the obvious disadvantages of having been betrothed to a murderer.

While Mottisfont talked, and her own lips formed civil replies, her mind was busy over the problem. Not even to herself would she admit that she had jockeyed Stephen into proposing to Valerie, but she had not spent several hours at Lexham without realising that his brief infatuation had worn itself out. She would not put it beyond Stephen, she thought, to jilt Valerie, if he were not first arrested for murder. The trouble was that although Valerie was as pretty as a picture she lacked the intelligence to hold the interest of a man of Stephen's type. Mrs Dean faced that truth unflinchingly. The child hadn't enough sense to see on which side her bread was buttered. She demanded flattery, and assiduous attentions, and if she did not get them from her betrothed she would be quite capable of throwing him over in a fit of pique.

When, shortly before teatime, Mrs Dean went up to her room, she was still thinking deeply; and when she heard her daughter's voice raised outside her door in an exchange of badinage with Roydon, she called her into the room, and asked her if she had been with Stephen all the afternoon.

'No, and I don't know where he is,' said Valerie, studying her reflection in the mirror. 'Probably getting off with Mathilda Clare. I've had a simply foul afternoon, doing nothing, except for listening to Paula reciting bits of Willoughby's play, and talking to the Inspector.'

'Talking to the Inspector? What did he want?' demanded Mrs Dean.

'Oh, nothing much! I must say, he was a lot more human than I'd expected. I mean, he absolutely understood about the hateful position I'm in.'

'Did he ask you any questions?'

'Yes, about what I did with Stephen's mouldy cigarette-case, but not a bit like that other one did. He didn't disbelieve every word I said, for instance, or try to bully me.'

Mrs Dean at once felt that Inspector Hemingway was a man to beware of, and set herself to discover just what information he had extracted from her daughter. By the time she had elicited from Valerie a more or less accurate description of her conversation with him, she was looking more thoughtful than ever. There could be no doubt that the Inspector's suspicions were centred on Stephen, and, taking the terms of Nathaniel Herriard's will and the damning evidence of the cigarette-case into account, there seemed to be little chance of his escaping arrest.

She was a woman who prided herself on her power of making quick decisions, and she made one now. 'You know, darling,' she said, 'I don't feel quite at ease about this engagement of yours.'

Valerie stopped decorating her mouth to stare in astonishment at her parent. 'Why, it was you who were so keen on it!' she exclaimed.

'That was when I thought it was going to be for your happiness,' said Mrs Dean firmly. 'All Mother cares about is her little girl's happiness.'

'Well, I must say I've utterly gone off the idea of marrying him,' said Valerie. 'I mean, money isn't everything, is it? and anyway, I always did like Jerry Tintern better than Stephen, and you can't call him a *pauper*, can you? Only I don't see how I can get out of it now, do you? It would look rather lousy of me if I broke it off just when he's in a jam, and it would be bound to get about, and people might think I was a foul sort of person.'

This admirable, if inelegantly phrased, piece of reasoning almost led Mrs Dean to hope that her daughter was acquiring a modicum of sense. She said briskly: 'No, pet, it would never do for you to jilt Stephen; but I am sure he will understand if I explain to him that as things are now I cannot allow my baby to be engaged to him. After all, he *is* a gentleman!'

'You mean,' said Valerie, slowly assimilating the gist of this, 'that I can put the blame on to you?'

'There's no question of blame, my pet,' said Mrs Dean, abandoning hope of dawning intelligence in her first-born. 'Merely Mother doesn't feel it right for you to be engaged to a man under a cloud.'

'Oh, Mummy, how *too* Victorian! I don't mind about that part of it! The point is I don't really *like* Stephen, and I know he'd be a hellish husband.'

'Now, you know Mother doesn't like to hear that sort of talk!' said Mrs Dean repressively. 'Just give Mother your ring, and leave it to her to do what's best!'

Valerie drew the ring somewhat regretfully from her finger, remarking with a sigh that she supposed she would have to return it to Stephen. 'I rather loathe giving it back,' she said. 'If he says he'd like me to keep it, can I, Mummy?'

'One of these days I hope my little girl will have many rings, just as fine as this one,' said Mrs Dean, firmly removing the ring from Valerie's grasp.

Upon this elevated note the conversation came to an end. Valerie returned to the all-absorbing task of reddening her lips, and Mrs Dean sallied forth in search of Stephen.

She was prepared to expend both tact and eloquence upon her delicate mission, but she found that neither was required. Stephen, looking almost benign, met her more than half-way. He wholeheartedly agreed that under the existing circumstances he had no right to expect a sensitive child to go on being engaged to him, cheerfully pocketed the ring, and acquiesced with maddening readiness in Mrs Dean's hope that he and Valerie might remain good friends. In fact, he went further, announcing with a bland smile that he would be a brother to Valerie, a remark which convinced Mrs Dean that, fortune or no fortune, he would have made a deplorable son-in-law.

She was not the woman to give way to indignation when it would clearly serve her interests better to control her spleen, and as she was obliged to remain at Lexham until the police saw fit to give Valerie permission to go, she came down to tea with her invincible smile on her lips, and only a steely light in her eyes to betray her inner feelings.

The news of the broken engagement had by that time spread through the house, and was received by the several members of the party with varying degrees of interest and emotion. Mottisfont said that he did not blame the girl; Roydon, who, in spite of writing grimly realistic plays, was a romantic at heart, was inclined to deplore such disloyalty in one so lovely; Paula said indifferently that she had never expected the engagement to come to anything; Maud greeted the tidings with apathy; Mathilda warmly congratulated Stephen; and Joseph, rising as usual to the occasion, insisted on regarding his nephew as one whose brave spirit had been shattered by treachery. When he encountered Stephen, he went towards him, and clasped one of his hands before Stephen could frustrate him, and said in a voice deepened by emotion: 'My boy, what can I say to you?'

Stephen rightly understood the question to be rhetorical, and made no reply; and after squeezing his hand in a very feeling way, Joseph said: 'She was never worthy of you! Nothing one can say can bring you comfort *now*, my poor boy, but you will find, as so many, many of us have found before you, that Time proves itself a great healer.'

'Thanks very much,' said Stephen, 'but you are wasting your sympathy. In your own parlance, Valerie and I are agreed that we were never suited to one another.'

If he entertained any hope of thus quelling Joseph's embarrassing partisanship he was speedily disillusioned, for Joseph at once smote him lightly on the shoulder, saying: 'Ah, that's the way to take it, old man! Chin up!'

Mathilda, who was a witness of this scene, feared that Stephen would either be sick or fell his uncle to the ground, so she hastily intervened, saying that she thought both parties ought to be congratulated on their escape.

Joseph was quite equal to dealing with Mathilda. He smiled at her, and said gently: 'Ah, Tilda, there speaks one who has not known what it is to suffer!'

'Oh, do for God's sake put a sock in it!' said Stephen, in a sudden explosion of wrath.

Joseph was not in the least offended. 'I know, old chap, I know!' he said. 'One cannot bear to have one's wounds touched. Well! We must forget that there ever was a Valerie, and turn our faces to the morrow.'

'As far as I am concerned,' said Stephen, 'the morrow will probably see my arrest on a charge of murder.'

Mathilda found herself quite unable to speak, so horrible was it to hear her unexpressed fear put crudely into words. Joseph, however, said: 'Hush, my boy! You are overwrought, and no wonder! We are not even going to consider such a frightful possibility.'

'I have not had your advantages. I have not spent a lifetime learning to bury my head in the sand,' said Stephen brutally.

Mathilda found her voice. 'What makes you think that, Stephen? How can the police know who murdered Nat until they discover how anyone contrived to get into that room?'

'You'd better ask them,' he replied. 'I shall be hanged by my own cigarette-case and Uncle Nat's will. Jolly, isn't it?'

'I will not believe it!' Joseph said. 'The police aren't such fools! It isn't possible that they could arrest you on such slender evidence!'

'Do you call a hundred and sixty thousand pounds or so slender evidence?' demanded Stephen. 'I should call it a pretty strong motive myself.'

'You knew nothing of that! Over and over again I've told them so!'

'Yes, my dear uncle, and if you had not previously told Valerie that I was the heir I daresay the Inspector might listen to you. As it is, I have just sustained a cross-examination which leaves me with the conviction that not one word I said was believed.'

'But you are still at large,' Mathilda pointed out.

'Being given rope to hang myself, no doubt.'

'Don't be absurd!' she said sharply. 'I don't believe any of this! They'll have to find out how Nat was murdered behind locked doors before they can arrest you!'

'From the trend of the questions put to me,' said Stephen, 'I infer that I entered the room through one of the windows.'

'But they were all shut!' Joseph said.

'A pity I didn't get you to verify that fact,' said Stephen. 'The police have only my word for it.'

Joseph smote his brow with one clenched fist. 'Fool that I was! But I never thought – never dreamed – Oh, if one could but look into the future!'

Maud, who came into the room at that moment, overheard this wish, and said: 'I am sure it would be very uncomfortable. I once had my fortune told, and I remember that it quite upset me, for I was told that I should travel far across the seas, and I am not at all fond of foreign travel, besides suffering from sea-sickness.'

'Well, that is a very valuable contribution to our discussion,' said Stephen, with suspicious amiability. 'On the whole I prefer the Empress.'

At the sound of this word Maud's placid countenance clouded over a little. 'It is a most extraordinary thing where that book can have got to,' she said. 'I am sure I have looked everywhere. However, the Inspector, who is a very civil and obliging man, has promised to keep his eyes open, so I daresay it will turn up.'

Mathilda's ever-lively sense of humour overcame the gloom induced by Stephen's morbid prognostications, and she burst out laughing. 'You haven't really told the Inspector to look for your book, have you?' she asked.

'After all, dear,' said Maud mildly, 'it is a detective's business to look for things.'

'My dear, you shouldn't have taken up the Inspector's time with such a trivial matter!' said Joseph, a little shocked. 'You must remember that he is engaged on far, far more important work.'

Maud was unimpressed. Seating herself in her accustomed chair by the fire, she said: 'I do not think that it will do anyone any good to know who killed Nat, Joe, for as he is dead there is nothing to be done about it, and it will only create a great deal of unpleasantness to pry into the affair. Like Hamlet,' she added. 'Simply upsetting things. But the *Life of the Empress of Austria* belongs to the lending library, and if it is lost I shall be obliged to pay for it. Besides, I hadn't finished it.'

This was so unanswerable that beyond begging her, rather feebly, not to waste the Inspector's time in such an absurd fashion, Joseph allowed the matter to drop. The rest of the party began to assemble in the room for tea, and everyone's attention was diverted from the major anxiety of the moment by Valerie's simple but effective way of carrying off what could only be regarded as a difficult situation. Surveying the company with cornflower blue eyes of limpid innocence, she said: 'Oh, I say, has Stephen told you that we're unengaged? I expect you probably think it's fairly lousy of me to call it off just because the police think he murdered Mr Herriard, but actually it wasn't me at all, but Mummy. And anyway, we'd completely gone off each other, so it doesn't matter.' She smiled in a dazzling way, and added: 'The funny thing is that I like him much more now that we're not engaged. As a matter of fact, I was loathing him before.'

'Both sentiments, let me tell you, are entirely reciprocated,' said Stephen, grinning.

'I'm afraid,' said Joseph sadly, 'that you haven't learnt yet, my dear, what it is to care for someone.'

'Oh gosh, yes, I have. I've been simply madly in love often and often. I mean, utterly over at the knees!' Valerie told him.

'Young people nowadays,' pronounced Maud, 'do not attach so much importance to engagements as they did when I was a girl. It was considered to be very fast to be engaged more than once.'

'How quaint!' said Valerie. 'I expect I shall be engaged dozens of times.'

'Well, when you get married, I will give you a handsome wedding present,' said Stephen.

'Oh, Stephen, you are a lamb! I do hope they don't go and convict you!' said Valerie, with a naïve sincerity that robbed her words of offence.

She then settled down to flirt with Roydon, in which

agreeable occupation she was uninterrupted until her mother came into the room, radiating brassy good-humour and a somewhat overpowering scent.

It took a strong-minded hostess to prevent Mrs Dean usurping the centre of the stage, and as Maud was not strong-minded, and refused to look upon herself as a hostess, that forceful lady at once assumed the functions of a doyenne. Seating herself in a commanding position, she encouraged conversation, directed people to suitable chairs, and suggested that in spite of the tragic circumstances under which they had all met they ought to try to get up a few quiet games to play after dinner. 'After all, we must not forget that it is Christmas Day, must we?' she asked, with a toothy smile. 'It does no good to sit and brood. Of course, there must not be anything rowdy, but I know some very good paper-games which I know you young people will enjoy.'

This suggestion smote everyone dumb with dismay. Paula was the first to recover the power of speech, and said, with her customary forthrightness: 'I abominate paper-games!'

'Lots of people say that to begin with,' said Mrs Dean, 'but they always join in in the end.'

'Mummy's absolutely marvellous at organising things,' explained Valerie, quite unnecessarily.

'No one,' said Paula, tossing back her hair, 'has ever yet succeeded in organising me!'

'If you were one of my girlies,' said Mrs Dean archly, 'I should tell you not to be a silly child.'

The expression on Paula's face was so murderous that

Mathilda, feeling that she had borne enough emotional stress during the past twenty-four hours, got up, on a murmured excuse, and left the room. She had barely crossed the hall when she was joined by Stephen.

'Did your nerve fail you?' he asked.

'Badly. She behaves like a professional hostess at a hydro.'

'Paula will settle her hash,' he said indifferently.

'I've no doubt she will, but I'm not feeling strong enough to watch the encounter. Let it be understood, Stephen, that if there are to be Quiet Games I shall go to bed with a headache!'

'There won't be. I may not be master in this house for very long, but I am tonight.'

'I make all allowances for your perverted sense of humour, but I wish you wouldn't talk like that!'

He laughed, and pushed open the library door. 'Go in. I'll send for tea here.'

'Do you think we ought to? It'll look rather rude.'

'Who cares?'

'Not you, I know. I'm past caring.'

He rang the bell, regarding her with an expression in his eyes hard to read. 'Can't you take it, Mathilda?'

'Not much more of it, at all events. There's a good deal to be said for Maud's point of view. This kind of thing is sheer hell. What did that policeman say to you?'

He shrugged. 'Just what you'd expect. I rather fancy that he came to me fresh from an illuminating chat with Sturry.'

'I detest Sturry!' Mathilda said.

'Yes, so do I. If I get out of this imbroglio, I shall sack

him. I caught him with his ear to the keyhole yesterday, when Uncle was favouring us with his opinion of Roydon's play. He won't forgive that in a hurry.'

'I've always thought he was the sort who'd stab you in –' She broke off short, colour flooding her face.

'Go on!' he encouraged her. 'Why not say it? My withers will be wholly unwrung.'

She shook her head. 'Can't. It's too grim. I suppose Sturry gave the Inspector a garbled account of what Nat said to you.'

'Not much need to garble it. Uncle said he wouldn't have me in the house again.'

'We all know he didn't mean it!'

'You try telling that to Inspector Hemingway. I think I'm for it, Mathilda.'

She said, with sudden, irrational fury: 'It's a judgment on you for being such a silly, damned fool! Why the hell do you have to quarrel with everyone?'

He did not reply, for the footman came in just then, in answer to the bell. He gave a brief order for tea to be brought to them, and for a moment or two after the man had gone away stood staring down into the fire.

'Sorry!' Mathilda said, surprised to find herself oddly shaken. 'I didn't mean it.'

He gave a short laugh, as though he thought what she had said to be of no account. 'Do you think I did it, Mathilda?'

She took a cigarette from her case, and lit it. 'In spite of all the evidence piling up against you, no.'

'Thanks. I imagine you're practically alone in your opinion.'

'There is one person besides myself who knows you didn't do it.'

'Very neat,' he approved. 'Ever been watched by the police? Most unnerving performance.'

'I suppose we're all under supervision.'

'Not you, my girl: you're not a suspect.'

She decided that her cigarette tasted of garbage, and pitched it into the fire. 'It's you who can't take it, Stephen. You talk as though Black Maria was at the door, but I maintain that the police haven't got enough evidence even to detain you.'

'I hope you're right. I may add in passing that if I'd wanted to murder anyone I'd have started on Joe.'

'I admit that he's a bit trying. It's a depressing reflection that overflowing affection should arouse the worst in normal breasts. If you come to think of it, it's all his fault. The ghastly result of good intentions! If it hadn't been for Joseph, I don't suppose Nat would have made his will, and I'm sure he wouldn't have thrown this party. But for him, Valerie wouldn't have known that you were the heir, and Roydon wouldn't have maddened Nat by reading his play to him. Trivial circumstances, whose appalling consequences no one could have foreseen, and all, by a fiendish turn of fate, combining to put you on the spot! It's enough to make one turn cynic! But they haven't anything like enough on you yet, Stephen!'

Oddly enough, Inspector Hemingway had reached much the same conclusion, although he did not share Mathilda's unreasoning faith in Stephen. He had found him very much on his guard during his brief interview with him, and although he realised that this was understandable, it did not prejudice him in Stephen's favour. Stephen was reticent, and he weighed every question before answering it. The Inspector, not a bad judge of men, thought him remarkably cold-blooded, and was inclined to the opinion that of all the ill-assorted persons gathered together at Lexham, he was the one most capable of committing murder. But in spite of what certain of his superiors thought an unholy predilection for all the more turgid aspects of psychology, the Inspector was far too good a detective to allow his theories to run away with him. He might (and very often did) talk in the airiest fashion, advancing opinions wholly unsubstantiated by fact, and indulging flights of the purest fantasy, but anyone rash enough to assume from this that he had attained his present position more by luck than solid worth would very soon have discovered that appearances, in Inspector Hemingway's case, were more than ordinarily deceptive.

He was profoundly dissatisfied with Stephen Herriard's evidence; he mistrusted the valet; and, in spite of being so far unable to prove it, still suspected that there might have been collusion between the two. With this in his mind, he had already dispatched Ford's finger-prints to London, and had obtained from him the names and addresses of his last two employers. These had been given so readily that it did not seem probable that this line of investigation would prove fruitful, but the Inspector was not the man to leave any stone unturned.

Questioned, Ford had stated that he had firmly shut all the

windows in Nathaniel's bedroom on the previous afternoon, adding that he did so every day, the late Mr Herriard having had no opinion of the beneficial effects of night-air. This was borne out by Sturry, who said that while he was quite unable to account for the activities of the valet or any of the housemaids, it was his rule to close all the sitting-room windows at five o'clock precisely throughout the winter. 'Such,' he said, 'being the late Mr Herriard's orders.'

Hemingway accepted this statement, but bore in mind two distinct possibilities. If the valet had been Stephen's partner in crime, no reliance could be placed on the truth of his statements; if he had not, Stephen, who had left the drawing-room some time before Nathaniel, might have been able to have gone up to his uncle's room unobserved, and to have opened one of the windows there.

That it would have been impossible for anyone to have climbed up to the windows without a ladder, the Inspector had already ascertained; it now remained to discover whether there was a ladder upon the premises.

He had told his Sergeant to find this out for him, and by the time he had brought his interview with Stephen to an end, Ware was waiting to report the result of his investigations to him.

'There's nothing of that sort in the house, sir: only a pair of housemaid's steps, and they wouldn't have reached, not anywhere near. But I snooped around the outhouses, like you told me, and I found one all right.'

'Good!' said Hemingway. 'Where is it?'

'Well, that's it, sir: I can't get at it. There's a disused

stable near the garage, and the chauffeur tells me that the head-gardener keeps his tools in it, and such-like. Only he went off home yesterday at noon, and he won't be back till the day after tomorrow, and no one seems to know where he keeps the key. There's a small window, but that's bolted. I saw the ladder when I peered through it.'

'He's probably got a special place for the key: most of them have.'

'Yes, but I've hunted high and low, and I can't find it. The chauffeur thinks he keeps it on him, because he won't have people borrowing his tools, nor getting at the apples he's got stored in the loft.'

'Where does he live?' Hemingway asked.

'Village about two miles to the north of this place.'

'Seems to me I'd better have another little chat with the Lord High Everything Else.'

Correctly deducing that his superior was referring to the butler, Sergeant Ware at once went off to find this personage. But Sturry, when informed that Inspector Hemingway had need, for unspecified reasons, of a ladder, was not helpful. He said that he regretted there was nothing of that nature in the house. His tone did not imply regret, but rather an unexplained contempt of ladders.

The Inspector knew well that Sturry was trying to put him in his place, but beyond thinking that he would have made a perfect stage-butler, and had clearly missed his vocation, he paid little heed to his forbidding manner. 'I didn't suppose you had one in the house,' he said, 'but I've seen an orchard, and my reasoning powers, which are a lot keener than you might think, tell me that there must be a ladder somewhere on the estate.'

'No doubt you would be referring to Mr Galloway's ladder,' said Sturry tolerantly.

'No doubt!' said the Inspector. 'Who's Mr Galloway?'

'Mr Galloway, Inspector, is the head-gardener, a very respectable man. The late Mr Herriard employed two under-gardeners, and a Boy, but they, if I may say so, Do Not Count.'

The Inspector gathered from the gracious bestowal of a title upon the head-gardener that he was a person to be reckoned with, but being wholly uninterested in the niceties of social distinctions in the servants' hall he said disrespectfully: 'Well, where does this Galloway keep his ladder?'

'Mr Galloway,' said Sturry, impersonating an iceberg, 'keeps all his tools under Lock and Key. Being Scotch,' he added, in explanation of this idiosyncrasy.

'Where does he keep the key?'

'I am sure I could not take it upon myself to say,' said Sturry repressively.

'Well, what happens when he's off duty, and someone wants a pair of clippers, or something?'

'That,' said Sturry, 'is an eventuality which Mr Galloway does not Hold With, him being very particular, and Gentlemen notoriously careless with tools.'

The Inspector eyed him smboulderingly. 'Did you ever read the story of the frog that burst?' he asked ominously.

'No,' replied Sturry, meeting his gaze squarely.

'You should,' said the Inspector.

Sturry bowed. 'I will bear it in mind, if ever I should have the leisure,' he said, and withdrew in what Hemingway was forced to admit was good order.

'I'm sorry for you, my lad,' Hemingway told his Sergeant. 'It looks as though you'll have to go and call on this Galloway, and find out if he's got the key of the stables on him. I'll have a look at the place first, though.'

Together they left the house, and made their way through the melting snow to the stableyard. A modern garage had been built on one side of this, with a flat above it for the chauffeur; at right angles to it a rather dilapidated building presented forbiddingly shut doors, and small windows, thickly coated on the inside with dust and cobwebs. One permitted a peep into an old harness-room; another enabled the Inspector to obtain a restricted view into the stable, and there, sure enough, laid flat along one wall, was a substantial ladder, quite tall enough to reach to the upper storey of the Manor.

Having felt under the door-sill, looked for a cache under the penthouse roof, and even searched two potting-sheds and a row of glass-houses, the Inspector, baulked in his quest for the key, looked carefully at the stable-window. It was a small sash-window, and although it would not have required any great degree of skill to have slipped a knife-blade between the two halves, and to have forced back the bolt, even the most confirmed optimist must have rejected this solution. It was plain that the window had not been opened for many a long day. Had any further proof than the undisturbed dust been needed, it would have been found in the presence, on the interior, of a cobweb of great size and antiquity.

'And now,' said Hemingway, 'you'll find that the gardener's had the key on him ever since midday yesterday. A fine sort of case this is!'

The Sergeant said, hiding a grin: 'I thought you liked them difficult, sir.'

'So I do,' retorted Hemingway. 'But I like something you can catch hold of! Here, every time I think I've got a line on something, it slips out of my grasp like something in a bad dream. If there's a sliding panel in that room, I'll eat my hat; I'd go to the stake no one tampered with that door-key; and now it begins to look as though the window wasn't touched either. It's witchcraft, that's what it is, or else I'm getting past my job.'

'It is a fair stinker,' agreed the Sergeant. 'No use thinking about the chimney, I suppose?' The Inspector cast him a look of dislike.

'Or the roof,' suggested the Sergeant. 'There are attics above the bedrooms, and there are dormer-windows. Could a chap have got through the one over Mr Herriard's room, and reached the window below?'

'No, he couldn't,' said Hemingway crossly. 'I've already looked into that, which just shows you the sort of state I'm getting into, for a more fatheaded idea I've never met. You'll have to go off and interview this gardener, but you can drop me at the station first.'

'All right, sir. But I can't help feeling that I shall find he's had the key all the time.'

'If you didn't, I should very likely drop down in a fit,' responded Hemingway.

They drove back to the police-station in depressed silence. Hemingway alighted there and went into the building. He found Inspector Colwall fortifying himself with very strong tea, and thankfully accepted a cup of this beverage.

'How are you getting on?' asked Colwall.

'I'm not,' replied Hemingway frankly. 'It reminds me of the Hampton Court maze more than of anything else. It doesn't matter what path you take: you always find your-self back at the starting-point again. Seems to me I'm trying to catch up with a regular Houdini. Handcuffs and locked chests would be nothing to this bird.'

'I don't mind telling you I was glad to hand over the case to you,' confided Colwall. 'Of course, detection isn't, prop-erly speaking, my line.'

'It won't be mine by the time I'm through with this,' said Hemingway, sipping his tea. 'Here I've got no fewer than four hot suspects, and three possibles, all without alibis, and most of them with life-size motives, and I'm damned if I see my way to bringing it home to any of them.'

'Four hot suspects?' said Colwall, working it out in his mind.

'Young Stephen, his sister, Mottisfont, and Roydon,' said Hemingway.

'You don't reckon the fair young lady could have done it?'

'I've put her in as a possible, but I wouldn't lay a penny on her myself.'

'Who are your other possibles, if you don't mind my asking?'

'The valet and the butler.'

Colwall seemed a little surprised. 'Sturry? What makes you think he might have had a hand in it?'

'Vulgar prejudice,' responded Hemingway promptly. 'He handed me a very dirty look this afternoon, so very likely I'll pin the murder on to him, if all else fails.'

Inspector Colwall recognised a joke, and laughed. 'You do talk!' he said. 'Myself, I had a hunch it was young Herriard. Ugly-tempered chap, he is.'

'He's got the biggest motive,' conceded Hemingway. 'Though murder isn't always committed for high stakes, mind you! Not by a long chalk. There's young Roydon, wanting money to back his play.'

'Yes; I went into that before you came down, but it seemed to me a bit unlikely. Of course, Miss Herriard could have done it, I suppose. I shouldn't think she'd stick at much.'

'I'm quite willing to arrest her, or Mottisfont, if you'll just tell me how either of them got into the room,' said Hemingway.

Colwall shook his head. 'It's a mystery, that's what it is. You don't think the old lady had anything to do with it, do you?'

'What, Mrs Joseph Herriard?' exclaimed Hemingway. 'Talk about far-fetched ideas! No, I don't. What would she do it for?'

'I don't know,' Colwall confessed. 'It only struck me that she hadn't got an alibi either, and neither you nor I ever suspected her at all. I suppose she might have had a motive.'

'Well, it hasn't come to light,' said Hemingway. 'What's more, it won't help me if it does. I've plenty of motives already, not to mention one damaging piece of evidence, in the shape of Stephen's cigarette-case. Not that it's any good to me, unless I can discover *how* the murder was committed.'

'No, I see that,' agreed Colwall. 'And there was a good deal of uncertainty about the cigarette-case, wasn't there? Seems young Herriard had lent it to Miss Dean, and anyone might have picked it up.'

'Yes, I've heard all that, but I don't think much of it,' said Hemingway. 'People don't go picking up cigarette-cases that don't belong to them: at least, not in that kind of society, they don't. It was identified as Stephen's, and he owned it; and I haven't so far heard that anyone else's finger-prints were found on it.'

'No, they weren't,' said Colwall. 'There weren't any finger-prints on it at all, as I remember.'

Hemingway set down his cup and saucer. 'There must have been *some* prints! Do you mean they were too blurred to be identified?'

Colwall stroked his chin. 'I remember seeing the report on it last night, and I'm pretty certain it said there were no marks on it at all.'

'Look here!' Hemingway said. 'On their own admissions, young Herriard and Miss Dean both handled that case! Are you telling me they left no prints?'

'Well, I'm only repeating what was on the report,' said Colwall defensively.

'And you saw that report, and never thought to mention that there was a curious circumstance attached to it! Why wasn't I shown it?'

'You could have seen it if you'd asked for it. There

just wasn't anything to it. We'd established that the case belonged to Stephen Herriard; the experts didn't find any finger-prints on it; and that's all there was to it.'

'I should have known better than to have taken anyone's word for it!' said Hemingway in bitter accents. 'Didn't it strike you that it was highly unusual, not to say suspicious, that there weren't any finger-prints on the case?'

'I suppose,' said Colwall, whose brain moved slowly, 'it must have been wiped.'

'Yes,' retorted Hemingway. 'That's just what I suppose, too! And if you think young Herriard dropped it, all accidental-like, first taking the precaution of wiping his finger-prints off it, all I can say is that you've got a nice, unsuspicious nature, Inspector!'

Colwall bridled a little at this, but as the inference of Hemingway's words sank into his mind, he flushed, and said: 'Of course, it's your business to spot things like that. I don't deny that what with one thing and another it just didn't occur to me that it was funny, not finding any prints on the case. Couldn't have got wiped off in young Herriard's pocket, could they?'

'No,' Hemingway said positively. 'They might have got a bit blurred, but you'd be bound to find some trace. Ever cleaned a bit of silver, and tried to get your own finger-prints off it? It takes some elbow-grease, I give you my word.'

'That's right, it does,' nodded Colwall. 'Same with brass-work. But this was a gold case. One of those large, flat ones, with a monogram on it.'

'I ought to have had a look at it in the first place,'

Hemingway said, annoyed with himself. 'Come on! Let's go and have a talk with your expert!'

But no expert was needed to convince him that the cigarette-case had been wiped clean of all betraying marks. It was still held in the crutch in which it had been placed upon discovery, and its smooth golden surface showed no smudge or blemish.

'Might just have come out of the shop,' grunted Colwall. 'Looks like new, barring a few scratches. Well, none of my men destroyed any prints, that I will answer for!'

'I don't suppose they did. This case has been carefully polished.'

'Well, that has torn it!' Colwall said. 'Do you figure it was planted in the room to throw suspicion on young Herriard?'

'That's about the size of it,' said Hemingway. 'One thing's certain: he didn't leave it there himself.'

'Then it pretty well clears him,' said Colwall regretfully. 'I must say, I thought all along it was him. A bit disheartening, isn't it?'

'I wouldn't say that,' replied Hemingway, who seemed to have recovered his cheerfulness. 'In fact, I regard it as a highly promising development.'

'I don't see how you make that out,' said Colwall, staring at him.

'I was beginning to think that this was going to be the one case where the guilty party didn't once slip up. Well, he did slip up,' said Hemingway, pointing an accusing finger at the cigarette-case. 'Just like a lot of others before him, trying to be too clever. The way I see it, planting this case was an unrehearsed effect. If he'd thought of it when he worked out the rest of his details, I daresay he'd have arranged for us to have found Stephen's finger-prints on the case. We can take it that Miss Dean's testimony was correct: she put the case down on the table at her elbow. Our unknown friend saw it there, and thought it would make a nice piece of evidence against Stephen. He picked it up, and probably slipped it into his pocket, either forgetting not to touch it with his bare hand, or not having the time to handle it through his handkerchief. But when it came to planting it, he wasn't the man to forget that he mustn't leave any prints on it, so he polished it good and hard. Well, it's restored my belief in the fundamental stupidity of murderers. They all slip up sooner or later, though I admit this one's sharper than most.'

'That's all very well, but I don't see how it's going to help you.'

'You never know,' said Hemingway, lifting the cigarette-case out of the crutch, and regarding it with a loving eye.

'What are you going to do with it?' asked Colwall.

'Give it back to young Stephen,' replied Hemingway coolly.

'Give it back to him?'

'That's right. Then I'll sit back to watch results.'

'What results do you expect?' asked Colwall, out of his depth.

'I haven't the least idea, but I hope they'll be helpful, because this case is beginning to get on my nerves.'

'Yes, but I don't see –'

'Up to now,' interrupted Hemingway, 'it must have been obvious to one and all that the hot favourite for the nine-o'clock-in-the-morning stakes was young Herriard, which was a highly satisfactory state of affairs for the real murderer, not calling for any exertion on his part. All he had to do was to lie low, and act natural. Well, now I'm going to let it be deduced that I don't fancy Stephen after all. Throwing the lead, so to speak. If I know anything about the minds of murderers, I ought to get some interesting reactions.'

Fourteen

THE SERGEANT, RETURNING FROM HIS VISIT TO Galloway's cottage, came in with a face of settled gloom, and told his chief that it was just as they had feared. Galloway had taken the key home with him, and it was even now hanging up on one of the hooks of his kitchen-dresser.

'So it doesn't look as though our man got in through the window at all,' he said. 'I suppose you haven't discovered anything fresh, have you, sir?'

When he learned what the Inspector had, in fact, discovered, he was interested, but inclined to agree with Colwall's view, that beyond eliminating one of the suspects it was not likely to prove to be of much use. 'If you ask me, sir, the man who did this job isn't the sort to lose his head,' he said.

'I didn't ask you, but you're quite at liberty to have your own opinions,' said Hemingway tartly. 'I've already had the satisfaction of proving that he can make a silly mistake: well, now we'll see if he can't be rattled a bit. So far he's had it all his own way: he shall have it my way, and see how he likes it.'

'Are you going up there again this evening, sir?'

'No,' said Hemingway, 'I'm not. This is where I put in a bit of quiet thinking, while that lot up at the Manor wonders what I'm up to. There's nothing like suspense for shaking a man's nerve.'

The Sergeant grinned. 'You wouldn't, I suppose, be thinking of the turkey they've got roasting at the Blue Dog, would you, Chief?' he ventured.

'If I have any insubordinate talk from you,' said Hemingway severely, 'I'll give you a job to do up at the Manor that'll keep you there till midnight. It wasn't the turkey I was thinking of at all.'

'I'm sorry!' apologised the Sergeant.

'So I should think. It was the ham,' said Hemingway.

The inmates of the Manor were, accordingly, left to their own devices, if not to peace. Peace did not flourish under the same roof as Mrs Dean, and by the time she had bullied Joseph, Mottisfont, Roydon, and her own daughter into playing paper-games, and had driven both the young Herriards and Mathilda into taking refuge in the billiard-room, an atmosphere of even greater unrest pervaded the household.

Christmas dinner, with all the associations which turkey and plum-pudding conjured up, inspired Maud to remark that she wished Nathaniel had not been murdered at such an awkward time, because although it seemed almost heartless to eat Christmas fare there was nothing else to be done, since there it was, and would only go bad if left. She added that they had better not set light to the pudding this year;

and Sturry, approving this decree, added his mite towards the drive for sobriety by removing the sprig of holly from the pudding.

Everyone went to bed early, but no one looked next morning as though the long night's rest had been of much benefit. Mottisfont said several times that he could not think what the police were hanging fire for, by which observation he was understood to mean that he thought Stephen ought by this time to have been in the County gaol. Valerie said that she had hardly closed her eyes all night, on account of the ghastly dreams which had haunted her. Roydon looked pale, and wondered audibly when the police would allow them all to go home.

Breakfast was not served until nine o'clock, and before anyone had reached the toast-and-marmalade stage, Sturry entered, rather in the manner of a Greek chorus, to announce the arrival of doom in the person of Inspector Hemingway. The Inspector, he said with relish, would like to have a Word with Mr Stephen.

The inside of Mathilda's mouth felt dry suddenly and the muscles of her throat unpleasantly constricted. Joseph drew in his breath sharply.

'He might have let me finish my breakfast,' said Stephen, laying down his napkin. 'Where is he?'

'I showed the Inspector into the library, sir.'

'All right,' Stephen said, and got up.

Paula thrust back her chair, and rose, in one of her jerky, impetuous movements. 'I'm coming with you!' she said abruptly.

'Get on with your breakfast: I don't want you,' Stephen said.

'I don't care a damn what you want!' she said. 'I'm your sister, aren't I?'

He took her by the shoulders, and thrust her into her chair again. 'Get this, and get it good!' he said roughly. 'You're to keep out of this!'

'There's no more reason for him to suspect you than me! Uncle accused me of wanting to murder him, not you!'

'You keep your misguided trap shut,' said Stephen. 'You're a good kid, but boneheaded.' His sardonic gaze flickered over the other members of the house-party, taking in Joseph's look of misery, Mathilda's white rigidity, the thinly-veiled satisfaction in Mottisfont's eyes, the relief in Roydon's. He gave a short laugh, and went out.

The Inspector was looking out of the window when Stephen entered the room, but he turned at the sound of the opening door, and said: 'Good-morning, sir. Looks like the thaw has set in properly.'

Stephen eyed him in some surprise. 'How true!' he said. 'Shall we cut the cackle?'

'Just as you like, sir,' Hemingway replied, 'What I came for was to give you back your cigarette-case.'

He held it out as he spoke, and had the satisfaction of seeing that he had succeeded in startling this uncomfortably brusque young man.

'What the hell!' Stephen demanded, his eyes lifting from the case to Hemingway's face. 'What kind of a damned silly joke do you imagine you're playing?'

'Oh, I'm not playing any joke!' responded Hemingway.

Stephen took the case, and stood holding it, 'I thought this was your most valuable piece of evidence?'

'Yes, so did I,' agreed Hemingway. 'And I don't mind admitting that it's very disappointing for me to have to give it up. But there it is! A detective's life is one long disappointment.'

Stephen smiled, in spite of himself. 'Would you like to explain a little? Why do I get my case back? I thought you had me booked for the County gaol.'

'I don't deny that's about what I thought too,' Hemingway admitted. 'And if only you'd left a finger-print or two on that case of yours, I daresay I'd have had the handcuffs on you by now.'

'Didn't I?' said Stephen, frowning in a little perplexity.

'Not one!' said Hemingway cheerfully.

Stephen glanced down at the case, turning it over in his hand. 'I don't seem to be very bright this morning. Am I to infer that my finger-prints had been wiped off?'

'That's about the size of it, sir.'

He encountered a very hard, direct look. 'Mind telling me if there were any finger-prints on it at all?'

'No,' said Hemingway; 'I'm not one to make a lot of mystery. There weren't any.'

'Oh!' said Stephen. Again he looked at the case, his frown deepening. 'A plant, in fact!'

The Inspector fixed him with a bright, enquiring gaze. 'Got any ideas about that, sir?'

Stephen slipped the case into his pocket. After a moment's hesitation, he said: 'No. Not immediately. When I *do* get an idea –'

'Now, you don't want to go taking the law into your own hands, sir!' interrupted the Inspector. 'What do you think I'm here for? If you know anything, you tell me, and don't start any rough-houses on your own, because though I can't say I'd blame you, I'd have to take you up for disturbing the peace, which, properly speaking, isn't my line of business at all.'

Stephen laughed. 'What would you do if you found that someone had tried to do the dirty on you to this tune, Inspector?'

The Inspector coughed. 'Report it to the proper quarters,' he said firmly.

'Well, I'd rather rub his damned nose in it!' said Stephen.

'As long as you don't go farther than that, I've no objection,' said Hemingway, with the utmost cordiality. 'And if you want a bit of advice, don't go leaving any more of your things about! It puts highly unsuitable ideas into people's heads, besides setting the police off on wild-goose chases, which is a very reprehensible thing to do, let me tell you!'

'Sorry!' Stephen said. 'Very annoying for you: you must now be back exactly where you started.'

'Oh, I wouldn't say that!' Hemingway replied.

'No, I don't suppose you would: not to me, at any rate. If it's all the same to you, I'd now like to go back and finish my breakfast.'

The Inspector signifying that it was quite the same to him, Stephen returned to the dining-room, where the rest of the party was still seated at the table. Every face turned towards him as he entered, some asking a mute, anxious question, some avidly curious. He sat down in his place, and told Sturry, who had found an excuse to come back into the room, to bring him some fresh coffee.

'Gosh, I quite thought you'd be under arrest by now!' said Valerie, putting into words what everyone else had been thinking.

'I know you did, my pretty one,' Stephen answered.

'What happened, Stephen?' Mathilda asked him, in a low voice.

He favoured her with one of his twisted smiles, and took out his cigarette-case, and opened it, and selected a cigarette. As he tapped it on the case, every eye became riveted on it. Mathilda looked quickly up at him, but saw that he was not paying any heed to her, but rather letting his challenging gaze wander round the table, dwelling for a moment on Roydon's face, travelling on to Mottisfont's, and resting there for a moment.

Again it was Valerie who found her voice first. 'Why, that's your cigarette-case! The one the police took!'

'As you say.'

'Do you mean they've given it back to you?' asked Roydon, in bewildered accents.

'Yes,' said Stephen. 'They've given it back to me.'

'I never heard of such a thing!' exclaimed Mottisfont. 'It can't be the same case! You're trying to pull our legs, for some reason best known to yourself! The police would never have relinquished the real case!'

'I'd give it to you to look at, only that the Inspector warned me to be more careful with my property in future,' said Stephen. 'When I leave my things about, they have an odd way of transporting themselves – isn't that nicely put? – into quite different parts of the house.'

'What the devil do you mean by that?' demanded Mottisfont, half-rising from his chair.

'Do you believe in poltergeists?' asked Stephen, still smiling, but not very pleasantly.

'Stephen!' Joseph said, his voice trembling with emotion. 'Stephen, my boy! Does it mean that they don't suspect you after all?'

'Oh, I gather that I am wholly cleared!' Stephen replied.

It was not to be expected that Joseph would greet such news as this in a restrained manner. He bounced up out of his chair, and came round the table to clasp his nephew's hands. 'I knew it all along!' he said. 'Thank God, thank God! Stephen, old boy, you don't know what a weight it is off my mind! If – if the worst had happened, it would have been my fault! Oh yes, it would! I know that. My dear, dear boy, if it were not for that one great sorrow hanging over us, this would be a red-letter day indeed!'

'But I don't understand!' Paula said. 'Why are you in the clear? Are you sure it isn't some kind of a trick?'

'No, there's no trick about it,' he answered.

'Why should there be a trick?' Joseph said. 'Can it be that *you* doubted Stephen's innocence? Your own brother!'

'How did it come to be in Uncle's room?' Paula asked, disregarding Joseph. 'You may as well tell us, Stephen! We must all have guessed!'

'Clever, aren't you? I'm a child in these matters myself, but I gathered from the Inspector that in his opinion it was planted there.'

Paula flashed a look round the table. 'Yes! That has always stood out a mile!' she declared.

'I don't believe it!' Mottisfont said, reddening angrily. 'That's what you chose to hint from the outset, but I consider it a monstrous suggestion! Are you daring to imply that one of us murdered Nat, and tried to fasten the crime onto you?'

'It's so obvious, isn't it?' Stephen said.

Joseph, who had been looking from one to the other, with an expression of almost pathetic bewilderment on his face, was so shocked that his voice sank quite three tones. 'It *couldn't* be true!' he uttered. 'It's too infamous! too terrible for words! It was Nat himself who took your case up! It must have been! Good God, Stephen, you couldn't believe a thing like that of anyone here – staying with us – invited here to – No, I tell you! It's too horrible!'

At any other time Mathilda could have laughed to see Joseph's roseate illusions so grotesquely shattered. As it was, the situation confronting them seemed to her to be too grim to admit of laughter. She said in a studiedly cool voice: 'What gave the Inspector this idea?'

'The absence of any finger-prints on the case,' answered Stephen.

It took a minute or two for the company to assimilate the meaning of this, nor did it seem from Maud's blank face, or from Joseph's puzzled frown, that its full import had been universally realised. But Roydon had realised it, and he said:

'It's the meanest thing I ever heard of! I hope you don't imagine that any of *us* would stoop so low?'

'I don't know at all,' said Stephen. 'I shall leave it to the Inspector to find out.'

'That's all very well!' struck in Paula. 'But if there were no finger-prints on the case, how is he to find out?'

'He seems quite optimistic about it,' Stephen replied.

It now seemed good to Valerie to declare in agitated tones that she could see what they were all getting at, but if anyone thought she had killed Mr Herriard they were wrong, and she wished that she had never been born.

Mrs Dean, whom Stephen's announcement had cast into a mood of bitter reflection, was forced to wrench herself from her thoughts to frustrate an attempt on her daughter's part to break into strong hysterics. Valerie cast herself on the scented bosom in a storm of noisy tears, saying that everyone had been beastly to her ever since she had set foot in this beastly house; and, with the exception of Joseph, who fussed about in an agitated and useless manner, the rest of the party lost no time in dispersing.

Maud told Mathilda, on her placid way to the morning-room, that she thought it was a good thing Stephen was not going to marry Valerie, since she seemed an uncontrolled girl, not at all likely to make him comfortable. She seemed to have no comment to make on the new and lurid light thrown on to Nathaniel's murder, and Mathilda was unable to resist the impulse to ask her if she had grasped the meaning of what Stephen had told them.

'Oh yes!' Maud said. 'I always thought something like that must have happened.'

Mathilda fairly gasped. 'You thought it? You never said so!'

'No, dear. I make a point of not interfering,' Maud explained.

'I must confess it hadn't occurred to me that any of us could be quite so base!' Mathilda said.

Maud's face was quite inscrutable. 'Hadn't it?' she said, uninterested and unsurprised.

Valerie, meanwhile, had been led upstairs, gustily sobbing, by her mother, who vented her own annoyance at having so precipitately jettisoned Stephen on Joseph, telling him that although she was never one to make trouble she felt bound to say that her girlie had been treated at Lexham with a total lack of consideration.

Poor Joseph was stricken to incoherence by the injustice of this accusation, and could only gaze after the matron in shocked bewilderment. He was recalled to a sense of his surroundings by the entrance of the servants, to clear the table, and went away to look for someone with whom he could discuss the latest developments of the case.

He was fortunate enough to find Mathilda, and at once took her by the arm and led her off to the library. 'I'm getting old, Tilda – too old for this kind of thing!' he told her. 'Yesterday I thought that if only the cloud could be lifted from Stephen, nothing else would matter. Today I find myself with a possibility so horrible – Tilda, *who*, I ask of you, could bear such a grudge against Stephen?'

'It might not be so much a question of a grudge as an instinct of pure *sauve qui peut*,' she pointed out.

'No one but a snake in the grass could do such a thing!'

She said dryly: 'Anyone capable of stabbing his host in the back would surely be quite capable of throwing the blame on to someone else.'

'Mottisfont?' he said. 'Roydon? Paula? How can you think such a thing of any one of them?'

'I envy you your touching faith in human nature, Joe.'

She was sorry, however, that she had said that, for Joseph took it as a cue, and said in a very noble way that he thanked God he had got faith in human nature. While she did not doubt that his trusting disposition had sustained a severe shock, and could even be sorry for his distress, she was in no mood to tolerate play-acting, and soon shook him off. Between his relief at knowing Stephen to be exonerated and his dread of discovering that his beloved niece, or his old friend Mottisfont, or poor young Roydon was the guilty party, he was so spiritually torn that the optimism of a lifetime seemed to be in danger of deserting him.

Of the three people now, presumably, equally suspected of having murdered Nathaniel, Paula showed the most coolness. She discussed, with a cold-bloodedness worthy of Stephen, the chances of Roydon's having done the deed, and said that, speaking from an artistic point of view, she hoped that he hadn't, since he had a Future before him.

'I imagine I must be out of the running,' she said, walking about the room in her usual restless way. 'No one could suspect me of trying to throw the blame on to my own brother! If there had been any bequests to them in Uncle's will, I should have said that one of the servants had done it, probably Ford; but as it is they none of them had the slightest motive.' She turned her brilliant gaze upon Mathilda, adding impulsively: 'If one wasn't a suspect oneself, wouldn't it be *interesting*, Mathilda? I think I could actually enjoy it!'

'Neither Joe nor I are suspects, and I can assure you we aren't enjoying it!' said Mathilda.

'Oh, Joe! He's an escapist,' said Paula scornfully. 'But you! You ought to be able to appreciate a situation that shows us all up in the raw!'

'I don't think,' said Mathilda, 'that I care for seeing my friends in the raw.'

'I believe that this experience will be very valuable to me as an artist,' said Paula.

But Mathilda had never felt less inclined to listen to a dissertation on the benefits of experience to an actress, and she very rudely told Paula to try it on the dog.

It was now nearly eleven o'clock, and all the discomforts of a morning spent in a country house with nothing to do were being suffered by Lexham's unwilling guests. Outside, a grey sky and melting snow offered little inducement to would-be walkers; inside, a general hush brooded over the house; and everyone was uneasily aware of Scotland Yard's presence. While suspicion had centred upon Stephen, everyone else had been ready to discuss the murder in all its aspects; now that Stephen had apparently been exonerated, and the field was left open for his successor, an uneasy shrinking from all mention of the crime was visible in everyone except Paula. Even Mrs Dean did not speak of it. She joined Maud in the morning-room presently, and, without receiving the slightest encouragement, favoured her with the story of her life, not omitting a list of her unsuccessful suitors, the personal idiosyncrasies of the late Mr Dean, and all the more repulsive details of two confinements and a miscarriage.

Roydon, who had mumbled something about getting a breath of fresh air, had gone up to his room, on leaving the breakfast-table, thus making an enemy of the second housemaid, who had only just made his bed, and wanted to bring in the vacuum-cleaner. Being a well-trained servant, she withdrew, and went off to complain bitterly to the head-housemaid about visitors who knew no better than to come up before they were wanted, putting one all behind with one's work. The head-housemaid said it was funny, him coming up to his room at this hour; and on these meagre grounds a rumour spread rapidly through the servants' quarters that that Mr Roydon was looking ever so queer, and behaving so strange that no one wouldn't be surprised to hear that it was him all the time who had done in the master.

All this made a very agreeable subject for conversation at the eleven-o'clock gathering for tea in the kitchen and the hall; and when one of the under-gardeners joined the kitchen-party with a trug of vegetables for the cook, he was able to enliven the discussion by recounting that it was a funny thing, them speaking of young Roydon like they were, for he had himself just seen him going off for a walk on his own. He had come upon him down by the potting-sheds and the manure-heap, and he had somehow thought it was queer, finding him there, and Roydon hadn't half started when he had seen him coming round the corner of the shed. Adjured by two housemaids, one tweeny, and the kitchenmaid, all with their eyes popping out of their heads, to continue this exciting narrative, he said that it was his belief young Roydon had been burning something in the incinerator, because he had been standing close to it, for one thing, and for another he'd take his oath he'd heard someone putting the lid on it.

This was so well received, with such delighted shudders from the tweeny, accompanied by exclamations of Go on, you never! from the two housemaids, that the gardener at once recalled that he had thought Roydon's manner queer-like at the time, and said to himself that that bloke wasn't up to no good, messing about where he had no call to be.

In due course, an echo of these highly-coloured recollections reached Inspector Hemingway's ears, by way of his Sergeant, who, by means of a little flattery, had managed to put himself on excellent terms with the female part of the staff. The Inspector, with the simple intention of unnerving the household, was spending the morning pervading the house with a notebook, a foot-rule, and an abstracted frown. His mysterious investigations were in themselves entirely valueless, but succeeded in making everyone but Maud and Mrs Dean profoundly uneasy. Mottisfont, for instance, took instant and querulous objection to his presence in his room, and fidgeted about the house, complaining to anyone who could be got to listen to him of the unwarrantable licence taken by the police. Breaking in upon the two ladies in the morning-room, he tried to enlist their support, but Mrs Dean said that she was sure she had no secrets to hide; and Maud merely expressed the hope that in the course of his investigations the Inspector might find her missing book.

The Inspector had not found the book, and, if the truth were told, he had begun to share the opinions of the rest of the household with regard to it. Since he had first encountered Maud, he had met her five times, and had on each occasion not only to sustain an account of when and where she last remembered to have had the book in her hand, but anecdotes culled from it as well. He darkly suspected that it had been hidden by the other members of the house-party, and told his Sergeant that he didn't blame them.

When the kitchen-gossip about Roydon was reported to him, he was not inclined to set much store by it, but he told the Sergeant that he had better keep a sharp eye on Roydon.

The Sergeant did more than this: he went down the garden to the potting-sheds, and took a look at the incinerator.

This was a large galvanised-iron cylinder, mounted on short legs, and with a chimney running up the centre, through the lid. In theory, by setting light to a little paper, stuffed into the gap left between the sides of the cylinder and its base, any amount of refuse, thrown in the top, would be slowly consumed into the finest ash. In practice, the fire thus kindled usually died out before half the contents of the cylinder had been burnt, so that what came out at the bottom was not ash, but charred and very often revolting scraps of refuse.

From the languid wisp of smoke arising from the chimney, the Sergeant correctly assumed that the fire was burning but sluggishly this morning. He lifted the lid, and found that the incinerator had been stuffed full of kitchen-waste. Somewhere below the unappetising surface the fire, judging by the smell, was smouldering. The Sergeant looked round for a handy stick, and, finding one, began to poke about amongst the rubbish. After turning over some grape-fruit rinds, a collection of grocers' bags, cartons, and egg-boxes, the outer leaves of about six cabbages, and the contents of several wastepaper-baskets, his stick dug up a blood-stained handkerchief, obviously thrust down beneath the litter, but as yet untouched by the fire.

The Sergeant, who had really not expected to find anything of interest in the incinerator, could scarcely believe his eyes. If he had not been a very methodical young man, he would have hurried back to the house immediately, to lay his find before his superior, so excited did he feel. For the handkerchief was not only generously splashed with blood: it also bore an embroidered R in one corner. It was dirty, from its contact with the kitchen-refuse, but the Sergeant felt no repulsion at handling it. He shook some used tea-leaves out of it, folded it carefully, and put it in his pocket. Then he went on poking amongst the rubbish until he had satisfied himself that no other gruesome relics were hidden in the noisome depths of the incinerator. To make quite sure, he raked the bottom out, not, judging by the smother of ash, before it was time. The fire was not burning evenly, and from one side of the cylinder some charred remnants fell out amongst the ash, including a scorched and blackened book. The boards of this had been consumed, and the outer pages crumbled away when touched, but when the Sergeant, idly curious, stirred what remained with his stick, he saw that although the edges had been burnt the inner pages were still perfectly legible. *Coronation in Hungary*, he read, across the top of one right-hand page. Opposite, heading the left page, he saw in the same capital italics: *Empress Elizabeth.*

A grin dispelled the natural solemnity of his countenance. He picked up the sad remnant of Maud's book, and took it back to the house with him, to show to the Inspector.

Confronted with the handkerchief, Hemingway showed a disappointing absence of enthusiasm.

'It's Roydon's all right,' the Sergeant pointed out. 'It's got his initial in the corner, and he's the only R in the house, sir. The blood's dry, too, you see.'

'There's enough of it, at all events,' remarked Hemingway, dispassionately surveying the handkerchief.

'I figure he must have wiped that knife with it, sir.'

'You may be right.'

'And there's no doubt he put it in the incinerator this morning, just as the gardener said.'

'Took his time about getting rid of it, didn't he?'

The Sergeant frowned. 'Yes,' he admitted. 'But maybe he didn't think it was vital to destroy it while Stephen Herriard was still under suspicion. After all, if he murdered old Herriard, and planted that cigarette-case in the room, he'd be pretty sure he'd diverted suspicion from himself, wouldn't he? It was you letting it be known that Stephen was more or less in the clear that sort of stampeded him, like you thought it might.'

'Ah!' said Hemingway, stirring the handkerchief with his pencil.

A little crestfallen, the Sergeant said: 'You don't think it's important, Chief?'

'I don't say that. It may be. Of course, I'm not an expert, but I'd have liked these highly lavish bloodstains to have gone a bit browner. However, I'll see Roydon as soon as he comes in, and if I don't get anything out of him we'll get this tested. Anything else?'

'Yes,' said the Sergeant, his slow grin spreading once more over his face. 'This!'

Hemingway saw the mutilated book in his hand, and ejaculated: 'You aren't going to tell me – Well, I'll be damned!' He took the book from the Sergeant, and flicked over the scorched pages. 'I told you so!' he said. 'Someone in this house couldn't take it. I'm bound to say I couldn't either. Well, it's your find, my lad. You can give it back to the old lady, and get the credit for a piece of smart detection.'

'Thank you, Chief, but considering the state it's in it doesn't seem to me there's going to be much credit attached to it!' Ware retorted. 'I'd just as soon you gave it back to her.'

'The mistake you made was in rescuing the thing at all,' said Hemingway. 'It just serves you right. You go and give it back to Mrs Herriard, and don't let me have any backchat about it either!'

The Sergeant sighed, and went off to find Maud. She had by this time escaped from Mrs Dean's toils, and was knitting in the library, exchanging desultory remarks with Mathilda. Joseph was seated on the broad window-seat with Paula, trying to amuse her with anecdotes of his career on the stage. Paula, who was far too profound an egotist to see anything pathetic in his reminiscences, did not even pretend to be interested. Beyond saying Oh! once or twice in an abstracted voice, she paid no heed to him. Her face wore its most brooding look, and it was obvious that her mind was solely occupied with her own stage-career.

The Sergeant coughed to draw attention to himself, and trod over to Maud's chair. 'Beg pardon, madam, but I think you said you'd lost a book?'

'Yes, indeed I have,' said Maud. 'I told the Inspector about it, and he promised to keep a look-out for it.'

Feeling absurdly guilty, the Sergeant proffered the wreck he was holding. 'Would this be it, madam?'

For almost the first time in their acquaintanceship, Mathilda watched Maud's face register emotion. Her pale eyes stared at the book, and her jaw sagged. It was a moment before she could find her voice. 'That?' she said. 'Oh no!'

'I'm afraid it's got a bit damaged,' said the Sergeant apologetically.

This tactful understatement made Mathilda choke. Almost shrinkingly Maud took the book, and looked at it. 'Oh dear!' she said distressfully. 'Oh dear, dear, dear! It *is* my book! Joseph, look what has happened! I cannot understand it!'

Joseph, who had already crossed the room to her side, said tut-tut, in a shocked voice, and asked the Sergeant where he had found it.

'Well, sir, I'm sure I don't know how it got there, but it fell out of the bottom of the incinerator.'

A stifled gasp from Mathilda brought Joseph's head round. He was looking suitably grave, but when he met her brimming eyes his gravity vanished, and he gave a sudden chuckle.

'I must say, Joseph, I don't know what you find to laugh at!' said Maud.

'I'm sorry, my dear! It was just a piece of foolishness. It's most annoying for you – really, very tiresome indeed! But never mind! After all, we have things so much more serious to worry about, haven't we?'

This well-meant comfort entirely failed in its object. 'No, Joseph, I cannot agree with you. I was particularly inter-ested in the Empress's life, and, as you see, all the first and last pages have been burnt away. And, what is more, it is a book from the lending-library, and I shall have to pay for it.' A slight flush reddened her plump cheeks; she sat very straight in her chair, and, directing an accusing stare upon the Sergeant, said: 'I should like to know who threw my book into the incinerator!'

The Sergeant knew himself to be blameless in every respect, but his feeling of guilt grew under the indignant old lady's gaze. 'I couldn't say, madam. Perhaps it was thrown away by accident.'

'That would be it!' exclaimed Joseph, seizing gratefully this explanation. 'No doubt it got picked up with the news-papers, or – or fell into a wastepaper-basket, and that's how it happened.'

'I shall ask the servants,' said Maud, rising from her chair. 'If that is what happened, it is most careless, and they will have to pay for it.'

'I shouldn't, if I were you,' said Paula. 'They'll give notice in a bunch. Besides, I'll bet Stephen did it.'

Joseph shot her an anguished look. 'Paula! *Must* you?'

Maud halted in her tracks. 'Stephen?' she said. 'Why should Stephen destroy my book?'

'No reason at all, my dear!' said Joseph. 'Of course he didn't!'

'Well!' Maud said. 'I have always thought him a very tiresome young man, making a great deal of trouble through nothing but ill-temper, but I never supposed he would be wantonly destructive!'

At that moment Stephen walked into the room. Paula said: 'Stephen, did you chuck Aunt Maud's book into the incinerator?'

'No, of course I didn't,' he answered. 'How many more times am I to tell you that I never touched the damned thing?'

'Well, someone did.'

His lips twitched. 'Oh no, not really?'

Maud mutely held out what remained of the *Life of the Empress Elizabeth*. Stephen took one look, and burst out laughing. The Sergeant seized this opportunity to escape from the room, and went back to tell his superior that from the looks of it Stephen Herriard had done it.

'Young devil!' said Hemingway.

Meanwhile, Maud, quite incensed by Stephen's laughter, was delivering herself of her opinion of him. It was evident that she was very much put out. Stephen said, with unaccustomed penitence, that he was sorry he had laughed, but that he was guiltless of having tampered with the book. Mathilda did not believe him, but she saw that Maud was really upset, and at once supported Joseph's theory that the book had been thrown away by accident. Maud reiterated her resolve to question the servants, and Paula said impatiently, 'What on earth's the use of making a fuss about it now that the damage is done? If you ask Sturry whether he put your book in the incinerator, he'll give notice on the spot.'

'You go and ask him,' Stephen advised Maud. 'You can't do any harm, because he's just given me notice.'

This announcement provoked an outcry. Joseph wanted to know what could have induced the man to do such a silly thing; Mathilda ejaculated: 'Snake!' and Paula said he would be a good riddance.

'I think very badly of him for giving notice at such a time as this!' said Joseph. 'It is very selfish of him, very selfish indeed!'

'It is annoying, because I meant to give him the boot before he could do it,' said Stephen. 'What's more, he'll be wanted to swear to Uncle Nat's will, before it's admitted to probate.'

'Why?' asked Paula.

Stephen made a slight, contemptuous gesture towards his uncle. Joseph said: 'I'm afraid that's my fault, my dear. It's so long since I read my law that I've become shockingly rusty. I very stupidly forgot that it's usual to insert an Attestation Clause. It doesn't really matter, only it means that both witnesses will be wanted before we can get probate.'

'Well, he can go and swear his piece before a Commissioner for Oaths,' said Stephen. 'Not that it's necessary. As long as we know where to find him, he can still do his swearing even though he isn't any longer employed here.'

'You make him swear before he leaves!' advised Mathilda.

'I wouldn't put it past him to try to put a spoke in your wheel somehow!'

'My dear, what a dreadful thing to say!' exclaimed Joseph. 'He may have his faults, but we've no reason to think him dishonest!'

'He loathes Stephen,' Mathilda said obstinately.

'Nonsense, Tilda! You really mustn't say such things!'

'Do, for God's sake, stop looking at everyone through rose-coloured spectacles!' said Stephen. 'Sturry's hated me ever since I told Uncle Nat he was watering the port, and you know it!'

'Well, but that isn't to say that he would deliberately try to harm you, old man!' protested Joseph.

'You see to it that he goes and swears whatever it is he's got to swear,' said Mathilda.

'All right, I will. It'll annoy him,' said Stephen.

'All this,' said Maud, 'has nothing to do with the *Life of the Empress Elizabeth!*'

'If you put it like that,' said Stephen, 'nothing so far has had anything to do with that thrice-accursed female!'

'I do not know why you should speak of the Empress in that rude way,' said Maud, with tremendous dignity. 'You know nothing about her.'

'No one who has been privileged to live under the same roof with you for the past three days,' said Stephen, losing patience, 'can claim to know nothing about the Empress!'

This outrageous remark very nearly precipitated a quite unlooked-for crisis. Maud's bosom swelled, and she was just about to utter words which her fascinated audience felt would have been shattering to anyone less hardened than Stephen, when Sturry entered the room with the cocktail-tray. Even under the stress of powerful emotion Maud knew that a lady never permitted herself to quarrel in front of the servants; and instead of scarifying Stephen, she held out the *Life of the Empress* to Sturry, and asked him if he knew how it had found its way into the incinerator.

Looking outraged, Sturry disclaimed all knowledge. Maud requested him to make enquiries amongst the staff, to which he bowed, without, however, vouchsafing any reply.

'Just a moment!' said Stephen, as Sturry was about to withdraw. 'I'm informed that you and Ford will be required to swear to the signature of the late Mr Herriard's will. In the existing circumstances, it will be more convenient for you to do so before a Commissioner for Oaths than to wait until the will's admitted to probate. I'll run you into the town tomorrow, and you can do so then.'

Sturry cast him a cold look. 'Might I enquire, sir, the nature of the oath required of me?'

'It's only a formality,' Stephen answered. 'You have merely to swear that Mr Herriard signed his will in your presence.'

Sturry drew in his breath with a sucking sound, and said with an air of quiet triumph: 'I regret, sir, I could not see my way to do that.'

No one had really believed Mathilda's grim prognostication, and a startled silence fell upon the company. Joseph broke it. 'Come, come, Sturry!' he said. 'Is that quite worthy of you? Of course you must do it! The Law requires it of you.'

'I beg your pardon, sir,' Sturry said, with careful courtesy, 'but I understood Mr Stephen to say that I should be required to swear that the late Mr Herriard signed his will in my presence.'

'Well?' said Stephen harshly.

'I regret, sir, that I could not reconcile it with my conscience to do that.'

'But, Sturry!' gasped Joseph.

'What the devil do you mean?' demanded Stephen. 'You witnessed the signature, didn't you?'

'In a manner of speaking, sir, yes. But if it comes to taking my oath I feel myself bound to state that neither Ford nor myself was present when the late Mr Herriard signed his will.'

'But, Sturry, that's absurd!' Joseph cried, very much flustered. 'You may not have been actually in the room, but you know very well that I brought the document straight out to you, in the upper hall, and you both knew what it was, and signed it! I mean, it's the silliest quibble to say Mr Herriard didn't sign it in your presence! You know how ill he was, and how much he disliked having a lot of people in his room! I told you exactly what you were doing, and you must have known perfectly well that Mr Herriard *had* signed it, for there was his signature for you to see!'

'I am not aware, sir, that I should be obliged to Go on Oath about it,' replied Sturry inexorably. 'I regret to appear Disobliging, sir, but I trust you will Appreciate my Position.'

He then bowed again, and left the room, softly closing the door behind him.

'That,' said Stephen, 'has properly torn it!'

'You fool, Joe!' Mathilda exclaimed, jumping up from her chair. 'Don't you *know* how important it is that the witnesses should actually *see* the signing of a will?'

'But Tilda – but Stephen – !' stammered Joseph. 'I never thought – it was difficult enough to get Nat to draw the will up at all! If I'd tried to make him agree to having Ford and Sturry in to watch him doing it – well, you know what Nat was! Of course I know that technically one ought to see the actual signing, but in this case – I mean, no one is going to contest the will! I'm sure it will be all right. I shall simply have to explain the circumstances, and –'

'You'll be clever if you can explain how Ford and Sturry saw through a wall,' interrupted Stephen.

'Do you really mean that the will is no good, just because the witnesses didn't watch Uncle signing it?' Paula asked incredulously.

'Yes, my sweet, that is just what I mean,' Stephen replied. 'In plain words, your Uncle Joseph has mucked it.'

Fifteen

~

THIS WAS SO STARTLING THAT EVEN MAUD MOMENTARILY forgot the loss of her book. Paula demanded: 'Then who gets Uncle Nat's money?'

'I don't know,' answered Stephen. 'His next of kin, presumably.'

'But I'm his next of kin!' exclaimed Joseph, much agitated. 'It's absurd! I don't want it! I shouldn't know what to do with it! Really, Stephen, you're taking a most exaggerated view of things! I feel quite sure that when the matter is explained –'

'No, Stephen's right,' Mathilda said. 'I know what a fuss there was when my Aunt Charlotte died, leaving a will on half a sheet of notepaper. The Law's extremely sticky about wills. Besides, how can you explain such a piece of lunacy as not admitting the two witnesses into the room?'

'But, Tilda, it was hard enough to bring Nat to the point of making a will at all!'

'Well you'd better keep quiet about that,' said Mathilda unkindly. '*We* know you persuaded him with the best intentions, but it might not sound so good to anyone who hasn't the pleasure of knowing the Herriard family.'

Joseph looked quite stunned, and was for once bereft of the power of speech. Maud's flat voice made itself heard. 'Well, I am sure Nathaniel never meant Joseph to inherit all his money,' she said. 'It is not at all what he wished, for he did not consider that Joseph had any sense of money.'

'Do you mean to tell me,' said Paula ominously, 'that I shan't get my legacy after all?'

'Not a penny of it,' replied Stephen. 'You may, of course, be able to bully Joe into disgorging it.'

That roused Joseph into exclaiming: 'How can you, Stephen? As though I should have to be bullied into it! If you are right about this unlucky business – but I feel sure you're not! – you can't think that I should let the matter rest at that! I know well what poor Nat's wishes were!'

'If you are about to offer restitution, don't!' said Stephen grimly. 'I'm not taking any.'

Paula suddenly surprised everyone by breaking into a peal of jangling laughter. 'How damned funny!' she said. 'Nat's been murdered, we've been torn and rent by fear and suspicion, all for nothing!'

Mathilda regarded her with disfavour. 'It may be your idea of humour. It isn't mine. I don't for a moment suppose that you want my advice, but before you all rush to extremes, might it not be as well to discover just how the law does stand towards intestacy?'

'He didn't die intestate!' Joseph said. 'Just because there's a small irregularity –'

'That's rather a good idea of yours, Mathilda,' said Stephen, as though Joseph had not spoken. 'I'll get on to Blyth, and ask him.'

He left the room. Paula was still laughing, with more than a suggestion of hysteria in her voice. Joseph tried to put his arm round her, but was fiercely shaken off. 'Leave me alone!' she said. 'I might have guessed you'd muddle everything! Fool! Fool!'

'If you don't shut up, I'll empty this flower-vase over your head!' threatened Mathilda.

'Can't you see the exquisite irony of it?' Paula said. 'He did it all for the best! Oh, my God, what a second act it would make! I must tell Willoughby! He at least will have the perception to appreciate it!'

Roydon, however, was not immediately to be found, nor, if Paula had found him, would her idea for a second act have been met with any enthusiasm. His thoughts were far from playwriting. He was confronting Inspector Hemingway, rather white about the gills, and with his Adam's apple working convulsively.

'I think,' said Hemingway, laying a bloodstained handkerchief on the table between them, 'that this is yours.'

'No, it's not!' replied Roydon, in a frightened voice. 'I never saw it before in my life!'

Hemingway stared disconcertingly at him for a moment, and then straightened the handkerchief, and pointed with the butt of his pencil to the embroidered letter in the corner.

'I don't know anything about it!' Roydon said obstinately.

'Laundry-marks, too,' observed Hemingway. 'Easily identified.'

There was an awful silence. Nothing in Roydon's experience had fitted him to cope with such a situation as this. He was badly frightened, and showed it.

'You put it into the incinerator by the potting-sheds, didn't you?' said Hemingway.

'No!'

'Come, come, sir, you're not doing yourself any good by telling lies to me! I know you put it there.'

Roydon seemed to crumple up. 'I know what you think, but you're wrong! I didn't murder Mr Herriard! I didn't, I tell you!'

'How did your handkerchief come to be in this state?'

'I had a bad nose-bleed!' Roydon blurted out.

The Sergeant, who was a silent witness, turned his slow gaze upon Hemingway, to see how he would receive this explanation.

'Do you burn your handkerchiefs every time you have a nose-bleed?' asked Hemingway.

'No, of course I don't, but I knew what you'd think if you found it! I – I lost my head!'

'When did you have this nose-bleed?'

'Last night, after I'd gone up to bed. I put the handkerchief in my suitcase, and then I thought – I thought if you were to find it there it would look suspicious. I heard you were searching the house, and – and I thought I'd better get rid of it!'

'Did you tell anyone about your nose-bleed?'

'No. No, naturally I didn't! It isn't anything to make a fuss about. As a matter of fact, I often get them.'

'But this morning, when you were afraid I might find the handkerchief, didn't you think to mention to anyone what had happened?'

'Yes, but I couldn't say it then! I mean, it would have sounded odd. At least, I thought it would. Everyone would have wondered if it was true, or if I was only trying to account for the blood on my handkerchief. Oh, I know I behaved like a fool, but I swear I had nothing to do with the murder!'

'Haven't you ever heard of blood-tests?' asked Hemingway.

'Yes; but suppose my blood and Mr Herriard's belong to the same group?' objected Roydon. 'I thought of that, and it seemed much safer to get rid of the damned thing. Because it could only lead you down a side-track, honestly!'

'Well, if your story's true, you've given me a great deal of trouble through behaving so foolishly,' said Hemingway.

'I'm sorry. Of course, I see now that it was silly of me, but the fact of the matter is that this whole affair is getting on my nerves.' A sense of grievance overcame him. 'I don't think I've been treated at all well!' he complained. 'I was invited down here to a friendly party, and first Mr Herriard was damned rude to me, and then he got himself murdered, and now I know very well I'm under suspicion, and it has nothing whatsoever to do with me!'

'Well, this handkerchief has a good deal to do with you,' said Hemingway sternly. 'You deliberately tried to conceal it, and that doesn't look any too good, let me tell you!'

'But I didn't do it! I swear I didn't do it! It isn't Mr Herriard's blood: it's my own!'

'That'll be for others to find out,' said Hemingway, and dismissed him.

The Sergeant drew a breath. 'Do you believe him, sir?'

'It's about what I thought had happened when you first showed me the handkerchief,' admitted Hemingway.

'But that story he put up, about being afraid you'd find it!'

'Might easily be true.'

The Sergeant looked disappointed. 'You made a point when you asked him if he'd mentioned his nose-bleed to anyone.'

'I didn't really, but I wanted to see what he'd do if I rattled him. Nose-bleeding's a silly sort of kid's complaint: you don't go round bucking about it.'

'Then you do believe him!'

'I've got what wouldn't do you any harm, my lad: an open mind! This is a job for the scientists. Until they tell me that this blood belongs to old Herriard's group, there's nothing I can do about it. You'd better come along, and get some lunch now.'

The Sergeant, feeling rather dissatisfied, followed him out into the hall, where he was pounced on by Mottisfont, who said in a complaining tone that he had been waiting to speak to him for a long time.

'Yes, sir, what is it?' asked Hemingway, eyeing him dispassionately.

'I don't know how much longer you propose to take over your investigation,' Mottisfont said sarcastically, 'but I must point out to you that my time is not my own. I'm a very busy man. I came down here merely to spend Christmas, not to remain indefinitely. I have an important business engagement in town tomorrow, and with all due deference to you I propose to leave in the morning.'

'I've no objection, sir,' said Hemingway calmly. 'You're not being kept here.'

'I understood that no one was allowed to leave the house!'

'Did you, sir? Not from me, I'm sure. Of course, I shall want your address, but I shouldn't dream of keeping you here.'

Mottisfont looked as though the wind had been taken out of his sails, and was beginning to grumble that he had been misled, when Paula came down the stairs, and interrupted him.

'I suppose you have heard the latest news?' she said. She was not laughing now; she looked hard and angry, and it was evident that she meant to vent her displeasure on as many people as possible.

'What news?' said Mottisfont.

'Oh, so you haven't! Well, you may be interested to hear that Stephen is *not* the heir, and that I do *not* get my legacy!'

Mottisfont stared at her. 'Do you mean that a later will has been discovered?'

'Oh no! Nothing like that! Merely that this one is invalid!' said Paula savagely.

'Indeed! I am very sorry to hear it, but I can hardly suppose that it concerns me,' said Mottisfont.

She laughed shortly. 'Not interested, in fact!'

The Inspector said: 'Well, I'm interested, at all events, miss. In what way is the will invalid?'

She was too angry to care what she said, or to whom. 'It's invalid because it wasn't signed in the presence of the witnesses. That fact has just been disclosed to us by our engaging butler.'

Mottisfont gave a slight titter. 'How typical of Joseph!' he remarked. 'Quite a blow to you and Stephen, I fear!'

'Quite!' said Paula through her teeth.

'You have all my sympathy,' he said. 'But it is never wise to anticipate, is it?'

'Oh, get out!' she said rudely.

He shrugged, and walked away. The Inspector said: 'Well, well, this is quite a surprise, I must say, miss! Very unfortunate for all concerned. How did it come about that the will wasn't witnessed? Mr Blyth never said anything.'

'He didn't know. My precious Uncle Joseph, who started life in a solicitor's office, remembered just enough law to realise that witnesses would be wanted, and he got Sturry and Ford to sign as witnesses. But my Uncle Nat apparently wouldn't have them in his bedroom, and they waited outside to do their stuff. Now it seems that my dear uncle forgot some clause or other, and on account of it the witnesses will be required to swear that they saw Uncle Nat sign his will. And of course, Sturry, as soon as he heard of it, seized the opportunity to queer my brother's pitch, and said he couldn't perjure himself. So that is beautifully that. It would be funny if it weren't so damnable.'

The Inspector, who had listened to this with an expression of absorbed interest on his face, said sympathetically that it was a bit of a facer. 'I am not what you'd call a whale on these matters myself, miss. What happens to the late Mr Herriard's estate now?'

344

'I don't know, and I don't care. I know nothing about law. My brother's telephoning to Mr Blyth now. He thinks my Uncle Joseph will inherit everything, as next of kin. I expect he's right. It's the sort of ironic thing that would happen!'

'Well, I think, if it's all the same to you, miss, I'll wait to hear the result of this telephone-call,' decided Hemingway, laying his hat down on the table.

She shrugged. 'Please yourself!'

He had not long to wait. Stephen appeared a moment or two later. In spite of her professed indifference, Paula pounced on him at once, and demanded to know what Blyth had said.

He lifted one eyebrow at the Inspector. 'Taken Scotland Yard into your confidence?'

'What the hell does it matter?' she said impatiently.

'That's right,' interjected Hemingway. 'You don't want to make a stranger out of me, sir.'

'I should find it difficult, shouldn't I?' said Stephen. 'You're getting to be quite like one of the family. You remind me of a broker's man.'

'Ah, I wouldn't know anything about them!' Hemingway retorted, not in the least resentful of this insult. 'I've never had one on my premises. They don't like you to in my profession.'

Stephen grinned. 'You win that round, Inspector, on points.'

Paula shook his arm. 'Oh, do shut up! What did Blyth say?'

'Refrain from mauling me about. Under the new circumstances I appear to be the only loser.'

'Do you mean Uncle Joseph doesn't pouch the lot?' she asked incredulously.

'Far from it. Under the Law of Intestacy, Uncle Nat's property will be divided equally between his next of kin. That means that Joe will get half, and you and I will share the half that would have gone to Father, were he alive today.'

Her eyes were fixed on his. 'Are you sure?'

'No, I'm not sure of anything. That's what Blyth says.'

She lifted her hands to her temples, pushing back the thick waves of her hair. 'Good God, then we shall all be rich!'

'Depends how you look at it. You and Joe will be comparatively rich, while I shall be comparatively poor. Death duties will be heavy. I doubt if it will work out at more than eighty thousand pounds for Joseph, and forty thousand pounds to you and to me.'

'Will you be able to keep on this place?' she asked.

'Hardly. It will be sold, and the proceeds pooled, I suppose.'

'Oh, I'm sorry about that!' she said mechanically.

His lips twisted. 'How sweet of you!' he mocked. He glanced towards Hemingway. 'Interested, Inspector?'

'I'm always interested,' Hemingway responded.

Maud chose that moment to come into the hall from the wide corridor leading past the billiard-room to the servants' quarters. She was still carrying her mutilated book, and it was evidently still absorbing her attention, for she said without preamble: 'They all say they know nothing about it. If you did it, Stephen, it would be more manly of you to own up to it.'

'God's teeth, how many more times do you want to be told that I never touched your book?' Stephen demanded.

'There is no need to swear,' Maud said. 'When I was a girl gentlemen did not use strong language in front of ladies. Of course, times have changed, but I do not think for the better. It's my belief someone wantonly destroyed this book.' Her pale gaze drifted to the Inspector's face. 'You don't seem to be doing anything,' she said, on a note of severity. 'I think you ought to discover who put my book into the incinerator. It may not seem important to you, but as far as I can see you aren't getting any further over my brother-in-law's death, so you might turn your attention to this for a change.'

'Good God, Aunt, you surely don't expect Scotland Yard to bother itself about a miserable book!' exclaimed Paula. 'We're all sick and tired of hearing about it!'

'And I,' said Maud, quite sharply, 'am sick and tired of hearing about Nat's murder, and Nat's will!'

'In that case,' said Stephen, 'we can't expect you to be interested in Blyth's verdict.'

'No, I am not interested,' Maud replied. 'I do not want a large fortune, and I do not want to be obliged to continue living in this house. I shall write to town for a copy of the *Life of the Empress* at once, and when I have finished reading it, I shall give it to the library in place of this one.'

Joseph, who was coming down the stairs, overheard this, and threw up his hands. 'Oh, my dear, are we never to hear the last of that book? I thought we had decided to forget about it!'

'You may have decided to forget about it, Joseph, but it was not your book. I was very much interested in it, and I want to know what the end was.'

'Well, my dear, and so you shall,' promised Joseph. 'When all this stress is over, I'll get you a copy, never fear!'

'Thank you, Joseph, I will get one for myself, without waiting for anything to be over,' said Maud, walking away.

The Inspector picked up his hat again. Joseph said: 'Ah, Inspector! Just off? I mustn't ask you if you've discovered anything, must I? I know you won't keep us in suspense longer than you need.'

'Certainly not, sir. I understand I have to congratulate you, by the way.'

Joseph winced. 'Please don't, Inspector! What has happened isn't in the least what I wanted. But it may all come right yet.'

'I hope it may, I'm sure, sir. I'm sorry about Mrs Herriard's book, and I'm afraid she thinks I ought to bring someone to justice about it.'

Joseph smiled wearily. 'I think we've all heard enough about that book,' he said. 'Unfortunately, my wife has a way, which the young people find tiresome, of recounting stray pieces of what she has read. The least said about it the better. She'll soon forget about it.'

'For the last time,' said Stephen dangerously, 'I – did – not – touch – the – book!'

'Very well, old chap, we'll leave it at that,' said Joseph in a soothing voice.

The Inspector then left the house, accompanied by Sergeant Ware. During the drive back to the town, he was unusually silent, and the Sergeant, stealing a glance at him, saw that he was frowning. Over a lunch of cold turkey and ham at the Blue Dog, Hemingway continued to frown until the Sergeant ventured to ask him what he thought about the morning's work.

'I'm beginning to get some very queer ideas about this case,' replied Hemingway, digging into a fine Stilton cheese. 'Very queer. I wouldn't wonder if I began seeing things soon.'

'I was thinking myself of something you once said to me,' said the Sergeant slowly.

'If you thought more about what I say to you you'd very likely get to be an Inspector one of these days,' replied Hemingway. 'What did I say?'

'You told me that when a case got so gummed up that it looked hopeless you liked it, because it meant that something was going to break.'

'I won't say it isn't true, because very often it is, but it won't do you any good to remember that kind of remark,' said Hemingway severely.

'Well, sir, is this case gummed up enough for you yet?'

'Yes,' said Hemingway, 'it is.'

'You've got something?'

'I've got a strong feeling that things moved a bit too fast for someone this morning,' said Hemingway. 'It's no use asking me how I get these hunches: it's what they call a *flair*. That's why they made me an Inspector.'

The Sergeant sighed, and waited patiently.

'While I was prowling round the house today, more like a Boy Scout than a policeman, I treated myself to a nice quiet review of the case.' Hemingway poised a piece of cheese on his knife, and raised it to his mouth. 'And taking one thing with another, and adding them up together with a bit of *flair*, and a knowledge of psychology, I came to the conclusion that I was being led around by the nose. Now, that's a thing I don't take kindly to at all. What's more, the Department wouldn't like it.' He put the cheese into his mouth, and munched it.

'Who's leading you around by the nose?' asked the Sergeant, intent, but bewildered.

Hemingway washed the cheese down with some beer. 'Kind old Uncle Joseph,' he answered.

The Sergeant frowned. 'Trying to put you off young Stephen's scent? But –'

'No,' said Hemingway. 'Trying to put me off his own scent.'

'But, good lord, Chief, you don't think he did it, do you?' gasped the Sergeant.

Hemingway regarded him pityingly. 'You can't help not having *flair*, because it's French, and you wouldn't understand it,' he said, 'but you ought to be able to do ordinary arithmetic.'

'I can,' said the Sergeant, nettled. 'Begging your pardon, sir, I can add two and two together and make it four as well as anyone. What I can't do is to make it five. But I daresay that's French too.'

'No,' said Hemingway, quite unruffled. 'That's Vision, my lad. You haven't got it.'

'No, but I know what it is,' retorted the Sergeant insubordinately. 'It's seeing things, like you warned me you were beginning to.'

'One of these days I shall get annoyed with you,' said Hemingway. 'You'll be reduced to the ranks, very likely.'

'But, Chief, he *couldn't* have done it!' the Sergeant pointed out.

'If it comes to that, they couldn't any of them have done it.'

'I know; but he's the one man who's got an alibi from the moment Herriard went upstairs to the moment when he was found dead!'

'When you put it to me like that, I can't make out why I didn't suspect him at the outset,' said Hemingway imperturbably.

The Sergeant said almost despairingly: 'He was talking to Miss Clare through the communicating door into the bathroom. You aren't going to tell me you suspect her of being mixed up in it?'

'No, I'm not. What I am going to tell you, though, is that when you get a bunch of suspects only one of whom has had the foresight to provide himself with an alibi, you want to keep a very sharp eye on that one. I admit I didn't, but that was very likely because you distracted me.'

The Sergeant swallowed something in his throat. 'Very likely,' he agreed bitterly.

'That's right,' said Hemingway. 'You stop giving me lip, and think it over. Whichever way you turn in this case, you come up against Joseph. You must have noticed it. Take the party itself! Whose bright idea was that? You can ask any of the people up at the Manor, and they'll all give you the same answer: Joseph! I never met the late Nathaniel when he was alive, but I've heard enough about him to be pretty sure he wasn't the kind of man who liked Christmas parties. No, it was kind old Uncle Joseph who thought it would be nice to have a real old-fashioned Christmas, with a lot of good-will floating around, and everyone making up old quarrels, and living happily ever after. Young Stephen wasn't on good terms with Nathaniel, on account of his bit of fluff; Paula had been worrying the life out of him to put up the cash for Roydon's play; Mottisfont had been getting his goat by selling arms to China, in a highly illegal fashion. So Joseph gets the bright idea of asking all three of them, plus two of the causes of the trouble, down to Lexham. You can say he was being well-meaning but tactless, if you like; on the other hand, you can widen your horizon a bit, and ask yourself if he wasn't perhaps getting together all the people most likely to quarrel with Nathaniel, to act as cover for himself.'

'Why, sir, he's nothing but a soft old fool!' protested the Sergeant 'I've met his sort many times!'

'That's what he wanted you to think,' said Hemingway. 'What you're forgetting is that he's been an actor. Now, I know a bit about the stage. In fact, I know a lot about it. Joseph can tell me all he likes about playing Hamlet, and Othello, and Romeo: I don't believe him, and, what's more, I never did. He's got Character-part written all over him. He was the poor old father who couldn't pay the rent in The Wicked Baron, or What Happened to Girls in the 'Eighties; he was the butler in about half a hundred comedies; he was the First Grave-digger in Hamlet; he was –'

'All right, I get it!' the Sergeant said hurriedly.

'And if I'm not much mistaken,' pursued Hemingway, 'his most successful rôle was that of the kind old uncle in a melodrama entitled Christmas at Lexham Manor, or Who Killed Nat Herriard? I'm bound to say it's a most talented performance.'

'I don't see how you make that out, sir, really I don't! If he'd got his brother to make a will leaving everything to him, there might be some grounds for suspecting him. But he didn't: he got him to leave his money to Stephen Herriard.'

'That's where he was cleverer than what you seem to be, my lad. In spite of having started life in a solicitor's office, he forgot the little formality of providing witnesses to see that will signed. You don't need to know much about law to know you've got to have the signature to a will properly witnessed. You heard Miss Herriard telling me that he also forgot to put in some clause or other. What she meant was an Attestation Clause. That meant that the witnesses to the will would have to swear to Nathaniel's having signed it in their presence before it was admitted to probate. So if Stephen didn't get convicted of the murder, Joseph had still got a trump-card up his sleeve. In due course, by which I mean when the case had been nicely packed up one way or another, it would transpire that the will wasn't in order after all.'

'Yes, but it didn't transpire in due course,' objected the Sergeant. 'It transpired today, and the case isn't anything like packed up.'

'No,' said Hemingway. 'It isn't. I told you I had a hunch things had been happening just a bit too quickly for someone. Kind Uncle Joseph hadn't reckoned with the Lord

High Everything Else. For some reason, which I haven't yet had time to discover, something brought the matter up, and Sturry blew the gaff. I don't fancy Joseph wanted that at all. He wouldn't like Sturry cutting in ahead of his cue.'

The Sergeant scratched his head. 'It sounds plausible, the way you tell it, sir, but I'd say it was too cunning for a chap like Joseph Herriard.'

'That's because you think he's just a ham actor with a heart of gold. What you ought to bear in mind is the possibility that he's a darned good actor, without any heart at all. You go back over all we've heard about this Christmas party! You picked up plenty of stuff from the servants yourself.'

'I don't know that I set much store by what they said,' said the Sergeant dubiously.

'I don't set a bit of store by any of the information they thought they were giving. But they told you a lot they didn't set any store by themselves, and that was valuable. What about Joseph hanging up paper-streamers, and bits of holly all over the house, until Nathaniel was fit to murder him?'

'Well, what about it?' asked the Sergeant, staring.

'It all fits in,' Hemingway said. 'Kind old Uncle Joseph going to a lot of trouble to make things bright and cheerful for a set of people whom even he must have known wouldn't like it any more than Nathaniel did. Kind old Uncle Joseph, in fact, working his brother up into a rare state of bad temper. He got on Nathaniel's nerves. He meant to. He did everything he knew Nathaniel didn't like, from decorating the house to clapping him on the back when he had lumbago.'

'Yes, but he's the sort of chap who always does put his foot into it,' interposed the Sergeant.

'That's what you were meant to think,' said Hemingway. 'You wait a bit, because I'm going to show you that kind Uncle Joseph's tactlessness is the predominant feature in this case. Piecing together all the information we've picked up, what do we get?'

'Joseph trying to keep the peace,' answered the Sergeant promptly.

'Not on your life we don't! Joseph throwing oil on the flames, more like. A man who wants to keep the peace doesn't invite a set of highly incompatible people down to stay with a bad-tempered old curmudgeon who's already got his knife into most of them.'

'But everyone says he was always trying to smooth rows over!'

'Thanks, I've heard him doing that for myself, and anything more calculated to make an angry person look round for a hatchet I've yet to see!' retorted Hemingway. 'Why, he even got on my nerves! But I haven't finished, not anything like. Having got the whole party into a state when anything might have happened, he does a bit more pseudo-balm-spreading by hinting to Stephen's blonde that Stephen's due to inherit his uncle's fortune, and it's up to her to keep him quiet. Looked at your way, that's more of his peacemaking; looked at my way, it's a nail in Stephen's coffin. No man could be as big a fool as to think that what you said to that girl wouldn't come out at the wrong moment. He was making sure that we should discover that Stephen had reason to think he was the heir.'

'Look here, sir, that's going too far!' the Sergeant exclaimed. 'The one thing that does stand out a mile is that he fair dotes on his nephew! Why, look at the way he would stick to it the murder had been done from outside! And the way he kept on saying that his brother must have taken Stephen's cigarette-case up to his room himself!'

'I am looking at it,' said Hemingway grimly. 'Two of the silliest theories I've ever had to listen to. They wouldn't have convinced a child in arms.'

'But you can't get away from the fact that he's fond of Stephen!'

'I'm not meant to get away from it,' replied Hemingway. 'I've had it thrust under my nose at every turn. The only thing I haven't yet been privileged to see is any reason for all this overflowing affection. I've seen a good bit of kind Uncle Joseph and his nephew since I came down here, and I haven't yet heard Stephen do other than treat him like dirt. That young man loathes the very sight of Joseph, and he takes no trouble to hide it. I've met some rude customers in my time, but anything to touch Stephen's rudeness to Joseph I've never seen. But it doesn't matter what he says: Joseph doesn't take a bit of umbrage; he just goes on loving his dear nephew.'

'Well, after all, he *is* his nephew, and when you've known a chap since he was a kid –'

'Now you have gone off the rails!' said Hemingway. 'When Stephen was a kid, Joseph was drifting about the world creating a sensation with his masterly portrayal of Mine Host of the Garter Inn, and Snug the Joiner, and very likely a First Citizen as well, not to mention a Soothsayer, and William, a Country Fellow. He wasn't within a couple of thousand miles of this country. If he knew that he'd got a nephew, that's about all he did know of Stephen until he planted himself on Nathaniel a couple of years ago. And if you're going to tell me that an affinity sprang up between them, you can spare your breath! Stephen never had a bit of time for kind Uncle Joseph, as you've heard over and over again from the servants. Went out of his way to be rude to him. In return for which, I'm being asked to believe that Joseph fair doted on him. Well, as far as I'm concerned, he overdid his doting. It isn't in human nature to dote on a young chap who does nothing but hand you out offensive remarks on a plate. In fact, that's where all kind Uncle Joseph's highly organised plans began to come a bit unstuck. Stephen wouldn't co-operate. However, Joseph banked on a lot of half-baked people like you thinking that he was a saint, and letting it go at that. The trouble is, I'm not half-baked, and I don't believe in saints who carry on like Joseph, playing up to the gallery all the time, till you feel you ought to give him a round of applause.'

'When you put it like that –' began the Sergeant slowly.

'You keep quiet, and listen to me. It's my belief Joseph meant to fasten this murder on to Stephen from the start, but just in case anything should go wrong, he first saw to it that his brother's will shouldn't hold water, when it came to be admitted to probate, and next that we should be provided with a few other likely suspects, to fall back on if the case against Stephen fell through. Thus we have Miss Herriard, and that limp playwright of hers, all ready to hand, not to mention Gun-running Mottisfont. And if I'm not much mistaken it was Joseph who egged Roydon on to read his play aloud on Christmas Eve, well knowing that it would drive Nathaniel to a frenzy.'

'You've got nothing to go on to make you say that, sir,' protested the Sergeant.

'I've got this to go on: that he didn't stop Roydon! I'll bet he could have done so, if he'd wanted to. He let him read it, and the balloon went up with a bang. Nathaniel, having had one row with Mottisfont, had another with Miss Herriard, and threw in a few mean cracks at Stephen, just for good measure. In fact, kind Uncle Joseph had got his stage nicely set, and all he had to do then was to stick a knife into Nathaniel, and sit back while we made fools of ourselves.'

'And you don't know how he managed to stick that knife into Nathaniel!' interjected the Sergeant.

'No, I don't; but for the moment I'm leaving that out of the discussion. It's safe to say that he did it damned cleverly, because it's got me baffled up to the present. But he chose a time when everyone else would be changing for dinner, and thus unable to produce alibis; and, further, he gave himself an alibi by carrying on a conversation with the one person who was obviously out of the running as a suspect.'

'Might be something in that door,' mused the Sergeant, thinking it over.

'What door?'

'The one between his dressing-room and the bathroom he shared with Miss Clare. I mean, she didn't actually see him, did she?'

'If you're thinking that she was listening to a gramophone, it's a possibility, but not a very likely one. What's more, I haven't so far found a gramophone on the premises.'

'Well, if he really was in his dressing-room all the time, how did he do it?'

'Never mind how he did it. We'll come to that presently. Just now I want you to consider his behaviour ever since the murder. He first arranges that Stephen shall be one of the three to discover Nathaniel's body. That gave him the opportunity to tell me, when the proper time came, that Stephen didn't turn a hair at finding his uncle dead.'

'He told you that?'

'Not half as crudely as that. He said his dear nephew was not one to show his feelings, which left me with the impression that Master Stephen had been pretty callous. But there! I pick up impressions a lot quicker than Joseph knows, and I'd already picked up the impression that Stephen had been rather fond of his Uncle Nathaniel, and was a good deal more upset by his death than he meant to give away. But of course there was more to getting Stephen into Nathaniel's room than that. Stephen inspected the windows and the bathroom door, just as any man would, while Joseph pretended to be mourning over his brother's body. That made it possible for Stephen to have had the chance to tamper with the fastenings. All Joseph had to do was to tell me that he was sure the windows were shut. When I asked him, as I was bound to, whether he'd actually seen them, he said no, but his dear nephew had, which came to the same thing. He knew it didn't come to the same thing, anything like, but it sounded well: just what a soft old fool would say. Oh, you have to hand it to him!'

'It makes him out to be pretty black,' said the Sergeant, awed.

'Well, you don't suppose a man who sticks a knife into his brother's back is a gilded saint, do you?'

'But, sir, I still can't see it altogether your way! I'd swear the one thing Joseph dreaded was that we should bring the murder home to Stephen! I mean, he went out of his way to explain that Stephen's rough manner didn't mean anything, and he was always sticking up for him!'

'Of course he was! That was his rôle, and very well he played it. But did he convince you that Stephen hadn't had anything to do with it?'

'No, I can't say that he did.'

'The point is,' said Hemingway, 'that the excuses he made for Stephen were so weak that they made us more suspicious than ever about him, which was all according to plan. The most damaging things I found out about Stephen I found out either *from* his uncle, by way of artless conversation, or *through* his uncle, like when it came out he'd hinted to Miss Dean that Stephen was the heir. He'd even taken care to hint the same to Mottisfont, knowing Mottisfont would spill it the instant he got the wind up on his own account.'

'There was never anything you could actually take hold of, though.'

'No; I told you we were up against a very clever customer.'

'Yes, but – Look here, sir, what about the will? If he was as clever as you make out, he must have known how the money would be divided up once the will was found to be no good! And he doesn't get the lot: he only gets half.'

'You're developing some very large ideas, aren't you?' said Hemingway. 'If you think eighty thousand pounds is a fortune to be sneezed at, I'll bet Joseph doesn't! Why, he's been sponging on his brother for the last two years, which means he's broke, or as near to it as makes no odds! Eighty thousand pounds would be as good a reason for murder to him as one hundred and sixty thousand pounds.'

'Well, I don't know. I'd have expected him to have got his brother to have made the will out in his favour, somehow.'

'Don't you ever take to crime, my lad, because it's easy to see you wouldn't make a do of it! If he'd come in for the whole fortune, instead of only half, it would have looked suspicious. I don't suppose he even thought of trying for the lot. He's far too downy a bird.'

The Sergeant appeared to consider the matter, fixing his superior with a grave, unblinking stare. After a prolonged and ruminative silence, he said: 'I don't deny it sounds convincing, the way you put it, sir. And you do have a knack of spotting your man.'

'*Flair,*' corrected Hemingway coldly.

'All right, *flair.* And I don't deny that I never fancied Miss Herriard, nor Mottisfont, nor that young Roydon. But what I do say, Chief, is that there isn't a bit of real evidence against Joseph, because you don't know how he did it, or when he found the time to do it.'

'That,' said Hemingway, 'is what we are now going to discover.'

'Well, I hope you're right, sir; but we've been at it the best part of two days now, and we're no nearer discovery, not as far as I know. Every line we had, or thought we had, broke down. The door-key hadn't been tampered with; the ladder couldn't have been got at; and there isn't a secret way into the room. I'm blessed if I know how we're ever going to make any headway.'

'That's right,' said Hemingway cheerfully. 'And all the time I wouldn't be a bit surprised if the clue to the whole mystery has been under our noses from the outset. Probably something so simple that a child could have spotted it. Life's like that.'

'If it's as simple an all that it's a wonder you haven't spotted it,' said the Sergeant sceptically.

'It's very likely too simple for me,' Hemingway explained. 'I was hoping you'd hit on it.'

The Sergeant ignored this. 'If only we had some fingerprints to help us!' he said. 'But everything was gone over so carefully, it doesn't seem to be any use trying that line again. I did think we might have got something from the dagger, but the hilt was as clean as a whistle. And it was plain the other dagger hadn't been touched, nor the sheath of the one he used. Well, we saw how easily it slipped in and out of the sheath, didn't we? I could have drawn the blade out without touching the sheath, if I'd wanted to, when I took the whole thing down. In fact, now I come to think of it, I never used my left hand at all, and I'll bet he didn't either.'

'Just a moment!' said Hemingway, frowning. 'I believe you've got something!'

'Got what, sir?'

'Your left hand. Do you remember just what you did do with it when you were up on that chair?'

'I didn't do anything with it, barring –' The Sergeant stopped, and his jaw fell. 'Good lord!'

'When you stretched up your right hand, to take the knife down, you steadied yourself with your left hand against the wall. And that, my lad, is ten to one what kind Uncle Joseph did too, without thinking about it any more than you did! Come on, we've got to get hold of the finger-print boys!'

The Sergeant rose, but he had been thinking deeply, and he said: 'Hold on a minute, sir! That's raised a point in my mind. I had to stretch up a good bit to reach that knife. Joseph couldn't have got near it, not on a chair.'

'Then he didn't use a chair,' replied Hemingway impatiently. 'I never met anyone like you for trying to throw a spanner in the works!'

'What did he use, then?'

Behind Inspector Hemingway's bright gaze his brain moved swiftly. Once more his excellent memory stood him in good stead. 'Christmas decorations: step-ladder!' he said. 'Same one Nathaniel fell over on his way up to dinner. Come on!'

Sixteen

WHEN THE UNEASY HOUSE-PARTY AT LEXHAM AROSE
from the luncheon-table that afternoon, Maud, as
usual, went upstairs for her rest, and Mottisfont took possession of the library by the simple expedient of stretching
himself out in the easiest armchair and disposing himself to
slumber. Paula dragged Roydon away to discuss the casting
of *Wormwood*. Mrs Dean, in whom the events of the morning had induced a reflective mood, said that she must have a
talk with dear Stephen, now that things were so mercifully
altered, and suggested that they should go to the morning-
room for a cosy little chat. Even Valerie seemed to feel that
this was a trifle blatant, for she said frankly: 'Oh, Mummy,
you are the limit!' Stephen said, with more presence of mind
than courtesy, that he was going for a walk with Mathilda,
at the same time directing such a menacing look at Mathilda
that she meekly acquiesced in this arbitrary plan for her
entertainment, and went upstairs to put on a pair of heavy
shoes and a thick coat.

They left the house by the garden-room door, and travers-
ing the gardens struck out into the small park. The melting

snow had made the ground spongy under their feet; the sky was dull; and the bare tree-branches dripped moisture; but Mathilda drew a long breath, and said: 'It's good to get out into the fresh air again. I find the atmosphere in the house rather too oppressive for my taste. Do you think you are definitely in the clear, Stephen?'

'Mrs Dean does,' he replied. 'Do you realise that that she-wolf was going to tie me up to Valerie again?'

'Of course, you're such a defenceless creature, aren't you?' she retorted.

'Against battering-rams, I am.'

'What did you do it for?' she asked.

'Get engaged to Valerie? I never meant to.'

'Little gentleman! A fairly raw deal for her, wasn't it?'

'I don't flatter myself she's broken-hearted.'

'No,' she conceded. 'You treated her pretty rough, though. You're not everybody's money, you know, Stephen.'

'By no means.' He turned his head, and looked down at her. 'Am I yours, Mathilda?'

She did not answer for a moment or two, but strode on beside him, her hands dug into the pockets of her coat. When she thought she could trust her voice, she said: 'Is that a declaration?'

'Don't come the ingénue, Mathilda, my love! Of course it is!'

'A bit sudden, isn't it?'

'No, it's belated. I ought to have made it five years ago.'

'Why didn't you?'

'I don't know. Took you for granted, I suppose.'

'Just a good sort,' she remarked.

'You are – a damned good sort. I always looked on you as a second sister.'

'You are a fool, Stephen,' she said crossly.

'Yes, I knew that as soon as I saw you beside my pretty nit-wit.'

'Came on you in a flash, no doubt.'

'More or less. I never realised until this hellish house-party. I don't want to have to live without you.'

'I suppose,' said Mathilda, staring gloomily ahead, 'I might have known that when you did propose you'd do it in some graceless fashion peculiarly your own. What makes you think I want Valerie's leavings?'

'My God, you are a vulgar wench!' Stephen exclaimed, grinning.

'Well?'

'I don't know. I shouldn't think you would want me. But I want you.'

'Why? To save you from further entanglements with glamorous blondes?'

'Hell, no! Because I love you.'

'Since when?'

'Always, I think. Consciously, since Christmas Eve. I've never quarrelled with you, Mathilda, have I? Do you know, I've never wanted to?'

'That must be a record.'

'It is. I won't ever quarrel with you, my sweet. That's a promise.'

'It's irresistible.'

He stopped, and swung her round to face him, holding her by the shoulders. 'Does that mean you'll marry me?'

She nodded, looking up at him with a faint flush in her cheeks. 'Somebody's clearly got to keep you in order. It may as well be me.'

He pulled her rather roughly into his arms. 'O God, Mathilda, do keep me in order!' he said, in a suddenly thickened voice. 'I need you! I need you damnably!'

She found that her own voice was unsteady. 'I know. You are such a fool, Stephen: such a dear, impossible fool!'

'So are you, to care a damn for me,' he said. 'I never thought you did. I can't think why you do.'

She took his face between her hands, looking up at him a little mistily. 'I like savage creatures.'

'Bull-terriers and Stephen Herriard.'

'That's it. What do you see in me? I'm an ill-favoured woman, my love, and you will have to confront my ugly mug across your breakfast-table all the days of your life.'

'You have a beautiful plainness, Mathilda. Your eyes laugh, too. Did you know?'

'No, I didn't know. Tell me more!'

He laughed, and, pulling her hand through his arm, held it, and strolled on with her across the spongy turf. 'I shan't be able to offer you this for your home.'

'It's all right with me. But you love it. You ought to have it.'

'Don't think I could keep it up as things are. It will be sold, anyway, and the proceeds split between the three of us.'

'You couldn't buy it in?'

He shook his head. 'Couldn't run it on what was left if I did. I don't mind. I've got you.'

They walked on. 'If Paula and Joe didn't want it sold – if they were willing to forgo their share of the price, you could keep it. Nat meant you to have it. I always thought that was why he bought it.'

'It was, originally. It's all right, Mathilda: I shan't mind – much. The only thing I couldn't bear would be to see Joe here.'

'Well, you won't: he doesn't like the place.'

The saturnine look came back into his face. 'You know nothing of what Joe likes or dislikes. None of us does.'

'He's never made any secret of the fact that historic houses don't appeal to him.'

'Reason enough to assume they do. I fancy Joe would like enormously to be Lord of the Manor. But he shan't be. Not unless he chooses to buy it. I'll stand out for a sale – and run the bidding up, too!'

'Why do you hate Joe so bitterly, Stephen?' she asked quietly.

He glanced down at her, a derisive expression in his hard eyes. 'I hate Joe for his hypocrisy.'

'Do you think he can help acting? It's second nature, I believe.'

'My God, Mathilda, can't you see the truth? Are you fooled too?' he asked incredulously.

'I don't like Joe,' she confessed. 'He means well, but he's an ass.'

'He is not an ass, and he doesn't mean well. You think he likes me, don't you? Well, I tell you that Joe hates me as much as I hate him!'

'Stephen!' she exclaimed.

He laughed. 'Think I'm brutal to Joe, don't you, Mathilda? When he tries to paw me about, and mouths his sickening platitudes, and drips affection all over me! You don't see that Joe's out to do me down. He nearly managed it, too.'

'But he's always trying to convince everyone that you couldn't have killed Nat!'

'Oh no, Mathilda! Oh no, my love! That's only the façade. Think it over! Think of all that Joseph's said in my defence, and ask yourself if it was helpful, or if it only served to make the police think that he was desperately trying to shield a man whom he knew to be guilty. Who do you think planted my cigarette-case in Uncle Nat's room? Have you any doubt? I haven't.'

Her fingers tightened on his. 'Stephen, are you sure you're not letting your dislike of Joe run away with you?'

'I'm quite sure. Joe was my enemy from the moment he set foot in this house, and discovered that I was Uncle Nat's blue-eyed boy. I was, you know.'

'But you quarrelled with Nat! Always, Stephen!'

'Sure I did, but without prejudice, until Joe came.'

She was silent for a moment, not doubting his sincerity, yet unable to believe that he was not regarding Joseph with a distorted vision. 'He got Nat to make a will in your favour.'

'Do you always believe what Joe tells you?' asked Stephen. 'He worried him into making *a* will. I don't know what happened: I wasn't there. Joe saw to that. But I can imagine Uncle Nat giving in to Joe, and then making the will out in my favour.

That would have been a joke he'd have appreciated. Only Joe was clever, and he saw to it that the will should be invalid.'

'You've never spoken a word of this!'

His lips curled. 'No. Only to you, and you think I'm unhinged, don't you? What do you suppose everyone else would think? I can tell you, if you don't know.'

She looked up at him, dawning horror in her eyes. 'Yes, of course I know. If you're right, it puts a hideous complexion on so much that has happened! I haven't stayed here often enough to be able to judge. I always ascribed the trouble that Joe has such a knack of starting to incurable tactlessness. But I see that your explanation might be correct.'

'You can take it from me that it is. If anyone but you had provided Joe with his alibi, I would, moreover, have been ready to swear that it was he who murdered Uncle Nat.'

'It isn't possible, Stephen. When he wasn't chatting to me he was humming snatches of song.'

He lifted her hand to his lips, and fleetingly kissed it. 'All right, my sweet. Yours is the only word I would take for that.'

They had come in sight of the house again by this time, and in a few minutes they entered it, through the front door, just as Inspector Hemingway was seeing a finger-print expert and a photographer off the premises.

The Inspector was looking more bird-like than ever, and there was a satisfied gleam in his eye, for under a dusting of powder the panel above the billiard-room mantelpiece had revealed the imprints of four fingers and a thumb. He cocked an intelligent eyebrow at Stephen and Mathilda, and drew his own conclusions.

'You are quite right, of course,' said Stephen, correctly interpreting the look in the Inspector's eye. 'But we feel – at least, Miss Clare does – that an announcement at present would not be in the best of good taste. Why the camera-man?'

'Just a bit of work I wanted done, sir. If I may say so, you don't waste your time, do you?'

Stephen laughed. 'As a matter of fact, I've wasted too much time, Inspector. How are you doing?'

'Not so badly, sir,' replied Hemingway. He turned to Mathilda. 'I want to have a talk with you, miss, if you please.'

'Very well,' she replied, rather surprised. 'I'll join you in the morning-room as soon as I've changed my shoes.'

This did not take her long, and she presently walked into the morning-room to find not only the Inspector there, but Stephen also, looking dangerous. She said at once: 'Take that scowl off your face, Stephen: you're frightening the Inspector.'

'That's right, miss,' said Hemingway. 'I'm all over goose-flesh.'

'I can see you are. No one is going to convict me of murder, Stephen, so relax! What is it, Inspector?'

'Well, miss, in checking over the details of this case, I find that I omitted to take your evidence. That won't do at all: in fact, it's a wonder to me how I came to leave you out. So, if you don't mind, I'd like you to tell me, please, just what you did when you went upstairs to change for dinner on Christmas Eve.'

'She gave her evidence to Inspector Colwall,' Stephen said.

'Ah, but that won't do for the Department, sir!' said Hemingway mendaciously. 'Very strict we are, at Scotland Yard.'

'I'll tell you what I did with pleasure,' Mathilda said. 'But I'm afraid it isn't helpful. First I had a bath, then I dressed, and lastly I came down to the drawing-room.'

'And I think Mr Joseph Herriard was able to corroborate that, wasn't he, miss?'

'Yes. We went upstairs together, and while I had my bath he continued to talk to me from his dressing-room. In fact, I don't recall that he ever stopped talking, except now and then, when he hummed instead.'

'Even when you had gone back into your bedroom? Did you go on talking to each other?'

'He went on talking to me,' corrected Mathilda.

'Do you mean that you didn't answer him?'

'I said Oh! at intervals. Occasionally I said Yes, when he asked me if I was listening.'

'Were you in the habit of talking to Mr Joseph while you were in your room, miss?'

'I didn't do it the night before, and I haven't done it since, but three days isn't really long enough for one to contract a habit, do you think?'

'I see. And you came downstairs together on Christmas Eve?'

'Arm in arm.'

'Thank you, miss; that's all I wanted to know,' said Hemingway.

Stephen, who had been frowningly regarding him, said: 'Just what are you driving at, Inspector?'

'Checking up on my facts, sir, that's all,' Hemingway replied.

But when he saw Sergeant Ware, a few minutes later, he shook his head, and said: 'No good. He took care to establish a cast-iron alibi all right.'

'There you are, then!' said the Sergeant, not altogether disappointed.

'No, I'm not!' Hemingway replied with some asperity. 'On that evening, and on that evening only, Joseph made a point of holding forth to Miss Clare, while she was dressing for dinner, and if possible, I'm more than ever convinced that he's the man I'm after.'

The Sergeant looked at him almost sadly. 'I've never known you to go against the evidence before, sir.'

'What you don't see is that I haven't got all the evidence. I've got a lot, but there's a vital link which I've missed. Well, I can't do any more until those lads 'phone through the result of developing that plate.'

'Of course, if it does turn out to be a print of Joseph's hand, it will be strong circumstantial evidence,' conceded the Sergeant. 'But not nearly strong enough, to my way of thinking, to convict him without our finding out how he could have got into Nathaniel's room to murder him. What's more, there's still that handkerchief of Roydon's.'

But Hemingway was plainly uninterested in Roydon's handkerchief. While awaiting the telephone-call from the police-station, he was sought out by Valerie, who wanted to know whether she could go home. He assured her that he had not the least objection to her immediate departure, an announcement which greatly cheered her. She went off to persuade her mother to leave Lexham on the following morning, and found that that redoubtable lady had at last succeeded in cornering Stephen, and was manoeuvring for position. As she entered the drawing-room, she heard Mrs Dean say: 'I know that you understood a mother's anxiety, Stephen. I'm afraid I'm very, very jealous of my girlie's happiness and future welfare. I could not have reconciled it with my conscience to have let the engagement continue as things were. But I'm sure you're chivalrous enough to forgive a mother's natural prudence.'

From the look on Stephen's face this did not seem to be very probable. Before he could answer, Valerie said: 'Oh, Mummy, I do wish you'd shut up! I keep on *telling* you I don't want to marry Stephen! And anyway we can go home: that angelic Inspector says so.'

In whatever terms Mrs Dean might later censure her daughter's mannerless interruption, even she was compelled to realise that after this forthright speech there could be no hope of renewing the engagement. She expressed a pious wish that they would not both discover that they had made a mistake they would regret, and left the room to overcome her chagrin in private.

Valerie said that for her part she was dead sure she wouldn't regret it.

'I shan't either,' said Stephen. 'You're a lovely, my pet, but you'd have driven me to suicide within a month.'

'Well, I thought you were pretty stinking, if you want to know,' said Valerie candidly. 'I expect you'll end up by marrying Mathilda.'

'I feel that I owe it to you to tell you that you're quite right.'

'Good God, you haven't gone and proposed to her already, have you?'

'I have; but you needn't spread it about yet.'

She stared at him 'Gosh, so that's why you're suddenly looking almost human! Are you really feeling a hundred per cent, just because you've proposed to Mathilda Clare?'

'No, my pretty nit-wit – because she accepted me.'

'You are a sickening swine, Stephen!' she said, without rancour. 'You never looked in the least like that when you were engaged to me.'

'I didn't feel in the least like this. I now feel so brimful of human kindness that if it wasn't Boxing Day I'm damned if I wouldn't drive in to the Free Library, to see if I could find a copy of the *Life of the Empress* there for Aunt Maud.'

'Well, you needn't bother, because she's writing to London for one,' said Valerie.

In this she was not quite accurate. Maud had indeed set out to write such a letter, but as she unfortunately could not recall either the author or the publisher of the book, and the title pages had been consumed in the incinerator, an insuperable bar seemed to have arisen in the way of her obtaining the volume. She appealed to everyone to supply her with the necessary details, but as no one knew them, no one could come to her rescue. Joseph announced in tragic accents that the book would always conjure up such painful recollections that he hoped she would refrain from introducing it into the house again. Stephen at once astonished everyone by promising to scour London for all the books that might have been written about the Empress, and to send them down to her.

'Now, now, old chap, I can't have you teasing your aunt!' said Joseph, shaking a finger at him.

'You're mistaken. I'm perfectly serious. You shall have innumerable lives of the Empress, aunt.'

'It is very kind of you, Stephen, but I don't want innumerable lives of her. I merely wish to replace the copy that was burnt. And I think that the person who wantonly destroyed it is the person who ought to replace it.'

'I am not that person, but I am in a very sunny mood, and I will replace it,' said Stephen.

'Indeed, you shall do no such thing!' Joseph said. 'We can't have him wasting his money like that, can we, my dear? No, I think if you very much want it I shall have to charge myself with procuring you a copy. You shall have it for your birthday! How will that be?'

'Thank you, Joseph, but my birthday is not until April, as you are very well aware, and I want the book now,' Maud replied. 'I shall write to Bodmin's, and describe what the book looked like, and I daresay they will know the one I mean.'

Joseph patted her hand. 'But, my dear, surely it was quite an old book? I'm afraid you are likely to find that it has been out of print for some years. I can see I shall have to prowl round second-hand bookshops on your behalf. Only be patient, and you shall have it, if I can possibly manage it! I shouldn't worry about writing to Bodmin's, if I were you: I'm quite sure they won't be able to supply it.'

As Maud showed a tendency to argue the point, and he was already bored by the whole subject, Stephen lounged out of the room, just in time to meet Inspector Hemingway, coming away from the telephone-room. The Inspector's eyes were bright with triumph, a circumstance which Stephen at once noticed. Stephen said: 'You look remarkably pleased with yourself, Inspector. Found a valuable clue?'

'The trouble with you, sir, is that you want to know too much,' said Hemingway severely. 'If you're looking for Miss Clare, she went upstairs a couple of minutes ago.'

'Don't get waggish with me, I implore you! My temper isn't proof against that kind of badinage. I am not looking for Miss Clare. I am escaping from the Empress of Austria.'

The Inspector smiled. 'What, you aren't going to tell me she's got lost again?'

'No; but in her present condition she's of no use to my aunt, and as my aunt cannot recall the name of her author, we have now reached an *impasse*, discussion of which will very shortly clear this house of its guests. Of course, if you were any good as a detective, you would have discovered by this time who cast the Empress to the flames.'

'Yes, that's what Mrs Herriard as good as told me,' said Hemingway. 'I'm sorry I can't see my way to obliging her, but there it is! my time's not my own, as you might say. Why doesn't she ask them at the library who wrote the book? They'll be bound to know.'

'Inspector,' said Stephen, 'you are a great man! During the whole course of our exhausting discussions, not one of us thought of that simple expedient. I don't want to hear any more tit-bits about the Empress, but I shall pass on your advice to my aunt, partly because I feel mellow, and partly because my Uncle Joseph wants to hear about the Empress even less than I do, judging by his strenuous opposition to Aunt's getting another copy of the book.'

Hemingway's shrewd gaze was fixed on his face. 'You don't pass up many chances of annoying your uncle, do you, sir?'

'None, I hope,' said Stephen coolly.

'What makes you do it, sir, if I may ask?'

'Mutual antipathy.'

'Mutual?' repeated Hemingway, lifting an eyebrow.

'Did I say mutual? A slip of the tongue.'

Hemingway nodded, as though fully satisfied with this explanation. Stephen turned to go back into the drawing-room, but before he reached the door it opened, and Maud came out.

Her small mouth was folded closely, and she looked at Stephen with a stony expression in her eyes. He said: 'I was coming to find you, Aunt. Inspector Hemingway advises you to enquire at your library for the name of the author of that book.'

Maud's countenance relaxed a little, and the glance she cast at Hemingway was almost one of approval. 'I must say that is a very sensible idea,' she said. 'But I still consider that the person who destroyed the book ought to own up. It was a very shabby trick. I should not have thought it of anyone at Lexham, even of you, Stephen.'

'My good aunt, rid your mind of this obsession!' he said wearily. 'Why should I have burnt it?'

'Joseph told me that you said –'

'Joseph told you!' he exclaimed, his brow growing thunderous. 'I've no doubt! You will probably find that he burned the book himself for the pleasure of casting a fresh aspersion on to me!'

Maud seemed quite unresentful of this accusation. She said mildly: 'I'm sure I don't know why he should do that, Stephen.'

He gave a short laugh, and strode away in the direction of the billiard-room.

The Inspector watched him go, a thoughtful look in his eyes. As Maud continued her progress towards the stairs, he turned to look at her, saying: 'Very unfortunate the way young Mr Herriard seems to have his knife into your husband, madam. And his uncle so fond of him!'

But Maud was not to be drawn into discussion. She met the Inspector's look with a blank stare, and said in her flattest voice: 'Yes.'

He made no further effort to detain her, but went to find his Sergeant. 'They were Joseph's finger-prints,' he informed this worthy.

The Sergeant's lips formed a soundless whistle. 'That does look fishy, sir,' he admitted. 'Very fishy indeed. But unless you can break down his alibi –'

'Forget it!' said Hemingway. 'What have I missed? That's what I want to know.'

The Sergeant scratched his head, 'I lay awake half last night, trying to spot something,' he said. 'But I'm blessed if I could, I don't see what you can have missed.'

'Of course you don't! If you could see it, I'd have seen it for myself, long ago!' Hemingway said irritably. 'I've got a feeling the whole time that it's right under my nose, too, which is enough to make a saint swear. The trouble is I'm getting distracted, what with all the engagements being made and broken off, and Mrs Herriard worrying me to find out who burned her ruddy Empress, and I don't know what beside. What I need is a bit of peace and quiet. Then I might be able to think.'

The Sergeant hid a smile behind his hand. 'Mrs Herriard been at you again, sir?' he asked sympathetically.

'Not to mention young Stephen. I did think he'd more sense. Anyone would think I'd nothing better to do than to look for missing property!'

'Who *was* this Empress anyway?' asked the Sergeant.

'How should I know? Look here, if you're going to start badgering me about her, I may as well book myself a nice room in a mental home, because I'll need it. I got hold of you to talk over a murder, not to have a chat about a lot of foreign royalties. What would you say was a predominating factor in this case?'

The Sergeant could not resist this invitation. 'Something that keeps on cropping up, sir? Well, I don't quite like to say.'

'Why the devil not?' demanded Hemingway. 'What is it?'

'Well, sir – the Empress!' said the Sergeant apologetically.

'Now, look here, my lad,' Hemingway began, in an awful tone, 'if you think this is the time to be cracking silly jokes –' He broke off suddenly, and his brows snapped together. 'You're right!' he said. 'By God, you are right!'

'I didn't mean it seriously, sir,' the Sergeant said, surprised. 'It was just a silly joke, like you said.'

'Perhaps it wasn't quite such a silly joke,' Hemingway said. 'Come to think of it, there *is* something queer about that book. Why did anyone want to burn it?'

'You said yourself, sir, you didn't blame anyone for getting rid of it, the way the old lady would keep on talking about it.'

'You want to cure yourself of this ridiculous habit you've got into of remembering all the things I say which it would do you more good to forget,' said Hemingway. 'The only member of this outfit who might have pitched the book into the incinerator because he was tired of hearing about it is young Herriard, and he didn't do it.'

'How do you know that, sir?'

'He said he didn't – that's how I know it.'

'Seems to me you've only got his word for it,' objected the Sergeant.

'Thanks,' Hemingway said bitterly. 'I may not be much good as a detective – in fact, I'm beginning to think I'm lousy – but every now and then I do know when a chap's lying and when he's speaking the truth. Stephen didn't burn that book, and it's no use trying to get me to believe that it was thrown into the incinerator by mistake, because that's a tale I never did believe, and never shall. Someone tried to get rid of that book, for some other reason than the one Stephen would have had, if he'd done it.' His countenance suddenly assumed a rapt expression the Sergeant knew well. He shot out a finger. 'Now, Joseph doesn't want the old lady to get hold of another copy, which is why his loving nephew Stephen's out to help her to do so. My lad, I believe we're on to something!'

'You may be, sir, but I'm damned if I am!' said the Sergeant. 'I mean, what *can* a book about some Empress or other have to do with Nathaniel Herriard's death? It doesn't make sense!'

'Look here!' Hemingway said. 'Who *was* this Empress?'

'That's what I asked you, sir, and you ticked me off properly for wasting your time.'

'Elizabeth. That was the name,' Hemingway said, quite unheeding. 'She had a son who went and committed suicide at some hunting-lodge, with a girl he wanted to marry, and couldn't. I know that, because Mrs Herriard told me that bit.'

'Do you mean that that might have given the murderer some idea how to kill Nathaniel?' asked the Sergeant.

'That, or something else in the book. Something the old lady hadn't got to, is my guess. Wait a bit! Didn't some foreign royalty get murdered in Switzerland, or some place, once?'

'When would that be?' said the Sergeant. 'They're always getting themselves bumped off, these foreign royalties,' he added disparagingly.

'It was some time in the last century, I think. What I want is an encyclopedia.'

'Well, there's sure to be one in the library here, isn't there?' suggested the Sergeant.

'That's what I'm hoping,' Hemingway said. 'And I've only got to find the volume I want missing to be dead sure I'm on to something!'

There was no one in the library when they entered it a few minutes later, and the Inspector was gratified to discover a handsomely bound encyclopedia on one of the bookshelves which lined the walls of the room. The required volume was not missing, and after flicking over a great many pages devoted to the lives of all the Elizabeths in whom he had no interest, and whose claims to fame he was strongly inclined to resent, the Inspector at length came upon Elizabeth, Empress of Austria and Queen of Hungary, born at Munich, December 24th, 1837; assassinated September 10th, 1898, at Geneva.

'Assassinated!' ejaculated the Sergeant, reading the entry over his superior's shoulder.

'Don't breathe down my neck!' said Hemingway, and carried the volume over to the window.

The Sergeant watched him flick over some more pages, run a finger down a column, and then begin to read intently. The expression on his face changed slowly from one of expectant curiosity to one of almost spellbound surprise. The Sergeant hardly knew how to contain his soul in patience, but he knew better than to intrude upon his chief's absorption, and he waited anxiously for the reading to come to an end.

At last Hemingway looked up from the volume. He drew a long breath. 'Do you know how this woman was killed?' he said.

'No, I don't,' said the Sergeant shortly.

'She was stabbed,' said Hemingway. 'An Italian anarchist rushed up to her as she was walking along the quay at Geneva to board one of the lake steamers, and stabbed her in the chest, and made off.'

'They do that kind of thing abroad,' said the Sergeant. 'Look at that King of Yugo-Slavia, for instance, at Marseilles! Bad police-work.'

'Never mind about that! You listen to me!' said Hemingway. 'She was stabbed, I tell you, and the man made off. She staggered, and would have fallen, if the Countess with her hadn't thrown an arm round her. Have you got that? She'd no idea she had been stabbed. The Countess asked her if she was ill, and it says here that she replied that she didn't know. The Countess asked her if she would take her arm, and she refused. Now, get this, and get it good! *She walked on board that steamer*, and it wasn't until she was on it, and it had begun to move, that she fainted! Then, when they started loosening her clothes, they found that there were traces of blood. She died a few minutes later.'

'Good lord!' the Sergeant gasped. 'You mean that you think – you mean that it's possible –'

'I mean that Nathaniel Herriard wasn't stabbed in his bedroom at all,' said Hemingway. 'Do you remember that the medical evidence was that death probably followed *within a few minutes*? Neither of the doctors ever said that death was instantaneous. It wasn't. After he'd been stabbed, he walked into his room, and locked the door, and that door was never opened again until Ford and Stephen Herriard forced the lock.'

The Sergeant swallowed twice. 'And Joseph gave himself an alibi!'

'Joseph gave himself an alibi for the whole time between the locking of that door and the breaking of it open, having already committed the murder.'

'But when did he do it?' demanded the Sergeant. 'Miss Clare went upstairs with him, don't forget that! He can't have done it with her looking on!'

'Get her!' said Hemingway, shutting the encyclopedia with a snap. 'You'll probably find her in the billiard-room with young Stephen.'

The Sergeant did find her there, and returned to the library presently escorting not only Mathilda, but Stephen too. He indicated to Hemingway, by a deprecating gesture, that he had been unable to leave Stephen behind, and cast a reproachful look upon that wholly impervious young man.

'Look here, Inspector!' said Stephen, with an edge to his voice, 'when you've quite finished annoying Miss Clare with futile interrogations, perhaps you'll let me know!'

'I will,' promised Hemingway. 'There's nothing for you to get hot under the collar about, sir. Since she's bound to take you into her confidence anyway, I don't mind you staying here, as long as you behave yourself, and don't try to waste my time protecting her from the cruel police.'

'Damn your impudence!' Stephen said, grinning reluctantly.

'You sit down, and keep quiet,' said Hemingway. 'Now, miss, I'm sorry to bother you again, but there's something I want you to answer. You've told me what happened after you got upstairs to your room on the evening Mr Herriard was murdered: what I want you to tell me now is what happened *before* you went into your room. As I remember, you stated to Inspector Colwall that you went upstairs with Joseph Herriard?'

'Yes, I did,' she answered. 'That is to say, he caught me up on the stairs.'

'Caught you up?'

'Yes, he went first to put a step-ladder in the billiard-room, out of harm's way.'

The Inspector's eyes were very bright. 'Did he, miss? Was Mr Nathaniel Herriard anywhere about at that moment?'

'He had just gone up to his room.'

'Did you see him go?'

'Yes, certainly I did,' she said, a little puzzled.

'Where were you, miss?'

'In the hall. Actually, standing in the doorway of this very room. I was enjoying a quiet cigarette in here after the somewhat strenuous time we'd been through over Mr Roydon's play. The rest of the party had gone up to change, I think. Then I heard Nathaniel and Joseph Herriard come out of the drawing-room together.'

'Go on, if you please, miss. What were they doing?'

'Quarrelling. Well, no, that's not quite fair. Mr Herriard was still very angry about the play, and – and one thing and another, and Mr Joseph Herriard was doing his best to smooth him down.'

'Did he succeed?'

'No, far from it. I heard Mr Herriard tell him not to come upstairs with him, because he didn't want him. Then he fell over the step-ladder.' A tiny chuckle escaped her. She said remorsefully: 'I'm sorry: I ought not to laugh, but it really was funny.'

'Where was this step-ladder?' asked Hemingway.

'On the first half-landing. Joseph had left it there, and – well, it was just the last straw, as far as Nathaniel was concerned, because he didn't like having paper-streamers hung up all over the house, and the wretched steps tripped him up. I don't quite know how: Joseph said he knocked them over on purpose, and I must admit it would have been quite like Nathaniel to have done so.'

'Did you actually see this happen, miss?'

'No; I heard the crash of the steps, and I came out into the hall to see what was going on.'

'Well, miss? What was going on?'

She regarded him with a crease between her brows. 'I don't quite understand, Mr Joseph Herriard was helping his brother up from his knees, and trying to apologise for having left the steps in such a stupid place.'

'And Mr Herriard?'

'Well, he was very angry.'

'Did he say anything?'

'Yes; he told Joseph to take the decorations down, and said he was a clumsy jackass.'

'Did he appear to you to have been hurt by the fall?'

'I don't know. To tell you the truth, he had a way of pretending that he was practically crippled with lumbago whenever anything happened to annoy him, and he certainly did clap his hand to the small of his back, and –' Her voice faltered all at once, and she gave a little gasp, and clutched at a chairback. 'Inspector, what are you asking me all these questions for? You surely don't mean – But such a thing isn't possible!'

Stephen, whose eyes had been fixed on her face throughout, said harshly: 'Never mind that! Go on, Mathilda! What happened next?'

She said in a shaken tone: 'He went upstairs. Rather slowly. He held on to the banister-rail all the way. I thought he was putting over one of his crippled acts. I heard him slam his door when he got upstairs, and I – I laughed. You see, I thought –'

'That doesn't matter,' Stephen interrupted. 'What did Joe do? Did he know you were watching?'

She turned her head. 'No. Not till I laughed.'

'And then? What did he say?'

'I don't remember. Nothing in particular, I think. He gave a little start, but that was quite natural. Oh yes, and he did say that Nat had knocked the steps over on purpose! Then he carried the steps away to the billiard-room. I collected my handbag from this room, and put out my cigarette, and went up to change. Joseph overtook me at the top of the stairs. But – but it isn't possible! It couldn't have happened then!'

Stephen said: 'Is it possible, Inspector? Was he stabbed then?'

'You've got no right to ask me that, sir, and you know it. What's more, I'll have to warn you both –'

'– to keep our mouths shut! You needn't trouble!'

'But the knife!' Mathilda said. 'I never saw it! What could he have done with that?'

'Easy enough to have concealed it from you!' Stephen said. 'Up his sleeve, or even flat against the inside of his arm, with the hilt held downwards in the palm of his hand. You'd never see it!' He turned to the Inspector. 'Would it have been possible for my uncle to have walked upstairs after having been stabbed?'

'A doctor could answer that better than I can, sir.'

'Nevertheless, that is what you suspect. What put you on to it?'

'When I've proved it to my satisfaction, sir, maybe I'll tell you. Until then, I'm asking you and Miss Clare to behave as though we hadn't had this highly illuminating interview.'

'You needn't worry!' Stephen said, his eyes glittering. 'Not for worlds would I do anything to impede the course of justice! Not – for – worlds!'

'I think,' said Mathilda, rather shakily, 'that I'll retire to my room with a headache. I don't feel like meeting Joseph, and I certainly couldn't act a part. I feel slightly sick.'

'That's right, miss, you go upstairs,' said Hemingway. 'It's the best thing you could do.'

She moved to the door. Stephen opened it for her, and as she stepped into the hall, she gave an uncontrollable start, for Joseph was there.

'Ah, there you are, Tilda!' Joseph said. 'I was just coming to look for you! Tea-time, my dear! Hallo, Stephen, old boy! Now, what mischief have you two been hatching, I should like to know?'

'Mathilda's got a bit of a head; she's going to lie down,' Stephen said, closing the door behind him. 'Did you say tea was ready?'

'Oh, poor Tilda!' Joseph exclaimed, concerned. 'Can I get you anything for it, my dear? Would you like an aspirin? I'm sure Maud has some.'

'I shall be all right if I lie down,' Mathilda replied. 'It's nothing much: I often get these heads.'

'Come on, Joe, leave her alone!' said Stephen, opening the door into the drawing-room. 'Tea!'

'With you in one moment, old man!' Joseph said. 'I'm just going to wash my hands.'

Mathilda had gone upstairs. Stephen heard her cross the hall above, and go into her room. He watched Joseph follow trippingly in her wake, smiled grimly, and went into the drawing-room.

The Inspector, emerging from the library, found the coast clear, and went at once to the first half-landing. Dropping on his knees there, he closely scrutinised the stair-carpet. It was a thick, grey pile, and here and there a few small stains were visible on it. The Inspector discovered two brown spots on the half-landing, and, having looked at them through his magnifying-glass, produced a safety-razor blade from a small case in his pocket, and carefully cut these away from the carpet. He placed the severed tufts of pile in a container, and rose from his knees. 'I'm going back to the station,' he said briefly. 'You stay here and keep your eye on our clever customer. It's just on the cards he may have been listening outside the library door. Tail him!'

The Sergeant, who had been thinking deeply, said: 'Chief, if it's true – why did he stab him in the back? That wasn't how that chap killed the Empress, according to what you read out!'

'Because, for one thing, any sharp pain in the back Nathaniel would think was his lumbago. For another, I'd say kind Uncle Joseph put in a bit of anatomical research, and chose the best place for his purpose.'

'But what a risk!' said the Sergeant. 'Suppose it hadn't come off? Suppose the old man had dropped down there?'

'He wasn't likely to do that. If he'd turned faint at once, no doubt Joseph would have helped him up to his room, and left him there. Don't forget he thought he'd got rid of the rest of the house-party! He had to take a risk. Keep your eye on him!'

He left the house, and a minute later the Sergeant heard the police-car outside start up and drive away.

It was nearly three hours later when Inspector Hemingway again entered Lexham Manor. He was admitted by Sturry, who said, in a portentous voice, that he was glad to see him.

'Well, that's something new,' said Hemingway. 'Quite brightens up my day. Ask Mr Stephen if he can spare me a moment, will you?'

'I will inform Mr Stephen that you are here, Inspector,' said Sturry. 'In the meantime, a very Peculiar Thing has occurred, of which I feel you should be instantly apprised.'

'You can't apprise me of anything I don't already know, so don't try!' said Hemingway briskly. 'Get hold of Mr Stephen for me!'

Swelling with affronted majesty, Sturry walked away.

In a very few minutes Stephen came into the hall. 'Thank the lord you're back!' he said. 'Joseph's disappeared. We've no idea where he is. Hasn't been seen since he went up to wash his hands before tea.'

'Well, you don't need to worry about him, sir, because I know where he is, which is all that matters.'

'Where?' Stephen demanded.

'Locked up,' replied Hemingway. 'That's what I came to tell you.'

'Good God!' said Stephen. 'I hand it to you, Inspector: I thought you had let him slip through your fingers. He must have heard what we were saying in the library, and made a bolt for it. Where did you pick him up?'

'Oh, I didn't pick him up!' Hemingway answered. 'Sergeant Ware arrested him at Frickley Junction nearly a couple of hours ago. Somehow I thought he might have been doing a bit of eavesdropping, so I left Ware to keep an eye on him. And a very instructive time he had, doing it. Your Uncle Joseph, sir, left the house by the garden-door, all unobtrusive-like, and carrying a suitcase, not twenty minutes after I'd gone myself. I won't bother you with all the details, but I'll tell you this: when he came out of one of the potting-sheds, which was where he made for first, poor Ware thought he was seeing things, or else it was a lot darker than what he'd thought it was. Talk of talented performances! Why, by the time your Uncle Joseph had dolled himself up in a nice brown wig, and moustache, and had darkened his eyebrows, Ware tells me you wouldn't have believed it could be the same man.'

'Old theatrical props!' said Stephen.

'I wouldn't wonder. Luckily, Ware's sure, even if he isn't quick, and as soon as he found that there weren't any snakes or pink rats about, he kept right on after your uncle. The first chance he had to telephone through to me was at Frickley Junction, where they'd got to by a slow train. Not properly heated either, judging by Ware's remarks. By that time, I'd had a highly instructive chat with the police-surgeon, not to mention another highly instructive chat with a pathologist, who'd been putting some scraps of that stair-carpet of yours through a few tests. And what that chap had to say about being dragged out on Boxing Day is nobody's business!'

'Blood?' Stephen asked.

'That's right, sir. Same group as Mr Herriard's, found by me where the blow was struck. Probably a couple of drops from the knife, since Mr Herriard hardly bled at all externally. That being that, and various items adding up to the required total, I told Ware to arrest your Uncle Joseph on a charge of murdering his brother, and to bring him along, instead of catching another slow train up to London, which was what he'd been afraid he'd have to do. And now, if you don't mind, sir, I've got to see Mrs Herriard, and break the news to her.'

'Just a minute!' said Stephen. 'How the devil did you get on to it?'

'You read the *Life of the Empress Elizabeth of Austria* instead of grumbling at other people for doing so, and maybe you'll find out,' said Hemingway. 'Your Uncle Joseph read it – all of it, which is more than he allowed his wife to do. Where is she, sir?'

'In the drawing-room. Miss Clare's with her. Was the Empress murdered, then?'

'I'm not going to spoil the story for you,' said the Inspector firmly. 'Besides, I haven't time. You'll find it all in the encyclopedia.'

'Damn you!' Stephen said, and took him to the drawing-room.

When she saw the Inspector, Maud looked steadily at him, her hands folded in her lap, her face quite expressionless. Mathilda moved instinctively to her side, but when the Inspector told her briefly, but as gently as he could, that her husband was under arrest, she showed no sign of agitation. For a moment she did not speak. Then she said: 'I did not see how Joseph could have done it.'

Taken aback, Mathilda exclaimed: 'You thought he *might* have?'

'Oh yes!' Maud replied matter-of-factly. 'You see, I have lived with Joseph for nearly thirty years. You none of you understood him.'

Mathilda looked at her in blank astonishment. 'Didn't you – didn't you like him?' she asked.

'I liked him when I married him, naturally,' Maud answered. 'I have disliked him very much for many years now, however.'

'Yet you went on living with him!'

Maud rose, rearranging the scarf she wore round her shoulders. A small, tight smile just widened her little mouth. 'I was brought up to believe that one married for better or for worse,' she said. 'I daresay you thought that because I used to be an actress I didn't care about such things. But I have always believed in doing one's duty. Joseph was not unfaithful to me, you see.' She walked across the room to the door. 'I shall not come down to dinner,' she stated. 'It would make you all feel uncomfortable, if I did. Is there anything more you wish to say to me, Inspector?'

'No, madam, nothing more,' Hemingway said, as astonished as Mathilda.

'Would you like me to come up with you?' asked Mathilda.

'No, thank you, dear. Just tell them to send dinner to my room, please, and don't worry about me. I shall be quite happy, making plans for the little house I've always wanted to live in.' She paused, and glanced up at Stephen, who was holding the door open for her. She smiled again. 'By myself!' she said simply, and walked out of the room.